"Let's be frank. You're hardly a matrimonial prize, Mr. Bowman. All the same, innocent young girls and others who should know better are thrilled when you make them the object of your attentions. Each thinks that she will be the one to reform you. They're all doomed to disappointment."

"I don't want to be reformed!"

"Of course you don't. Bad boys never do. And if those London debutantes and their foolish mothers would only read the *Journal*, they'd soon come to realize that your case is hopeless."

She didn't think he was angry, but something had darkened his eyes, something quick and dangerous. When he snagged her wrist, she sucked in a breath.

"That sounds like a challenge," he said.

He wasn't wearing gloves, and the heat of his skin on her bare skin was highly unsettling. With a will of its own, her pulse began to flutter.

He said softly, "If I kiss you, will you write about it in your paper?"

"No," she managed in a credibly calm tone. "I'll shoot you."

He laughed. "A word of advice, Mrs. Chesney. If you want to preserve your good name, don't take mine in vain."

Also by *Elizabeth Thornton*

SHADY LADY

ELIZABETH THORNTON

Bantam Books

New York Toronto London Sydney Auckland

SHADY LADY
A Bantam Book / February 2004

Published by
Bantam Dell
A Division of Random House, Inc.
New York, New York

ISBN 0-553-58490-1

Manufactured in the United States of America
Published simultaneously in Canada

OPM 10 9 8 7 6 5 4 3 2 1

For all the saints at First Church,
and their overwhelming support.
A heart-felt 'thank you.'

Shady Lady

Prologue

He knew the precise moment that a stray comment from one of the other guests struck a chord in her infallible memory. Something shifted in her eyes—not suspicion, not comprehension. *Speculation* would be closer to the word he wanted. Then the look was gone. But he knew Chloë. She had stored the tidbit of information away for future reference.

He had to kill her before she worked everything out.

He couldn't afford to be squeamish, and he couldn't afford to waste time, not in this case. She had to be silenced before she broadcast her suspicions to the world.

It was time to go to bed. Footmen were on hand with candles to light the way upstairs. No one lingered. The house party was over. Some guests had already left. The few who remained were packed and ready to leave first thing in the morning.

Once in his bedchamber, he lay on his bed, fully dressed, with his hands behind his neck, listening to the sounds of the house settling in for the night. He waited half an hour, got up, and left his room.

After dismissing the maid, Chloë sat down at the escritoire, opened her notebook, and began to make notes on the dinner just past. She described the menu, the china, the guests—what they wore, how they looked, and what they said. They were influential people with friends in high places. There had been quite a bit of bragging about these friends, and she duly noted that too.

One conversation in particular stayed in her mind, something Lady Langston said. As the memory came back to her, she put down her pen. Thoughts chased themselves in quick succession through her mind. It hardly seemed possible. Her memory might be at fault. She couldn't accuse anyone without checking on a few facts.

But if she was right, she could be in mortal danger.

A moment before, she'd felt quite warm. Now she was chilled to the bone.

Her whole body jerked when someone knocked softly on the door.

"Chloë?"

His voice!

"I want to talk to you. Open the door, Chloë."

Not in a month of Sundays!

Moving swiftly, she crossed to the window and closed the drapes, then she sat down at the escritoire and rummaged in one of the drawers for paper. The box of stationery that she found was of the best quality vellum and had Lord Brinsley's coat of arms stamped on each page. In other circumstances, she would have been impressed. The thought wrung a shaky sob from her.

It took her only a moment or two to write what she had to say. She hoped, prayed, that this letter would be redundant, that she'd live to tell the tale herself. She didn't want to involve Jo, but there was no one else she could turn to now.

Lady Brinsley had offered to post her guests' letters. All they had to do was leave them on the hall table.

Maybe she was panicking for nothing. Maybe she should invite him in to talk things over.

The doorknob rattled. "Chloë, I know you're still up. I saw the light under your door. I'd like to talk to you."

"Just a moment."

Thank God the door was locked.

She thrust her diary into the escritoire and left her letter on the mantelpiece, hoping that the maid would take care of it for her. Snatching up her cloak, she glided soundlessly through the door that gave directly to the servants' staircase.

As she descended the stairs, her mind worked like lightning. If she screamed at the top of her lungs, would anyone hear her? And if they heard her, would they get to her in time? Would they believe her? Where should she go and what should she do?

She left the house by the back door. After a few steps, she halted, giving her eyes time to adjust to the dark. Her skin prickled. She wasn't alone.

A shadowy figure stepped in front of her. "Chloë?" he said. There was a smile in his voice.

As his hands reached for her, she ducked beneath his outstretched arms and began to run.

Chapter 1

I should have known you would be a woman."

Jo Chesney, publisher and proprietor of the *Avon Journal*, looked up with a start. She was in her office, at her desk, studying the latest edition of the newspaper, hot off the press, and was taken aback by the stranger's presence as much as by his offensive words. This was Thursday, the day they got the paper out. She hadn't time for interruptions.

Her first thought was that he was an actor. He had that look—tall, dark, and dramatic rather than handsome. He had presence. And this was, after all, Stratford-upon-Avon, Shakespeare's birthplace, and at this time of year there was always a play being performed in the theater or in the open air.

She wasn't unduly alarmed when he took a step toward her. There were plenty of people about, and Mac Nevin, the managing editor, was in his office

across the hall, or in dispatch. All she had to do was call
out and someone would come running.

All the same, she was aware that he had her at a
disadvantage. For one thing, he was immaculately
turned out and she was wearing a smock to protect her
clothes. For another, he was looming over her like a
great beast of prey. She evened the odds by getting to
her feet.

Obviously, he was laboring under a misunderstanding. He must have entered the wrong building and
mistaken her for someone else. Misunderstanding or
no, she took exception to his insulting manner and
tone of voice. She was a respectable lady who also happened to run a successful business. No one talked to
her like that.

Her gaze as chilly as his own, she said, "These are
the offices of the *Avon Journal*. If you've lost your way,
I'd be happy to give you directions."

"I haven't lost my way. You are J. S. Chesney, I presume, the owner of this scurrilous piece of refuse?"

She hadn't noticed that he had a copy of the *Journal*
tucked under one arm, not until he tossed it on the
desk.

Scurrilous piece of refuse. If he wasn't an actor, he must
be a politician. No normal person spoke like that. He
was trying to be offensive. He couldn't have known
how well he was succeeding. The *Journal* was more
than a paper to Jo. It was her late husband's pride and
joy. When John died, it seemed that the *Journal* would
die with him. She wouldn't allow it. Against everyone's
advice, she'd stepped into the breach and kept the paper going. In her mind, John and the *Journal* were inseparable.

"Yes," she said. "I'm Mrs. Chesney. I own the *Journal.*

What did we do, misspell your name? Give you a bad review?"

"A bad—" His brows slashed together. "You think I'm an actor?"

Obviously not, but since the idea seemed to annoy him, she added fuel to the fire. "You certainly look the part." She studied him for a moment. "You could pass yourself off as the hero if you stopped glaring and minded your manners."

For a moment, she thought she'd gone too far. His lips compressed, but only momentarily. He said slowly, "I was right. You don't know me at all, do you, Mrs. Chesney?"

"Should I?"

"You write about me as though you know me . . . intimately."

She didn't like his choice of words. But whether the innuendo was deliberate or unintentional was debatable. She decided to give him the benefit of the doubt.

She lifted her chin a notch. "If you have a complaint, I suggest you talk to Mr. Nevin, our managing editor. I'm the publisher. I don't have control of everything that goes in the paper."

"A typical female response! If all else fails, find some man to bail you out of your difficulties. Oh, no, Mrs. Chesney. Your name is on every edition of the *Journal*—J. S. Chesney. You're the one who will pay the toll, unless, of course, you are married. Then your husband, poor devil, will be held to account for your misconduct."

She wanted to lash out and scourge him with a few well-chosen words. What stopped her was the sudden realization that he was serious. This sounded like litigation, the courts, punitive damages. She had to hear him out.

"I don't stand in any man's shadow," she said quietly. "I'm a widow, as I'm sure you've already discovered."

"No, I didn't know." He seemed to be hesitating, as though he were about to apologize, but went on instead. "It doesn't make any difference. I want this stopped."

He reached out and flipped the *Journal* over so that she was staring down at the back page. LONDON LIFE, the heading blazed. This was fairly new, an unapologetic commentary on the comings and goings of London's rich and famous. Readers, it seemed, even those who lived as far afield as Stratford-upon-Avon, couldn't get enough of these celebrities—what they wore, what they ate, where they lived, what they did.

It was her friend Chloë who had come up with the idea and Chloë who wrote the rough copy using the pen name Lady Tellall and sent it by express from London every other week. She was ideally suited for the job. Though now a widow, Chloë had married well and moved in the upper reaches of polite society.

Polite society, according to Chloë, was anything but polite, except on the surface. Beneath the surface raged dangerous currents, explosive passions, tempestuous liaisons. In short, Chloë said with a laugh, everything that made life interesting. And every week, Jo published enough from Chloë's correspondence to fill the back page with the salacious secrets of the rich and famous.

Since the inception of London Life, the *Journal*'s circulation had soared.

Now Jo understood. The irate stranger must be one of Chloë's glamorous celebrities, and he had obviously taken exception to what Chloë had written about him. But which one was he?

She sank into her chair, rested her linked fingers on the desk, and made a slow perusal. She saw an athletically built man in his early thirties, immaculately turned out in a black coat and beige trousers. She couldn't see his boots, but she knew they would be Hessians, possibly with gold tassels, and polished to a mirror shine. His hair was dark, but it wasn't black. There were shades of mahogany in those crisp locks that brushed his collar. On his left cheek, close to his mouth, was a small scar. But most telling of all, and something she *should* have noticed and *would* have noticed if she hadn't felt under attack, was that he was leaning heavily on a cane that had a distinctive silver handle.

"You're Waldo Bowman!" she declared.

When he inclined his head in acknowledgment, the small knot of tension between her shoulder blades gradually receded. He might look reckless and dangerous, but according to Chloë, the only thing he was guilty of was taking advantage of the fact that he was irresistible to women. A breaker of hearts, Chloë called him, but she said it without malice. She admired Waldo Bowman.

Chloë had a fondness for rakes that Jo did not share.

He was studying her with as much interest as she studied him. She knew she looked a frump in her smock, with her awful red hair swept severely off her face and tied back with a ribbon. She wasn't going to apologize for how she looked. Getting a paper out was a messy business. There was no reason for her to feel awkward or embarrassed.

There were ink stains on her fingers. She resisted the impulse to wipe them surreptitiously on her smock.

Her eyes jerked up to meet his. "I didn't hear that. What did you say?"

There was a short silence while he regarded her thoughtfully. At last, he said, "You don't move in my circles, so I know you are not the author of this scandal sheet." He shook the paper. "Her name, Mrs. Chesney. Give me her name, and you and I shall be quits."

She shook her head. "My sources are confidential. You won't get her name out of me."

He splayed one hand on the desk. His eyes had chilled by several degrees. "Let there be no misunderstanding between us. I won't tolerate having my name bandied about in a second-rate broadsheet that can only appeal to the vulgarly curious. Have you no conscience? Or is your only object to sell papers?"

The reference to her conscience left her unmoved. It was the word *broadsheet* that fanned the flames of her temper. Broadsheets were one-page news sheets and were lurid beyond belief, and generally despised by intelligent people. He had delivered the ultimate insult.

When she rose to confront him, two spots of color burned in her cheeks. He had the foresight to take a step back before she rounded the desk.

Her voice was low and trembling with anger. "I publish the news, Mr. Bowman, and you happen to be news just like"—she snatched the newspaper from the desk and held up the front page—"just like William Hogg, who murdered his wife and buried her body under the floor of his barn. So don't talk to me about conscience. If you had one, you wouldn't appear in my paper."

His eyes narrowed unpleasantly. "You're comparing me to a murderer?"

"Of course not! The point I'm trying to make is that you've developed a following. My readers want to hear about you, just as they want to hear about the Duke of Wellington or the prince regent."

"You never write anything derogatory about them."

"I don't publish anything derogatory about anyone, not even Mr. Hogg. I publish the truth."

An insolent smile curled his lips. "The truth as you see it."

She mimicked his smile exactly. "Correct me if I'm wrong. Did you or did you not present your latest flirt with an emerald pendant when you ended the affair?" His jaw seemed to have locked, so she went on deliberately, "And did you or did you not, only last month, fight a duel with Lord Hornsby in Hyde Park?"

He unlocked his jaw. "If you print that in your paper, I'll sue you for defamation of character!"

"Hah! You'd lose! How can I defame the character of a rake?" She folded her arms under her breasts and stared doggedly into his eyes, challenging him to contradict her.

He moved his cane to his other hand and studied her face. Gradually, the heat died out of his eyes and he began to look amused. "You're not going to print the story of our duel?"

"No."

"Not to save me embarrassment, I'll wager. Then it must be to protect Hornsby. Do you mind telling me why?"

"I wouldn't lift a finger to protect Hornsby."

"They why—"

She said impatiently, "Lady Hornsby has been shamed enough by her husband's indiscretions. I've no wish to add to her humiliation."

"You don't want to shame Lady Hornsby," he said slowly, "but it's all right to shame my relations?"

"You're not married."

"I have a mother and sisters."

"It's not the same."

"How is it different?"

"The difference is . . ." She floundered a little. "The difference is . . ."

"Yes?"

"Oh, you know what the difference is. Your indiscretions can't hurt a mother or sister the way they can hurt a wife."

His voice rose fractionally. "At the risk of sounding redundant, may I point out that I'm not married."

"No," she said, warming to her subject, "and that's all to the good. Let's be frank. You're hardly a matrimonial prize, Mr. Bowman. All the same, innocent young girls and others who should know better are thrilled when you make them the object of your attentions. Each thinks that she will be the one to reform you. They're all doomed to disappointment."

"I don't want to be reformed!"

"Of course you don't. Bad boys never do. And if those London debutantes and their foolish mothers would only read the *Journal,* they'd soon come to realize that your case is hopeless."

She didn't think he was angry, but something had darkened his eyes, something quick and dangerous. When he snagged her wrist, she sucked in a breath.

"That sounds like a challenge," he said.

He wasn't wearing gloves, and the heat of his skin on her bare skin was highly unsettling. In polite society, members of the opposite sex did not touch each other in this intimate manner unless they were closely related.

Intimate! That word again! She shivered for no apparent reason.

"What?" She'd lost the thread of their conversation.

He was no longer amused, but frowning faintly. "You're trembling."

"No. I think it's you."

It was a lie but the best she could come up with to

save face. She wasn't going to give him something to laugh about.

It was that thought that kept her from crying out when he tugged on her wrist and brought her closer. He grinned, lethally, and with a will of its own, her pulse began to flutter.

He said softly, "If I kiss you, will you write about it in your paper?"

"No," she managed in a credibly calm tone. "I'll shoot you."

He laughed and let her go. "A word of advice, Mrs. Chesney. If you want to preserve your good name, don't take mine in vain."

She took the precaution of hiding her hands in the folds of her smock. "Are you threatening to spread lies about me?"

"You do have a low opinion of my character, don't you? No. I was thinking of the *Journal*'s good name. If I sue and you lose, your paper will be discredited."

"I won't lose."

His lips quirked. "Is that another challenge?"

They were interrupted when the door opened to admit a young gentleman, also in the height of fashion, whom Jo knew quite well. Henry Gardiner, at thirty-two, was the most eligible bachelor in the county, largely because his father, Sir Robert, *owned* half the county, or so the locals claimed.

"Waldo!" exclaimed the newcomer. "Ruggles said this would only take five minutes." He smiled at Jo. "It's a pleasure to see you again, ma'am. I hope you don't mind the intrusion, but our coach is waiting, and the wedding can't go forward without my friend here."

For some odd reason, Jo had been feeling that Mr. Gardiner had caught her red-handed. On hearing his last remark, however, she brightened considerably.

"Wedding?" she said, eyeing Waldo speculatively. "Who is the lucky lady?"

A look of amusement crossed Waldo's face. "You're way off the mark, Mrs. Chesney. I'm not getting married."

"Eh?" Mr. Gardiner stared, then gave a chortle of laughter. "I beg your pardon," he said, regaining his composure. "I suppose anything is possible. No, no, ma'am. A mutual friend is to be married today in Warwick, and Mr. Bowman is to be his groomsman."

"Warwick?" she said. "That's at least eight miles away. Then I won't delay you." She smiled brilliantly. "Goodbye, Mr. Gardiner, Mr. Bowman. Have a pleasant journey."

Jo curtsied, the gentlemen bowed. As soon as they had quit the room, she sagged against the desk, then straightened almost at once when Waldo Bowman reappeared.

"What is it now?" she asked, rattled.

He smiled slowly, as though he knew how unsettling his presence was. "I'll be in Warwick overnight," he said, "but I should be back in Stratford tomorrow. Perhaps we could make up a party and take in a play or whatever Stratford has to offer?"

She bared her teeth in a patently false smile. "Don't waste your charm on me, Mr. Bowman. I'm immune to it. Nothing you say or do will get my correspondent's name out of me."

He stared at her reflectively for a moment or two. Finally, he said, "A simple no would have sufficed. Is it me you fear or yourself?"

Her voice rose a notch. "I've heard of vanity, but you—"

He put a finger to his lips, silencing her. "Don't rage. Henry is right outside the door. We wouldn't want to give him the impression that we're having a lovers' tiff."

He moved to the door and paused with his hand on the doorknob. There was no grin now to set her pulse fluttering. "I meant what I said, Mrs. Chesney. Be careful what you print in your newspaper. Don't go looking for trouble."

She stayed rooted to the spot, scarcely breathing, till she heard the sound of footsteps and voices receding along the corridor and finally a door closing. She was more than a little confused. One moment he was flirting with her, the next he was threatening her.

He wasn't anything like she expected. Chloë had misrepresented him or, at the very least, underestimated him. He wasn't all charm. When he wanted to be, he could be intimidating. Now that she'd met him in person, she was unlikely to forget that he'd served with Wellington in Spain. That's how he'd come by his lame leg and, she supposed, where he'd acquired a core of steel that no amount of charm could conceal. Such men were used to having their orders obeyed.

But not by her, and he would do well to remember it. Besides, the war had been over for two years.

She looked at her wrist. It really, *really* annoyed her to recall how she'd trembled at his touch, not in fear—she could have excused that—but because he'd made her aware of him as a man. She wasn't used to men like Waldo Bowman. The gentlemen in her circles treated her with deference, knowing that she was devoted to her husband's memory.

Don't go looking for trouble.

She wasn't afraid for herself as much as for Chloë. If he sued the *Journal*, he would lose. Chloë never claimed to be telling the truth but only reporting the latest gossip. But if he sued and Chloë's identity was revealed, that could prove awkward for her friend. She could well be ostracized by society.

No. He would put the blame squarely where it belonged—the owner of the paper that published Chloë's pieces.

He was making a mountain out of a molehill. Chloë wasn't snide or malicious. If she had a fault it was that she was gushing. She truly admired the people she wrote about. There must be something she was missing, a more compelling reason for Bowman to threaten legal action if his name appeared in the *Journal* again.

She almost jumped when the door opened, but it was only Billy, the apprentice printer, who had brought the post.

"Mostly bills," he said cheerfully, setting the burlap mailbag down on her desk. " And a letter from your friend Lady Webberley. I recognized her writing."

A letter from Chloë. That was unusual. Chloë's personal letters usually went to the house on Church Street, and not to the *Journal*'s offices. Jo thought no more about it. She hadn't time to read it right now. She'd get to it later.

She put the letter in her pocket and a hand on Billy's shoulder. "If we get everything out and away before noon, there'll be an extra sixpence in your pocket."

Billy beamed. He was thirteen years old and his mother's sole support. An extra sixpence would go a long way in their frugal household.

"You're on," he declared.

They moved quickly—through the door, down the corridor, and into the room used for dispatch. Long tables were laid out with sections of the paper, and everyone who worked for the *Journal*—printers and their apprentices, paper sellers, cleaners, clerks, and editors—was involved in either assembling the paper or tying stacks of newspapers into bundles and carting them outside to waiting wagons.

Jo paused fleetingly to savor the moment. Mac Nevin, shirt sleeves rolled up, gave her a cheery wave. He was in his sixties, ruddy of complexion, with a thinning mane of silver hair. Some people thought that *managing editor* was too grand a title for the editor of a small, provincial paper. Not Jo. She knew how much she owed Mac. Without him, she wouldn't have known how to begin publishing a newspaper.

At one time, Mac had been sought after by every paper in the land. His fondness for the brandy bottle, however, eventually put paid to that. He'd returned to his home town a shade of his former self. Now he was sober, and the *Journal,* he once confided, had been the saving of him. Jo could have said much the same about herself.

She observed the chaos in dispatch with a smile on her face. Everything she wanted in life was right here. She rolled up her sleeves and set to work.

Chapter 2

"What was that all about?" demanded Henry as the coach moved off.

"He didn't like what the lady wrote about him," replied the Honorable Douglas McNab, better known to his friends as "Ruggles." His accent was English and cultured, but with his red hair and freckles he looked as though he might have been plucked from the Highlands of Scotland, as indeed he had, but that was many years ago, when he was a schoolboy. He went on, "And since we were passing through, he decided to tell her face-to-face. Only, he didn't know she was a female until he met her."

"What?" asked Henry, mystified.

Ruggles, who was sitting on the opposite banquette, reached over to give Henry a copy of the *Journal*. "Back page. Lady Tellall."

Henry glanced at the page, then tossed the paper aside. "Balderdash! Waldo doesn't give a hoot what people say about him. So what's the real reason for your interest in Mrs. Chesney, Waldo?"

"Mmm?"

Waldo was only half listening. He was thinking that he didn't often meet a woman who didn't give a damn for his good opinion. In fact, she'd judged him and found him wanting. *You're hardly a matrimonial prize.* He agreed with her, but there were plenty who wouldn't. He was the heir to a sizable fortune and estate. In the eyes of ambitious mothers with daughters to marry off, those were virtues that covered a multitude of sins.

Something else he found curious. She was beautiful yet took no pains with her appearance. It hardly mattered. The drab smock couldn't conceal her womanly curves or detract from that glorious flame-red hair and gray green eyes. As for those daubs of ink on her chin—did she know they were there? Would she care? Of course she wouldn't! She was a woman with a mission. She had a paper to produce.

He yawned. He preferred something quite different in a woman. His eye was invariably drawn to women who knew how to flaunt their beauty, women with charm to spare who knew how to please a man, women like his latest flirt, Caroline Walters.

They'd enjoyed a short affair that had foundered when he spent a month in Scotland last year with Ruggles. But he hadn't forgotten Caro, and she hadn't forgotten him.

Just thinking about Caro improved his humor.

Much to his annoyance, his thoughts kept straying to Jo Chesney. He was curious about her, that's all it amounted to. He wondered if it was all men she despised or only men like him, men who knew how to enjoy life. *Bad boys,* she called them.

He looked at Henry. "How long has she been a widow, Henry?"

Silence, then Henry hooted with laughter. "You'll get cold comfort there, my friend. Three years, if you must know, but much good it will do you. Better men than you have tried, yes, and *their* intentions were honorable. John Chesney was the great love of Jo's life. She'll be wedded to him till the day she dies."

Waldo slanted his friend a patient smile. "Rein in your imagination, Henry. I'm not in the habit of trifling with respectable young women."

He meant what he said. He'd spent what were supposed to be the best years of his life fighting for king and country. He was now in his thirties, and all he wanted was to make up for lost time. Respectable young women were a hazard he tried to avoid.

"Jo?" murmured Ruggles. "Sounds to me, Henry, that you know the widow pretty well."

Henry grinned. "No, but not for the want of trying. The only thing she truly cares about is perpetuating her husband's memory by making a success of the *Journal*."

Ruggles said, "Is she a war widow?"

"No," answered Henry. "John was carried off by a lung fever. He was a big, robust fellow, but he got caught in a storm one night and came home soaked to the skin. It was quite a shock when he died only two days later. At any rate, Jo is now her own mistress. She can pretty well do as she pleases, and it pleases her to run her husband's newspaper. In fact, she has turned it around. It wasn't going anywhere till she took over. She's a gallant little thing."

"She's one of these 'new women,' is she?" remarked Ruggles, distinctly amused.

"New women?" Henry looked baffled. "Never heard of them. Who are they?"

"You'll meet two of them at the wedding," observed Waldo laconically. "Hugh Templar's wife, Abbie, and Case's bride. Abbie runs her own rare-book business, and Jane writes articles for various publications."

Henry's jaw went slack. "For money?"

"Oh, yes, for money. I'm told it makes them feel self-sufficient. It seems not every woman is content to spend her time arranging flowers, playing the piano, sewing a fine seam, and so on. They want to be useful."

Henry shook his head. "Good grief! I don't know what the world is coming to! But I don't think that description fits Jo. She's not running the paper to be useful but to honor her husband's memory, as I told you."

Waldo was silent, remembering his encounter with Jo. *New woman.* Very definitely not his type.

"You still haven't told me," said Henry, "why you went to see her. And don't give me that flummery about objecting to what she wrote about you in her paper."

Waldo spread his hands. "But that's *exactly* why I went to see her. I've had a very unpleasant experience because of what she wrote, and I've no desire to repeat it."

Waldo's silence prompted Ruggles to take up the story. Eyes twinkling, he said, "To cut a long story short, Waldo's mother received a letter from a friend congratulating her on Waldo's approaching nuptials. She'd read about it in the *Journal*, you see—the friend, I mean—or rather, she'd read the speculation about it. And that was enough for her."

Henry nodded, indicating he understood only too well. "And your mother started hounding you, I suppose, and got your father into the act. Poor Waldo. I truly commiserate."

Henry had got the story half right. His mother's dearest wish was to see her son married. His father, on the other hand, had washed his hands of his son and heir a long time ago.

Ruggles said, "It was worse than that. His mother, unbeknownst to Waldo, invited the girl and her family for a house party, when Waldo was to be there."

Henry was aghast. "That is positively *wicked*! Who was the girl?"

"Lady Elizabeth Beauchamp," intoned Ruggles.

"Not the one with the traveling harp?"

"The same." Though Ruggles's expression was stoic, his shoulders began to shake.

Henry's face crumpled, then he slapped his knee and burst out laughing. Ruggles soon joined him. When their laughter died away, Henry said, "I'm surprised you didn't wring Jo's neck, Waldo."

"The thought crossed my mind."

"I'm sure, now that you've explained things to her, she'll be more careful in future. She's a good sort."

Waldo didn't contradict his friend, but he was of the opinion that if Mrs. Chesney ever discovered how much trouble she'd caused him, she would use every opportunity that came her way to do it again.

Ruggles said, "I know that smile, Waldo. What are you plotting in that devious mind of yours?"

"Mmm?" Waldo's smile turned into a grin. "I was planning my strategy, you know, deciding how I can discover the name of the woman who has caused me so much grief."

"You won't get her name out of Jo," declared Henry.

"Are you willing to bet on it?" It was a facetious comment, and not meant to be taken seriously. But that was not how Henry heard it.

"No," he said, frowning. "Leave Mrs. Chesney alone. She's not one of your high flyers, Waldo. She's a simple country girl."

Waldo made a small sound of derision. "You're right about her not being a high flyer, but she's anything but simple. If she's done all you claim she's done, she's a shrewd businesswoman."

Ruggles said, "I'll take you up on your bet, Waldo. Ten guineas says you won't get Lady Tellall's real name from Mrs. Chesney. And just to make it interesting, let's put a time limit on it. Let's say by midnight on Sunday. That's three days from now."

"I wasn't in earnest," protested Waldo. "It was just a manner of speaking. And I wasn't thinking of applying to Mrs. Chesney. She wouldn't give me the time of day. I was thinking I might approach the managing editor, Mr. Nevin, you know, man-to-man."

Henry smirked. Ruggles yawned. Waldo sighed.

"All right," he said. "Ten guineas it is. Satisfied?"

"I am," said Henry, beaming. "Ruggles, you should have wagered a hundred guineas. You can't lose. Jo won't tell him anything."

"We'll see about that," said Waldo, but his voice lacked conviction.

Chapter 3

The *Journal*'s offices were still busy when Jo left to go home for dinner. Usually she worked only till noon, but Thursday was their busiest day.

It was raining when she stepped out, but not heavily, and anyway, she'd come prepared. She unfurled her umbrella and struck out briskly toward Holy Trinity Church on the bank of the river Avon. There were a few stragglers going her way, pilgrims mainly, who wanted to pay homage to Stratford's bard. Shakespeare was buried in Holy Trinity's chancel. Jo did not enter the church. The grave she wanted was in the churchyard, by the south wall. The inscription on the headstone was simple:

Sacred to the memory of
John Saxon Chesney
1783–1814
In God we trust

* * *

This was the third anniversary of John's death.

Here, in the lee of the church, the air seemed warmer, the rain less driven. There were clumps of daffodils massed along the walls. John would have liked that—shades of Wordsworth, his favorite poet. She'd preferred Shelley, until he ran off with some woman and broke his wife's heart. After that, much to John's amusement, she refused to read Shelley.

There were no other Chesneys buried here. John's family came from Bath, and his only surviving brother was in America. The reason he'd made his home here was because an uncle had left John the house on Church Street. And the *Journal.* That was the draw.

John wouldn't have appreciated her marking his passing in this way. He was the least sentimental person of anyone she knew—no tears, and no maudlin sentiments.

She swallowed and said, "The *Journal* is doing really well. At this rate, we'll soon have the funds to buy one of those Stanhope presses that you always wanted."

John would have a chuckle over that.

The rain had stopped. She was struggling to let down her umbrella when something slammed into her back with enough force to make her stumble. She righted herself and turned quickly to see a towheaded boy of about seven or eight summers disappearing around the corner of the church. She knew who he was. He was Eric Foley, and he lived with his grandmother in a cottage not far away on Orchard Street.

She looked down at her feet. He'd thrown an onion at her. Last time, it had been an egg. At least he hadn't taken to throwing stones yet. Horrid, horrid little boy!

Her troubles with Eric started almost from the day

he arrived in Stratford, about a month ago, and she knew who to blame for that. Mrs. Foley, his grandmother, had taken a dislike to Jo just because the vicar had asked her to act as convener for the altar guild. It seemed that Mrs. Foley thought the position should have gone to her. In Jo's opinion, it was a fuss about nothing. All her little guild had to do was arrange for fresh flowers in the sanctuary every Sunday. She would gladly have relinquished the position, but in a fit of pique, Mrs. Foley retired from the guild and that was that.

All this happened years ago, when Jo came to Stratford as a bride, but Mrs. Foley had never forgiven Jo for usurping her position on the guild. And now it seemed that Eric was taking up cudgels on his grandmother's behalf.

Jo's first encounter with Eric was when she found him in the *Journal*'s offices at one of the presses. He wasn't too thrilled when she'd shown him the door. Her second encounter was after she'd spoken to his grandmother about his behavior. Little boys and printing presses were a dangerous combination, she'd told his grandmother. Next day, her front door was splattered with an egg. There was no sign of Eric, but she knew he was the culprit.

His grandmother had no control over him.

The blasted rain had started again! Jo now struggled to get her umbrella up. This done, she picked her way around gravestones and made for the church porch. Having spoken to the boy's grandmother to no effect, she decided to have a word with Mr. Sutherland, the vicar. Maybe he could succeed in checking the boy's waywardness before it landed him in serious trouble.

* * *

She left the church feeling thoroughly chastened. The vicar had told her that Eric's grandmother, who had a weak heart, had taken a bad turn. A neighbor was looking after Eric in the meantime, since Eric was an orphan and there were no relatives to take him in. On the following morning, Eric would be leaving for a school in Barnet.

In spite of everything, Jo's sympathies were stirred, and she ended up offering to help the unfortunate family in any way she could. The vicar thanked her for the kind thought but said that it wasn't necessary. He had everything in hand.

When she arrived home, her widowed aunt, Mrs. Daventry, was waiting for her in the morning room. "Come and warm yourself by the fire," she called out.

Mrs. Daventry was plump, good-natured, and an agreeable companion. She kept her own house in London, and she had one married son who lived close by in Oxford. From time to time, she would go there for a visit, but not for long since her daughter-in-law did not go out of her way to make her feel welcome. Jo, on the other hand, was always glad to see her aunt.

While Mrs. Daventry poured the tea, Jo helped herself to a macaroon. She felt a twinge in her back and winced. "Eric Foley again," she said in answer to her aunt's questioning look.

Mrs. Daventry sipped her tea while she listened to Jo's story. Finally, she said, "I've heard about the school Eric is going to. It's very strict. They say that Mr. Harding, the headmaster, is a fiend for discipline. Poor Eric."

Jo said, "I'm sure the vicar would not be sending him there if it was so bad. And there's nothing wrong with discipline. It's just what Eric needs."

Her aunt nodded. After a moment, she said,

"Where is the money coming from to send him to school? It's not a charity school. Someone must be paying the shot, and I don't think his grandmother is well off."

"The church." Jo tried to recall what the vicar had told her. "I'm sure that's what the vicar said. I offered to help, but he said there was nothing I could do now."

Mrs. Daventry's cup rattled in its saucer as she set them on the table. "Nothing you can do!"

"He said he has everything in hand and that Eric leaves for school tomorrow."

"Well, he hasn't left yet, has he? We still have time to make up a parcel for him, don't we?"

"What kind of parcel?"

"The kind of parcel a boy looks forward to receiving from home when he's away at school. Treats, Jo. You know what I mean—cake, sweets, sugarplums, jams, jellies. School fare can be pretty monotonous, and I don't suppose Mr. Harding indulges the boys."

"Isn't that rewarding Eric for bad behavior? That's what he'll think. Next time he'll throw rocks at me, hoping for a bigger and better parcel."

"Nonsense! You're not giving him a hundred pounds. Cake and a few sugarplums—you're laughing at me!"

"No. I'm laughing at myself. I don't even like the boy. And he certainly doesn't like me. Besides, I'm not sure that he'll accept anything from me. What I had in mind was to give the vicar a sum of money to use, anonymously, as he sees fit for the boy and his grandmother. I don't want anyone to feel beholden to me."

"The boy needs more than material things. He's an orphan, Jo. He needs a friend."

"Fine. Then you be his friend."

"Jo—"

"No." She sighed and gave a tiny shrug. "Aunt, you know me. I feel awkward around children. I never know what to say to them. And they take advantage of me at every turn. I don't find them innocent and sweet. I find them devious and mischievous. I'm sure the fault is in me, but there it is."

When her aunt's brows rose fractionally, Jo was sorry she had said so much. They both understood what the real problem was. It wasn't that she was awkward around children. The problem was that when she lost John, she'd lost her chance to have children too.

She and John had both wanted children. In fact, the first thing they did when they moved into the house was furnish the nursery. Then they'd settled down to wait for the arrival of their first child. And they'd waited and waited. They hadn't given up hope, or so they told themselves. They were still young. But after four years, the unthinkable happened.

Suddenly, the pain she thought she'd locked away flared up as though she'd lost John yesterday. This shouldn't have happened, not to John. He was a good man, good and decent and honorable. The world was full of scoundrels. Why was he taken?

She couldn't remember clearly the weeks that followed. She stopped eating. She didn't go out or have friends in. She knew that her friends and family were worried about her, but she couldn't seem to care. All she wanted was to be left alone.

The turning point came when the *Journal*'s managing editor gave notice six months after John's death. Without John at the helm, he said, the paper was failing and he had decided to move on.

When Jo couldn't find anyone to replace him, Chloë encouraged her to take over. Everyone else was shocked at the idea. Respectable ladies did not soil their hands with commerce. That was a man's job.

Thank God she had listened to Chloë. The *Journal* had given her a purpose. She hadn't had the time to wallow in self-pity. But as much as she loved what she was doing now, it could never take the place of John.

She stirred when her aunt got up. "What did you say?"

Mrs. Daventry's eyes were soft with understanding. She spoke gently. "Cook can help me put the parcel together."

Jo hastened to add, "And I'll give the vicar the sum of money I promised."

And that's how it was left.

While Mrs. Daventry went to confer with Cook, Jo went upstairs to change for dinner. After washing her hands and face, she studied her reflection in the mirror. Uncle Daventry had once said that she was the image of her mother, but Jo couldn't see it. It was true that they had the same gray-green eyes, but Mama's hair was as dark as mahogany. Her own hair was the bane of her existence. Not only could she do nothing with it, but she hated the color, neither red nor blond but something in between.

Her mother was an accredited beauty; everyone said so. Jo didn't want to be beautiful. What she wanted was to look intelligent. She wanted to be taken seriously.

It was the truth, but it wasn't the whole truth. What she didn't want was to be compared to her parents.

Her father, Sir Vivian Moore, was a celebrated playwright. Her mother had, at one time, been an actress. Their lives had never been settled, so Jo was passed from one relative to the next as they pursued their careers.

She had never forgotten Uncle Daventry's remark when, at six years old, she'd been introduced to him. "Good Lord! She's Gertrude's image! Let's hope that's where the resemblance ends." Aunt Daventry had shushed him, but the words had stuck in Jo's mind, words that were reinforced by other comments she'd overheard about her parents as she grew to womanhood.

At eighteen, she'd gone to live with her parents, and what a disaster that turned out to be. She'd learned that it wasn't only their careers they were pursuing, especially in her father's case. Women were attracted to him like bees to honey, while her mother found consolation elsewhere.

She'd returned home to her aunt Daventry's house much wiser than her eighteen years. She loved her parents, but she never wanted to be like them, or live like them. She wanted the settled life she'd never had as a child; she wanted stability and security, and she'd found those with John.

Since this was the anniversary of John's death, and she and her aunt would not be going out or receiving guests, she simply brushed her hair off her face and tied it with a fresh ribbon.

She was looking forward to spending an evening quietly at home. Her social engagements were becoming something of an ordeal, largely because her friends were determined to see her married again. At almost every function she attended now, there would be an unattached male, usually a widower, who was invited only because he might be induced to offer for her hand in marriage. Her friends meant well, but it was humiliating. It made her feel like a piece of merchandise in a shop window. And there never were any buyers, which was fine by her. If she couldn't have what she'd had with John, she didn't want anything.

When she came downstairs, it was to find a fresh pot of tea waiting for her. The servants were spoiling her today. They knew it was the anniversary of John's death.

Her maid had left the day's post beside the pot of tea. There were two letters. She sat down and opened the one with her mother's handwriting on it.

Sir Vivian and Lady Moore were visiting friends in Waterford and were evidently enjoying themselves immensely. There followed a list of the names of their new friends, whom Jo's mother described in rapturous terms. Jo could have quoted the last few lines of her mother's letter by rote, she'd heard them so often. There were so many young, smart gentlemen going about, her mother wrote, eligible gentlemen who knew how to charm a woman, and if Jo would only put her mind to it, she could be married within the month.

This put her in mind of Waldo Bowman, and she wondered what her mother would make of him. She'd probably try to add him to her list of conquests. Mama still thought she was the beauty she'd been thirty years ago.

There was more to him than one would have known from Chloë's description. His trademarks were supposed to be his whimsical humor and effortless charm, but he certainly hadn't bothered to waste them on her.

He'd invited her to make up a party to go to the theater, no doubt thinking he could worm Chloë's name out of her. Was he hoping that his charm would work where his threats had failed? She wasn't such a simpleton.

The next letter was from Lydia Langston. Jo had

never met Lady Langston, but she was familiar with the name. Her ladyship attended many of the events Chloë attended. They were both keen gardeners, and they had become good friends.

Jo scanned the letter quickly, then read it again more slowly. The gist of it was that no one knew where Chloë was. Chloë was known to be unpredictable and she might have met up with friends and gone off with them. All the same, one would have thought she'd send word to her servants—and they were the ones who had suggested that her ladyship write to Jo. To set all their minds at rest, her ladyship wrote, if she knew where Chloë was, would she please reply by return post? And if she didn't know, what should her ladyship do next? All things considered, maybe Jo could come up to town and sort this out?

Jo shook her head. There was so much Lady Langston had left out. How long had Chloë been missing? Who had last seen her? What did her friends and neighbors have to say?

Jo wasn't terribly alarmed. Chloë was not only unpredictable, she was also thoughtless, not in a mean sense, but unthinking of the consequences of her actions. Impulsive, shocking, amusing, and fun to be with—that was Chloë.

She read Lady Langston's letter again and decided that she might have been worried if she hadn't known that a letter had arrived from Chloë that very morning. It was still in the *Journal* offices, unopened. What hadn't arrived today, and she'd been expecting it, was Chloë's copy for the next two editions of the paper. Chloë could never be pinned down to writing every week. Occasionally, nothing arrived, and Jo was left scrambling to fill the back page. She wondered if the letter that had arrived this morning was an apology from Chloë for the delay. She'd meant to take it home but had forgotten. She'd have to go back to her office and get it so that she could write by return to Lady Langston and tell her that everything was fine.

But she'd do it after dinner. By that time, surely there would be a letup in the rain.

The light was fading and it was still raining when they set off, Mrs. Daventry going to the rectory with the parcel for Eric, and Jo to her office in Waterside to get Chloë's letter. The *Journal*'s offices were not far from the church, and the plan was that after they had done their errands, they would meet halfway and go home together.

All was quiet as Jo let herself in. She let down her umbrella and felt her way to the table in the corridor with the lamp on it. The tinderbox was kept in the drawer. She was groping for it when she heard something—a door opening, a step on the landing, something.

"Mac?" she called out. "It's me, Jo."

There was no response.

She must have been mistaken.

It took her only a moment to light the lamp and a few steps took her to her office. She set the lamp on her desk and went to the clothes closet where she kept her smock. The letter was still in the pocket.

She sat down at her desk, broke the wafer, and opened Chloë's letter. She noticed the stamp at the top of the page, a leopard's head, then she began to read.

My diary will explain everything.
Be careful, Jo. If I'm right, we could both be in mortal danger.

And that's where the letter ended.

Shocked, Jo sat back in her chair, then read the message again. Was Chloë interrupted? If so, who had sent this? And what did she mean—*we could both be in mortal danger?*

She knew all about Chloë's diary. It was a notebook that went everywhere with her. After every party, she would make notes to jog her memory when it came time to write her piece for the *Journal.* If the diary wasn't with Chloë, Jo didn't know where it could be.

She turned the note over and looked at the postmark. It had been posted in Oxfordshire, but that didn't tell her much. Some postmarks had dates. This one didn't. And all the country mail went through London. It wouldn't have taken more than two days to reach Stratford. Yet Lady Langston's letter implied Chloë had been missing for some time.

She looked again at the leopard's head at the top of the page. It could be a family crest. Or the sign of an inn.

She glanced up when the flame in the lamp fluttered. A cold draft streamed through the door.

"Mac?" she called out.

She was beginning to feel nervous, and no wonder after reading Chloë's note. The next instant, she froze. She heard the soft tread of steps going along the corridor, then the click of a latch.

She sat there for a long time, ears straining, heart racing. There was nothing. She got up and looked around for something to use as a weapon. There was a poker in front of the grate. It would do.

With the lamp in one hand and the poker in the other, she went cautiously from room to room. In the storeroom at the back of the building, she found a window half open. It hadn't been forced. Someone had carelessly—or deliberately—left the sneck off for the intruder to get in.

Other than that, nothing seemed to have been disturbed or taken.

Then who had been here and what did he want?

She made a more thorough search and found that something *was* missing—a folder with Chloë's notes for back copies of the *Journal.*

A name flashed into her mind—*Waldo Bowman.* She remembered how, not many hours ago, he had demanded to know who supplied her with information for the back-page gossip column, then he had threatened to take action against her.

Waldo Bowman! Her temper began to sizzle. She had no need of the poker now. She wasn't afraid of Waldo Bowman.

She didn't think for a moment he'd come in person to burglarize her offices. A man like that would hire others to do his dirty work for him. Besides, she couldn't see Waldo Bowman creeping away from anything, not even if he were caught in the act.

First the visit from Bowman, then the letter from Lady Langston, then Chloë's cryptic note, and now the break-in. She was thoroughly rattled.

London wasn't so far away. If she left early in the morning, she could be there by nightfall. Mac was capable. He could take care of things in her absence.

When she left, she made doubly sure that all the windows and doors were securely locked.

Chapter 4

*W*ith one thing and another, they did not leave for London till almost noon of the following day. There were simply too many things to do, too many details to take care of. One of those details was to collect a parcel of clothes from the vicar's wife, a parcel for Master Foley that the vicar had inadvertently left behind that morning when he set off with the boy. Since Barnet was not far out of their way, Jo was happy to deliver it.

All these delays meant that they would not reach London that night, not unless they were prepared to cross Finchley Common at dusk and risk being accosted by highwaymen. This neither Jo nor her aunt was prepared to do. Travel on the king's highways was risky in the best of circumstances so Mrs. Daventry, much to Jo's amusement, never set out on a long journey without her late husband's pistol concealed in her reticule—not that she knew how to use it, but it made her feel safe. But Finchley Common was so notorious that only seasoned soldiers or duelists thought nothing of crossing it after dark. There was nothing for it but to stay the night at Barnet, preferably at the Red Lion if a room was available. Once they reached London, they would stay at her aunt's house.

As their chaise bowled along, Jo paid little attention to the hamlets and villages they left behind. She was going through all the letters she had received from Chloë in the last month or two, looking for clues as to what could have prompted her friend to write that cryptic note. But there was nothing odd or out of the ordinary. Chloë loved shopping, entertaining, and going to parties. There wasn't a hint of anything suspicious or sinister, until that last letter.

She felt as though she were on a seesaw. One moment she felt confident that Chloë would turn up, hale and hearty, and be shocked to discover how she had alarmed all her friends. The next moment she feared the worst.

Waldo Bowman.

Now that he had Chloë's notes, he would know that Chloë was the author of London Life. If, in fact, he was responsible for the break-in . . .

"Why the sigh?"

Jo looked up with a start. Her aunt was gazing curiously at her. She'd told her aunt as much as she knew, but those were facts. She hadn't confided her suspicions.

"Waldo Bowman," she said simply. "I'm almost sure he was responsible for the burglary last night."

Mrs. Daventry was taken aback. "Surely not."

"He was determined to find out who supplied me with information for London Life."

"All the same, I can't believe he would stoop to that, not the Mr. Bowman I know."

Jo stared at her aunt. "You *know* him?"

"I *met* him, once, last year, when I was visiting Roger and Liza."

"Roger. Your son. My cousin?"

"Yes, dear. Why do you look so surprised?"

"You never mentioned it to me!"

"Oh, but I did. He was the gentleman who took me in to supper, you know, when Roger promised but forgot all about me."

Jo remembered the incident, but she'd forgotten the gentleman's name. It was before Mr. Bowman began to figure prominently in Chloë's reports. *The nice gentleman with the limp* was how her aunt had described him, and Jo had formed the impression of a kindly old gentleman who had indulged in a mild flirtation with a lonely old lady.

She looked at her aunt. "*That* was Waldo Bowman?"

Mrs. Daventry giggled. "I was the envy of every woman there. Oh, I know he's a rogue, but he's not a scoundrel. *He* can't help it if he has a way with women. And as far as I know, that's the only vice he has." There followed a long, languorous sigh. "I can honestly say that the hour I spent in Mr. Bowman's company was the highlight of my visit. If only I'd been ten years younger—well, maybe twenty years younger."

Brows knit, Jo stared at her aunt. Aunt Daventry was supposed to be like her—sane, sensible, and level-headed. That's why they got on so well. In all the years she'd known her aunt, she'd never known her to giggle or simper. She didn't know if she could bear it.

"Lord, child, there's no need to scowl. He made an old woman happy for an hour or two. What's wrong with that?"

"Nothing," replied Jo in a tone of voice that implied the opposite.

"Mmm." Mrs. Daventry gazed absently at the passing scenery. Finally, she said, "I will say this, though: There's a mystery there. What I mean is, Mr. Bowman works in some capacity at the Home Office, but he never speaks of it. No one knows what he does."

"Aunt, you got that from Chloë's column, and you know Chloë. She exaggerates to make her subjects sound more interesting than they really are."

"Did I? I believe you're right. But there are some things I *do* know about him. He's the only son in a family of five. Maybe that's why he appeals to women. He understands us."

Jo laughed. "With four sisters, I bet he was spoiled past redemption. Poor Mrs. Bowman, with four daughters to marry off."

"It's not Mrs. Bowman. It's Lady Fredericka. She is the daughter of an earl. As for the father, Mr. Bowman, he is very well connected, though, to be sure, he doesn't have a title. And only the youngest girl, Cecy, is unmarried. She'll be making her come-out this year."

Jo was not only amused, she was amazed. "Aunt," she said, "how do you know so much about him?"

"From Mr. Bowman himself, when he took me in to supper. And before you say something derogatory about him, no, he's not one of those men who only talks about himself. All he did was answer my questions."

Jo threw up her hands. "I didn't say a word."

Her aunt quickly retorted, "I can read your mind."

The conversation moved on to other things, but Jo couldn't get Chloë out of her mind. Had Chloë uncovered some damning secret about Waldo Bowman that he wanted to suppress? It made sense. It would explain

Chloë's cryptic letter as well as the break-in at the *Journal*.

It made sense, but...She didn't want it to make sense. For no good reason, she wanted to give Waldo Bowman the benefit of the doubt, and that annoyed her.

The light was fading when they pulled into the stable yard of the Red Lion in Barnet. The landlord advised them that he had only one room left, and they were lucky to get it. It was always like this, he said, at dusk. There were few travelers who were willing to brave Finchley Common at night, so rooms were scarce at every posthouse.

They didn't feel lucky when the chambermaid led them upstairs to a dark, shabby little room at the back of the inn. After a short conference, they decided to make do with it. As for dinner, no private parlors were available and no tables to be had in the public dining room. However, the chambermaid said, if they did not mind waiting for an hour or so, and they did not mind eating in their chamber, she would bring them soup, cold meats, and bread.

After washing and tidying themselves, they decided to go for a walk to stretch their cramped limbs. They took Eric's parcel with them and were agreeably surprised to learn from the landlord that the school was within walking distance.

"Mind, Aunt," Jo said as they struck out along High Street, "we're not calling on Eric, we're simply delivering a parcel for him. Anyway, it's more than likely that he'll be in bed."

"I'm sure you're right. And I don't particularly want to see Eric. After all, he'll hardly have had time to settle in. No. It's the school that interests me. Did you know that he was there before, but he ran away from it? The vicar's wife told me. That's why his grandmother took him in. And now that she can't look after him, he has to go back to the school."

Jo gave Mrs. Daventry a keen look. She knew her aunt only too well. She had a soft heart. People were forever taking advantage of her.

She said quietly, "The boy needs discipline. Those are the vicar's exact words, so let's not interfere in something that does not concern us."

As it turned out, they learned nothing about the school. A porter met them at the gate and refused to let them enter the building.

"Only by appointment," he said, and if they cared to return tomorrow, they could make an appointment to see the headmaster then.

This they could not do, since they would be setting out early the next morning. But at least the parcel would be passed on. There was a maid at the gatehouse who'd brought the porter his supper. She took the parcel from them and promised to give it to Eric.

On the way back to the posthouse, they said very little, absorbed in their own thoughts, but their spirits lifted when the chambermaid brought their dinner. Not only was there an excellent mulligatawny soup, but she'd also managed to procure a steak-and-kidney pudding with new potatoes and vegetables.

Mrs. Daventry went to bed soon after, but Jo was too restless to sleep, so she sat down at the table and reread Chloë's letters, going so far as to make notes. It didn't help. Chloë didn't seem to have a care in the world.

Until the last cryptic message.

She drummed her fingers on the table. She got up and took a few paces around the room. She felt cooped up, but there was nowhere for her to go, not without a chaperon. If she were a man, it would be different. She could come and go as she pleased.

Her paces slowed, then halted. She knew what Chloë would say, that she was the proprietor and publisher of a successful newspaper. She'd done things that other women could only dream about. Then why was she dithering like this? If she wanted to go for a walk to clear her brain, who was there to stop her?

She went to the closet and, after putting on her pelisse, gloves, and bonnet, quietly left the room.

The small town of Barnet, which sat at a crossroads, was bustling with travelers, most of whom were making for London. Every postinghouse and inn seemed to be doing a brisk trade, and no one paid any attention to Jo. She didn't intend to go far, only to the end of the High Street, where she'd turn and retrace her steps.

The walk helped. Instead of stewing about Chloë and the robbery at the *Journal,* she began to take an interest in the various inns and postinghouses she passed on the way. Lights blazed from every window. Vehicles of every description disgorged their passengers, then passed under the arches that led to the stable block. Wheels rattled over cobblestones; horses whinnied; ostlers and postboys were shouting across each other. It didn't look as though this thriving metropolis ever went to bed.

At one point she was caught up in a knot of people, some trying to enter the Green Man and others trying to leave it. Like a small boat buffeted by waves, she was tossed this way and that until one of the hotel's guests steadied her with one arm clamped around her shoulders. Breathless and laughing, she looked up at her rescuer. Her smile died and she pushed out of his arms.

"You!" she declared, making a profanity of the word.

Waldo Bowman tipped his hat to her. Her gaze moved beyond him. Two young *women*—they were wearing powder and paint, so she knew they could not be ladies—were each hanging on the arm of a tall, red-headed gentleman, and all of them were regarding her keenly.

Ladies or not, they were dressed in the height of fashion, in the kind of outfits Chloë might have worn, luxurious velvet pelisses and high poke bonnets with an abundance of satin ribbons. Jo was horribly aware that her own traveling ensemble was a dull gray coat, long past its prime. It was serviceable, and that was the best that could be said about it.

Why must she always look like a dowd when she came face-to-face with Waldo Bowman?

"Mrs. Chesney," Waldo said. "So you did take the road to Barnet. When I was told you had not registered at the Red Lion, I presumed you had decided to take the road through Oxford. I hardly expected to find you wandering around at this time of night without an escort, though."

Her eyes narrowed on his face. Those dark brows were slashed together and his lips were set in an un-compromising line. He was finding fault with her again! Then his words registered.

"You went to the Red Lion to look for me?"

"Some time ago. I must have missed you."

"Why?"

He smiled faintly. "We're both going to London. I thought that you would be glad of my escort, not to mention the comfort of my carriage. Where is Mrs. Daventry, by the way?"

Her voice was rife with suspicion. "How did you know about my aunt and that we are on our way to London?"

"Your maid told me when I called this morning, after I dropped Henry in Stratford. It seems I just missed you. I see from your expression that you have a few choice words you'd like to say to me. Fine. But not here. Allow me to see you to your hotel."

He said something to his companions, who turned around and went back into the hotel, then he gestured to a carriage that was drawn up at the edge of the pavement, indicating that she should enter it. As if on command, one of the coachmen descended from the box and opened the door for her. Apparently, Mr. Bowman and his companions had been on the point of resuming their journey when she'd literally bumped into them.

She turned back to him. Whatever she had been about to say died unsaid. There was a stillness about him that warned her to tread carefully here.

It was a relief when someone came between them and she was no longer held in his unsettling stare.

"Shall we go?" he said.

She hesitated, but only for a moment. She didn't want to make a scene in front of all these people, and her instincts were telling her that Waldo Bowman didn't care one way or the other whether she made a scene or not. This was one battle he intended to win.

Striving for dignity, she allowed him to lead her to the carriage.

Waldo had hardly settled himself on the banquette when she ripped up at him. "You are insufferable!

Arrogant! And without doubt, one of the most ill-bred men I have ever met!"

He replied mildly, "I must correct you on one point. I'm anything but ill-bred. In fact, my pedigree can be traced back to King Harold—you know, the one who lost the Battle of Hastings."

"I see," she said waspishly, "that you don't dispute that you're insufferable and arrogant."

He bit down on a smile. "I've been called worse."

She let out a frustrated breath.

He was fascinated by the way she responded to him—the baiting, the set-downs, the fiery looks from beneath her brows. This was not how most women treated him. If they weren't fawning over him, they were flirting with him. But most women did not consider him an adversary. This was a new experience for him, matching wits and wills with a sharp-tongued shrew. He was almost tempted to kiss her into silence. Or better yet, paddle her posterior. If he had some say in the ordering of her life, he would keep her on a tight leash. She shouldn't be wandering around Barnet at night without an escort. The place was teeming with young bucks looking for mischief.

Another thought occurred to him. If he had some say in the ordering of her life, he would insist that she cast off her drab mourning clothes and dress in the current mode. This devotion to her late husband was, in his opinion, unhealthy and not entirely credible.

It made him wonder about John Chesney....

She was looking at him expectantly, waiting for him to explain why he'd come after her. He wished he could explain it to himself. The wager hardly mattered. He could easily have paid Ruggles off when they arrived at her door only to learn from the maid that her mistress and her companion had left for London.

Instead, he'd set out after her, anticipating, he supposed, the pleasure he would get from crossing swords with this fiery termagant.

It was only a game, something to stave off boredom on the tedious drive from Stratford to London. And she hadn't disappointed him.

"Well?" she said impatiently, finally breaking the silence. "I'm waiting, Mr. Bowman. Why did you follow me to Barnet? And I want the truth this time, if you please."

Omitting all mention of the wager, which was irrelevant anyway, he said easily, "I told you, I went to your house on my way through Stratford, hoping to make amends for, shall we say, my manners the other day. Your maid told me you were on your way to London but would stay overnight in Barnet, at the Red Lion. You were not there, so I assumed you had taken the road through Oxford."

"That's no answer. Why go to so much trouble?"

He said patiently, "To offer you my escort to London. Finchley Common is not for the faint of heart, and two ladies on their own make an easy target for highwaymen." His eyes narrowed on her face. "What's on your mind?"

Her voice dropped a notch. "Where were you last night, Mr. Bowman?"

"You know where. In Warwick, celebrating a friend's wedding."

"Can someone vouch for that?"

There was a heartbeat of silence as he studied her. "Dozens of people," he said easily. "Why?"

"Someone broke into my office last night and stole some notes sent to me by our London correspondent—you know the one I mean, the one whose name you were so eager to obtain."

He said slowly, "And you think I might have had something to do with it?"

Her voice was flat and cool. "What I'm saying is that I don't believe in coincidences."

"You think I'd go that far just to get the name of a woman who is spreading gossip about me?"

"What if it's more than gossip? What if she's found out something damning about you, something incriminating that she was going to publish in her column? How far would you go to stop her, mmm?"

It happened so quickly, she didn't have time to cry out. He moved like lightning. Strong fingers clamped around her arms and she was dragged forward to perch on the edge of the banquette.

His voice was hard with temper. "Now, you listen to me, Jo Chesney. Talk like that can get you killed, and not only you, but your correspondent as well. What if I was the thief? What if I had something to hide? You're threatening me with exposure. If I was desperate to keep my secret, I'd have to get rid of you. Do you understand what I'm saying?"

She nodded mutely.

"Are you sure of your facts? *Do* you have incriminating evidence against someone?"

She said quickly, "No. It's only a theory I'm working on to explain the theft."

He heaved a sigh and let her go. "I'm sorry if I frightened you, but you went too far. You can't go around accusing people and expect them to ignore you. There are some bad people in the world, and you can't tell just by looking at them. Watch your step, and watch what you say."

She wasn't exactly feeling contrite, but she was coming to see that he'd given her good advice. Her unguarded tongue had led her into danger. If she'd picked on the wrong man, she could be a corpse right now.

"I'm sorry," she said. "I shouldn't have spoken to you like that. As I said, it's only a theory, and not a very good one either."

Her words did little to mollify him. It was true that he wanted to know the name of her London correspondent, but only because the woman was a nuisance. Jo Chesney had the gall to question his integrity. A thief! That's what she thought of him. Had she been a man, he would have had her by the throat right now.

She saw something in his eyes that made her wary. The coach was slowing. Before it had stopped, she was out the door. Once again, he surprised her. Lame leg or not, he could move like lightning. His hand cupped her elbow and she was forced to slow her steps.

"What is it now?" she asked, despising the quaver in her voice.

"My offer still stands. I'd be happy to take you and Mrs. Daventry up in my carriage and convey you to London."

The thought of being cooped up with him in a carriage for hours on end appalled her. "Thank you, no. We're fixed here for the night."

"I don't mind delaying until tomorrow morning."

When they came to the inn's back door, she turned to face him. "Your companions might have something to say about that."

"My...? Ah." He gave her a slow smile. "You mean my friend Ruggles and the charming ladies I left back at the Green Man. We shared dinner with them, and that's all we shared."

Her voice was thin. "You don't have to explain yourself to me."

As though she had not spoken, he went on to elaborate, "Miss Hill and Miss Evans won't be going with us. They are actresses, you see, and are on their way to Stratford, where they are performing in *The Tempest*."

She didn't want to get into a discussion about acting and actresses, she just wanted him to go away. "One of my favorite plays," she said brightly, then emphatically, "*Good night*, Mr. Bowman."

He raised his walking cane, effectively barring her from entering the hotel. He said seriously, "You haven't told me everything. I'd like to help. I know you're in some kind of trouble. Why don't you tell me about it?"

For a moment her resolve wavered, then her lips curled in a cynical smile. "Charm, threats, and now kindness. It won't work, Mr. Bowman. I'm *not* going to tell you who writes the gossip column for my paper."

He was unsmiling. "That was a game. This break-in is serious. Won't you let me help, Jo?"

She was too eager to be rid of him to correct him for using her Christian name. She shook her head. "You're imagining things."

He knew that he wasn't, and her reluctance to confide in him came, surprisingly, as a disappointment. He sighed. "Look, if ever you need a friend, you'll find me at the Albany on Piccadilly. I have rooms there."

She looked away. "Thank you. Now, will you let me pass?"

He lowered his cane.

"Good night, Mr. Bowman." And with that, she was gone.

Waldo walked back to his carriage, muttering under his breath. She was one of the most exasperating females he knew. He'd offered her his protection and she'd refused it as though he'd offered her a hot coal. A woman could be too independent for her own good.

Independent, stubborn, willful, and fiery—those were
the words that came to mind when he thought of Jo
Chesney. She was also gallant, or so Henry said, and
reckless—a lethal combination, in his experience.

Any fool could see that she was in some kind of
trouble. He couldn't just leave her in the lurch.

She hadn't mentioned the reason for this sudden
trip to London. He'd tried quizzing the maid, but either she had not known or she'd been told to be discreet. He wondered now if it had anything to do with
Lady Tellall. Someone, a thief, had discovered her
identity. Maybe Jo was posting down to town to warn
her. But why not send a letter? Why come in person?

There must be more to it than that.

In spite of the fact that she'd refused his help, his
own principles wouldn't allow him to accept her re-
fusal as final.

There was only one thing to do. He would ignore
her objections and call for her and her aunt first thing
in the morning and insist that they allow him to escort
them to London. With Ruggles and Mrs. Daventry in
the carriage to keep the conversation civilized, maybe
he could learn what was troubling her.

And if that didn't work, if she refused his offer of
help again, he'd walk away and never look back.

Jo raced up the stairs, entered the chamber she
shared with her aunt, and quickly shut the door. Her
breath was coming hard and fast. She was trembling.

Waldo Bowman. Was he deliberately trying to confuse her? He'd looked so sincere when he said he
wanted to help her that she'd almost blurted out the
whole sorry story about Chloë. She should know better. This was the man who had confronted her in her

office and threatened to sue her. He wanted Chloë's name. He'd followed her to Barnet. She couldn't trust him, mustn't trust him.

All the same, he'd seemed genuinely shocked and angry when she'd accused him of breaking into the *Journal*'s offices.

If ever you need a friend, you'll find me at the Albany.

He couldn't have known how much those words affected her. If only...

She shook her head. She didn't know what to believe, but until she learned more about Chloë's disappearance, she would be wise to trust no one but herself.

She took a few steps into the room and halted. No one was there. She was taken aback. All her aunt's clothes were gone, but she'd left her reticule. Jo picked it up. The pistol weighed heavily in her hand.

It didn't look as though her aunt would have gone far, not without her reticule. The thought had hardly registered when someone knocked at the door. It was the chambermaid with a note from Mrs. Daventry.

Jo read:

> *Eric Foley is in desperate need of our help, so I've gone to the school to rescue him. Hurry, Jo. This is serious. I'll wait for you there.*

With a muffled exclamation, Jo thrust the pistol into her own reticule and quickly left the room.

Chapter 5

There were lights showing in the east wing of the school when Jo arrived. She'd had the good fortune, when she'd left the Red Lion, to come upon a chaise that had just set down its passengers, and she'd hired it on the spot. Now, as one postboy looked after the horses, the other followed in her footsteps as she approached the porter's lodge. To her great surprise and relief, there was no porter on duty and the gate was unlocked.

She paused for a moment, marshaling her confidence, reminding herself that she was a woman of substance and used to being taken seriously. She didn't know what was waiting for her, but whatever it was, she was up to handling it.

All the same, she hoped that her fears were groundless and this was all a colossal misunderstanding.

The front door was opened by a maid in a white apron and mobcap, a girl of about fourteen summers or so, whose lips trembled and dark eyes filled with tears when she saw Jo. She seemed to know who Jo was and had been waiting for her to appear.

"You've got to help her," she cried, her tears running over. "They've sent the porter to fetch the constable. You see, she wouldn't leave quietly, not without the boy. And it's all my fault. I shouldn't have told her, but I didn't know who else to tell, see?"

"You spoke to my aunt?"

The girl sniffed. "She's so kind. I was here when you came with the parcel. I heard you talking. You was going back to the Red Lion to get your dinner. So, when no one was looking, I went and fetched her."

Jo remembered who the maid was now. She had taken the parcel from them to give to Eric.

"What has happened to Eric?" she asked gently.

The soft tones brought on a fresh bout of weeping. "Mr. Harding beat him something awful, then locked him in the closet. The poor mite was moaning and wheezing, and . . . and . . . I didn't know what to do."

Jo shook her head, hardly crediting that such things could happen in a place like this. This wasn't a grim, workhouse school. It was a substantial building, well cared for inside and out. Even the candles were the best quality. Beeswax did not smoke or stink like tallow. Only parents who were well off could have afforded to send their sons to a school like this.

She remembered her aunt saying that Mr. Harding was a fiend for discipline, and wondered if the maid had exaggerated what had happened.

"Why was Mr. Harding so angry with Eric?" she asked.

"Because he ran away from school."

"Where is Eric now?"

The girl pointed upstairs. "In the closet, next door to the infirmary."

"And Mrs. Daventry?"

She pointed to a door on Jo's left. "Through that door to the schoolrooms."

No sounds came from behind the closed door.

As though reading Jo's mind, the maid said, "They've gagged her and tied her to a chair until Constable Harding gets here."

Jo's jaw went slack. "Gagged and tied her to a chair?" she repeated faintly. Something else occurred to her. "Did you say Constable *Harding*?"

The maid nodded. "He's Mr. Harding's brother."

Stricken, Jo looked first at the postboy, then at the maid. This was turning into a nightmare. She'd been counting on the authorities to take charge if things got out of hand. They'd take charge, all right, but they'd probably arrest her aunt and leave Eric in the care of his wicked headmaster.

Jo was outraged.

The postboy said, "You don't want to tangle with Mr. Harding, miss. He's a real devil when his temper's up. And the law is in his pocket, if you sees what I mean."

This little speech acted like flame to tinder. Hot flags of color appeared in Jo's cheeks. "We'll see about that," she declared. "But first things first." She glanced upstairs, then looked at the door to the schoolrooms. "Eric," she said, "then my aunt. Come along. I'll need both of you to help me."

On the way up, she learned their names. The postboy, a small, wiry lad of twenty, was called Roy, and the maid was Phoebe. Phoebe was eager to lead the way, but Roy looked as though he would rather be anywhere but there. Jo also learned why there were no boys to be seen. The dormitories were on the other side of the schoolrooms, and only the boys in the infirmary were allowed on this side of the building.

No one hindered their progress, and in no time at all, Jo turned the key in the lock and opened the closet door. "You can come out now, Eric," she said.

The only response was a dry cough and a wheeze.

It was dark inside the closet, so she sent Roy to get a candle from one of the wall sconces. This done, she bent down with candle in hand and looked inside. All she could see was a bundle of rags.

"Eric," she said softly. "I've come to take you away."

The rags moved and a face appeared, a small white face with enormous eyes. "I want my mam," he cried. "Go away."

Oh, God, what was she supposed to say to that? She stretched out her hand, but it only made him cringe away.

"Hurry, ma'am," said Phoebe anxiously. "The constable may be here at any moment."

Jo felt utterly helpless. Eric wouldn't come to her, because he thought of her as his enemy. But he might go to Phoebe. She made her voice as gentle and as soothing as she could make it. "You like Phoebe, don't you, Eric? Well, she's going to take you away from this awful place, and Roy is going to help her."

In the end, it was Roy who got the boy out. Eric could hardly stand, and when Roy hoisted him into his arms, he whimpered pitifully. Jo felt his hand. It was ice cold.

She concealed her anger behind a smile. "We'll soon get you warm," she said. His eyes watched her warily as she stripped off her coat and wrapped it around him. "Now," she said, "let's get him out of here."

Before they had taken a step, they heard foot treads on the stairs.

"Matron," whispered Phoebe as a small dark woman with intense eyes rounded the corner. "Now we're done for."

"And who might you be?" demanded Matron, staring hard at Jo.

"Thank you," said Jo, plucking the glass of water that Matron held in one hand. "I presume this is for Eric?" She passed it to Phoebe. "I'm Eric's aunt," she went on politely. "Aunt Jo. How do you do."

Matron's eyes passed over them and moved to the open closet. "I'll fetch Mr. Harding," she said. "He'll soon deal with you."

She turned to go, but Jo was quicker. She grabbed the matron by the waist, hustled her into the closet, then quickly closed and locked the door. Matron immediately started banging on the door and crying for help.

Three pairs of eyes looked at Jo in wonder.

Eric said, "Are you really my aunt Jo?"

This was no time for involved explanations. "Of course," she replied.

She took the glass of water from Phoebe and put it to Eric's lips. "Drink," she said briskly. He did not flinch away from her this time. Still keeping his eyes on her, he took a long swallow, then another, before shaking his head, indicating that he'd had enough.

No one else accosted them on their way downstairs, and if they had, Jo would have had no qualms about holding them at bay with her aunt's pistol. In fact, having seen the sorry state Eric was in, she was angry enough to use it. Though there were no visible bruises and no limbs were broken, he whimpered at every step the postboy took on the way down.

At the bottom of the stairs, she told Roy to take Eric

to the chaise and wait for her, then she spoke quietly to Phoebe.

"You can't stay here now, Phoebe. You know that, don't you? Matron knows you helped me. Do you have relatives in Barnet, someone you can go to?"

Phoebe smiled. "Don't you worry about me, miss. I'm going to tell them that you *made* me show you where Eric was, and after what you did to Matron, I think they'll believe me, don't you?"

Jo's eyes gleamed. "Oh, yes, I think they'll believe you, but just to make sure you're in the clear, tell them I threatened you with my pistol."

Phoebe's eyes flared. "You don't mean...?"

"Oh, yes, I do. Right here." Jo removed the pistol from her reticule and held it out for Phoebe's inspection. "Don't look so worried. I don't think it's loaded. Now, here's what we're going to do. You're going to announce me, then you're going to untie my aunt and help me get her out of here. All right?"

Even as she said the words, Jo had her doubts. Nothing could be that simple.

Phoebe nodded, not very convincingly.

Jo hoped that her own fear was not as apparent as the maid's. Attempting to bolster Phoebe's confidence, she said, "Mr. Harding is a man who likes to pick on the weak and helpless. Well, he's in for the shock of his life if he picks on me. Think of Matron if you don't believe me."

Her words worked. "She's such a Tartar! I don't know how you did it," exclaimed Phoebe.

"Just watch me!" said Jo, very convincingly for a lady whose knees were beginning to knock together.

She hid the pistol in the folds of her gown. "Lead on, then, Phoebe. I'll be right behind you."

As Phoebe announced her, Jo took in the room at a

glance. It was typical of other schoolrooms she had known, with desks and chairs bolted to a sloping floor. Her aunt was tied to the master's chair, mumbling behind her gag. Her bonds didn't look too formidable, not rope or leather but strips of rags. When she saw Jo, Mrs. Daventry's eyes lit up.

Two gentlemen turned at her entrance. She had no trouble deciding which one was Mr. Harding. He was the elder of the two, and his pale plump face was marred by a scowl.

His voice matched his expression. "I didn't give you permission to enter. Who are you, and what do you want?"

"I'm Mrs. Chesney," she said, "and I've come to see what is keeping my aunt." She feigned a gasp. "Auntie! What have they done to you?" Then to Phoebe, "Untie her at once."

When Phoebe hastened to obey, Harding moved to block her. "Oh, no, you don't! This woman is demented! I've sent for the constable and—" His voice faded as Jo brought up the pistol and pointed it straight at his chest.

Her hand shook, but that was all to the good. A nervous woman was a dangerous woman. "I really don't want any trouble," she said, and was surprised at how steady her voice was. "Let's agree that there has been a colossal misunderstanding. I don't want to shoot anyone. All I want is my aunt."

The younger man looked gratifyingly terrified. "Mr. Harding," he said, "perhaps we should do as she says. I don't—"

Harding made a slashing movement with one hand, silencing his companion. His breathing was quick and harsh. "Have you lost your mind, woman? You must be crazy to come barging in here, threatening me with a gun. I'd advise you to put it away before I take it away from you."

She spoke in the deadliest voice she could muster. "Try it and see what happens."

Mrs. Daventry was on her feet and her gag was off. "I'm not leaving here without Eric," she declared.

Jo's mind was racing, trying to come up with a ruse that would give them time to get away. She didn't think she could manhandle Mr. Harding into a closet and, anyway, she didn't want to get too close to him in case he took her gun away.

"You there!" she said to Phoebe. "Show my aunt where the boy is. Now!"

Mrs. Daventry looked as though she might remonstrate with Jo for addressing Phoebe, whom she regarded as a friend, in such strident tones, but something in her niece's expression warned her to keep her tongue still. She left quietly with Phoebe.

Harding stood there, hands clenching and unclenching at his sides. Jo was counting the seconds, trying to calculate how much time her aunt would need to get to the chaise, regretting now that she hadn't told them to go without her at the first sign of trouble.

After a long, interminable silence, she gave a tiny shrug. "That wasn't so bad, now, was it? I'd advise you not to come after me."

As she spoke, she backed away from them. The younger man looked vastly relieved to see her go. Mr. Harding, on the other hand, kept pace with her. Her arm was cramping from holding the heavy pistol, but she dared not lower it yet.

In the hallway, she could hear the rumpus upstairs as Matron banged on the door. Harding's gaze swiveled toward the noise and Jo seized her chance.

She was through the front door before he could grab her.

Almost at once, she heard a shout and someone yelling for her to stop. This only had the effect of making her run faster. She was almost at the chaise when a hand clamped around her arm and dragged her back. Acting out of sheer animal instinct, she lashed out with her clenched fist.

Harding let out a howl of pain and covered his nose with his cupped hands. Blood streamed down his shirtfront. "You've broken my nose," he yelled.

"I'll do worse than that if you try to stop me." She was shaking so badly, she needed both hands to hold her pistol steady. "Put your hands in the air and back off," she commanded. "You too, Phoebe."

They both did as they were told, but Harding was reckless with temper. "You won't get away with this. Kidnapping is a capital offense. I'll see you hang for it!"

"Then I've nothing to lose if I shoot you, have I?"

Finally convinced that he was dealing with a lunatic, Harding backed up another step.

Jo entered the chaise. "Quick, get us back to the inn," she shouted to her postboys. She was careful not to give the inn's name.

The chaise jolted into motion and was soon rattling over cobblestones. Jo edged into the corner to give Eric more room. There was only one banquette, and he took up most of it. Although there wasn't much to see in the coach's dark interior, she could feel his eyes on her. She wanted to comfort him but, remembering how he'd reacted to her in the closet, she decided that her best course was to leave him to her aunt.

Mrs. Daventry cooed and made soothing sounds as she fussed over Eric. Satisfied that all was well with him, she said to Jo, "Thank the dear Lord you had the presence of mind to bring my pistol with you. I was in such a panic when I left, I never even thought of it."

"Yes, it certainly did the trick. I don't know what I would have done without it."

There was a thoughtful silence, then Mrs. Daventry said, "Do you think he'll press charges?"

"Oh, I don't think there's any doubt of that."

"Then what are we going to do?"

Jo tried to concentrate, but reaction was setting in, and she couldn't see further than the next hour or two. "What we're going to do," she said slowly, "is settle up at the Red Lion and leave for London before Harding sets his brother on us. He's the constable, by the way."

"Yes, I know. Phoebe told me. It's iniquitous, that's what it is. But, dear, you surely don't mean to cross Finchley Common at night? What about"—she looked down at Eric and whispered—"highwaymen?"

Jo was too tired to argue. "We have no choice. Besides, we have a pistol. If I see a highwayman, I'll shoot him."

Eric, who had been following the conversation with interest, piped up, "Aunt Jo isn't afraid of anything."

Mrs. Daventry laughed. Jo managed a weak smile.

They were passing the Green Man. There was no sign of Mr. Bowman or his carriage. He must have taken her at her word and decided to push on to town. She was wishing now that she'd been nicer to him and taken him up on his offer. She had so many burdens to juggle—Chloë, Eric, and now the authorities. It seemed to her that Waldo Bowman was the kind of man who would make short work of them all.

This was fatigue speaking. She didn't need a man to take care of her problems. She was quite capable of taking care of them herself. Not that that would impress Mr. Bowman. According to Chloë, his taste ran to alluring, fashionable beauties who had made a study of pleasing men. Women like her mother, she supposed.

Now, where had that last thought come from? Certainly not from Chloë.

The chaise hit a pothole, jerking them forward then back. Eric gasped and curled into Jo. Very tentatively, she put her arms around his thin shoulders to steady him. He didn't flinch or try to pull away, and she wondered if he knew who was holding him.

"Eric?" she said softly.

He stirred and turned his face up to her. "Mmm?"

Maybe he couldn't see her clearly. "It's me, Aunt Jo."

"What is it?"

There was an odd sensation in her chest. "Nothing," she said, and swallowed hard.

When the chaise turned into the Red Lion's stable yard, Mrs. Daventry took charge. "No, you stay where you are, Jo, and look after Eric. I'll settle up and get our boxes."

She went off with one of the postboys. Eric didn't say anything, but his breathing was quick and shallow, and Jo was becoming anxious. Her mind wouldn't be easy until he'd seen a doctor, but that would have to wait until they were clear of Barnet. If the authorities caught up to them, she had no doubt that they would take Eric away from her, and she wasn't going to let that happen.

As gently as she was able, she eased away from him and got her pistol. Cradling it in the crook of one arm, she kept her gaze fixed on the yard. So far, so good. They were still in the clear.

Mrs. Daventry returned, the boxes were stowed, and they were soon on their way. It wasn't until they'd left the lights of Barnet behind that Mrs. Daventry told her the bad news.

"The porter fellow from the school was there, Jo. No, he didn't see me. But I don't think it will be long before they're after us."

Eric's voice held a betraying quiver. "What are we going to do, Aunt Jo? Mr. Harding will kill me for running away this time. He told me so."

In the face of Eric's terror, her own fears were easily quelled. Her voice was light and easy. "I'll just have to shoot him."

A laugh was startled out of Mrs. Daventry. Eric smiled. And Jo yelled to the postboys to spring the horses.

Chapter 6

Viscount Morden shrugged his broad shoulders as his manservant brushed down the nap of his fashionably plain evening coat. Though the viscount was only in his early thirties, his receding hairline made him look older. He wasn't a handsome man, but he was compelling. As Earl Brinsley's only son and heir, he'd been raised from the cradle to become the head of a great and noble house as well as master of considerable estates and fortune. He knew his own worth and it showed.

He was in his suite of rooms in Piccadilly House, the magnificent home the Brinsleys occupied when they were in town, and he was dressing for a reception his parents were hosting for his betrothed and her parents.

"That will do, Bates," he said with his customary half smile. "I've been thinking about what you told me, and there are some points I'd like to go over. Shall we sit down?"

Bates took the chair the viscount indicated, close to the fire, but he declined the offer of brandy. Though he appreciated the gesture, he had a highly ingrained sense of what was proper between master and servant. There was mutual respect and trust here, but he did not aspire to be treated as an equal.

For over forty years, he had been in the family's employ, first as a bootboy at the age of eleven, then working his way up to his present prestigious position. He was more than a valet, more than a footman. He was his lordship's personal manservant and answered to no one but the viscount. Over time, he'd become the viscount's confidant. Lord Morden frequently referred to him as his right-hand man, and Bates tried to live up to that tribute. There was nothing he would not do for his master.

The business of Lady Chloë Webberley was a case in point. He did not know all the circumstances, and he did not want to know. When they alluded to her, they spoke in vague terms, though there was never any doubt in Bates's mind that she had sealed her own fate when she'd threatened to ruin the viscount. At any rate, Lady Webberley was no longer a problem. Now all that remained to keep his master's secret safe was to find and destroy Lady Webberley's diary and any correspondence that might be incriminating.

To this end, at his lordship's behest, he had personally hired an investigator. But Taggart had come up empty-handed. This did not seem to trouble the viscount overmuch. He believed that if anyone knew where the diary was, it would be Lady Webberley's closest friend, Mrs. Chesney. All they need do was wait for Mrs. Chesney to make her move.

The viscount took the chair on the other side of the hearth, drew on a cheroot he'd lit with a taper, and exhaled a stream of smoke. "This fellow Taggart," he said. "You're sure he can be trusted?"

"Quite sure, your lordship. We've used him before. He's not interested in finding out who is paying him, only that he gets paid."

The viscount nodded. "Then you can begin by telling me, again, precisely what happened last night in Barnet. He lost her. How can that be? And how does Waldo Bowman come into it?"

Bates spoke soothingly. "That was unfortunate. It appeared that the ladies had retired for the night, so Taggart decided to keep an eye on Mr. Bowman. He was curious to find out what the connection was there. It seemed suspicious to him that Bowman would turn up just when Mrs. Chesney made the move we've been waiting for."

"But there's nothing suspicious about their meeting?"

"Apparently not. According to Taggart, they met by accident. Words were exchanged, not a quarrel exactly, but close to it. Mr. Bowman insisted on driving Mrs. Chesney back to her hotel. Taggart could not follow because he was on foot, so he waited for Mr. Bowman to return to his friends. At some point, he overheard Mr. Bowman tell his companion, Mr. Ruggles, that they were to call for Mrs. Chesney in the morning and escort her to town."

The viscount's tone was dry. "So Taggart went to bed and, while he was sleeping, our quarry slipped away."

"I'm afraid so. Bowman didn't fare any better. When he called at the Red Lion this morning, he seemed genuinely surprised to learn that Mrs. Chesney and her companion had decided to push on to town last night." He hastened to add, "It's only a matter of time before he finds her, unless she has gone into hiding."

The viscount frowned. "Did she spot Taggart? Does she know she was followed?"

"No. Taggart thinks it's Mr. Bowman whom Mrs. Chesney is trying to avoid."

"I see." After a moment's reflection, the viscount went on, "Well, I hope we have someone keeping an eye on Lady Webberley's house. Mrs. Chesney is bound to turn up there sooner or later."

Bates allowed himself a faint smile. "That's already taken care of, m'lord. One of the gardeners is Taggart's man."

"It would be better if he were one of the inside servants."

"There are no footmen in Lady Webberley's employ, but she relies on the gardeners to help the maids with the heavy work."

"Just make sure he knows what Mrs. Chesney gets up to."

The viscount sipped his brandy and drew on his cheroot as he silently reflected on the course of action he had followed to protect his position in society and everything that mattered to him. He'd told Bates that Lady Webberley had threatened to ruin him. In fact, it had not gone that far. But he had no doubt that it would have if he had not stopped her before she could act. He knew she was Lady Tellall and wrote for the *Journal.* She would not have hesitated to publish what she knew in her column. Even if she could not prove anything, he could not afford the scandal that would arise, not when he was on the point of marrying the Marquess of Kintyre's daughter. Chloë was no longer a problem, but until he got his hands on her diary and destroyed it he would never feel secure.

To be fair to Taggart, he'd been thorough. They

might not know where Chloë's diary was, but they
knew where it was not. It was not in Chloë's house, nor
in Mrs. Chesney's house, nor at the *Journal*'s offices. Jo
Chesney was his last chance to tie up loose ends. If she
could not lead him to the diary, no one could. He
doubted that she would understand the threat to him.
Even Chloë had not understood until that last evening
of the house party.

If he'd been thinking straight, he would never have
taken up with her. She was older than he, more sophis-
ticated. And he'd been besotted. But besotted or not,
the thought of marriage never once crossed his mind.
He knew what he owed his family. His bride's reputation must be spotless. Chloë was a woman of the world.
It was too bad she could not keep her nose out of what
did not concern her.

He poured himself another brandy. Sipping slowly, he
focused his mind on Taggart's report. As the thoughts
occurred to him, he said, "Who is this boy, Eric Foley?
She went out of her way to visit his school. Why? And
what was in the parcel?"

"Taggart is looking into her connection to the boy.
It's probably quite innocent. The same goes for the
parcel. After all, it was the vicar's wife who gave it to
her."

"I'm aware of that. My point is that Taggart needs
help. The job is too big for one man. I can't afford to
wait while he checks things out. I need answers *now*."

Bates did not reply to this, though he thought that
the comment was unjust. His lordship hadn't wanted
more than one or two men on the job. *The fewer people
who know about that confounded diary the better* were his
exact words.

"No need to frown, Bates. I'm not alarmed. It's early

days yet. With any luck, Mrs. Chesney will lead us straight to what we want."

The viscount's charm worked. Bates's frown vanished and he gave a little nod.

"Now tell me about Mr. Bowman's visit to the *Journal.* He quarreled with Mrs. Chesney, you said?"

Bates swallowed a sigh. They'd been through this before. All the same, he said pleasantly, "Mr. Bowman was furious and didn't care who knew it. Seems he didn't like what the *Journal* had been printing about him and he was threatening to sue Mrs. Chesney."

"And they continued their quarrel when they came face-to-face in Barnet?"

"The quarrel was more on the lady's part, I believe."

The viscount was silent. He was calculating the odds, wondering if Bowman's quarrel with Mrs. Chesney could work to his advantage if anything were to happen to her. He didn't dwell too long on that thought. All going well, he would get the diary, destroy it, and that would be that.

"Sir?"

He had mangled his cheroot. With a grunt of derision, he threw it in the fire. "Bowman," he said, as if that explained the mangled cheroot. "You'd never know it, but he served with Wellington in Spain. Now look at him! The man is a thorough-going libertine. And does society care? Far from it. He's the most popular man in London. Ladies sigh over him, gentlemen want to call him 'friend,' and fond mamas trot out their unmarried daughters whenever he comes into their line of vision." He gave a mirthless laugh. "It's true what they say, then. Everybody loves a rogue."

Bates thought he understood, and sympathized. The viscount had been bred to be the kind of man his father wanted. Duty and loyalty to family came before everything. A marriage had been arranged to a most suitable young woman, but the viscount had not chosen the girl for himself. His father had done that. Perhaps he envied Bowman his freedom.

"Not everybody loves a rogue," Bates said. "Mrs. Chesney, for one. She was overheard by a postboy to say some very nasty things about Mr. Bowman. A jackass, I believe she called him."

"A jackass?" This time, the viscount's smile was genuine.

"Then there's his father. According to belowstairs gossip, there's no love lost there. No one knows what the origin of that quarrel is, but rumor has it that Mr. Bowman was sorry when the war ended, because it deprived him of a valid excuse to stay away from his home."

"But he's the heir. One day everything will come to him."

"True. But he won't exert himself to heal the breach or earn his father's favor."

His lordship shook his head. His own life was devoted to making his father proud of him. He looked at the clock, drained his glass, and got up. "Time to go," he said.

At the door, he said, "Tell Taggart to employ as many men as he needs. I want to know how Bowman and that boy fit into the picture. I want a watch on Mrs. Chesney at all times. Tell him."

"Yes, your lordship."

Bates waited until his master was descending the stairs before he shut the door.

If Viscount Morden wished to know how he would look in forty years, all he need do was look at his father.

What little hair was left to the earl was snowy white, but in everything else there was a close resemblance between father and son. Lord Brinsley was broad-shouldered and carried himself well. He had a piercing gaze that was known to transfix underlings who provoked his flash-fire temper. The viscount had been the object of that formidable temper on more occasions than he cared to remember. Tonight, however, his father was pleased with him.

They were in the earl's library, drinking brandy and sharing what should have been a companionable moment between father and son after the dinner guests had gone home and Lady Brinsley had retired for the night. The viscount, however, could never be comfortable with his father. He was always striving to please him. Even as a boy, he had never quite measured up to what his father wanted in a son. His betrothal to Lady Margaret, the daughter of a marquess and therefore a step above an earl, had helped his credit considerably.

The earl said, "Just remember, my boy, there must be no hint of scandal before the wedding, or there may not *be* a wedding. Your future father-in-law dotes on his daughter. He believes this is a love match, and I want him to go on thinking it until long after you and Lady Margaret have made your vows."

The viscount made no reply. Inwardly, he was reflecting on his parents' marriage. It was no love match either. But the earl and his countess seemed resigned to their lot. His mother could hardly be pried away from their country estate near Henley. His father preferred to live in town. Naturally, he had a mistress. What man didn't? But his father was discreet about it. And if his mother knew, she was too well-bred to let it show.

As if picking up on that thought, the earl said, "Lady Margaret may not be a raving beauty, but she's a well-bred girl. Add to that, she's an heiress. You couldn't do better."

The viscount, in all honesty, was able to reassure his father that he was perfectly satisfied with the girl who had been chosen for him.

A silence ensued, broken at length when the earl exhaled a long sigh. "We can only hope that the girl is also a breeder." He took a long swallow of brandy. "Because, without sons to carry on our line, the whole business becomes an exercise in futility." He looked at his son. "You know what I mean."

The viscount laughed and got up. "Don't worry, Father. I know my duty. Here, give me your glass; I'll top it up." He walked to the solid mahogany desk, replenished both glasses from a crystal decanter, then returned to his chair. "You'll have your quiver of grandsons before you know it."

"Hah!" The earl accepted the glass his son held out to him. "It's not as easy as that. Look at your mother and me. It's not that she didn't conceive, but she couldn't carry to term."

"Until I came along."

"When I was practically in my dotage and had all but given up hope. A vigorous dotage, you understand." The viscount and his father exchanged a quick smile. "We had to keep trying. People in our position . . ."

The viscount had heard it all before. Without a son to inherit, the estates and the title would pass to a distant relative, to a branch of the family that his father detested, who did not hold to the family motto of duty before everything.

It was his father's guiding principle, and his also.

That was why he had to get hold of Chloë's diary and destroy it. He would not see his family disgraced.

His thoughts drifted to Waldo Bowman. He wondered what principles guided his actions...and what was really behind his relationship with the Chesney woman.

Chapter 7

Not far from Piccadilly House, in St. James's Square, another party was in progress. The hostess, Caroline Walters, was feeling very pleased with herself. Contrary to expectations, Waldo had cut short his visit to Warwick and posted up to town to attend her reception. She took this as a compliment to herself and a clear indication that Waldo had decided to renew their affair.

She mustn't appear too confident. That's what had been Dulcie Congram's downfall. She'd made a fatal blunder when she'd tried to make Waldo jealous by encouraging Lord Hornsby's attentions. A duel had been fought. Lord Hornsby had come off the worse, but Dulcie's triumph was short-lived. All she had now was an emerald pendant to mark the end of her affair with Waldo. That happened more than a month ago. Now speculations were rife as the *ton* waited to see which lady would capture Waldo's fickle eye.

Supper was over and most of her guests were assembling in the salon, where they were to be entertained by Maria Fellini, the celebrated soprano from Milan. For those who didn't have an ear for music, there were cards in the cardroom, and that was where she knew Waldo would be.

She couldn't drop everything to be with him. As hostess, she had duties to perform, and she performed them with effortless grace. She liked to think that she was a woman of refinement and taste. Everything in her home had been chosen to convey that impression—the fine bone china, the Waterford crystal, the Aubusson carpets, and the ornately carved silver. Silver and lavender were the colors of her choice, because they set off to advantage the violet in her eyes and her pale magnolia complexion.

As she passed from the salon to the cardroom, she took a moment to assess her reflection in the pier glass. Tonight she wore violet silk, which rustled when she walked and set off her lovely throat and white shoulders. Vastly pleased with herself, she entered the cardroom.

Waldo was not at any of the tables. She scanned the room and found him beyond the French doors, on the terrace, smoking one of those thin cheroots with his friend Ruggles. Other gentlemen were there as well, with the same idea as Waldo. Knowing that a lady's presence would not be welcome when the gentlemen had gathered to smoke, she turned aside and exchanged a few words with her guests, but her eyes kept straying to Waldo.

He was careless about his dress, not nearly as fastidious as her late husband, but that only added to his appeal. He looked as though he'd be equally at home in a lady's boudoir or brawling in the stews of London.

He was active by nature, and it showed in his lean, muscular frame. His limp was an indication, if anyone should doubt it, that he was a man who lived dangerously.

She watched, fascinated, as that sensual mouth blew out a stream of smoke. His hair was dark, his features were bold and chiseled, but it was his brilliant eyes that mirrored his thoughts. They could be warm and inviting or devastatingly remote.

It made a lady watch her step.

She was recalled to her surroundings by the raucous voice of the dowager Countess of Allenvale. "You look famished, Caro. Well, you won't find supper on the terrace. I suggest you try the dining room."

The snide remark brought a few titters from the other dowagers at Lady Allenvale's table. Caro affected not to understand. She made some casual comment and sailed out of the cardroom.

"Old crow," she muttered when she was out of earshot.

Ruggles's admiring gaze trailed Caro Walters as she left the cardroom. "Lucky devil," he said, glancing at his friend. "She's yours for the taking. In fact, I'd say that most of the unattached females who are here tonight are yours for the taking. Would you mind telling me what you've got that I haven't?"

Waldo's smile was dry. "A gammy leg. They assume I got it in a brawl or a duel. For some obscure reason, it makes me seem glamorous in women's eyes."

"You're joking."

"Borrow my cane if you don't believe me."

Ruggles laughed. "You could try telling them the truth."

Waldo drew deeply on his cheroot, then flicked the stub into the shrubbery. "That it's a war injury? I have told them. You can blame Lady Tellall for distorting the facts in her column. She has made me out to be another Lord Byron—you know, mad, bad, and dangerous to know. I'd like to wring that woman's neck."

"Lady Tellall's?"

"Jo Chesney's."

Ruggles turned away to hide his smile. They'd stayed overnight in Barnet for the sole purpose of escorting Mrs. Chesney and her friend the rest of the way to London. First thing this morning, however, when they'd called at the Red Lion, they discovered that Mrs. Chesney had changed her mind and left the night before. Waldo had said very little on the drive home, except to say that Mrs. Chesney was the most exasperating woman of his acquaintance. His ill humor had improved when Ruggles suggested they take in Mrs. Walters's party, but all they'd done since they arrived was play cards, smoke, and drink champagne.

Waldo went on musingly, "Is she running from me or is she in some kind of trouble? That's what I keep asking myself."

Ruggles shrugged. He'd heard about the break-in at the *Journal* and how Mrs. Chesney had accused Waldo of being behind it. "If you really want to know, why don't you track her down and ask her?"

"I have no desire to track her down."

Ruggles regarded his friend curiously. "Fine. Then let her go. Look here, Waldo, you can't expect *every* female to fall at your feet."

Waldo made an expression of distaste. "I don't expect it. In fact, no woman has ever fallen at my feet, and if such a thing were to happen, I would summon a doctor."

"You're taking me literally! What I meant was—"

"I know what you meant, and I assure you I am not sulking because Mrs. Chesney has taken me in dislike."

"Dislike?" Ruggles hooted with laughter. "Face it, Waldo. She *loathes* you. She doesn't trust you. Not that you deserve it, of course. Blame Lady Loose Lips or whatever her name is. I bet Mrs. Chesney thinks you have designs on her virtue."

There was enough inflection in the last remark to make it sound like a question. Waldo gave a snort of derision.

He refused his friend's offer of snuff and gazed reflectively at the occupants of the cardroom. Ladies in diaphanous gauzes and shimmering silks caught his eye. He knew their skin would be soft and fragrant. Jo Chesney couldn't hold a candle to these alluring women, and he didn't know why he couldn't get her out of his mind.

"It's not working," he said absently, voicing his thoughts. "I shouldn't have come here."

"What?" Ruggles frowned, not understanding his friend's train of thought.

Waldo said, "Let's go to the Bell. I'm in the mood for masculine society, and that's where all our friends will be."

Ruggles was astonished. "You mean, you'd give up Caro Walters for a night of carousing with our friends?"

"I'm bored," replied Waldo, surprising himself with the truth of his remark.

Ruggles took a moment to think about it. "What friends?" He counted them off on the fingers of one hand. "Case is married, Richard is married, and Freddie and Robert are still in Warwick. That leaves just the two of us."

"Fine. Then let's go to my rooms in the Albany and have a party for two."

Enlightenment dawned and Ruggles grinned. "I see Mrs. Chesney has made quite an impression on you. My advice is to forget her. According to Henry, she'll be married to her late husband till the day she dies." He slanted Waldo a lazy look. "Pity, isn't it? So much beauty and passion shouldn't go to waste. We must hope for the best, that one day the right man will come along and he and Mrs. Chesney will live happily ever after. Don't look so cynical. It does happen."

"You're a romantic, Ruggles."

"So I am."

Waldo left the party without Ruggles, after making his apologies to his hostess. He wasn't the only one to leave. There were so many parties and assemblies during the Season that it was an established custom to try to attend as many as possible. He didn't tell Caro that he was going home to a party of one. All the same, she looked at him as if she could kill him. If she'd ripped up at him as he deserved, he might have changed his mind, but she lowered her lashes, and when they lifted, she gazed at him with those beautiful limpid eyes of hers.

And he wanted to yawn.

Once in his rooms, he poured himself a large glass of brandy and sat down beside the fire to enjoy it. *He was bored.* He tested the thought gingerly and decided there might be some truth in it. After two years of indolence, two years of kicking over the traces, he was bored.

He wasn't giving Jo Chesney the credit for putting the thought in his mind. It had been there for some

time, only he hadn't wanted to acknowledge it. He
didn't feel guilty about his mode of living; he didn't
want to be reformed. What he missed was the direction
and purpose he'd had when he served with Wellington.

For more than seven years he'd been a soldier, and
in that time he'd been completely focused. They'd
been supremely confident then, he and his friends,
young men all, handpicked by Wellington for special
assignments or to serve as his aides. That's when his
and Ruggles's paths had crossed, when they'd been se-
lected for special assignments. Until then, he hadn't
really appreciated the quiet, unflappable Scot who
kept to himself. It hadn't taken him long to discover
that when the going got rough, there was no one he
would rather have defending his back.

Then suddenly, the war was over, and with it the
sense of purpose that drove them on. Back in England,
they were at a loose end. They'd tried to pick up the
threads of their old lives, but there was no going back.
The world had managed very well without them, and
the world had moved on.

For a while, they had both continued to serve with
the secret service, but he had found his heart wasn't in
it. The sense of purpose and urgency was gone. Spying
in times of peace did not have the same clarity as when
there was a war to be won. So he'd resigned from the
service. Ruggles had accepted a position with Special
Branch. This was a new venture that had been established in the last year or two, a police force within the
police force, to root out subversives and assist local authorities with difficult cases. He'd been asked to join as
well, but he'd requested time to think it over.

Now he had to decide what he wanted to do with the
rest of his life. He sipped his drink slowly as he considered his options.

* * *

He came awake instantly, fully alert, sensing another presence, and his hand went automatically to his holster for his pistol. Only there was no pistol and no enemy creeping up on him. This was England. He was in his library, having dozed in his favorite chair, and Mellowes, his manservant, had entered the room, no doubt to see if there was anything his master wanted before he went to his own bed.

Waldo stretched his cramped muscles, rubbed his lame leg, then frowned when he observed his manservant's expression. "What is it, Mellowes?"

"There's a Runner from Bow Street who wishes to speak to you."

"At this time of night?" He got up.

He wasn't alarmed. Before he'd resigned from the secret service, he'd had dealings with the Bow Street Office from time to time and knew most of the magistrates and officers who worked there. But this was the first time that one of them had called at his rooms.

"Well, show the officer in, Mellowes."

The gentleman who entered looked more like a blacksmith than an officer of the law. His old-fashioned tricorne hat was stuffed under one arm. His big, fleshy hands matched the rest of him.

"It's Officer Stoppes, is it not?"

The Runner nodded.

"What brings you here?"

"It's about your sister. Magistrate Vine thought you'd want to know. We've locked her up for resisting arrest."

Waldo was astonished. "There must be some mistake, or one of my friends is playing a practical joke on me."

"This is no joke, sir. She's facing serious charges—abducting a minor and disturbing the peace."

Waldo's jaw sagged. "What? *Maude?*"

"No, sir. Your other sister, Mrs. Chesney."

"Mrs...." Waldo swore under his breath. "It *is* a practical joke," he said. "I'm sorry you've been put to so much trouble. I'm afraid my friend Ruggles—that is, Mr. McNab—has set this up."

"I don't know nothing about that, sir. But I can tell you that this is no joke. She's got the Bow Street Office in an uproar, and Magistrate Vine is fit to be tied."

Waldo was beginning to add things up. "And she's mentioned me by name?" he remarked.

Officer Stoppes's brow wrinkled. "Why, yes, sir," he said. "And told Mr. Vine where to find you."

"What else did she say?"

Stoppes shifted his tricorne to his other arm. "Only that you would stand bail for her."

Something came and went in Waldo's eyes—not amusement, but something close to it. "Now, this I have to see," he said. "Mellowes, my hat and cane, if you please."

Though Waldo plied Officer Stoppes with questions on the short drive to Bow Street, he learned no more about the circumstances leading to Jo's arrest than he'd already been told. It was Magistrate Vine, Stoppes said, who had sent him to fetch Waldo. As for Mrs. Chesney, she was locked up in a cell until Mr. Vine could decide what to do with her.

Waldo did not believe for one moment that Jo could have got herself into anything that could not be smoothed over. She wasn't a criminal. He knew from experience, however, that if someone got on her wrong side, she could be a spitfire. In his opinion, tact and diplomacy were all that was required to put things right. And Mr. Vine was a good sort. He knew him well.

His steps slowed when he entered the building. It was Saturday night, and London's criminal element had obviously been out in force. Thugs, ruffians, drunkards, many of them in shackles, as well as prostitutes and their pimps were more numerous than the officers who guarded them. The air was ripe with the stench of sweat, candle smoke, and gin. No lady of quality should have to endure these indignities.

Officer Stoppes led Waldo to the magistrate's chambers. "He's expecting you," he said, took one look at Waldo's face, and beat a hasty retreat.

The man who rose at Waldo's entrance was stout, verging on corpulent, and with his snowy white hair and cheeks wreathed in a smile, might have been taken for someone's favorite uncle. It wasn't a false impression, but it wasn't accurate either. Magistrate Vine could be as hard as granite when the occasion or culprit warranted it.

Without expression, without inflection, Waldo said, "Was it really necessary to lock her up in one of your cells?"

Vine sat down at his desk, laced his plump fingers together in front of him, and smiled up at Waldo. "Sit down, Waldo. If it weren't for the fact that she has broken the law and continues to defy me, I'd be quite taken with your Mrs. Chesney. When did she become your sister, by the way?"

Waldo took the chair on the other side of the desk. "You must have frightened her badly, Archie, before she told you that."

"Frighten Mrs. Chesney? Don't make me laugh. When she gets on her high ropes, there is no restraining her." He leaned forward to make his point. "All I ask, Waldo, is that you take her off my hands as soon as possible and make damn sure she stays out of trouble."

This was too easy. After a considering silence, Waldo said, "Let me see if I've got this right: You'll let her go if I do—what?"

Vine laughed and shook his head. "No tricks, Waldo. Just post a thousand-pound bond—"

"A thousand pounds!"

"—to ensure the lady's good behavior."

"A thousand pounds!"

"And get the boy and hand him over to his head-master—"

"What boy?"

"—and I'll drop all charges against Mrs. Chesney."

Waldo let out a long-suffering sigh. "Five hundred pounds," he said, "and not a penny more."

"Done," replied Vine, beaming, "but only because you're an esteemed colleague."

Waldo had his doubts about that but decided to leave it for the moment. "Now tell me exactly what happened."

It took Vine only a few minutes to sketch the story. The boy was Eric Foley, and it seemed that Jo and an older lady had abducted him from his school, at gun-point, all because the headmaster had whipped the boy for running away from school in the first place. Naturally, the authorities had been informed, and when they'd caught up with Mrs. Chesney, she'd held them off at gunpoint too, allowing the older lady and the boy to make their escape. Where they were now, no one knew, except Mrs. Chesney, and she refused to say.

Waldo was appalled. This was really serious. "There must be more to it than this," he said.

The magistrate got up. "Those are the facts. It

doesn't matter what the provocation was; she resisted arrest. I'm hoping you can talk some sense into her. It's imperative that the boy be returned to his school as soon as possible. Officer Stoppes will take you to her. You must impress upon her that if she comes before this bench again, you will lose your bond and she will go to prison."

At the door, Waldo halted. "What's the real reason you're letting Mrs. Chesney go?" he asked.

Vine's lips thinned momentarily, then he heaved a sigh. "She had the temerity," he said, "to threaten to lampoon me in her newspaper, and not only me but also this office. We'd be called bullies for picking on a poor defenseless woman and child. Oh, yes, I can just see how well that would sit at the Home Office. I'd have your people on my neck before I could turn around."

Waldo shook his head. "And all for the sake of one small boy."

Vine's voice hardened. "She's as stubborn as a mule. I hope you can talk some sense into her." He turned away, then turned back. "One more thing." His eyes gleamed. "I hope you'll invite me to the wedding." And with a hearty laugh, he shut the door.

"Very funny," Waldo told the door.

He paid the bond to one of the clerks, found Officer Stoppes, who then escorted him to Jo's cell.

There was a small window in the door, and he took a moment to study her through the bars. She didn't look much like the spitfire Magistrate Vine had described. She looked like a waif of the street. She was sitting on a stool, head and shoulders bowed, hugging herself to keep warm.

When the door creaked as he pushed into the cell, her head lifted. The only light came from a candle on the center of the table. It warmed her skin and dusted her hair with flecks of pure gold. She looked as though the slightest touch would break her.

There flashed into his mind a picture of Jo at their first encounter, proud, defiant, daring him to do his worst, and he was incensed that she had been brought to this.

Their eyes met. He could hear her indrawn breath, see the relief flooding through her, then the look was gone and she straightened her spine.

"You took your time getting here," she said.

"I came as soon as I heard you were here."

She got up. "It seems like an eon. That's what happens when you're in prison. You lose track of time. I'm sorry if I snapped at you. Thank you for coming. I didn't know if you would."

A closer look at the cell appalled him, as did the frigid temperature. The only furnishings were the stool, a broken-down table, a straw pallet on the floor, and a chamber pot.

His mind strayed to the party he'd attended that evening, to the elegant surroundings and the pampered, perfumed ladies. That's where Jo Chesney belonged, not in a place like this. The thought was vaguely irritating.

She looked past him to the open door. "Am I free to go?"

"You've been released into my custody." He wasn't harsh, but he wasn't gentle either. She must be made to understand how things stood between them.

A tiny frown furrowed her brow. "I—what?"

"You've been released into my custody."

"What does that mean?"

"It means that I've posted a five-hundred-pound bond as surety for your good behavior, and if you don't obey the law, I'll lose it. That's not going to happen, because I'm going to keep a close eye on you until..."

"Until what?"

He had been about to say *until the boy is back where he belongs,* but he knew that would provoke a scene and she might find herself locked up for the night, so he said instead, "until I get to the bottom of this." He cut off her protest by putting a finger to her lips. "We'll talk later. Now let's get out of here before they decide to lock us both up. Where is your coat?"

He carried his point but only, he suspected, because she was either dazed with fatigue or suffering from latent shock.

She took a quick breath, hesitated, then said, "They took it away from me."

"Then let's get it."

Chapter 8

Waldo hailed a hackney.

"Where to, g'uv?" the driver asked.

Waldo looked at Jo. "Where is the boy?"

She hesitated, but only for a moment. "With my aunt, Mrs. Daventry."

Another moment of silence. "Jo?"

She let out a puff of breath. "Greek Street. Just off Soho Square."

"Greek Street," he told the driver, and after handing Jo up, he climbed in after her. "Now," he said, as the hackney moved off, "tell me exactly what happened in Barnet after I left you."

Her eyes flashed briefly with anger, but whether that anger was directed at him or at the memory of what happened in Barnet, he could not tell.

She said, "A maid from the school came to the Red Lion when I was out walking. She found my aunt alone. She was there, you see—the maid, I mean—at the school, when we delivered a parcel of clothes for Eric."

"The parcel the vicar's wife gave you?"

"How do you know about that?"

"Your maid told me before I left Stratford. That was the reason for your detour to Barnet, wasn't it?"

"Yes. But we didn't see Eric then. In fact, we saw no one but the porter, and he wouldn't let us in."

"But the maid saw you?"

"Yes. She took the parcel from us and afterward came to the inn. She told my aunt that Eric had been savagely beaten for running away from school. Phoebe—that was her name—was truly alarmed. She'd helped Eric get away the first time, you see. She says that Mr. Harding was always picking on Eric, making an example of him, but this time he'd gone too far." She paused, gathering her thoughts, then went on, "My aunt left a note for me, telling me to come to the school at once, and that's what I did."

Her hands curled into fists. "There was a bit of a row, but we got Eric away. He was locked in a cupboard, in a pitiful state. I couldn't leave him to those brutes. We knew they'd be after us, so we set off at once."

She was looking at him in a challenging way.

"A bit of a row?" he said easily. "What does that mean?"

"It means," she said crisply, "that I threatened to shoot the first person who tried to stop me."

"You had a pistol?"

"No. My aunt did. I borrowed it."

Again, that challenging look. He let it pass for the moment and said, "Magistrate Vine said something about resisting arrest. How did that happen?"

"Anyone can say they are officers of the law. It's not

as though Runners wear uniforms. They burst in on us this morning when we were sitting down to breakfast."

"Where was this?"

"At the Clarendon Hotel on Bond Street. When we arrived in London last night, it was too late to rouse Mrs. Daventry's servants from their beds and get the house ready for us, so we decided to put up at a hotel for the night."

He took a moment or two to consider her words. Finally, he said, "Tell me about the Runner who tried to arrest you. You were at breakfast. Then what happened?"

"He tried to take Eric away, to send him back to that awful school. I did what any decent person would do. I held him off while Aunt Daventry and Eric made their escape."

"The pistol again?"

She nodded.

"I thought you said that the boy was in a bad way."

"He revived a little when we got him away from that... *prison.*"

He shook his head. "I don't think you know much about boys' schools. The discipline may seem harsh, but if it weren't, the teachers would soon lose control. And a whipping does more damage to a boy's dignity than to his backside."

"Is that how you're going to raise *your* children, with whippings?"

"No, I shall probably—"

"What?"

He grinned. "Who said I was going to have any children?"

"You are an only son, are you not, and your father's estates are entailed?"

"Where did you hear that?"

She practically smirked. "I read it in the *Journal.* It's your duty to produce the next crop of Bowmans to keep your estates and fortune intact."

"There's no law says I have to do my duty."

She tilted her head to get a better look at him. "That's the thing about you, Mr. Bowman. One never knows whether you are serious or amusing yourself."

He folded his arms across his chest. "In the matter of Eric Foley, I am in deadly earnest. If this isn't resolved to Magistrate Vine's satisfaction, I could lose a considerable sum of money and you could be charged with a serious offense. Now, begin at the beginning and tell me exactly who did what and how a respectable lady came to be locked up in a cell in Bow Street."

Mrs. Daventry's house was a modest three-story building with a handsome bow window on the ground floor. The maid who opened the door fought back tears when she saw Jo.

"Oh, miss, I'm that glad to see you," she choked out.

"No more glad than I am to see you, Rose. Where is Mrs. Daventry?"

Jo's matter-of-fact tone seemed to steady the maid. Her tears dried. "Upstairs, with the boy."

They were met by Mrs. Daventry at the top of the stairs. When she saw Waldo, her jaw went slack. "Mr. Bowman," she said faintly.

"It's all right, Aunt." Jo put her arm around Mrs. Daventry's shoulders. "Mr. Bowman is here to help us. I'll explain later. Now, take us to Eric. How is he?"

"Sleeping."

Waldo said, "It's true, Mrs. Daventry. I'm here to help."

Mrs. Daventry continued to stare at Waldo. By degrees, all trace of anxiety left her face and a slow smile curved her lips. "Who says God doesn't answer prayer? Come this way. He's restless. Now that you're here, Jo, he may settle."

Mrs. Daventry stayed in the background as Jo and Waldo crossed to the bed. Jo took the chair and stared down at the sleeping child. After a moment, she felt his brow.

"He's fevered," she said, "and his nightshirt is wet with perspiration."

"Has the physician been sent for?" Waldo asked.

"Yes," replied Mrs. Daventry. "I don't know what's keeping him." She bit down on her lip. "I didn't know what to do for the best. I didn't realize Eric was fevered."

Waldo said soothingly, "It's probably nothing at all. Children are prone to odd fevers. All the same, let's send for another doctor. Try Mercer on Baker Street and use my name."

"I'll see to it at once," said Mrs. Daventry.

As Mrs. Daventry went off to find a servant to fetch Dr. Mercer, Jo rummaged in a drawer and came back to the bed with a clean nightshirt. "It belongs to my aunt's grandson," she said.

When she said Eric's name softly, he began to moan. "Mam?" he whispered. "Mam?"

Jo said, "It's Jo, Eric. I'm going to change your nightshirt, then you'll feel more comfortable. All right?"

He opened his eyes and blinked up at Jo. "You broke Mr. Harding's nose," he said.

"No. That's what he said, but I only tweaked it a little."

"There was blood everywhere," replied Eric feebly but with obvious relish.

"Yes. There was, wasn't there? And if he comes near you, I'll do it again."

Waldo pressed a hand to his eyes and shook his head. "Jo," he said in a warning tone.

At the sound of Waldo's voice, Eric gave a little cry and tried to haul himself up. Jo put a steadying arm around his shoulders. "Look who is here," she said. "Mr. Bowman. He is our friend. He's here to help us. If it hadn't been for him, I'd still be locked up in Bow Street. He won't let anything bad happen to you, will you, Mr. Bowman?"

Waldo spoke to the boy. "We'll talk when you're feeling better," he said gently. There was nothing gentle about the look he flung at Jo. It promised a swift retribution for making promises on his behalf, promises he might not be able to keep.

Mrs. Daventry returned with a glass of warm chocolate. "For his sore throat," she said.

"Let's change him first," said Waldo. "Ready, Jo?"

Eric mewed like a hurt kitten as the nightshirt came off.

"I know," said Waldo, copying Jo's matter-of-fact tone, "you're hot and tired and want to be left alone, but you see, Eric—" The shirt was off, and Waldo's voice suddenly died.

"Get the candle," he said tersely to Mrs. Daventry, "and hold it up."

Eric cringed from that light and tried to slip beneath the covers, but Waldo was firm. "What have we here?" he said.

There were ugly fresh welts across the boy's shoulders and back, but that was not what held Waldo's interest. A huge dark bruise ran from under his breastbone to his groin.

Waldo's hands hovered but he did not touch the bruise. "How did you get this, Eric?" His voice was as pleasant as before and gave no indication of the murderous rage that seethed beneath the surface.

"Mr. Harding threw me down the stairs."

Jo was shocked. "This is the first I've heard of it. Eric, you should have told us!"

Her outburst seemed to alarm the boy, for he cried out, "I won't do it again."

"Do what, Eric?" asked Waldo gently.

"Run away from school."

Waldo turned fierce. "No, you won't, because you're never going back there. And if Mr. Harding shows his face here, I shall make him sorry that he ever heard the name Eric Foley."

Eric looked at Jo. She sniffled and said, "He means that he'll hurt Mr. Harding much worse than I did. Now, let's get you changed, then you can drink your chocolate."

While they were waiting for the doctor to arrive, Waldo put a number of questions to Jo and her aunt to get a clearer idea of what might be involved in solving the problem of what to do about Eric Foley. It soon became evident that they knew very little about the boy's circumstances except that he was an orphan and that he'd become a ward of the church.

"Are you sure of that?"

Jo and her aunt exchanged a quick look. "Well, no, we don't know for sure," said Jo. "That's why we refused to hand him over to the authorities. They were going to return him to that dreadful school until everything was sorted out. And there was no question of Eric going back to that school, not for a day, not for an hour."

Waldo agreed. He'd had his share of whippings as a schoolboy, and they in no way resembled what Eric had suffered.

They spoke in hushed whispers at one end of the room so that they would not waken Eric. When he turned in his sleep, however, he visibly flinched and whimpered.

In a voice trembling with suppressed anger, Jo said to Waldo, "Now do you see what I mean? I'm going to make Harding pay for what he did to Eric."

Her aunt said, "But what can you do, dear, a mere female?"

Though Jo was careful to keep her voice down, she made no attempt to conceal her wrath. "I'll use the power of my newspaper to shame him, yes, and bring him to justice if the magistrate won't act."

Waldo said sharply, "You'll do nothing without my consent. I have a considerable stake in ensuring your good behavior, Jo. Don't forget it!"

"Money!" she declared. "Is that all you can think about?"

"No. But I don't want to stir up trouble needlessly, not at this point. Think, Jo. If the authorities discover where Eric is hiding, they'll take him away and return him to the school. We'll deal with Harding later, after Eric is well out of his reach."

He was right, of course, but it was against her nature to do nothing. She didn't want any boy to suffer as Eric had.

Mrs. Daventry tactfully steered the conversation in another direction. "You haven't told me what happened at Bow Street. How did you come to be involved, Mr. Bowman?"

"Jo sent for me," he said, and had the pleasure of watching the color bloom in Jo's cheeks.

She said, faltering a little, "I thought... it seemed... well, I knew Mr. Bowman had influence, and when the magistrate turned nasty—"

"After you threatened him," Waldo cut in.

"—I remembered Mr. Bowman—"

"Please," Waldo interrupted yet again. "After all we've been through together, surely it wouldn't choke you to call me by my Christian name?"

It almost did, but she went on anyway. "I remembered *Waldo* told me that if ever I needed a friend, I should call on him."

"So here I am," added Waldo cheerfully.

Jo said, "I was amazed at the change in the magistrate after I mentioned Mr. Bowman's name." She slanted Waldo a sideways look. "All doors opened for me and I was free to go."

"Not exactly free. As I keep reminding you, there are conditions attached."

Mrs. Daventry was looking from one to the other, her expression oddly innocent. At that point, Eric's plaintive voice brought the focus of attention back to him. "May I have more chocolate?"

Not long after, the doctor arrived and confirmed Waldo's suspicions. The boy's ribs were bruised, though none appeared to be broken. Dr. Mercer showed Jo how to bind Eric's painfully thin rib cage, prescribed quiet and rest, then left.

When Eric was settled again, Waldo asked Jo to see him out. He wanted a word with her in private, out of earshot of Eric and Mrs. Daventry. He wanted to warn her not to get her hopes up, that if Eric had a guardian there was only so much he could do. Above all, he wanted to impress upon her the importance of keeping out of trouble. Magistrates and Runners were not to be trifled with, let alone held off at gunpoint.

In the hallway, he picked up a candle and led the way into what appeared to be a small breakfast room. He set the candle on the mantelpiece. She gazed up at him expectantly, waiting for him to begin. Her cheeks were without color; her eyes were dark.

"I've changed my mind," he said. "This can wait. Get a good night's rest, then we'll talk."

She squinted up at him. "You won't betray us to the magistrate, will you? I mean, you won't tell the authorities that we're here?"

The words were hardly out of her mouth when she wished them back. His expression had not changed, but she could feel his anger, sense it in his controlled response.

"I'm going to excuse that remark because I know how tired you must be. But I should like to know what reason you have to mistrust me."

"I don't mistrust you. I wasn't thinking. Can't we just leave it at that?"

"Do you still suspect me of breaking into your office?"

"No!" There was no hesitation in her response. She added quickly, "A man like you would use other means to get the information he wanted!"

His voice was like silk. "A man like me?"

He was pressing her, and that made her more frank than wise. "You're a . . . what I mean is, you have a way with women. Oh, you know what I mean!"

"That I'm a rake, in fact?"

"Well . . . yes."

She watched in some apprehension as he set aside his cane. "What are you doing?" she asked warily.

"Proving a point."

When his warm hands cupped her shoulders, she went rigid and raised her hand to shove him away. He would not budge. Emotions glittered behind the thick veil of his lashes—temper and, she thought, a curious irony. When his lips took hers, she was too startled to struggle. Eyes wide, she stared up at him.

He didn't kiss a woman's mouth, he made love to it, opening her lips with the gentle pressure of his, nibbling, using his tongue to separate and gently probe. It was sweetly erotic, then not so sweet as the kiss became wetter, hotter, more demanding. She leaned into him, just to get her balance. Her head was swimming.

His lips left hers and began to explore the hollow of her throat, her cheeks, her eyes. Cold reason tried to intrude, but her mind was dulled by fatigue. There was something here beyond her knowing, something she couldn't control, or didn't want to control.

She was suddenly set back on her heels. Shocked, befuddled by fatigue and arousal, she stared up at him. "What in blazes do you think you're doing?" She massaged her throat in a vain effort to control her breathing.

He said calmly, "I'm living up to my wicked reputation. But you'll notice, I know when to stop. Do you?"

When he picked up his cane and made for the door, she went after him. "Now, you listen to me, Waldo Bowman." She could hardly contain her frustration. "You've got the wrong idea about me and I won't have it. I'm not one of your light-skirts."

He replied easily, "No, but I think you'd like to be."

She was taken aback, then she was livid. "I'm a respectable widow. Do you think I'd take up with a rake? I have more respect for myself, yes, and more respect for my late husband."

"Ah, the saintly John. I wondered when you would throw him in my teeth."

He turned so quickly that she bumped into him, then she quickly retreated a step.

Laughter lurked in his eyes. "Didn't he ever pounce on you and kiss you until you thought your heart would burst?"

"Yes," she said sweetly, "but he had marriage on his mind. What do you have in mind, Mr. Bowman, mmm?"

His brows rose. "In the interests of self-preservation, I don't think I should answer that question." He turned and walked to the front door.

Seething, insulted, she went after him. "Just stay away from me. Do you understand? Just stay away."

His hat and gloves were on the hall table. He picked them up and turned to face her. There was plenty of light to read his expression. His eyes were hard, giving the lie to the velvet in his voice.

"I understand you perfectly. That's not important. More to the point, do you understand *me*? You've been released into my custody and I've posted a bond for your good conduct. Think of me as your guardian and yourself as my ward. Naturally, we'll be seeing a great deal of each other, at least for the next little while."

Jo's fierce green eyes met his cool gray eyes in a wordless battle of wills.

"I didn't set these terms," he said mildly. "The magistrate did. If you don't like them, I suggest you take it up with him."

"That won't be necessary."

"No, I thought not. One other thing. I may be gone for a day or two while I make inquiries about Eric. I trust you'll do nothing in that short time to bring Magistrate Vine's wrath down on our heads?"

She breathed through her teeth.

A flicker of a smile touched his lips. "Such control! But I'm not fooled, Jo Chesney. I've tasted your passion."

She held the door for him. On the front step, he turned back to her. "But you kiss like a novice. Why is that?"

She shut the door in his face.

He struck out along Greek Street to Soho Square, where he found a hackney to take him home. It wasn't far, but their progress was slowed by a plethora of vehicles coming and going to various houses along the route. The London Season was in full swing, when anyone who aspired to fashion or celebrity status was obliged to attend a series of balls, receptions, musicales, parties, and so on in order to be seen or talked about.

There was no escaping the Season. One had a duty to one's parents and one's unmarried sisters. Especially one's unmarried sisters. By this time next week, he would be squiring his mother and sisters from one function to another. He wondered what his family would make of Jo Chesney. The question was irrelevant because his family would never meet her. It shouldn't take long to settle the problem of what to do with Eric, then he and Jo Chesney need never meet again.

The kiss had been a mistake. She'd thrown out one of her irresistible challenges and, naturally, he had taken it up. They'd been throwing darts at each other from the moment they'd met. It was a game that he'd enjoyed. She looked down her nose at him because he was a rake, or so she supposed, and he held her up to ridicule because she was a prude.

All he'd wanted was to teach her a lesson. What he'd got was more genuine passion than he'd tasted in an age. It would be a long while before he forgot that kiss.

Nothing could come of it. No one could live up to her saintly husband. Besides, a woman like Jo Chesney wouldn't settle for anything less than marriage. If he'd told her what was on his mind, she would probably have broken his nose—or worse.

His lips quirked.

His half smile faded when he remembered how she'd looked when he found her in Bow Street. That must not be allowed to happen again. He would be out of town for at least a day, maybe two. Surely, he could trust her to stay out of trouble until he returned?

There was something else—the business of the break-in at the *Journal*'s offices. She still hadn't confided in him, still hadn't told him the reason for this sudden trip to London.

It was inevitable that his next thought would be of Sergeant Harper, a battle-scarred veteran of the Spanish Campaign, now on leave from Special Branch because of injuries received on his last assignment. Sergeant Harper could turn his hand to anything. He blended in with the scenery. As a result, when there was someone to be watched or protected, his name always came to mind.

Sergeant Harper. The more he thought about it, the more it seemed to be the perfect solution.

She was sure that she would fall into bed and sleep for a hundred years. Instead, she tossed, she turned, and every few minutes, or so it seemed to her, she awakened with her heart thundering and her breath catching, as though a thunderbolt had just passed through her brain.

At one point, she got up, pulled on her dressing gown, and went to check on Eric. Their rooms adjoined, and she'd left the door open in case he needed help or cried out in the middle of the night. There was a candle burning on the mantel so that, if he wakened, he would know where he was. She tiptoed to the bed and looked down on the sleeping child.

Strands of fair hair fell across his brow. She resisted the urge to brush them back with her fingertips. He looked so small and innocent. *Angelic* wasn't an exaggeration. It seemed beyond belief that anyone would wish to harm an innocent child.

If it hadn't been for her aunt, Eric might still be locked up in that closet in Mr. Harding's school. She liked to think that she was kindhearted and generous by nature, but in Eric's case, she'd seen only a boy who'd been making a nuisance of himself—instead of a boy crying out for help.

How could she have been so blind?

Things were different now. He would soon know that she meant what she said. Whatever happened, she would not desert him.

After drawing the eiderdown over his thin shoulders, she tiptoed back to her own room and her own bed. Sleep still eluded her.

There were so many things to think about, and each weighed heavily on her mind. What was she going to do about Eric? What was she going to do about Chloë? And what was she going to do about Waldo Bowman?

She'd learned something about herself tonight that was highly unsettling. A man could appeal to her senses even when love didn't enter into it. She knew that such things could happen—her own parents were proof of that—but she would never have believed it could happen to her. It seemed to her now that by surrendering to the kiss of a rake, she had defiled John's memory.

Saintly, Waldo had called John. She didn't know where he got that idea, but it wasn't from her. Like any man, John had had his share of weaknesses. He was hopeless with money, so he soon turned their household accounts over to her. He forgot birthdays and anniversaries, but he always made up for it. He was never punctual and was too easygoing for his own good. But in the things that really mattered, he was as solid as a rock.

One thing was certain. Women had never been John's weakness, not like some men she could name.

She missed him, missed his calm good sense that could be counted on in any crisis. She missed his quiet humor and those evenings spent on long walks, or discussing books and their favorite authors, in front of the fire. But most of all, she missed the loving....

Eyes closed, she tried to bring his face into focus. It wasn't John's likeness that came to her but Waldo's.

She abruptly pulled the covers up to her nose and willed herself to sleep.

Chapter 9

I am not like my mother. That was what came to Jo's mind the instant she awakened, but she could not connect it to anything in particular, and as soon as she pushed back the covers, other thoughts battled for precedence—Chloë, Eric, and the humiliating prospect of having to defer to Waldo Bowman's wishes as though he were her guardian.

She hurried through her ablutions and minutes later entered Eric's bedchamber. Her aunt was there, with her mending basket. Eric was asleep.

Mrs. Daventry spoke in a soft undertone. "He was awake earlier and drank down two glasses of chocolate."

"Is that good for him?"

"It won't do him any harm, and I'm hoping when he wakens you'll be able to tempt him to eat *real* food."

"Me?" Jo looked at her aunt. "What can I do?"

"You've made a conquest there." Mrs. Daventry

chuckled. "All he can talk about is how you stood up to Mr. Harding. I must say, I was impressed too. I don't think there's anything Eric wouldn't do to please you now."

Jo looked down at the sleeping boy and felt her heart clench. He looked so small in that big bed, small and frail.

"I won't let anything happen to him," she said softly, more to herself.

Mrs. Daventry cocked her head and studied Jo for a moment or two. Finally, she said, "With you and Mr. Bowman to champion him, I'm sure Eric will do very well. Which reminds me, he was here earlier—Mr. Bowman, I mean."

"Here? Why didn't you wake me?"

"Because he asked me not to."

"What did he want?"

"I'd tell you if you'd let me catch my breath." Mrs. Daventry paused, and when Jo pressed her lips together went on, "He said that he was leaving for Stratford to see Eric's grandmother and confer with the vicar. All going well, he should be back tomorrow, at which time he'll look in on us and tell us what he has found out. That's what he told me. He told Eric that he was safe now and that he'd nothing to fear from Mr. Harding. He would make sure of it."

"That was kind of him," Jo said dutifully.

"I thought so."

"Yes, but..." Jo sighed. "Can we believe him?"

"Why shouldn't we?"

"I'm not saying he doesn't mean well, but a man in his position..." Jo shrugged. "Oh, you know what I mean. He's a celebrity. He's in demand. One small boy and his problems are not likely to hold his thoughts for long."

Mrs. Daventry considered for a moment, then shook her head. "No, dear. I'm sure you're wrong. Mr. Bowman doesn't strike me as banal or frivolous. When he says he'll do something, he'll do it."

A ghost of a smile touched Jo's lips. "I see. You've formed a favorable opinion of his character just because he once took you in to supper?"

"You have a short memory," responded Mrs. Daventry. "Have you forgotten that only last night he rescued you from Bow Street? Don't you remember how shocked he was when he saw poor Eric's injuries? What I can't understand is why you are so determined to mistrust his motives."

Color flooded Jo's cheeks. "I'm not. That is...we hardly know him. All I'm saying is we shouldn't expect too much."

"Then you won't be disappointed?"

Jo gave a light laugh. "What *can* you mean by that remark?"

Mrs. Daventry's attention returned to her mending. She took a few tiny stitches before replying. "You know what I mean, Jo. You compare every man you meet with John and, of course, no man can ever measure up to John." She looked up at her niece with twinkling eyes. "I think if you give Mr. Bowman a chance, you might be surprised."

"Give him a chance!" Jo gave a snort of derision. "Aunt, he's a rake. He fights duels. He changes his lady loves as often as he changes his neckcloths."

Her aunt went on in the same placid way. "Don't confuse Mr. Bowman with your father. In his conduct to us, he has behaved like a perfect gentleman." She cocked her head to the side, studying the slow blush of color in Jo's cheeks. "So, that's the way of it!" she declared.

"I don't know what you mean."

"Don't you? Ah. Eric is wakening. Look who is here, Eric. Aunt Jo." She set aside her mending and got up. "Boiled beef and egg custard, Jo. See if you can persuade him to eat."

For a long moment, Jo stared at the doorway that her aunt had just disappeared through. At length, heaving a sigh, she brought her attention back to Eric. His big brown eyes were gazing up at her with complete and utter confidence. She was well aware that he regarded her as something between his own guardian angel and the warrior queen Boadicea. How could she live up to that?

"Eric," she began with a patently false smile, and faltered. She felt like a woman who would use her wiles to get a man to go against his own principles just to do what she wanted.

"What?" His brows were down as though he knew what was coming and was disappointed in her.

She cleared her throat. "How would you like to earn a sixpence?"

There was something to be said for bribery and corruption, thought Jo. Eric ate every morsel and everyone was happy.

"It's not," Jo told her aunt, "that he doesn't like boiled beef or egg custard. It's just that he's never had them."

She'd spent a good half hour with him before he'd fallen asleep, trying to discover what his favorite foods were so that she wouldn't have to bribe him to eat every meal. It was a pathetically small list.

"Bread, potatoes, cabbage soup, and porridge— that's what they fed him at school." Her voice held a bitter edge. "With sausage once a week and occasionally fish or a meat pie. No wonder he's thin and pale. No wonder he doesn't want to try new things. Do you know, Aunt, any boy who doesn't eat everything that's put in front of him is fed by force? The masters actually force it down their throats." She ground her teeth together. "I wish I *had* broken Harding's nose. What I can't understand is why the law doesn't do something. Schools like that shouldn't be allowed to exist!"

"I don't think the food at Harrow or Eton is much better," Mrs. Daventry replied. "That's why parents send parcels to their sons, you know, to add variety to their diet."

"Is that what you did with Roger when he was at school?"

"Of course. And that's why I suggested that we make up a parcel for Eric. He doesn't have parents to look out for his interests."

Jo's voice trembled with indignation. "I wonder that parents can be so heartless as to send their sons to such places."

"But boys want to go," protested Mrs. Daventry. "And their fathers insist on it."

"Well, Eric doesn't want to go to school, and he doesn't have a father."

"No, Jo. Eric doesn't want to go to Mr. Harding's school, because of the beatings. Let's wait and see what Mr. Bowman has to say. He won't let any harm come to Eric."

Jo stayed with Eric while her aunt went to church, but after lunch she left Eric in her aunt's care and took a hackney to Chloë's house. It was across the river, close to Lambeth Palace, and much grander than the

house on Greek Street. Chloë's late husband, Sir
Ralph, had inherited his wealth. There was no entail,
so when he died, everything passed to Chloë.

It sat in its own grounds, a three-story Georgian
mansion with an extensive conservatory at the back.
Most of the rooms were shut up and the furniture under Holland covers. The house was too big for one person, but Chloë couldn't bear to part with it. It held too
many happy memories, she said. She could close her
eyes and sense Ralph's presence. She couldn't possibly
sell the house and turn him over to strangers.

It sounded morbid, but Chloë was anything but
morbid. In fact, she was a pleasure to be with. Her energy and love of life were infectious. She had, however,
one major failing. She would go off by fits and starts
without telling anyone what she was up to.

Jo had intended to pay this call as soon as she arrived in town, but that was before she'd become em-
broiled in Eric's troubles. In fact, when she came up to
town, she usually stayed with Chloë, not with her aunt.

She stopped the hackney at the gates to Webberley
House, paid off the driver, and walked up the gravel
drive to the front door. It was opened by the parlor
maid. There were no manservants in Chloë's employ,
except Sykes—the old, decrepit gardener—and his
helpers. A woman on her own, Chloë said, had to be
doubly careful about provoking the wrong sort of gossip. It was acceptable to have one's name linked with a
blue blood, but not with a footman.

It was mostly talk. Chloë loved to shock people out
of their complacency.

"Any word from Lady Webberley?" asked Jo as the
maid helped her off with her coat.

"No, ma'am. We were hoping you might have news

for us. Mrs. Paige is that worried, though she tries not to show it. She'll be glad to hear you've arrived."

Like the housekeeper, Jo tried to hide from the servants how worried she was. "Then I'd best speak to her right away." She groped in her mind for the maid's name. "Tell her I'll be in the morning room, Libby."

"Yes, mu'um."

When Libby hesitated, Jo said, "What is it, Libby?"

"I don't see your boxes."

"My . . . oh, my valise? Well, I'm staying with my aunt on this visit."

A look of disappointment crossed Libby's face, and Jo hastened to add, "For the rest of the week anyway. Then we'll see."

The maid curtsied and hurried away. Jo let out a long breath and took a moment to absorb her surroundings. Light streamed in from a Venetian window on the half landing, adding a glow to the gracious interior. The walls and stair carpet were done in pale gray, a perfect background for the brilliant splashes of color from the crimson upholstered pieces and the hothouse flowers in a crystal vase on the round boulle table. Chloë had an unnerving eye for color. She could have been an artist or earned her living as a landscape gardener.

Flowers were one of Chloë's passions. The conservatory was a wedding present from her husband and, Jo suspected, the main reason Chloë could not be parted from Webberley House. Her friend knew more about the care and propagation of her plants than the gardener did, which was not surprising. These were not ordinary, garden-variety English flowers. These were exotic specimens, transplanted from foreign shores— all the places, in fact, where Sir Ralph had served as a British diplomat.

There were flowers in the morning room as well, or rather, flowering plants in terra-cotta pots—creamy blooms on long, woody stems. *Orchis* or something like it is what Chloë called them. They were supposed to be priceless, because few people in England had them. Rare plants were more precious to Chloë than rubies or diamonds.

The morning room was the hub of the house. It served as a breakfast room, an office, and a snug little parlor. French doors gave onto the terrace, with its vista of immaculate lawns and profusion of flowering plants and, at the end of the property, the magnificent Gothic conservatory.

Jo walked to the French doors and opened them. It was a perfect spring day. The sun was warm, birds were chirping on their perches, and the air was fragrant with the mingled scents of daffodils, hyacinths, and flowers she could not name. It was so warm that the fires had not yet been lit, though that would change when the sun went down.

She had a flash of recall: Chloë, with scissors in hand, clipping the dead heads off flowers, waving her over to see something.

She shut the French doors with a snap and turned back to survey the room. If Chloë were here, it would have been overflowing with books, periodicals, and, of course, the latest copy of the *Journal.* Letters would have been strewn over the top of the rosewood escritoire, as well as invitations to various functions. Obviously, the maids had tidied everything away.

She couldn't avoid it. She had to go through Chloë's things, but she was reluctant to begin. It made her worst fears seem closer to coming true.

Chloë's calendar of engagements was in the top drawer. Jo eagerly turned the pages till she came to the dates she wanted. There were only two entries: Lady Brinsley, Oxfordshire, and Jo, Stratford. If she'd kept to this itinerary, Chloë would have been in Stratford more than two weeks ago.

Jo sat back and let the thought turn in her mind. After Chloë had visited Lady Brinsley in Oxfordshire, had something else come up? An invitation that Chloë couldn't resist? A new man in her life? In spite of Chloë's expression of undying love for her late husband, she was attractive to men and attracted by them. Jo could not be sure, but from things Chloë had let slip, she'd wondered whether Chloë had taken the odd lover since she'd become a widow. Before she could prevent it, a picture of Waldo flitted into her mind. Chloë would have taken his kiss in stride, because it would have meant as little to her as it had to him. In fact, in some respects, she and Waldo were one of a kind, except that Chloë was mostly talk and Waldo lived up to his reputation.

Elbows on the escritoire, she rested her chin on her linked fingers, thinking of Chloë and how they'd come to be such close friends. It shouldn't have happened. They were as different as night from day.

The *Journal* had brought them together. Having been raised in Stratford, Chloë became a faithful subscriber, and whenever there was an appeal for some deserving cause, she never failed to respond generously. But her letters were never simple. She asked questions and made comments on articles the paper carried that required a response, and John had given Jo the job of answering them. So began a delightful correspondence that ranged from the trivial (how to get a mustard stain out of white silk) to the serious (why Britain was at war with France).

John was surprised at their friendship, especially

when he first met Chloë. He thought she must be
something like Jo's mother. She dressed to the nines;
she was flirtatious; she was a beauty. But that's as far as
the resemblance went. Chloë's mind was as sharp as a
needle. She was interested in everyone and everything.
Jo's mother's main occupation was to preserve her leg-
endary allure.

A month after John's death, Chloë turned up on
Jo's doorstep. She'd stayed for a week, cajoling and
threatening, getting Jo to eat, forcing her to leave the
house if only to go for a walk. As soon as she returned
to London, however, Jo sank back into her lethargy.
The next time Chloë came to see her, it was at Jo's re-
quest, when the *Journal* was on the verge of bank-
ruptcy. And it was because of Chloë that she'd found
the confidence to take over John's paper and make a
success of it.

She owed a lot to Chloë.

Chloë, where are you? she whispered into the silence.

If something interesting had come up, Chloë
wouldn't have been breaking any engagements to accept it. If she turned up in Stratford, well and good. If
not, Jo never worried about it. It wasn't that kind of invitation. She and Chloë never stood on ceremony with
each other.

She supposed Chloë had kept her appointment
with Lady Brinsley at her country estate. Maybe Lady
Langston had been there too. They were all keen gardeners. Was that the connection? Was there a house
party?

Then where had Chloë gone next?

There were other entries in the calendar, parties
and dos that Chloë had missed, and some that were
just coming up. This was the height of the London Season. Chloë wouldn't have missed it for anything.

Then where was she?

Jo went through the escritoire drawer by drawer. There were a few bills, several invitations to balls and musicales, but not what Jo was looking for, nothing that resembled a diary.

A quick perusal of the bookcase wasn't much help. She found exactly what she expected to find: one shelf devoted to literary works and the rest an untidy hodge-podge of books and folios, all dealing with some aspect of gardening and the care and propagation of hot house plants.

She went to the closet next and couldn't help smiling at the disorder that met her eyes. On the lower shelves, there were stacks of old newspapers and periodicals, in no particular order. Above them were wooden boxes. Jo fetched a chair and climbed up to get a better look. All she found were receipts and an odd assortment of household articles and clothing that looked as though Chloë was storing for the parish poor.

On top of the sideboard was a silver salver with a number of calling cards. These would have come from ladies who had visited the house when Chloë was away. Chloë's visitors had one thing in common. They all lived in Mayfair, the most prestigious residential district in London. Jo recognized only one name, Lady Langston's. She wondered if Lady Brinsley had come up to town after the house party at her country estate. Or perhaps there was no house party. She knew that Chloë and Lady Brinsley were friends. Perhaps . . .

These endless speculations were driving her mad. She had to find answers. She had to trace Chloë's movements before she vanished. But where to begin?

There was a tap at the door and the housekeeper entered. Mrs. Paige was in her early fifties, tall, handsome, and, so Chloë always said, a credit to her profession.

The house ran like a well-oiled clock, even with no mistress in residence. Many ladies had tried to lure Mrs. Paige away from Chloë and failed. The secret of keeping good servants, Chloë once told Jo, was to pay them well. She was only partly right, thought Jo. Chloë's servants adored her.

"Come in, Mrs. Paige," she said, "and let's see what we can make of this conundrum."

Not only did she question the housekeeper, but she also questioned the inside servants. There were gardeners, but as they did not live on the premises, she left them out of it for the moment.

What she heard confirmed her own thinking. More than two weeks had passed since Chloë had set off for Oxfordshire, in the company of friends, to take in Lord and Lady Brinsley's house party. And that was the last they had heard or seen of her. When the housekeeper became anxious—though she would hardly say she was alarmed—she had prevailed on Lady Langston to write to Jo and put the whole matter before her. So now the onus was on Jo to decide what to do.

She listened, nodded, and asked them one by one whether they knew where Lady Webberley kept her diary. No one did. No one saw the point of her question, and she did not enlighten them.

After this, she went from room to room, not in a desultory way, but to search for the diary, beginning with the dining room, then the drawing room, and finally the bedrooms. The housemaids had kept everything spotless. Nothing caught her eye; nothing seemed out of place.

In Chloë's bedroom, she stood at the window, looking down on Chloë's sanctuary, her beautiful and charming walled garden. Everything seemed in harmony, everything except Jo and her vague uncertainties. Would Chloë have left her garden unattended for so long?

It was time to call in the authorities. She would have to go to Bow Street and talk to the magistrate. No, that wouldn't do. They wouldn't take her seriously, not after all the trouble she'd given them.

If only she had something solid to show them. There was Chloë's letter, but she didn't think that would galvanize them into action, not coming from her.

So what should she do?

She would begin, she decided, by paying a call on Lady Langston, and after that, as many of Chloë's friends as she could manage. Their names were all on the cards they had left in Chloë's absence. And since they all lived in Mayfair, or on the edges of Mayfair like her aunt Daventry, the task wouldn't be too onerous.

Though she was impatient to get started, she had to wait until the following day. No one visited on a Sunday unless by invitation. All the same, now that she'd decided how to go on, she felt her spirits lift. She returned to the morning room, found a large envelope, and filled it with all the cards, invitations, and other pieces of correspondence she'd found in Chloë's escritoire. The desk calendar wouldn't go into it, so she tucked it under her arm.

One way or another, she was going to track her friend down. On that resolute thought, she left the room.

As soon as he saw Mrs. Chesney leave in a hackney, Jacob Fry—not his real name—left the conservatory and presented himself at the back door. He'd been hired on as a part-time odd-job man when the regular man met with an unfortunate accident, which Fry had contrived only a week ago. It was just a broken arm, but it prevented Mr. Cable from performing his duties. In addition to taking care of the heavy work in the garden, the odd man had to stoke the furnace for the conservatory, bring in wood and coal for the many fireplaces, clean and fill the oil lamps, and generally make himself useful. It was a perfect cover for someone who wanted to have the run of both the house and grounds without rousing anyone's suspicions.

Of course, he had to evade the vigilant eyes of old Sykes and Mrs. Paige, but Jacob was good at avoiding detection. That's what made him so highly sought after. He was a Bow Street Runner turned bad. If the price was right, he was game for anything.

Today, Sunday, he had a free hand. Sykes wouldn't be in till tomorrow, and Mrs. Paige would be reading her Bible. Nobody would be keeping an eye on him.

On this occasion, he didn't want access to the various rooms in the house. He'd already been through them, searching for anything that might look like a diary. He'd found nothing. What he wanted now was information.

He couldn't help thinking that whoever found that diary could make his fortune by selling it to the highest bidder.

Libby opened the door to him. He knew how to play her. She was only a servant, but he treated her as though she were a duchess.

He'd already removed his cap. "I'd best clean and oil those lamps now," he said, "unless there's something else you'd 'ave me do?"

She ushered him inside with a laugh. "You never stop, do you, Mr. Fry?"

"That's what I'm paid for, Miss Libby. An honest day's work for an honest day's wages, that's what I say."

"You sound just like my da." A wistful look came over her face. "He's been gone five years now and I still miss him something fierce."

Fry was well aware of it. "A man after my own heart," he said, and was rewarded with a grateful smile.

"I'll put the kettle on," she said, "and when you've seen to the lamps, we'll have a nice cup o' tea before you go."

That was exactly what Jacob wanted to hear.

An hour later, when he left the house, he was feeling let down. It didn't look as though he'd be selling the diary to the highest bidder after all. Mrs. Chesney had asked all the servants if they knew anything about her ladyship's diary, but no one had.

All he could do now was make his report. Mrs. Chesney didn't know where the diary was. She didn't know where Lady Webberley was, or so she said. He was sure he could frighten the information out of her if only he could get her alone. It would have to be away from the house. The conservatory came to mind.

It was something to think about. Meantime, he had a report to make.

Chapter 10

The following morning, Jo dressed with care. This was London at the height of the Season. She would be calling on fashionable society ladies. She didn't want them to think she was a country bumpkin.

Even at the best of times, her wardrobe lacked panache. That's what Chloë called it, *panache*. By that she meant flair and style. The trouble was, after John died, she'd become involved with the newspaper, and there didn't seem much point in dressing up when there was no one special to please. She wasn't a dowd by any means, but she didn't keep up with the latest fashions. Now, as she studied her reflection in the looking glass, she wished she'd listened to Chloë. She looked like a colorless little governess.

The day was warming up nicely when she descended from her hackney in Berkeley Square, right outside Lady Langston's house. She paid off the driver, mounted the stairs, and was admitted by a cheerful maid who told her to wait and she would see if her mistress was at home. This was a polite way of saying that the maid would ask whether her mistress wished to receive this particular visitor or not. On this occasion, Jo was sure of her welcome. After all, it was Lady Langston who had sent for her.

She was just beginning to feel the awkwardness of perhaps being turned away when the rustle of skirts on the staircase alerted her to the presence of, she presumed, Lady Langston.

"My dear Mrs. Chesney," said that lady, coming forward and offering Jo her hand. "I am delighted to make your acquaintance at last. Chloë has told me so much about you. I have a snug little dressing room, so much more comfortable than the drafty drawing room. And I feel as though you are a friend. No need for ceremony between us." And in this warm and effusive vein, she led the way upstairs.

The dressing room turned out to be a cozy parlor and reminded Jo of Chloë's morning room. The escritoire was littered with correspondence; there was an untidy welter of books on the bookcase and sideboard, and the same pots of orchis on a table close to the window but not too close. It would never do for rare plants to catch a chill.

"Let me ring for refreshments," Lady Langston pulled the bell rope beside the fireplace as she spoke.

Jo's focus shifted to her ladyship. She judged her to be in her mid to late fifties. Her chubby cheeks were bunched in a smile; her eyes mirrored a friendly interest. She wore a fussy taffeta gown of dark plum that did nothing to flatter her buxom figure. Jo had a vision of the overstuffed maroon-colored sofa in her mother's drawing room. It was very comfortable.

When they were both seated, her ladyship began. "What news of Chloë?"

Jo shook her head. "I think you must know more than I do. It was only yesterday I learned that she'd visited Lady Brinsley at her place in Oxfordshire."

"Brinsley Hall," her ladyship confirmed with a nod. "Didn't I mention it in my letter?"

"No, not one word."

"Oh, dear." Lady Langston's face lost some of its animation. "I think I took it for granted that you knew. It was a house party, just a small group of us, all members of the Horticultural Society. Elinor had invited us to show off the improvements she'd made to her conservatory. The earl was there, but he didn't stay long, and we had a lovely time talking about gardens and walking around the grounds. The place is steeped in history, you know."

"Elinor? That would be Lady Brinsley?"

"Yes. And her son was there, Viscount Morden. A nice young man."

Jo knew all about the Horticultural Society. It was one of Chloë's passions. That's where she'd met Lady Brinsley. There was a method in this, Chloë said, because it opened doors for Lady Tellall. She would have been making copious notes in her diary for her London Life column.

"Is the viscount a member of your society?"

Lady Langston laughed. "I can't see Morden getting his hands and boots grubby. He's too fashionable for us, and we're too old for him. No. Elinor had prevailed on him to be our guide. I told you the place is steeped in history. The Romans were there first, though there's little left of them but a few statues and such like. The monks came next and built a monastery on the ruins of the Roman villa. Morden knows everything, and he's very good about showing visitors around. It's quite an education."

"What happened to the monastery?"

"That became Brinsley Hall—all done over, of course, to make it comfortable."

The thought that occurred to Jo couldn't be voiced aloud. She was thinking that Chloë was, like Morden, too young for the gardening crowd.

She knew about Morden from Chloë's column, but all that she could remember was that he came from a proud and illustrious family and was about to marry into another proud and illustrious family. Blue bloods, Chloë said, cared about things like that. He wasn't colorful in the way that Waldo was colorful. Come to think of it, Chloë was colorful too.

She said, "When did you last see Chloë?"

"That last night, before we all went to bed. But I knew she wanted to get away early the next morning, so when I didn't see her for breakfast, I thought nothing of it. Since then, I've talked to Elinor and to several of our mutual friends, and they haven't seen or heard from her either."

"You talked to Lady Brinsley?"

"I did."

"Here, in town?"

"Yes. But she's not here now. Elinor finds town life too harrowing. She prefers the country. All the same, there are engagements she must press herself to attend. She was here only a day or so ago to preside at a reception for her son's betrothed. There are other functions planned that she must attend, so I expect to see her in town before long."

"I see." It didn't sound as though she would be speaking to Lady Brinsley in the near future.

Lady Langston looked down at her clasped hands.

When she looked up her expression was grave. "You're like me, aren't you?" she said. "You think that something dreadful must have happened to Chloë, some terrible accident?"

"I don't know what I believe," Jo said.

She debated whether to tell Lady Langston about Chloë's alarming note and decided against it. Chloë had warned her to be careful, that she might be in danger, and she took that warning to heart.

But the note reminded her of something.

She said carefully, "I'm surprised Chloë didn't write to me from Brinsley Hall, just to advise me when to expect her. And she knew I'd love to have a sample of Lady Brinsley's notepaper."

Lady Langston looked at her blankly for a moment or two before enlightenment dawned. "Oh, you mean with the earl's crest emblazoned on the top?"

"A leopard's head," supplied Jo.

"Yes. I believe you are right. Perhaps she meant to take a sample of notepaper with her when she left."

That was one piece of the puzzle solved. Chloë had written that note when she was at Brinsley Hall, probably that last night. Then the letter should have arrived more than two weeks ago, not four days ago. What was the reason for the delay?

This was hopeless. One problem was solved only to be replaced by another.

Jo said, "Lady Langston, you must have been one of the last people to see Chloë. I want to know what went on at that house party. I want to know the names of those who were there, what was said, and if anything out of the ordinary happened. Someone must have seen Chloë leave. She can't have disappeared into thin air. Take your time and tell me everything you remember."

Lady Langston regarded Jo sadly for a moment, as though she understood her reluctance to think the worst, then she began to speak. "Chloë and I were fortunate to be invited by Lord and Lady Skene to travel up with them. We arrived in the evening in good spirits, and after unpacking, we dressed for a late-night supper, which was laid out in the dining room." She stopped and shook her head. "This is impossible. We went for walks. We played cards in the evening, or entertained ourselves at the piano. We spent part of every day in Elinor's conservatory, or admiring the grounds and gardens. I don't know what else to tell you."

Jo understood the older woman's frustration. She didn't know where to begin either. After thinking about it for a moment, she said, "What happened that last night? Who was there? Who said what? Perhaps someone invited Chloë to another house party or planted the idea in her mind of going off somewhere else. Don't try to pick out what's important. Just go over that last evening as you remember it."

Lady Langston tried to remember, but it was obvious she was beginning to feel harried. However, two facts came to light. The first was that Chloë had hired a chaise to take her to Stratford, since she wouldn't be returning with the others to London. The second fact was that her boxes were not at the Hall.

"Her boxes?" said Jo.

"For her clothes. Everyone's boxes had been brought down the night before, for those who wanted to get an early start. Chloë's boxes were not there. When I asked about it, I was told that Chloë had left long before breakfast."

"Who told you that?"

"I . . . one of the servants, I think."

They were interrupted when a footman and maid

arrived with the tea things. Jo could see why her hostess was well upholstered. Tea and biscuits turned out to be a veritable feast. There were cream buns, buttered scones, macaroons, seedcake, and finally, an array of biscuits, all displayed to mouthwatering perfection on a three-tiered stand.

As they demolished one tier of dainties after another, the conversation became general, but Jo soon brought it back to what most interested her, the Brinsleys' house party. There were only a dozen guests, and most of the names were known to her, but the ones that stood out were the ones she'd read about in Chloë's column or were among the ladies who had left their calling cards at Chloë's house.

"As I told you," said her ladyship, "they know as little as I, at least the ones I've talked to. No one is particularly perturbed. Everyone seems to think that Chloë will turn up in her own good time." A thought struck her. "You should talk to Elinor. She will be in town soon to make arrangements for a ball she'll be giving next month to mark her son's engagement to Lady Margaret Kintyre—you know, the marquess's daughter?"

Shortly after this exchange, Jo rose to leave. Her ladyship walked her to the front door. They parted with promises on each side to keep in touch and let the other know if anything turned up.

Once on the pavement, Jo looked at her watch and decided that there was more than enough time to pay a call on the ladies whose cards she'd taken from Chloë's house, or at least those who were also at Brinsley Hall at the crucial time. But it was really Lady Brinsley she wished to question. She'd just have to wait until her ladyship came to town.

Chapter 11

She was back in Greek Street within the hour, out of patience, out of humor, and, she grudgingly admitted, a trifle hurt. Crushed was a more accurate description, but she didn't want to start feeling sorry for herself, so she focused on her ire.

Not one of the ladies she had called on had been "at home," only she suspected they were *all* at home. The trouble was, not only had she no cards to present to the supercilious maids who answered the door, but she wasn't dressed for the part of a fashionable lady. She could guess what they'd told their mistresses, because, in very short order, she was shown the door.

She despised London society and all its affectations.

She wasn't done yet, though. She was a newspaper woman, and she wasn't going to give up so easily. Besides, this wasn't about a story. This was about Chloë.

Rose helped her off with her pelisse. In a voice she might have used to pass on state secrets, she whispered,

"He's here, ma'am. Mr. Bowman, I mean. He's with master Eric. Such a fine, polite gentleman."

A burst of childish laughter had them both looking up at the ceiling. "And," added Rose, "he has a way with children. Master Eric ate all his luncheon, every last bite of it, as though he hadn't seen food in a year."

Jo made a harrumphing sound, decided she was being churlish, and managed a smile. "Mr. Bowman has a way with everyone, Rose."

"Doesn't he, though? Oh, Mrs. Daventry said I was to tell you she's gone out shopping for clothes for Master Eric. Mr. Bowman said he'd stay with the boy till one of you got back. He's such a fine gentleman."

"Very thoughtful," Jo agreed.

She went to her own chamber first, then, after arranging her hair, she made for Eric's room just along the corridor. Much to her surprise, he wasn't in bed but up and dressed and playing cards with Waldo at a small table in front of the fire.

She crossed the room on a rustle of skirts and plumped herself down on the edge of the bed before Waldo had a chance to get to his feet. She was thinking of his lame leg and how he shouldn't stand up out of politeness just because a female had entered the room. She needn't have worried. No one seemed to be aware of her existence. They were both concentrating on their cards.

She let out a little hiss of breath. "Good afternoon, Mr. Bowman," she said, "Eric." She nodded in Eric's direction. "Oh, don't let me disturb you."

Apart from a murmured greeting, they took her at her word.

Fulminating now, she said, "So, how did things go in Stratford? What did the vicar have to say?"

Waldo looked up with a lazy grin. "I've arranged

everything to our satisfaction. Mr. Sutherland couldn't be happier. I'll tell you all about it as soon as this game is finished."

Eric chimed in, "I don't have to go back to Mr. Harding's school, Aunt Jo. I don't have to do anything Uncle Waldo doesn't want me to do."

"And Aunt Jo," Waldo amended with a disarming smile. "Her opinion counts too." A small interval of silence, then, "No, Eric, you can't play that card. Here, let me show you."

Jo watched in silence as the game progressed. Evidently it was her day to be ignored, first by the ladies of the *ton* and now by Eric and Waldo. She watched them as they played their cards. *Pique* was too strong a word for what she felt. *Disappointed* was closer to the mark. It wasn't often that she was made to feel invisible.

Waldo's preoccupation took care of one problem, though. He was pretending that the kiss had never happened. She was glad, because it saved them both a great deal of embarrassment.

Finally, she could no longer contain herself, and she said, aggrieved, "Is that all you have to tell me? You've arranged everything? The vicar is happy? And Eric doesn't have to go back to Mr. Harding's school? What have you arranged? Why is Mr. Sutherland happy? What's going on?"

Another lazy smile from Waldo. "Patience, Jo, patience. I'm fighting for my life here. Eric is poised to annihilate me. I can't let that happen. When the game is over, then we'll talk." He gave her a speaking look. "In private."

His words rebuked her. She was in the wrong, of course. Obviously, he didn't want Eric to know what he'd found out.

Another silence as the game went on. Jo grew restless. She wasn't happy with the idea of Eric learning to play cards when most boys would be doing their lessons.

She voiced the thought. "Wouldn't Eric's time be better spent in reading or doing arithmetic?"

"He *is* reading and doing arithmetic. Just watch him."

It was true. There was a pencil and paper in front of Eric with words and numbers on it. Not only that, but he was counting his cards.

Waldo said, "The point of getting an education is to put it to use. That's what we're doing. If Eric can't read and count, he can't play cards—not with me, at any rate."

This newfound camaraderie between Eric and Waldo made her feel distinctly out-of-sorts. It seemed that she and Waldo had very different views on how to raise a boy.

She couldn't keep the edge from her voice. "There must be better uses for an education than playing cards!"

Eric said, "All the boys at school know how to play cards."

"That's no reason for you to follow their example."

Waldo looked at her with a frown in his eyes. "That's where you're wrong, Jo. A boy must fit in with his peers. He must be able to hold his own."

"Trump!" Eric suddenly yelled, making Jo jump. "I won! I won!"

"Fair and square," Waldo conceded.

"Well," said Jo, relenting a little. "I suppose it's harmless enough when there's no gambling involved. But since you've made a miraculous recovery, young man, it's lessons for you tomorrow."

Eric's brilliant smile died. "But..." He looked at Waldo.

Unconcerned, Waldo said, "I've promised to teach him how to fight. Now, don't look as though you've swallowed a prune. It's a sport. Every self-respecting gentleman knows how to defend himself."

Eric piped up. "I want to know how to fight, Aunt Jo, so those boys will leave me alone."

"And so they will," said Waldo emphatically.

His look spoke volumes. Jo understood. No doubt Eric had met with his share of bullies at Harding's school. All the same, it was a bit galling to have Waldo take charge without consulting her.

Both Waldo and Eric were watching her closely, waiting for her to respond. "I abhor violence in all its manifestations," she said.

Waldo's brows climbed, then he hooted with laughter. "Tell that to Magistrate Vine and Mr. Harding."

"I—" she huffed. "What else could I do? I couldn't let them take Eric away, could I?"

"No!" cried Eric.

"Certainly not," Waldo responded. "You did the right thing. Sometimes a show of force is the only honorable recourse that is left to us. Win or lose, we've got to fight." He added gently, "All I'm teaching Eric is how to defend himself."

His eyes saw too much. He was well aware that she resented his influence. She let out a breath and shook her head. "I can hardly wait to see it. A fine pair you make: you Eric, with your bruised ribs, and you with your—" She stopped and colored faintly.

"Gammy leg," supplied Waldo easily. "Don't be embarrassed. I think it's more awkward when people don't mention it."

Eric's eyes shone with excitement. "Uncle Waldo

didn't let that stop him during the war. At the siege of Bada...Bada—whatever—he and Major Somerset drew their swords and fought off all the bad men who were trying to hurt the governor's daughters."

"The siege of Badajoz," Jo murmured and smirked.

Chloë had written about the incident in her column, but it had slipped Jo's mind. Now it all came back to her, how Captain Bowman and Major Somerset had fought off the scum of the victorious British army to save the governor's daughters from being dragged off and ravished. Badajoz would be forever remembered as a black day in the annals of the British army even though Wellington had hanged the worst offenders.

Laughter lurked in the look she gave Waldo. "You mustn't believe everything you read in the papers, you know."

"The incident was mentioned in dispatches," he protested. "Anyway, the point I was trying to impress on Eric was that a man of honor always protects the weak, whatever the consequences."

"That's what I'm going to be when I grow up," said Eric, "a man of honor, just like you, Aunt Jo and Uncle Waldo."

She started to laugh, saw that he was in earnest, and dipped him an elegant curtsy instead. "Why, Eric, that is the nicest compliment a gentleman has ever paid me."

Eric beamed.

Waldo got up. "I shall ring for Rose," he told Eric, "and you can tell her you may have a demitasse of chocolate. Not a whole cup, but a demitasse. Understood?"

Eric nodded.

"So," said Jo, "that's how you got Eric to eat his lunch. That's blackmail."

"I don't know why you're smirking. All I did was take a leaf out of your book. Yes, Eric told me. But sixpence is a little steep for me."

She snorted, as only a well-bred lady knew how. "And the chocolate won't cost you a penny."

"Clever girl."

Eric said, "Are you leaving, Uncle Waldo?"

"Yes, but I'll see you tomorrow. In the meantime, you can practice those card tricks I showed you. And remember, don't tell a soul how they work. It's our secret."

"Cross my heart," replied Eric with feeling.

Jo led the way to a small sitting room a few doors down. "Eric likes to know that we're close by," she said. "In fact, he'll hardly let us out of his sight. Would you like something to drink—tea, coffee, or something stronger?"

"Thank you, no. Mrs. Daventry has already plied me with tea and crumpets."

"Ah." She was beginning to feel nervous and she didn't know why. In Eric's bedchamber, he'd seemed relaxed, almost playful. Now he looked . . watchful.

When she sat down on one of the chairs that flanked the empty grate and he took the other, the look was gone. He said in that easy way of his, "We missed you at lunch."

Sensing a trap, she said carefully, "I lunched with Lady Langston. Do you know her?"

"Only by name. Is she your secret scribe, Jo?"

"My secret—No! And that's all I'm going to tell you."

He regarded her thoughtfully, then went on, "You went out alone, without a maid to chaperon you."

She laughed. "I'm past the age of needing a chaperon!"

"In the country, perhaps. But not in London." He put a finger to his lips when she made to speak. "A lady with your reputation can't afford to put a foot wrong."

This unsubtle reminder of her incarceration in Bow Street put her teeth on edge. "If you are referring to my...my contretemps with the law, may I remind you that, not a moment ago, you were applauding what I'd done."

A smile tugged at the corners of his mouth. "What I'm referring to," he said, "is the fact that I stand to lose a considerable sum of money if you run afoul of the law again."

"That's not going to happen."

"I'm glad to hear it, but in this you will obey me. When you go out, you will take your maid with you."

Her eyes narrowed unpleasantly. She'd debated with herself about taking him into her confidence, but this high-handed attitude stayed the impulse. He might forbid her to go on with her investigation, and she wasn't going to allow that to happen.

He said, "If you don't like my terms, Jo, you can always go home to Stratford. In fact, that's what Magistrate Vine would prefer."

And by implication, that's what he would prefer too. So would she, but not before she'd discovered what had happened to Chloë.

"I came up to town," she said, "to visit a few friends and do a little shopping, and that's what I intend to do," and without a pause, she went on, "So, what arrangements have you made for Eric?"

Her mistake was to give him a direct look. She was caught in his stare, and his searching eyes seemed to penetrate all her defenses. She wasn't aware that she'd stopped breathing till he released her with a flick of his lashes.

"Let me set your mind at rest," he said. "The vicar is Eric's trustee. There's a small sum of money that Eric's father left for his son's education, and Mr. Sutherland won't be spending it on Mr. Harding's establishment, not after what I told him. So, with Mr. Sutherland's consent, I've applied to Chancery for temporary guardianship of the boy. There's no rush, of course, but the first thing I'll do is look for a suitable school for him."

This did not set her mind at rest. "It's a family that boy needs, not another school. He needs love, not discipline. If I were his guardian and he came to live with me, he could see his grandmother as often as he likes. When you think of it, it makes perfect sense. A man in your position doesn't have the time to look after a small boy. I do. And when his grandmother—"

"Jo," he cut in, "his grandmother is deathly ill. She may never recover."

This brought her up short. After a moment, she sighed. "Poor Eric. Then he'll have no one. It isn't fair. He's such a good boy. My aunt and I are amazed at how well he's fitting in. He doesn't seem cowed or afraid. His parents would be proud of him if they could only see how well he's turned out."

"I'm sure they would."

"He never speaks of them, and we don't like to pry. It's as though he has drawn a veil over that part of his life. You must have learned something of his background from the vicar. What did he tell you?"

He took a moment to adjust his coat, and the thought flashed into her mind that if Waldo had accompanied her that morning, they would have gained admittance to every door that was shut against her. He wasn't a fashion plate, but the cut of his blue coat and beige trousers was impeccable. That wasn't all. He had an air about him that commanded respect—not arrogance exactly, but an assurance that was entirely unconscious.

She rarely thought about her appearance, but in Waldo's presence she always felt inadequate. And now, after being turned away at every house she had called on, she was wishing that she had something more striking to wear than the plain grim kerseymere she had donned that morning.

"Eric is illegitimate," he said.

"What?" She was shocked.

"Didn't you work it out? His grandmother's name is Foley. So is his mother's."

She shook her head. "I thought Mrs. Foley was Eric's grandmother on his father's side."

"No."

He seemed reluctant to go on, but she was too curious to be put off by that. "What about his father? Don't tell me, I suppose he was already married!"

"Something like that. But he always provided for Eric and his mother. He was a decent man, Jo. He left money for Eric's education and money to support Eric's mother."

"Little enough if you ask me." She lapsed into silence. After a while, she looked up with an appeal in her eyes. "Can't you see that it would be better if I were Eric's guardian? There's an excellent school in Stratford, the Grammar School, the school that Shakespeare once attended. Eric could go there as a day boy and come home to me every evening. Why do you keep shaking your head?"

"Because you're not thinking. You're a widow, a single woman. There isn't a court in the land that would allow you to become Eric's guardian, not unless his father had stipulated it in his will, and that didn't happen."

"Well, of course it didn't happen! I never knew Eric's father!"

"Don't get angry with me! I didn't make the laws."

Her gaze was hostile. His was veiled.

She was first to break the silence. In a more conciliatory tone, she said, "I was thinking of an informal arrangement. If you and Mr. Sutherland are agreeable, the law won't stand in our way."

"But I'm not agreeable."

Her hands curled into fists. "Do you mind telling me why?"

"Not at all. You've known Eric for only a short while. What if you discover, as time goes on, that he's not what you thought he was?"

"I wouldn't abandon him, if that's what you think. When I make a commitment, I keep it."

"Yes, I know. That's one of the things I like about you."

"Then why are you being so difficult?"

A slight smile curved his lips, but it was fleeting. "I might ask why you are being so unreasonable. No, listen to me, Jo. All that the vicar and I are trying to do is honor the wishes of Eric's father."

She leaned toward him, an appeal in her eyes. "He couldn't have foreseen this situation, where Eric is alone in the world with no family to turn to."

"I think he did, but even if he didn't, it won't do. A single woman with a child would arouse the worst kind of gossip."

"As though I care about that!" she retorted.

"You may not, but you can bet your last farthing that the vicar does. And it wouldn't be good for Eric either."

There were other arguments she might have used, but she saw that his mind was made up and nothing she said would change it. So she marshaled her dignity and asked him about the schools he considered suitable for Eric. None of them was anywhere near Stratford. She thought it must be deliberate.

When there was a lull in the conversation, she said, "When do you expect Eric to go away to school?"

"There's no hurry. His ribs have to heal first. But I'd rather he stayed in London where I can keep an eye on him, so if you're planning to return to Stratford, let me know and I'll make other arrangements for Eric."

For a moment she was stunned, then she gasped and rushed into speech. "This is intolerable! If it hadn't been for my aunt and me, Eric would still be in that dreadful school, in that monster's power. We rescued him! Now you come along and suddenly you're his guardian and you're talking about taking Eric away from us?"

"I came along," he replied sharply, "because you invited me. And I don't remember saying anything about taking Eric away from you. He'll go to school, eventually, as all boys do. Until then, as his guardian, I am entitled to have some say in the ordering of his life. I'm fixed in London for the next little while. If you take him to Stratford, I'll hardly see him."

Eyes clashed and locked.

He was the one to cut the silence. "What is it to be, Jo?" he asked quietly. "Do you return to Stratford or stay in town?"

Her voice was like ice. "I'm not in a hurry to get back to Stratford."

"What about the *Journal*?"

"I have an excellent colleague who can manage on his own for a few weeks."

"Ah."

"What does that mean?"

He spread his hands. "I'm impressed. It's not every day I come across a lady who owns and runs a successful business enterprise."

She looked for mockery and saw none. "Thank you."

Another long silence ensued. She didn't know why he lingered. He must know she wanted him to go.

The thought was unworthy. Without his help, she didn't know what would have become of Eric, not to mention herself. She couldn't expect him to think like her in every particular. That was the trouble. It was irrational, but she *did* expect him to think exactly like she did, at least about Eric, and when he didn't, it rankled.

She was casting around in her mind for a neutral topic of conversation when he said conversationally, "Our mutual friend, Henry Gardiner, tells me that the *Journal* was foundering until you took the helm."

It was the truth, but it seemed disloyal to John to admit it. "I was lucky," she said. "I acquired a few writers who were writing what people wanted to read. It was as simple as that."

"Writers such as your friend Lady Tellall?"

She gave him another hostile look. She wasn't forgetting that he had once referred to the *Journal* as a broadsheet. The insult still stung. "Not everyone is a glutton for literary works, you know, or devoted to politics. Some of us like to read stories of real people. I don't take the *Times* as my model. If I did, most of my readers would cancel their subscriptions. I prefer the *Courier*. The serious news and the parliamentary report are still there, but not on the front page."

He said gently, "Jo, I'm not finding fault. I applaud

your success." He paused. "But Lady Tellall! She writes about real people, but she misrepresents them."

She tilted her head and looked at him quizzically. "You can always write a letter to the editor with your complaint, and I'll make sure it's published."

He grinned. "I wouldn't dream of lowering myself to her level!"

"Mmm. Pity. It would sell more papers. Or you could try suing me. You'd lose, of course, but that would sell more papers as well."

His lips thinned, then suddenly he laughed. When he got up, she did too, and followed him to the door. She said, "You said that you would make other arrangements for Eric if I returned to Stratford. What other arrangements?"

He was laughing when he turned to face her. "Do you never give up?"

"Never!"

"Eric could go to my sister and her husband. They have children of their own. I think Eric would like it there."

"I see." Her voice was coated with acid. "A husband makes all the difference!"

"I'm afraid so. Now, if you were to marry . . ." He left the words hanging, inviting a response.

She wondered where this was leading. He could be caustic when he wanted to be, and she had no desire for that acid tongue to make a mockery of her marriage.

"I doubt that I shall ever marry again," she replied carefully. "John and I were very happy. We were well suited. I don't expect to meet another who would suit me half as well. That's why I won't marry."

"He sounds like an exceptional man."

She heard something in his voice, not amusement

but a change of inflection. "If being good and decent is considered exceptional, then I suppose he was." She lifted her shoulders in a tiny shrug. "He wasn't like you. He wasn't a man of the world. He wasn't particularly handsome or charming." She smiled to herself. "He could be quite gruff when he wanted to be. He was also kind, generous, and as straight as an arrow. That was John." She looked at him curiously. "Why do you want to know?"

There was a change in him. The clear gray eyes became veiled, but only for a moment. Then he was the Waldo she knew, cynical and mocking.

"No particular reason," he said, "except that I was under the impression that yours was a grand passion. I think I was misled. Was I?"

His flippant rejoinder was more hurtful than annoying, but her pride wouldn't allow her to show it. She tried to make her smile as easy as his. "Passion is transitory, Mr. Bowman. Haven't you discovered that yet? John and I were friends as well as lovers. Our marriage was grounded in friendship and mutual respect."

"Is that yes or no?"

Now he had gone too far. "Don't mock what you don't know!" Her voice was tight.

His was amused. "You took the words right out of my mouth. *Passion*, Jo. If you haven't experienced it, you've been cheated." When he lowered his head to hers, she held her ground. "Now I know why you kiss like a novice," he whispered.

He was chuckling when he left her.

She took a moment or two to compose herself before she joined Eric. They played cards, but her mind wasn't on the game. She was thinking up annihilating rejoinders to wipe the laughter from Waldo's eyes. As her temper cooled, however, it occurred to her that he had not answered her question. Why was he so interested in John?

When Waldo turned the corner of Greek Street into Soho Square, Sergeant Harper fell into step beside him. He was in his early forties, and his sun-baked face wore a perpetual frown. His garments were well-made and tailored to fit his stocky frame, but he never appeared to be comfortable in them. When he was in uniform, however, he was an imposing, compelling figure.

They walked the short distance to one of the coffee shops that had recently sprung up in the area. Waldo's mind was preoccupied. He was thinking of John Chesney and how Jo had put her husband on a pedestal. No man could live up to what Jo expected in a mate. He'd been hard on her for her own good. He was perfectly sure that John Chesney had been a good, decent man, but he'd been in his grave for three years. It was more than time that Jo cut her ties to the past and looked to the future.

There was something else that irritated him, something that Eric had told him, in all innocence, when they were playing cards while both Jo and her aunt were out of the house. It seemed that the boy had overheard snatches of conversation that were definitely not meant for his ears. Aunt Jo was worried about her friend. No one knew where she was. That's why Aunt Jo had come up to town, to find her friend.

He had not mentioned it to her because he hadn't wanted to betray the boy, and he was hoping that she would mention it to him first.

Why hadn't she? That was the thought that nagged at him.

Harper led the way to a window table. Though they couldn't see Mrs. Daventry's house, they had a good view of the square. They would see anyone coming and going from Greek Street.

Waldo ordered coffee. Harper, who had not eaten yet, ordered the steak pie and new potatoes.

Harper knew the reason for Waldo's trip to Stratford, so Waldo spent the next few minutes relating the outcome. He ended by saying, "She's not going anywhere, not for the next little while. She won't leave the boy with the servants. She'll wait till her aunt comes home."

"Do you still think she may run off with the boy?"

"No. She has other things on her mind. But if I'm wrong, she'll go to Stratford, if only to take charge of the *Journal.* That paper means a great deal to her. It won't be difficult to find Eric there."

"Do you still want her watched?"

Waldo thought for a moment, then shook his head. "I'll keep an eye on her from now on."

Harper had always enjoyed a familiar relationship with all the officers he'd served under. Captain Bowman was a different case. He wasn't quite sure what to make of him. The man who now charmed his way through the most exclusive drawing rooms in London wasn't the man he'd known in Spain, when they'd both worked on special assignments for British Intelligence. Captain Bowman was known to have nerves of steel; he was cool under fire. He would not tolerate incompetence in the men who were under his command. The men who worked closely with him revered him. As for others, like Harper, who were not part of that inner circle, they sucked in their bellies and squared their shoulders whenever the captain came into their line of vision.

Waldo, who had been watching the emotions chase themselves across Harper's unhandsome face, said humorously, "Harper, you disappoint me. I've been led to believe that you're disastrously outspoken. Don't hold back on my account. There's a question you're burning to ask. What is it?"

"Two questions," said Harper, whose hard stare was just short of a glare.

"Well?"

"Why can't the boy go with Mrs. Chesney to Stratford? She seems fond of him and he of her, at least from what you've told me. It seems the best solution all round to my way of thinking."

Waldo gave him the answer he'd given Jo, that it would give rise to unpleasant speculation and gossip and the vicar would never allow it.

"If you're the boy's guardian," Harper went on doggedly, "then what the vicar wants don't count."

Waldo smiled and rested his linked fingers on the flat of the table. "Next question," he said.

Harper's bushy eyebrows climbed. "You've just answered it, sir. I was going to ask what happened to the Captain Bowman I knew in Spain, but I see he's still alive and kicking. You never confided in nobody then neither."

"Harper," Waldo gently remonstrated, "I was a secret agent. We're not supposed to confide in people."

"I'm not talking about those kinds of secrets. You know something that you're keeping to yourself."

"*Disastrously outspoken* doesn't do you justice. But enough of this cat-and-mouse game. You have a report to make, sergeant, and I'd like to hear it. So, what has Mrs. Chesney been up to in my absence?"

Harper sucked in his belly, squared his shoulders, and made his report.

* * *

Waldo was in his rooms in the Albany, dressed to go out for dinner, sipping a sherry while he waited for his friend Ruggles to call for him. He was thinking of Eric's artless remarks and Sergeant Harper's report. When he put them together, he had a very good idea of what was going on.

Chloë was missing. She was the friend Jo was worried about and the reason for this precipitous trip to town. According to what Harper had found out, Lady Webberley had waved good-bye to her servants a fortnight ago, and she had not been heard from since.

Chloë and Jo. He couldn't imagine them as friends. The Chloë he knew—and who didn't know Chloë?— was a high-flyer, the life and soul of every party. He couldn't see Jo as a party girl. But he could see a connection between Chloë and the *Journal*. Who better to tell tales on friends and acquaintances than the ever-present, much-in-demand worldly widow?

She had to be Lady Tellall. It all made sense.

His thoughts drifted to Eric and the heated words he and Jo had exchanged. She didn't know all the circumstances, and he could not explain them. As a consequence, she thought he was finding fault with her, and nothing could be further from the truth. He was well aware that she was genuinely attached to the boy. And that was the problem.

He got to his feet when he heard Mellowes open the door to Ruggles. He was dining with his friends at the Bell in Covent Garden. That was just around the corner from Soho Square. He could easily drop in on Jo on his way home. It was more than time that they had a heart-to-heart talk about Chloë Webberley.

Chapter 12

That same evening, as dusk was falling, Jo arrived at Chloë's house with maid in tow—twelve-year-old Maggie, a novice housemaid, and a sop to Waldo's edict that she never go out without a chaperon. She wasn't trying to circumvent the rules Waldo had laid down. It was simply that Mrs. Daventry didn't have a surfeit of servants, and Maggie was the only one who could be spared.

After conferring with Mrs. Paige and explaining the reason for her visit, Jo climbed the stairs to Chloë's chamber with Maggie at her heels. No one would object to what she was about to do. Chloë had always made it perfectly clear to her servants that Jo was like a sister to her and should be treated as such.

She had devised a plan for being accepted by Chloë's friends as one of their own. The first step was to dress the part of a fashionable lady of the *ton*. All the garments she required could be borrowed from

Chloë's extensive wardrobe. And it wouldn't be the first time she'd borrowed the odd gown from Chloë. A nip here, a tuck there, and no one would know that the gowns were not made for her. They'd know, of course, if she wore them in Stratford. Chloë's garments turned heads; Jo's garments were . . . practical.

What she really wanted was to move in to Chloë's house so that she could be on hand when visitors called. This was tricky, because she needed Waldo's permission and that meant she would have to take him completely into her confidence. She was tempted, but she couldn't ignore the warning in Chloë's note or the coincidence of Waldo appearing on the scene just when Chloë went missing. And if he refused her permission to go on with the investigation into Chloë's disappearance, she didn't know what she would do. No doubt he'd lose his bond or she would be back in Bow Street.

Though she'd always told herself that Chloë's gowns were a little too dashing for her taste, she found herself sighing with pleasure as she shook out first one outfit then another. The colors were rich, the fabrics sensuous to the touch. It didn't take her long to choose what she wanted. Maggie's words expressed exactly how Jo felt.

"I never seen anything so fine," the little maid breathed out.

Jo nodded her agreement. The bed was spread with garments in amber velvet, dark blue kerseymere, emerald taffeta, silver gauze, and a ravishing red silk evening dress with a matching long-sleeved cropped jacket that fastened below the bosom.

Though she knew, with her red hair, that she should not wear red—hadn't her mother always told her so?—her mouth began to water. Holding the dress in front of her, she stood in front of the cheval mirror, trying it this way and that as she gazed at her reflection. It was only a trick of the light, she told herself, but she actually looked elegant.

"Oh, mu'um, that dress was made for you," Maggie whispered reverently. "You look beautiful."

Jo sighed. Regretfully, she laid the dress aside. To Maggie's bewildered look, she replied, "It's new. I've never seen it before. I'm sure Lady Webberley would kill me if I borrowed it. Pack it away, Maggie."

Maggie sighed her disappointment and gathered the dress in her arms.

"Wait!" cried Jo. She fingered the silk and admired the way it shimmered in the candlelight. "It wouldn't hurt to try it on," she said.

Maggie beamed.

Off came the serviceable kerseymere and on went Chloë's red dress. *Elegant* wasn't the word for it. The silk clung to Jo's curves and hollows like melted wax. The wide expanse of white bosom that rose above the low bodice left nothing to the imagination. Now she knew why her mother had warned her not to wear red. She didn't look elegant; she didn't even look like a lady. She could quite easily have passed herself off as one of Waldo's light-skirts.

Maggie held out the cropped jacket. "This should make you look decent, mu'um."

Jo ignored the suggestion. Decent was the furthest thing from her mind. She loosened the ribbon tying back her hair and combed her fingers through her fiery tresses. Shameless coquette, she silently told her reflection, and batted her eyelashes. She dipped a curtsy and did a little pirouette. When she saw Maggie's face, she slowly, slowly, floated down to earth.

"If he could see me now," she said, "it would rock him back on his heels."

"Who, mu'um?"

She was thinking of Waldo. "Why, my prince, of course. Don't look so stricken. It's just a game, Maggie. Haven't you ever played dress-up?"

Maggie nodded. "When I was little. Shall I pack the dress away now?"

Jo was reluctant to give up the dress. "Let me think about it," she said.

Libby arrived at that moment with pincushion and pins. Her gaze roamed over Jo. "Not the red dress," she said doubtfully.

The maid's determination to deprive Jo of the red dress made her all the more determined to keep it. "Especially the red dress," she said emphatically. "I always wanted a red dress but was never allowed to have one."

When the selection was made, she was loath to don her drab little frock that made her look, in her opinion, like a country bumpkin, so she chose instead to cover herself with one of Chloë's diaphanous negligees. Then, with candle in hand, she floated out of the room.

She didn't go far, only next door to the bedchamber she occupied when she came for a visit. This room was not under Holland covers. It looked as though it had been made ready for her. She could smell the beeswax from the highly polished furniture, the lavender from the bedclothes and from the crystal bowl of potpourri, made by Chloë herself, that sat on the table in front of the window.

There was a candelabra on the mantelpiece, which she lit with the candle she'd taken from Chloë's room. The candles flickered then flamed, casting a golden glaze on the interior. It was a feminine room, done in green and apricot, but not too feminine. There were no frills or flounces. Everything was restrained.

Restrained. That was the story of her life. Just once, she'd like to break out of her mold and be the kind of woman Waldo would admire, the kind of woman she saw reflected in the cheval mirror. She didn't look like Jo Chesney or feel like Jo Chesney. She felt liberated, utterly feminine, and ready for anything.

This was how a woman of the world would look before her lover took her to bed. He would kiss her passionately, touch her intimately, and she would return his caresses in full measure.

She smiled and closed her eyes, enjoying the fantasy. When she realized that in her dream those were Waldo's lips and hands taking liberties with her person, she gasped and pulled back from the looking glass.

The knock at the door made her jump. "Come in," she called out breathlessly.

Mrs. Paige entered with a tea tray in her arms. "Would you like me to light the fire?" she asked as she set the tray down.

Jo cleared her throat. "That won't be necessary." She felt embarrassed, as though the housekeeper could read her mind. "I won't be staying long."

Mrs. Paige didn't seem to be aware of Jo's changed appearance. She didn't even blink, and Jo felt mildly disappointed.

"Tea and crumpets," said Mrs. Paige briskly. "I know they're your favorites."

Jo injected some warmth into her voice. "How lovely. Thank you, Mrs. Paige."

When the housekeeper left, Jo crossed to the table and looked down. Tea and crumpets—now, that was more in her style. Dress-up time was over. She helped herself to the tea and left the crumpets. As she slowly sipped the hot tea, she thought about Chloë.

Suddenly, she felt overwhelmed. She had the oddest feeling that if she retraced her steps, she would find Chloë sitting at her dressing table, brushing out her dark curls.

She inhaled deeply, gulped down a long swallow of tea, then another, and set the teacup down on the table in front of the window. This room was at the back of the house with a fine view of the garden, not that there was much to see at this time of night. She separated the gauze drapes and looked out.

The garden was Chloë's pride and joy. Sykes did all the heavy work, but Chloë did all the planning and a good part of the planting. She had no patience with the formal gardens of France, with their neatly laid-out hedges and borders. She was a disciple of the English landscape espoused by Capability Brown and other famous English gardeners. If one wanted to pick a quarrel with Chloë, all one need do was make a disparaging remark about Capability Brown.

The garden wasn't in darkness. Chloë enjoyed walking in the garden of an evening and had lanterns judiciously set out to light her way to points of interest—the lily pond, the grotto, the gazebo, the marble fountain, and, of course, the conservatory. When Chloë was away from home, as now, only a few of the lanterns were lit.

Another odd moment of disorientation gripped her. When she couldn't find Chloë in the house, she invariably found her in the conservatory. She shook her head. Chloe wasn't in the house and she wasn't in the conservatory. No one knew where she was or what had happened to her.

She'd talked to the inside servants, but she had yet

to talk to the gardeners. Maybe they knew something that the house servants did not. And at least one of them must be about or the lanterns would not be lit. Just then she saw a shadow move. The shadow became a man and entered the conservatory. It must be Sykes or one of his helpers.

She picked up her skirts and ran from the room. In Chloë's room, the maids were still working. On the bed was her own drab dress. She couldn't talk to Sykes in only a negligee, so she shrugged out of it, stepped into her own gown, and left again without exchanging one word with the startled maids.

When she came out of the back door, she halted. It had started to rain, not heavily, but enough to make her hesitate. There was a huge stretch of turf between the house and the conservatory. If it started to rain in earnest, she would be soaked.

"Sykes!" she called out. "Sykes!" There was no answer, but there was a light in the conservatory. She unhooked one of the lanterns at the back door and set off. When she was halfway across the sward, the light drizzle turned into a downpour, and within moments she was soaked to the skin.

That annoyed her. She should have had more sense than to come out in the rain without her coat or an umbrella. Her annoyance was swallowed up in alarm when something landed on her cheek.

Her panic subsided when she saw that it was only a moth that had fallen from a tree. All the same, her instincts were now humming. The few lanterns that were lit hardly made an impression on the Stygian darkness. There could be an army of men out there, hiding in the bushes, and she would never know it.

If she hadn't felt like a half-drowned rat, she would have turned herself around and hared back to the house. After all, she could always question the gardeners in the morning. As it was, she slowed her steps when she reached the entrance to the conservatory and soundlessly slipped inside.

It was like stepping into a tropical forest—not that Jo had ever been in a tropical forest, but that's how Chloë described the atmosphere inside her hothouse. It was balmy, it was humid and, Jo supposed, a perfect habitat for snakes and lizards, but, thankfully, Chloë had a dread of snakes and lizards. Jo had never liked the smell, something between a musty carpet and farmers' fields after a flood had receded. When the weather warmed up, it was different. The furnace was allowed to go out and the pipes went cold. She could tell by the temperature that the furnace must be going full blast.

A pool of water was forming at her feet. At this rate, she'd get pneumonia. She couldn't stay here. She had to go back to the house or go forward.

The rain was drumming on the glass roof. A wind was getting up. Someone was moving around up ahead. He was carrying a lantern. It had to be Sykes or one of the gardeners. She mustn't allow her imagination to run away with her. On that bracing thought, she raised her lantern high and went after the man ahead of her.

Chapter 13

T hough her lantern did not shed much light, the conservatory wasn't in complete darkness. Light from the lanterns outside filtered in, silvering the fronds and the trunks of palm tress that soared to the roof. There were paths going off in every direction, but Jo held to the one she was on, the one that led to the very center of the building, where she could hear the murmur of the miniature waterfall. This was Chloë's favorite haunt.

"Mr. Sykes?"

Her voice came out a hoarse croak. She breathed in and tried again. "Mr. Sykes?"

There was no response, but the light ahead of her suddenly went out. The silence that stretched out seemed to blanket everything—the sound of the waterfall, her breathing, the rain on the glass roof. All she could hear was the soft tread of footsteps coming her way, slow and stealthy.

Her mouth went dry; her heart leapt to her throat. The flickering shadows, the great Gothic arches, and the oppressive atmosphere brought all her instincts to the fore. He was stalking her as a predator stalks its prey. If she made a run for it, he would pounce on her.

On that thought, she blew out her lantern and stepped off the tiled path onto the boardwalk that ran behind the tiered flower beds. If he attacked her, she would use the lantern to bash his brains in.

If only her hand would stop trembling.

Moments went by, then a shadow moved, took the shape of a man, and flitted by her. She waited until she had control of her breathing, then she took the opposite direction, toward the waterfall.

She had spent many hours in the conservatory with Chloë, so she knew every nook and cranny. To get to the nearest exit, she had to leave the protection of the boardwalk and pass in front of the waterfall, leaving herself exposed. It was a risk she had to take. She had to get back to the house before he blocked her retreat. Soundlessly, she edged her way forward, her lantern held at the ready.

She screamed when a man's shadow loomed up in front of her.

Now was the moment to swing her lantern and bash his brains in. She couldn't do it. Instead, she threw down her lantern, gave him a mighty shove, and leapt past him. In the next instant, he grabbed her from behind and swung her round. She stumbled over something and she bumped her head as she went down. Stars exploded in front of her eyes.

"Jo," said Waldo Bowman, "what the devil's going on?"

She recognized his voice. "You," she breathed out. "You're the intruder."

He knelt beside her and grabbed her by the shoulders. "Are you all right?"

"Yes! No!" Her voice sounded as though it came from a long way off and she didn't know why. "I should have brained you with my lantern for frightening me like that!"

He sounded as angry as she. "You're lucky I didn't brain *you*. What do you think you're doing, creeping around in the dark?"

"I thought I saw Sykes!"

He raised her to her feet. She sniffed and looked up at him. She wasn't frightened now.

He stripped off his coat and draped it over her shoulders. "You're soaked through." His arms went around her in a comforting embrace. "What you need is a stiff brandy."

"No." She was trembling, but it wasn't only because she'd had a fright. Vestiges of the woman she'd seen in the mirror were still hovering at the edges of her mind, and the feel of that lean masculine body against hers intensified the image. This was Waldo, the man she wanted as she'd never wanted any man.

His hands were curled around the edges of his coat. It took very little effort to draw her closer. His voice was husky. His breath warmed her lips. "Then what do you want?"

"This," she replied, and she kissed him.

Her impulsive kiss caught them both off guard. There was a moment when she might have changed her mind, but his arms clamped around her, bringing her flush against his hard length, and her mind emptied of everything but the sensation of his lips on hers.

It was just like the first time he'd kissed her. She found herself yielding, not to him, but to something in her own nature that she had only come to know in the last hour. She didn't feel like a novice; she felt like the woman in the red dress, desirable, ravishing, eager for her lover's embrace.

She sucked in a breath when his fingers undid the buttons on her bodice. But that was as nothing when he cupped her bared breast and his thumb brushed over one hardening nipple. She swallowed a whimper and flung back her head in helpless abandon.

He was the one who broke the embrace. His chiseled face was right above hers, and though they were in shadow, it seemed to her to be clenched in pain. "This is madness," he said. His chest was heaving, his breathing was harsh. He gave a mirthless laugh. "I'm not usually so clumsy. It's the wrong time and the wrong place. We have to talk."

She shivered, not in fear but in anticipation. She didn't want to talk. Every inch of her body ached for his touch.

He held her at arm's length. "My God," he said. "What am I doing? You're shivering. You're in shock. I should be horsewhipped for taking advantage of you."

It wasn't what she wanted to hear. "It's not your fault." And that was not what she wanted to say. She felt crushed. One moment she was flying, the next she had fallen to earth with a thump.

"Jo, are you all right?"

"I feel . . . dizzy." And that was the truth.

He tightened one arm around her waist and swept her high against his chest, then, muttering curses under his breath and without breaking stride, as though his lame leg had been miraculously cured, he carried her to the house.

*   *   *

There is nothing like a warm fire, a glass of hot toddy, and a change of clothes to bring a woman to her senses. This was Jo's thought as she cast veiled glances in Waldo's direction. She was thinking of the red dress. If it hadn't belonged to Chloë, she would have bundled it up and tossed it in the fire. She'd heard of being seduced by a man, but no one had told her she could be seduced by the feel of silk on her skin. She'd never worn red before, hadn't realized that it would make her feel bolder, freer. Now that she was wiser, she vowed never to wear that dress again.

There was something else troubling her—John, the man who was supposed to be the love of her life. She knew that John wouldn't have minded her taking up with a good, decent man like himself, but this unhallowed longing for the embrace of an experienced man of the world would, she was sure, have shocked him as much as it shocked her.

She couldn't blame Waldo. In fact, he had acted like a perfect gentleman. Now, if only she could remember that she was a lady.

They were still in Chloë's house, in the morning room. She was reclining on a sofa in front of the fire, with one of Chloë's voluminous velvet robes covering her, and Waldo was standing with his back to her, a glass of brandy in his hand, gazing out at the gardens as Sykes and one of his helpers combed the grounds and conservatory for signs of an intruder.

She was torn between gratitude and annoyance by his unexpected arrival on the scene. He'd been spying on her. That's what it amounted to. Ever since he'd rescued her from Bow Street, he'd had someone watching her to make sure, in his words, that she did not abscond with the boy and land herself in *real* trouble, especially when he was not there to smooth things over. Naturally, the watchdog had followed her to Chloë's house, and Waldo's sharp mind had put two and two together. He knew that Chloë was Lady Tellall, he knew that she was missing and that she, Jo, had come up to town to find her. And because she was still shaken after what happened in the conservatory, she'd answered all his questions. So now he knew about Chloë's cryptic message as well. In fact, he knew as much as she did. But that didn't stop the barrage of questions. He was like a bulldog. Once he got his teeth into something, he wouldn't let go.

When he turned from the window and it looked as though the questions might begin all over again, she hastened to forestall him. He wasn't the only one who wanted his questions answered.

"Why didn't your guard dog rescue me tonight? Isn't that what he's supposed to do?"

"My—" A smile curled his lips. It seemed they were fated to strike sparks off each other. He had a good idea when it would stop, but he thought Jo was a long way from acknowledging why she used her sharp tongue to keep him at arm's length.

He took the stuffed armchair beside the fire and regarded her quizzically. "Didn't I tell you? I called him off. However, if I'd known that Chloë had sent you that alarming note, I would have doubled the guard. How one slip of a girl can get up to so much mischief boggles the mind."

Stung, she replied, "That's hardly fair. I didn't go looking for trouble. It found me."

"I believe you." Before she could snap at him again, he went on, "It was sheer luck that I came here. After dinner, I called in at Greek Street, and your aunt told me you were visiting Lady Webberley."

"My aunt *told* you? You must have browbeaten Chloë's name out of her!"

"Why the indignation? I thought you were glad to see me."

"I was, but I almost brained you with my lantern!"

Laughter filled his eyes. "Instead, you kissed me. Now, what am I to make of that?"

She should have known he wouldn't be able to resist gloating. "Nothing," she retorted. "I would have kissed a troll at that point if I thought he was rescuing me."

He shook his head and let out a long sigh. "Little liar! Jo, that kiss was wanton. No, no more fencing with me."

In fact, the kiss had gone a long way to dousing his annoyance when he learned that the reason she hadn't confided in him was because she suspected him of having something to do with Chloë's disappearance.

If she'd been afraid of him, she would have run away. Instead, she'd initiated an embrace that had taken him completely off guard. Everything had faded from his mind—his reasons for being there, Jo's rain-slicked gown, the housekeeper waiting anxiously for word, the gardener combing the grounds—and if he had remembered, he wouldn't have cared. He was sucked into Jo's passion like a man drowning in a whirlpool.

She was a dangerous woman, Jo Chesney, and if he had any sense, he would take to his heels.

After taking a swallow of brandy to hide his smile, he said, "I'm still not satisfied that I've grasped all the subtleties of your story. Let's start at the point where you surprised a burglar at the *Journal*'s offices."

They'd been over it all before, but whenever she deviated from her original story, he would pounce and ask her to clarify what she'd told him. So she went over everything in minute detail—Chloë's cryptic note with no dates or postmark, the intruder, the missing file, and what she had learned from Lady Langston of the Brinsleys' house party, and finally, she told him about the scheme she'd concocted for infiltrating the ranks of Chloë's friends.

His brows lifted. "So, you're willing to cast off your widow's weeds?"

She didn't correct him. His error saved her the mortification of explaining that the garments she wore were the finest she owned. "I'll do whatever is necessary to find Chloë," she said.

He nodded. "I'm not sure, though, about letting you move into Chloë's house. Let me think about it."

Though she kept her tongue between her teeth, she fumed. He had the upper hand, of course, but once Chancery settled Eric's guardianship, the threat of Magistrate Vine and her returning to Bow Street would be removed.

A flicker of a smile touched his lips.

She frowned. "Did I say something amusing?"

"Ah, no." In an altered tone, he went on, "How many people knew that Chloë was Lady Tellall?"

She was glad to change the subject. "Only three: Mac Nevin, who is my managing editor, my aunt, and myself. Chloë didn't want people to know, because they'd be afraid to say anything in her hearing in case she published it in her column."

"Well, someone knew she was Lady Tellall, someone with something to hide."

"I know." She shivered and reached for her glass of hot toddy.

He went on gently, "Let's leave that for the moment. Tell me about Chloë's note again, not the content, but the date it arrived."

"I told you. The letter arrived not long after you left my office, the first time we met."

"And by that time the Brinsleys' house party was long over, and Chloë had been missing for at least a week?"

"More like two weeks. What's your point?"

The faintest shadow of a smile touched his lips. "Patience, Jo. I'm simply trying to visualize what might have happened to delay delivery of the letter."

"Perhaps she gave it to someone to post and they forgot."

"Perhaps."

It was the content of the letter that disturbed her. Waldo said they should keep an open mind on what Chloë intended. He was trying to keep her hopes up, she supposed. That's how she'd felt until she'd talked to Lady Langston. Now, after tonight, she was convinced that Chloë was in some sort of danger.

Someone at the Brinsleys' house party had wanted to hurt Chloë. No. It was worse that that.

"What is it, Jo?"

She was feeling overwhelmed again, unequal to the task she'd taken on. "I was thinking..." She gave a helpless shrug. "Maybe it's time to call in the authorities. I'd hoped that that wouldn't be necessary, that it was just a misunderstanding and that Chloë would turn up at any moment. But after tonight, I'm beginning to fear the worst."

He spoke slowly and gently. "Leave it to me. I'll speak to Magistrate Vine and advise him that Lady Webberley is missing. But don't expect him to drop everything to look for Chloë. His jurisdiction doesn't stretch to Oxfordshire, and it's quite possible that that's where she went missing."

He had the kindest eyes. She'd never noticed that before.

Or maybe it was just a trick of the light.

She thought for a moment, then said, "What about Special Branch? They can investigate wherever they want, or so I've heard."

"True, but—you'll forgive me for being so blunt—without a body, there's not much they can do. Now, if she were a spy or a threat to national security, Special Branch would undoubtedly be interested."

"Chloë is not a threat to national security!"

"No, I didn't suppose she was, but she's a threat to someone, else why would he take the file of her notes? You're sure of that, Jo? You're sure that the file was missing?"

"Perfectly sure. But I don't know why anyone would want it—I mean, it was already published in the *Journal* for anyone to read."

"I see." He lapsed into silence and stared at the fire.

"Waldo," said Jo impatiently, "what are you thinking?"

He stretched his cramped muscles. "I was thinking about you and Chloë. You're so different from each other that I can't help wondering what made you such close friends."

She looked for mockery and found none. "Yes," she said softly, "I suppose Chloë and I seem unlikely friends. If we'd met in the usual way, at some assembly or in a lady's drawing room, we probably wouldn't have had anything to say to each other. She loves the social whirl, while I'm more of a stay-at-home." She frowned when he chuckled.

He spread his hands. "I'm sorry. You and Chloë are unlikely friends? Go on. I'm truly interested."

He seemed sincere, so she went on. "You could say our friendship began as a meeting of minds. Chloë subscribed to the *Journal* and wrote copious letters to the editor, letters that I answered. In time, we just wrote to each other." She smiled as a memory came back to her. "There was hardly a subject we agreed on—the war with France, the Corn Laws, the rights of women. And when we finally met, we didn't disappoint each other. We were opposites, all right."

Her face softened and she blinked rapidly. "None of that mattered in the slightest. Somehow or other, in our copious correspondence, we'd become close friends. In fact, we were like sisters."

She sat back and looked up at him. "It was Chloë who persuaded me to take over the reins of the *Journal* when John died. It was her idea to become Lady Tell-all. She's the best woman friend I've ever had. If our positions were reversed, she would move heaven and earth to find me. That's the kind of friend she is. And I won't give up looking for her either."

His smile brought a quick frown to her brow. "Now what are you thinking?" she asked.

"Lucky Chloë, to have a friend like you."

She gave a wistful sigh. "I think I'll need more than luck to find her. I hardly know where to begin."

"You've made an excellent beginning! Let's—how did you put it—infiltrate the ranks of Chloë's friends and make discreet inquiries. They're more likely to talk to us than magistrates or Bow Street Runners. But let's not be too obvious about it. We don't want to frighten anyone into doing something rash."

"We?" she said hopefully. "You mean, you'll help me?"

"How could I not?" He gazed at her through his lashes. "I never could resist a lady in distress."

She felt as though a great shadow had been lifted from her heart. They were in this together. She wasn't alone.

Libby entered at that moment. "Mr. Sykes is here," she told Waldo.

"Show him in." He got up.

Jo could tell that Sykes had spruced himself up for the interview. His thinning hair was neatly combed over his balding pate. His coat was clean and his boots were shined. He'd been with Chloë since before her marriage. She chided herself for not talking to him before this. He would feel Chloë's loss as keenly as anyone.

His face grave, Sykes said, "You was right, Mrs. Chesney. Someone as shouldn't be there was in the conservatory. Some of 'er ladyship's prize plants has been trampled. The work o' hooligans, I shouldn't wonder. There's lads in this neighborhood that's let out all hours o' the day and night. Too much money and too much time on their hands is what I says. Their parents should know better."

Jo looked at Waldo. He hadn't been convinced that there was an intruder in the conservatory. "What did I tell you?"

Waldo's gaze was fixed on Sykes. "Was anything else destroyed or trampled? Was anything of value taken?"

"Not as I could see. But them plants is valuable. Her ladyship won't like it when she finds out. She'd as lief they ran off with the silver than hurt her precious nurslings."

"How did they get in?"

Sykes shifted uncomfortably. "The doors are never locked." He hastened to add, "Her ladyship did not think it was necessary. Nothing like this has ever happened before."

"How many gardeners and outside workers are there?"

"Four, counting myself."

"Find them and meet me in the conservatory in, say, half an hour."

When Sykes left, Waldo sat down. His expression was grave. "From now on, I don't want you going anywhere alone. Do you understand?"

She said slowly, "It wasn't the work of hooligans, was it?"

"I don't think so. Hooligans aren't tidy. They run amok. They break windows in glass houses, not trample a few plants. This intruder was careful. He probably doesn't even know he trampled some of Chloë's precious plants. He doesn't want anyone to know he's been here."

When he paused, Jo said, "Do you think he was looking for Chloë's diary?"

"I don't think there's any doubt of it."

"In the conservatory? Why would she hide it in the conservatory?"

"I have no idea. Maybe she didn't, or maybe our intruder knows more than we do. Maybe he found it and that's the last we'll see of him."

"And maybe," she said fiercely, "he should look over his shoulder, because I'll be there. I won't stop until I've found him or found Chloë. I swear it."

There was a long pause, then Waldo smiled. "I wouldn't be in his boots for anything. Now, finish your hot toddy and I'll take you home. We'll talk in the carriage and decide where we go from here."

There was another thought circling his mind that he did not voice. Maybe the intruder had hoped to lure Jo into the conservatory and frighten her into telling him where Chloë's diary was hidden. And when he discovered that she didn't know, what then?

Chapter 14

The push to find Chloë began a few days later when Jo moved into her friend's house along with her aunt and Eric. She hated to impose on her aunt, but she couldn't afford to shock the very society she wanted to impress by living alone with only maids for company. A suitable chaperon was an essential accessory. Chloë was different. She was an original and could break society's rules, up to a point.

Waldo wasn't too happy with the idea, not after the episode with the intruder, but Jo was persuasive. If Chloë's friends came calling, she wanted to be there to receive them. As for repelling another intruder, she had borrowed her aunt's pistol and she wasn't afraid to use it. Waldo gave way, but only after making a few arrangements to ensure her safety. Sergeant Harper moved in as well, and extra gardeners were hired on, whose main job was to patrol the grounds when Harper could not be there.

Before they had unpacked, one interesting fact came to light. One of the gardeners, Jacob Fry, had, in Harper's words, taken off like one of Congreve's rockets.

"Do you think he was the intruder?" Jo asked.

Harper replied, "Captain Bowman thinks so."

"Maybe he found the diary and that's why he has run away."

"He didn't run away until he heard that he was wanted up at the house. Well, I was questioning all the gardeners, wasn't I? He has something to hide, that one."

After this conversation, she went through the house room by room, drawer by drawer, and still found nothing. The trouble was, she wasn't quite sure what she was looking for—a notebook, a diary, letters, a key— and as far as she knew, there were no secret drawers in any of the dressers or commodes.

In the meantime, she had plenty to occupy her. She sent letters to Stratford: one to Mac Nevin at the *Journal*, advising him of her situation and that it might be weeks before she returned, and the other to a friend and neighbor, Maeve Halliday, with a list of garments and other odds and ends to be sent on to augment her wardrobe. She spent the mornings with Eric, making sure he did his lessons or playing with him on the grounds, but her afternoons and evenings were to be reserved for Waldo.

She was anxious to begin questioning all Chloë's friends and acquaintances, not only those who were present at that fateful house party.

Waldo advised her to be patient. These people were the cream of society. It was better to establish herself before trying to gain admittance to their hallowed halls. His mother, he was sure, would help sponsor her when he put the whole matter of Chloë's disappearance before her. In the meantime, he was not idle. He was using his connections to find out about Chloë's movements before she disappeared.

Over the next little while, with Waldo as their escort, she and Mrs. Daventry went to the opera, the theater, museums, and art galleries, all in the cause of increasing Jo's circle of acquaintances. At first, it was nerveracking. She wasn't used to wearing fine clothes or making herself stand out in such exalted company, but day by day, her confidence increased, and to her surprise, she found that she was enjoying herself.

Much of the credit could go to Waldo. When she faltered, he would be there with a steadying hand on her elbow. When conversation lagged, he would unobtrusively fill in the gaps. When anyone asked her awkward questions, he would invariably lead her into answering vaguely though diplomatically. What he could not help her with were those moments of madness when a look from him, a gesture, would rekindle all those unsettling sensations she'd experienced when she'd worn the red dress.

It was the first time Jo had been out with Waldo unchaperoned. He'd arrived in his curricle, a vehicle that could seat only two comfortably, and had whisked her away before she had time to think. They were going to Hyde Park to see and be seen by all the fashionables who were out for a breath of fresh air. Jo knew she looked smart in her borrowed finery—an amber velvet pelisse with a matching bonnet. The color warmed her skin and made the red in her hair, in Jo's opinion, less fiery, and the gleam of admiration in Waldo's eyes was immensely satisfying.

It was now that Jo appreciated Waldo's strategy. As they made the circuit of the park, she was surprised at how many faces she recognized. From time to time, their curricle was waved to a halt and Waldo would introduce Jo. It was becoming hard to memorize so many names. There was one, however, that was familiar to her.

"Morden," said Waldo under his breath, "Lord Brinsley's heir, and the lady with him is his betrothed, Lady Margaret Kintyre."

The couple in question detached themselves from a small group of pedestrians at the edge of the drive and made their way to Waldo's curricle. As parasols bobbed in the warm breeze and ladies curtsied, Jo had a vision of a field of spring flowers in all their delicate colors. It made her feel quite dashing in her amber pelisse. She wondered if anyone would recognize it.

The viscount was, Jo judged, a year or two older than Waldo, above-average height, and well-built rather than athletic. His features were regular and commanded by a pair of piercing blue eyes. He might have been considered a fine figure of a man except that there was an air of complacency about him that spoiled the effect.

Lady Margaret was a perfect match for the viscount, at least as appearances went. She was tall with fair hair and fine hazel eyes, but her expression lacked animation.

Waldo made the introductions and by way of explanation added that Jo had come up to town to visit her friend, Lady Webberley, only Lady Webberley was nowhere to be found.

Lady Margaret seemed startled, but Morden took the news in his stride. "Yes, I'd heard something to the effect," he said. "My mother is quite anxious since, as far as we know, no one has seen Lady Webberley since she was a guest at our place in Oxfordshire."

Jo said, "I should very much like to speak with your mother, Lord Morden. There may be something she knows about Chloë—that is, Lady Webberley—or something she remembers that could help me find her. Is she still fixed at Brinsley Hall?"

Morden's eyes widened slightly. "No. She arrived in town yesterday, but I doubt that she knows anything or she would have told me. I shall certainly mention your concern to her, though." He seemed to search for words, then went on, "Unfortunately, her health is uncertain and I would not wish to upset her."

"I understood," said Waldo conversationally, "that Lady Brinsley is to preside at your annual ball?"

Blood darkened Morden's complexion. He answered abruptly, "Quite so. But ladies take pleasure in arranging balls. As I already told you, my mother is quite anxious about Lady Webberley, and I know I speak for my father as well when I say that we do not wish to add to that anxiety."

This time, it was Waldo who spoke abruptly. "Of course. You and your father, however, can have no objection to answering a few questions. Not here, certainly. I shall wait on you at your convenience."

Her eyes bright with curiosity, Lady Margaret said, "Should you not report your friend's disappearance to the authorities, Mrs. Chesney?"

There was real interest here, and Jo responded to it warmly. "That has already been done, Lady Margaret, but there isn't much they can do. You see, my friend comes and goes as she pleases. My own anxiety may be premature."

"All the same . . ." A look from the viscount had Lady Margaret stumbling to a halt.

"Come along, Margaret," said the viscount, his voice thin with impatience. "Your chaperon will be wondering what has become of us." Then to Jo, "A pleasure to make your acquaintance, Mrs. Chesney. Bowman." He tipped his hat and sauntered off with Lady Margaret on his arm.

"Well," said Jo. "What was that all about?"

"As you may have gathered, I cannot abide the man."

"Why not?"

Waldo flicked the reins and the curricle moved off. "Morden," he said, "has an exaggerated opinion of himself, an opinion, I may add, that was shared by his doting parents and the teachers at Eton, at least when I knew him well. He never got up to mischief like ordinary boys. His homework was always handed in on time, his desk was always neat. He didn't sneak out to the tuck shop when he should have been in school. In fact, he never put a foot wrong. You can imagine what his classmates thought of that."

"He sounds like a paragon of virtue."

"Yes, and who can like a paragon?"

She looked at him sharply, wondering if this was a reference to John, but Waldo gazed back at her with guileless eyes.

"We were in the same form," he said.

"I'm surprised. He looks older than you."

"No. In fact, he's a few months younger. What did you think of him?"

Jo made a face and Waldo laughed.

Someone called Waldo's name and Viscount Morden was forgotten as he reined in his team and the next round of introductions was made.

*   *   *

They were on their second circuit of the park when Jo remarked that Waldo had a wide circle of friends.

He slowed his team to a walk, following in the wake of a line of carriages. "If you were not sitting beside me, no one would pay me the least attention. It's you that has got them curious. You're fast becoming the talk of the *ton.*"

She wasn't sure how she felt about that. "What are they saying about me?"

"They're calling you the 'Shady Lady'"

"*What?*"

"It means *woman of mystery.*"

"I know what it means, but I don't see how I fit that description. I've only just arrived in town. What do they expect—my life history?"

He laughed. "In a word, yes. Even my family is curious." He thought for a moment, then added, "*Especially* my family."

"What have you told them?"

"I can't tell them what I don't know. As for what I do know, I've given them an edited version of the truth· namely, that we were introduced at some unspecified date in the past by a mutual friend in Stratford, that we met again on the road to town, and when you learned that your friend, Lady Webberley, was missing, not knowing anyone in London, you came to me for help."

"You didn't tell them about Bow Street," she blurted out.

He grinned. "No. I'm saving that for when they know you better. Nor did I tell them that you have an active role in running a newspaper."

She knew he was warning her for her own good. Ladies of fashion did not dabble in business. They whiled away the hours in a round of pleasure or devoted themselves to good works.

And just as though he could read her mind, he said, "Two of my closest friends are married to women who are much like you. One runs her own rare-book business, and the other writes pieces for various periodicals, yes, and makes a fair bit of money at it."

She was astounded. "And their husbands don't mind?"

"Apparently not."

She laughed. "Sounds to me, Waldo, that you're not sure whether you approve or not."

"Let's say I'm warming to the idea. What about your husband, Jo? Did he mind?"

"Oh, John would never have allowed it. Like most men, he believed that a woman's place was in the home. Things changed when I became a widow. I had to find something to occupy my time, and the *Journal* was right there." She looked at him quizzically. "Everyone needs something useful to do, Waldo, even you."

He treated her to one of his lazy grins. "I've already found something useful to do, Jo."

"Oh? What?"

"Keeping you out of trouble."

A white terrier dog suddenly crossed their path, frightening the horses, but Waldo's capable hands on the reins easily subdued them. Jo tensed then relaxed when she observed how deftly Waldo handled his team of bays.

A stray thought flitted into her head, and before she could stop it, those unsettling sensations were making her catch her breath. She was remembering those capable hands moving over her, touching her intimately, arousing her to an unbearable pitch. She gritted her teeth and started to count sheep.

She was just beginning to relax when Waldo said, "Now, don't be alarmed, but my mother and sisters are anxious to meet you. I've agreed to accompany them some afternoon this week. There's nothing to fear. They're determined to like you if only to please me."

She didn't know why there were butterflies in her stomach. She'd known that Waldo was going to introduce her to his mother and sisters, but not quite so soon.

"You mentioned sisters," she said. "Which ones?"

"A married sister, Maude, who has left her husband and sons in the country and come up to town to help my mother with Cecy. Cecy is the youngest, by the way, and I'm warning you now that, appearances to the contrary, she is a minx, so be on your guard."

She dredged up a smile. "I've heard all about you and your sisters from my aunt."

"Oh, what did she tell you?"

Her eyes glinted up at him. "Oh, everything was to your credit. Aunt Daventry is one of your greatest admirers."

"Now, there's a woman of discrimination."

Jo laughed.

A moment went by, then Waldo said, "Well, Shady Lady, are you going to keep me in suspense or are you going to tell me about yourself? Why are you so secretive?"

She let out a tight little breath. Finally, she said, "What do you want to know?"

"You can begin by telling me about your parents."

She exhaled another tight little breath. "My father writes plays. Sir Vivian Moore. You may have heard of him? He is retired now and lives with my mother in a nice little property just outside Dublin."

"Sir Vivian is your father? Gertrude Moore is your mother?"

"Is that so astonishing?"

"Frankly, yes."

She knew what he was thinking. Everyone knew about her parents and the wild lives they'd led. No one would ever take her for their daughter.

She looked at him as though she did not like him at all. "I suppose you assumed that my father was a vicar?"

He began to laugh. "Hardly. You're too enterprising to be a vicar's daughter, though I will say that sometimes you dress the part. I suppose you moved around a great deal when you were a child?"

She looked down at her gloved hands. "No. My parents moved around, but they wanted me to have a settled life. I was looked after by relatives, mostly by my grandmother and Aunt Daventry. So, you see, I had a perfectly normal, happy childhood."

He shifted slightly to study her profile. "Do I detect a note of bravado?"

Those alert gray eyes saw too much for her comfort. She shrugged. "I may have thought, when I was a child, that my parents had abandoned me, but as I grew older I realized it was for the best."

The line of carriages ahead of them was thinning, and for the next little while he concentrated on his driving. Before long, however, they were again obstructed by a row of carriages.

Jo's eye was caught by one that had drawn up at the side of the sward. There was only one occupant—a dramatic dark-haired beauty with an alluring smile, dressed all in violet to match her wide-set violet eyes. Though her carriage was hemmed in by a number of gentlemen, some on foot, some on horseback, that brazen smile was trained on Waldo, but the look she blazed Jo was like a blast from a blacksmith's furnace. Waldo acknowledged the lady by tipping his hat as they drove by, but he did not stop to chat.

Jo slanted him one of her rapier glances. "Who," she said, "is that?"

"Mrs. Caroline Walters," he replied easily.

She did not pursue the matter. There was no need. Even Stratford possessed its share of ladies of questionable virtue. But none as beautiful as the lady in the violet gown.

She sniffed, averted her head, and affected an interest in the passing scenery.

When Waldo dropped Jo at her front door, he returned to the subject of his mother and sisters.

"I could bring them tomorrow," he suggested.

That was too soon for comfort. "No, make it the day after." When he sighed, she went on quickly, "I want to spend time with Eric. He sees very little of me. Today it's Hyde Park. Tomorrow night we go to the theater. I can't expect my aunt to entertain Eric while I'm out enjoying myself."

"Then the day after tomorrow it is," he said.

A thought occurring to her, she said, "What have you told your family about Eric?"

"Very little. I didn't see the need."

"You'll have to tell them sometime that you're his guardian—unless, of course, you mean to leave him with me."

He gave her one of his clear-eyed gazes. "Let's find out what has happened to Chloë first, shall we, then we'll talk about Eric."

The vision of the violet-eyed beauty still fresh in her mind, she said coolly, "I can see why you want to send him away to school. There's no place for a child in your irregular mode of living. He'd be much happier with me."

All the humor drained out of his face. As cool as she, he replied, "You're quoting Chloë at me again. Have a care, Jo. One day you'll go too far and I'll live up to my wicked reputation. Good day to you."

A flick of the reins sent his gig bowling along the drive.

She stamped her foot in frustration, then marched into the house. She'd spoken out of pique because, fetching as she thought she was in her borrowed finery, one of Waldo's flames had put her in the shade. It was irrational for her to feel jealous. There could never be anything between Waldo and herself. What he wanted he got from women like Mrs. Walters, and what she wanted was back in Stratford.

After removing her pelisse and bonnet, she went straight to the morning room, to the closet where Chloë stored odds and ends, including back copies of the *Journal.* She found them under a stack of periodicals. Nearly everything that Jo knew about Waldo was in those newspapers.

She carried them to the table and, beginning with the latest edition, scanned each page. Though she'd meant to look only for Mrs. Walter's name, her eye was caught by the names of people she had met since coming up to town, or those she hoped to meet. Lord and Lady Brinsley, Chloë wrote, had retired to their country estate but planned to be in town for their annual ball. Their son and heir, Viscount Morden, had been seen at the theater with a most eligible heiress. Those in the know expected a happy announcement to be published in the *Gazette* before the Season was over. Chloë even mentioned herself. Lady Webberley, Chloë said, tongue in cheek, was the darling of society, and no party or function could be considered a success if she did not attend it.

Jo had read all this before, but most of it had gone over her head because she had not known the people involved. Now that she did know them, she found herself wondering how much was true and how much was invented.

She remembered putting that very question to Chloë, who had responded with a laugh that she might exaggerate a little but she never told outright lies. And some of what she wrote turned out to be self-fulfilling prophecies, such as the *on-dit* that no party could be considered a success if Lady Webberley did not attend it. Now she was invited everywhere.

In her mind's eye, Jo could see Chloë's dark eyes dancing and her generous mouth turned up in a smile. "Without exaggeration," she remembered Chloë saying, "I can claim to be a matchmaker. You'd be surprised, Jo, that sometimes something I've written has persuaded a cautious swain to offer for the lady of his choice."

They'd both had a good laugh about that.

It hadn't worked with Waldo. Jo soon found the reference, and others that she'd forgotten about. He wasn't nearly as handsome or the dandy Chloë made him out to be. As expected, his name was linked with a number of ladies, and not all of them suitable to bring home to his mama. Mrs. Walters wasn't mentioned by name, but there were many references to the lady in violet, and Jo made the connection.

The more she read, the more surprised she was that Waldo had shown such restraint when he cornered her in the *Journal*'s offices. If she had been in his shoes, she would have given herself a good shaking. No man wanted the intimate details of his private life aired in public. All the same, his wicked reputation was well documented. If even half of it was true, he was still a rake.

She read on. It wasn't all salacious. His war record was impeccable. His family was very respectable. His mother was the daughter of an earl and had married well, though the gentleman was untitled. Their palatial home, Palliser Park, was in Kensington, a ten-minute drive beyond the western boundary of Hyde Park. In their time, the Bowmans had raised five children— four daughters and one son—of whom only the youngest daughter still remained at home. Naturally, the family's hopes were all pinned on Waldo, for if he did not marry and beget heirs, the house and estates would pass out of the family to the nearest male relative.

Poor Waldo. The weight of all his family's hopes rested on him. It must be a terrible burden. She wondered what his family would make of her—the Shady Lady whom he was squiring around town. If Chloë were here, she would be gleefully reporting all the minute details of the mysterious lady who had captured Waldo's interest. And Jo's readers would lap it all up like a cat with cream.

The thought brought her up short. This week's edition of the *Journal* was already out, and, of course, there was no column from Lady Tellall. What if she, Jo Chesney, were to fill in for Chloë? She wasn't thinking so much of amusing readers so much as how she could use the *Journal* to find out what had happened to Chloë.

With no clear idea of what she was doing, she sat down at the escritoire, found pen and paper, and began to write. A moment later, she stopped. Her nib was dull. She found the pen cutter in a drawer, found a fresh nib, which she proceeded to sharpen to a fine

point, then started over. As far as possible, she copied
Chloë's style. She wrote about Waldo and his Shady
Lady; she mentioned Viscount Morden and Lady Mar-
garet Kintyre. She wrote about the Brinsleys' house
party and what she'd learned of it from Lady Langston.
She mentioned Chloë and hinted slyly that someone
fitting her description was seen on the ferry bound for
Calais and possibly Paris.

Once she started, she could not seem to stop. She
wrote about the people she'd met at the theater, the
opera, in the park, and if she didn't know anything
particular about them, she described what they were
wearing and put words in their mouths—all very innocent, nothing that would embarrass them. At the end
of an hour, she had more than enough for Chloë's column. Out of so much verbiage, only one thing
counted: the few lines she had written about Chloë.
Maybe it would jog someone's memory. Maybe someone would remember seeing Chloë, not on the ferry to
Calais, but somewhere else. And maybe that someone
would write to her.

That thought prompted her to conclude with: *Lady
Tellall loves to hear from her readers. Write to her at the Journal.*

She wasn't too hopeful of the outcome. On the
other hand, she had nothing to lose. After dinner,
she'd polish her prose and make any necessary addi-
tions or deletions, then she'd send it by express to Mac
Nevin in Stratford.

In his rooms at the Albany, Waldo was enjoying his
last cheroot before going to bed. He'd been trying to
read Walter Scott's latest novel, but he kept getting distracted by thoughts of Jo.

She was the daughter of Sir Vivian Moore and his actress wife. He knew all about Sir Vivian. The man was a legend in his own time, a baronet's son who had left his wealth and privilege behind when he ran off to London as a young man to join a troupe of actors. Eventually, he wrote plays, brilliant comedies that had taken London by storm. In their heyday, he and his equally famous wife had blazed a tempestuous trail through the leading salons of Europe.

It was incredible to think that Jo was their daughter. One thing was certain—she didn't want to be like her parents. In her own words, she was a stay-at-home. That's what she'd never had growing up, a stable home to call her own. A stable home, a stable man, and a stable life—those were the things Jo had wanted, and she'd found them with John Chesney.

So much was becoming clear to him now—the drab clothes to detract from her femininity; the conventional mask of respectability; her distaste for men of the world, men such as himself. She'd marked him down as a replica of her father, or near enough as made no difference. Part of him was flattered. Sir Vivian was a brilliant man. There was much to admire in him. Another part of him resented it. There was also much in Sir Vivian to deplore. He'd been notorious for his wenching. Lady Moore hadn't seemed to mind. She'd kept herself amused with a string of lovers.

It was all gossip, of course, and he knew how unreliable gossip could be. But there was no getting around the fact that the Moores had led colorful, unconventional lives.

He drew on his cheroot and watched the spiral of smoke as he slowly exhaled. She'd chosen the life she wanted with Chesney and it seemed to have satisfied her. In her own words, however, when John died, things changed.

That was an understatement.

After a moment's reflection, his lips twitched. He wasn't joking when he'd told her that keeping her out of trouble had become his main object. Jo Chesney was a force to be reckoned with, and if she hadn't been, he wouldn't be using all the means at his disposal to find her friend, Eric would still be incarcerated in Harding's school, and he wouldn't have applied for guardianship of a boy he did not know. That he was enjoying the experience was beside the point.

What on earth had got into him?

It was Jo. She might be a force to be reckoned with, but she had a way of looking at him that made him want to take all her burdens upon himself. It also made him wonder what would happen if he were to tap into that well of passion that lay just beneath the surface.

Chapter 15

Lady Fredericka Bowman considered herself an affectionate if not indulgent mother who took her family's best interests to heart. She did not meddle in her grown children's affairs, so she believed, unless the occasion demanded it. This was one of those occasions. Waldo had arranged to introduce her to Mrs. Chesney the following afternoon, but that did not suit her ladyship. For one thing, there might be other callers present, leaving little time to spend alone with Mrs. Chesney, and for another, she wanted to form her own opinion of the woman who had earned the soubriquet Shady Lady, without Waldo hovering over her and intimidating her with his flinty eye.

Consequently, when Waldo, all unsuspecting, sat down to a hearty breakfast in his rooms at the Albany, Lady Fredericka marshaled her two lovely daughters and they set off in their coach for town. They were hardly out of the gates of Palliser Park when Cecilia, the younger girl, asked her mother if it was true that Mrs. Chesney was an adventuress.

"Who told you that?" demanded her ladyship sharply.

"Miriam Woolcot, at Mrs. Towne's musicale last night. And she got it from her sister, Ruth."

"Ruth Woolcot..." began her ladyship wrathfully, and faltered. She shrugged helplessly. "That's what we're going to find out."

The elder daughter, Maude, made a small sound of impatience. She was a year younger than Waldo and had left her husband and children in the country— much to their relief—so that she could help her mother launch the youngest girl in society. There was a strong family resemblance among these ladies, but in other respects they were very different. Maude considered Cecy a mischievous halfling, neither woman nor girl. Cecy thought her sister was too staid by far and would have preferred Liza, another married sister, to chaperon her during her first Season, but this her father would not allow. Liza was giddy, he said, and would exert no control over her equally giddy sister. As for Lady Fredericka, she was the soul of kindness until she was provoked. Then, no one was left in any doubt that she was the daughter of an earl.

Lady Fredericka observed her elder daughter's expression and frowned. "What?" she demanded.

Maude said, "Do you really believe, Mama, that Waldo would introduce an adventuress to his mother and sisters? You're worrying for nothing, and this ill-thought-out visit will only annoy Waldo."

Lady Fredericka spoke with all the dignity of her rank, both as a mother and as an earl's daughter. "I am only doing my duty. And, of course, I don't think

Waldo believes that Mrs. Chesney is an adventuress. Men are blind when they want to be."

Maude shook her head. "You cannot believe he is in love with her."

"Is that so far-fetched?"

"With Waldo, frankly, yes. You know he is fickle."

"A fine opinion you have of your brother!"

A silence followed this reproof. When it lengthened, and it seemed to Cecy that the fascinating subject of Mrs. Chesney was closed, she observed helpfully, "Ruth also said that Waldo has deserted all his usual flirts, including Mrs. Walters, and everyone thinks it's because of Mrs. Chesney."

Her ladyship was so diverted by this piece of information that she forgot to chastise Cecy for her prurient interest in things a young girl should know nothing about. "Deserted Mrs. Walters, has he? Well, I'm very glad to hear it. I never could like that woman. There's something cold about her. I don't think she's capable of love."

After a moment, Maude said, "What do you make of this business with Chloë Webberley? Is there cause for alarm, or could it be a misunderstanding? You must admit, Chloë is erratic at the best of times."

"I don't know Lady Webberley all that well," responded her ladyship thoughtfully, "so I can't say. What I do know is that Waldo is taking her disappearance very seriously. He has reported her as missing to the authorities, but they don't know where to begin to look for her. That's why he has offered to help Mrs. Chesney find her friend." She paused, then added eloquently, "Or so he says. That's what I mean to find out."

A look of alarm crossed Maude's face. "Mother," she

said, "be careful what you say. If you embarrass Mrs. Chesney, Waldo will be very angry."

Lady Fredericka was momentarily taken aback. "I? Embarrass Mrs. Chesney? I assure you, Maude, I shall be the soul of tact."

Maude said nothing, but she was wishing that Waldo was with them to check their mother's wayward tongue.

Jo was in the garden, teaching Eric how to play cricket, when three elegant ladies suddenly appeared on the terrace along with Mrs. Daventry.

"Jo, dear, we have visitors," cooed her aunt, managing a tremulous smile.

Jo was startled. Ladies did not pay calls at this unearthly hour, nor did they barge into a lady's private domain uninvited. The drawing room was where ladies were entertained. She was perfectly sure her aunt would not have permitted them to see her like this unless they'd practically forced their way in. She wasn't dressed to receive visitors. She was dressed to field the balls Eric was batting all over the turf. Her cheeks were flushed from running, her hair was out of its pins, and the hem of her plain gray dimity was mired in mud.

As they drew nearer, something clicked inside her brain, and though she'd never met them, she knew who they were and why they'd come. Lady Fredericka was out in front—above-average height, dark-haired, with elegant bones that put Jo in mind of a Thoroughbred racehorse. Her daughters were a younger version of their mother. The elder, Mrs. Daviot, looked distinctly ill-at-ease, and Jo liked her the better for it. The younger girl looked as demure as a Dresden shepherdess, except that her dimples were winking.

Mrs. Daventry flashed Jo an anguished look before coming forward to make the introductions. There were curtsies all round, then it was Eric's turn. "My ward," Jo said, stretching the truth a little. She wasn't sure what Waldo had told his mother about the boy.

Lady Fredericka said, "I hope you'll forgive the intrusion, Mrs. Chesney. The fault is mine. I gave my coachman the wrong directions, so instead of taking us to my milliner, who has a shop just around the corner close to Vauxhall Gardens, he brought us here. It seemed a shame to waste the opportunity for a cozy tête-à-tête, just you and Mrs. Daventry and we three. I hope we haven't called at an inopportune moment?"

There was nothing Jo could do but accept Lady Fredericka's explanation. Besides, she couldn't afford to antagonize the woman who, she hoped, would sponsor her in society. So she swallowed her chagrin, made a suitable response, and invited them to join her in the drawing room.

"That was graciously done," remarked Lady Fredericka artlessly.

She had blue, blue eyes that were bright with intelligence—and possibly curiosity. Though her skin was smooth, there were laugh lines at the corners of her eyes. She had the look of a woman who enjoyed a joke. So did Jo, but not when the joke was on her.

Jo led the way, with Eric holding on to her hand. He hadn't said a word, but he rarely did with strangers present. She spoke to him quietly, observing conversationally that his batting was getting so good that she could hardly keep up with him.

Still no response.

Sighing, she said, "Why don't you go to the kitchen and ask Cook to make you some hot chocolate?"

His little face brightened. "A cup or a demitasse?"

"You choose."

He started forward, remembered his manners, and turned back to face Jo. "Thank you, Aunt Jo," he said with feeling, and he walked away as fast as his little legs could carry him.

The ladies hovered, observing Eric as he pushed through the door to the servants' quarters. Mrs. Daviot was right at Jo's elbow. Remembering that Waldo's sister had sons of her own, Jo said, "It won't do him any harm, will it? The hot chocolate, I mean."

Maude smiled. "Not in moderation. But even if he gorges himself on chocolate, he'll only make himself sick, and that will be a lesson to him. I speak from experience, you see."

When the laughter died away, Jo walked her visitors to the drawing-room door, then excused herself to fetch her Paisley shawl from her chamber. The moment the door closed, she whisked herself around and went tearing up the stairs. When she looked in the looking glass, she made a sound that was halfway between a groan and a moan. Oh, what must they think of her! She looked like a frump! First impressions were so important! It wasn't that she had disgraced herself. Waldo's mother had deliberately tried to catch her off guard, and she had succeeded.

Just wait till she saw Waldo! He should have warned her that something like this might happen. A man should know his own mother and sisters. They were due to go to the theater this evening. She'd ring such a peal over him that he wouldn't hear for a week.

Five minutes later, she was ready to descend the stairs. She'd washed her hands and face, changed her gown and shoes, and combed her hair. The shawl was draped loosely around her shoulders.

She breathed deeply as she approached the drawing

room. She knew what they were about. They were looking her over to see if she would make a suitable wife for the son and heir. She would soon put them right about that.

Jo was quite mistaken in her belief that she had made a bad first impression. In fact, the opposite was true. Only Cecy was disappointed. She had hoped that Mrs. Chesney would turn out to be a hussy. That would have given her a certain cachet with her friends. The Shady Lady was turning out to be not so shady after all.

On the way home, Lady Fredericka and Maude were discussing their impressions of Jo. "I was struck dumb when I first saw her," declared her ladyship. "I thought she must be one of the maids. Did you see the mud on her gown and boots?"

"What I saw," said Mrs. Daviot, eyes flashing, "was a woman who does not stand on her dignity but who can enter into a boy's games when I'm sure there were other things she would rather be doing."

She had liked Jo Chesney on sight, and her regard had only increased during the visit. It was obvious to her that Mrs. Chesney was a conscientious if somewhat anxious guardian who wasn't ashamed to ask for help in the task of raising her ward. There was affection there too. As a devoted mother, Mrs. Daviot could only approve.

"I think," she said, "it is to her credit that she has taken on the burden of raising a young boy. Eric is very fortunate."

"Well, of course he is," replied her ladyship impatiently. "That is just my point. I was so afraid she would turn out to be a fashion plate. It's a relief to know she is a good-hearted, sensible young woman with more on her mind than the social whirl. Waldo could do a lot worse."

"Mama." Maude enunciated each word carefully, "Mrs. Chesney made her sentiments as clear as crystal. Nothing will induce her to marry again. No one can take the place of her first husband. She didn't come up to town to be with Waldo but to find her friend Lady Webberley. I'm convinced that that is all there is to their friendship."

"On her part, perhaps, but I'm not so sure about Waldo's."

"Why not?" asked Cecy, her interest reviving.

After a moment's reflection, her ladyship said, "I don't really know, except to say that Waldo answers all my questions with such wide-eyed innocence that my suspicions are aroused."

"Mother," Maude said, "you are making too much of it. There's nothing to be suspicious about."

Lady Fredericka dismissed her daughter's words with a gesture of one hand. "And now that I have met her, I see where her attraction lies. She is devoted to her aunt, to her ward, to her friend, and even to her late husband. I've always admired loyalty."

"So you like her, Mama?" said Cecy.

"Very much indeed. And I particularly liked the way she greeted us when we surprised her in her garden. It showed great presence of mind. Mind you, I could wish that she was a few years younger and had never married, and that her father was not Sir Vivian Moore. But then she wouldn't be the woman Waldo admires."

Cecy pounced on this. "What's wrong with Sir Vivian?"

Her ladyship replied seamlessly, "Nothing, except that he and Lady Moore live so far away."

Feeling a trifle warm, Maude stripped off her kid

gloves, then fixed her mother with a hard stare. "Remember Miss Beauchamp, Mama? You got the wrong idea about her too. And before that it was Miss Reade. Need I go on? Whenever you push a female at Waldo, he invariably cuts the acquaintance."

Her ladyship bore the rebuke with smiling complacency. "And so I hoped he would. Waldo married to Sally Beauchamp? Or Henrietta Reade? I could not bear it!"

There was a moment of profound silence as her daughters digested her words, then they all began to laugh.

Sometime after breakfast, Waldo met up with Harper and Ruggles in one of the coffeehouses in St. James's, as previously arranged. He hadn't wanted to meet them at the Horse Guards, where Special Branch was located, because Special Branch wasn't involved yet. Ruggles was helping him out as a favor, and Harper was on an extended leave. He could do as he pleased.

After ordering coffee and Bath buns, they settled down to exchange notes.

"You go first, Harper," said Waldo.

Harper looked askance at the snuffbox Ruggles offered him and shook his head. He considered snufftaking a prissy affectation. Real men, in his opinion, smoked pipes.

"So far nothing," he said. "I've been to Bow Street and used my connections there to have them check with every constable and magistrate's office here and around Oxfordshire. There's no shortage of corpses, but not one of them fits the description of Lady Webberley. That don't mean much. She could have had an accident and be recovering in some hospice or other. How would we ever find out? There just aren't enough officers to police the city, never mind the home counties. That's what we needs, a national police force like they has in France."

Waldo nodded, sharing Harper's view. Most of the policing in Britain was done by the militia and local constables. The Bow Street Office with its Runners was a step in the right direction, but they were few in number. And Special Branch, for the most part, confined itself to matters of national security.

Waldo said, "Don't mention to Mrs. Chesney that we are investigating all suspicious deaths of women at the time her friend disappeared. I don't think she is ready yet to accept that Lady Webberley is probably dead."

Harper nodded. "I understand."

"I don't suppose you fared much better," Waldo said, addressing Ruggles.

"No," replied Ruggles, "although I spent an interesting hour or two at Brinsley Hall, interviewing the servants. There are two gamekeepers who were out that night hunting down poachers. They didn't see or hear anything unusual. In fact, there were no poachers. No one was about. Of course, they weren't keeping their eyes on the house. They were combing the woods and the banks of the stream behind the home farm."

"What about the chaise Lady Webberley ordered?"

"No luck there either." Ruggles smiled wryly. "We might as well be looking for a needle in a haystack. Letters have gone out to all the hostelries and posthouses we know about within a three-mile radius of Brinsley Hall. Only a fraction have responded, and they've responded in the negative."

He stopped speaking as a waiter arrived at their table with three steaming cups of coffee and a plate of

Bath buns. Like a true war veteran who had survived near starvation on campaigns, Harper automatically reached for the biggest bun. Suddenly remembering his manners, and realizing that he no longer had to wonder where his next meal was coming from, he grinned hugely and put the bun back.

"After you," he said politely, offering the plate of buns to his companions.

Waldo and Ruggles made their selections and generously left the biggest bun for Harper.

After a mouthful of coffee, Ruggles took up where he'd left off. "As far as any of the servants can remember, nothing unusual happened during the house party. No one knows anything of a letter that Lady Webberley may have written. In short, we've come up against a brick wall."

Harper said, "So what do we do now?"

Both he and Ruggles looked at Waldo.

Waldo wiped his fingers on his table napkin before responding. "There is no way around it. We have to question the Brinsleys and all the people who were guests at the house party. I want to know what happened to the chaise that was to take her to Stratford. Where are her traveling boxes? Did she leave anything behind or give someone a note to post? And so on and so on."

Ruggles gave a mirthless laugh. "Better you than me. It's one thing to go up to the Brinsley estate when you know they're not there and question their servants, and quite another to confront the earl in person."

"Fine. You take the house guests and leave Brinsley to me."

Harper was interested. "What's so special about Brinsley?"

"His connections," replied Ruggles at once. "He is a

personal friend of the home secretary. Fortunately for us, Waldo has friends in high places too. Brinsley will answer Waldo's questions where he won't answer ours."

Waldo said, "I doubt that police methods will work here. What is required in this situation is a light touch—you know, tact and diplomacy."

"You mean," said Ruggles, smiling in spite of himself, "the same methods we used when we were in the secret service?"

"Precisely."

Harper knew exactly what they meant. On the last case he'd worked on, he hadn't known they were anything more than they appeared to be—Ruggles, a manservant, and the captain, having retired from the service, an idler and a ladies' man. He'd been astonished when he discovered that they hadn't retired and that they were still working on a case. He'd learned a lot more since then, and he now considered them among the most dangerous men he knew.

He didn't think much of Brinsley's chances against Captain Bowman. Not that he would ever betray his admiration to his companions. He despised toadeaters. Besides, as an enlisted man, he considered it his duty to keep officers from getting too big for their breeches.

"Share the joke, Harper," said Ruggles

Harper's absent smile became a grin. "I was just wondering," he said, "if either of you gentlemen would like the last Bath bun?"

No one did, so Harper reached for it and bit down with relish.

Chapter 16

That same evening, Waldo arrived right on time to escort the ladies to the theater. He kept a closed carriage in town for just such occasions, and he'd had his coachmen spruce it up till it gleamed like new. He was determined that no lady of fashion would eclipse Jo. Not that she would have known that he'd taken so much trouble on her behalf, but his friends knew, and speculation was rife that Waldo's days as a single man were numbered.

He knew there was trouble brewing the moment he saw her. Color was high on her cheeks and she looked everywhere but at him. Mrs. Daventry didn't appear to notice Jo's silence. It was she who innocently put him wise to what was going on. His charming mother and sisters had called that morning and they'd had a comfortable coze, getting to know each other. Lady Fredericka was so thoughtful, so kind.

Not by a look or a word did he betray that he could

happily strangle his mother and think nothing of it. But her barging in uninvited wasn't his doing. Jo's wrath was misplaced.

He handed Mrs. Daventry up first. When it was Jo's turn, he tried to break the ice by remarking that she looked very nice. That was no exaggeration. In fact, she looked quite stunning in her silver tissue gown with its low bodice and puff sleeves. His compliment was rewarded by a frosty "Thank you." He tried again, this time by asking how Eric would amuse himself while they were away.

"Harper," she said, "is teaching him how to play chess." With that, she stepped into the carriage, sat down on the banquette, and immediately began an animated conversation with her aunt.

Face like granite, Waldo followed her in and shut the door with a snap.

It did not take long for Jo to come to her senses. A few eloquent looks from her aunt soon dampened her ire. As Mrs. Daventry had already pointed out, it was irrational to blame Waldo for the sins of his mother. Besides, what was the fuss about? Lady Fredericka and her charming daughters gave every indication that they'd enjoyed the visit.

Jo already knew all that, but what was so frustrating was that no one would accept that marriage was the furthest thing from her mind. Everyone seemed to think that she must be angling for Waldo because he was such a catch—Lady Fredericka, her daughters, and now Aunt Daventry.

She knew this wasn't Waldo's doing. She knew it was unfair. But she had to take her frustration out on someone, and he was right there.

By the time they arrived at the theater, however, she had given herself a mental dressing-down and was prepared to make amends by expressing her pleasure in everything—the well-sprung coach, the drive, the performance that evening, and the patrons she would meet. She would mind her tongue and behave with the utmost decorum.

When she alighted from the carriage, however, and looked into Waldo's cold eyes, she felt as though she had lost something precious and it could not be retrieved by guile. Only honesty would do.

Her voice was husky when she spoke. "I'm sorry. I behaved like the veriest child. I know you didn't send your mother and sisters to the house this morning to embarrass me. There's no excuse for me. I can't even explain why I get in such a taking."

The coldness in his eyes melted a little. He studied her face a moment longer, then rewarded her with one of his dazzling smiles. "Don't you? I do. Now, don't get fired up again. We're here to enjoy ourselves. Just for a little while, let's cry truce and stop trying to strike sparks off each other. All right?"

He was deliberately trying to strike sparks off her again with his provocative remarks. In the interests of harmony, she decided not to rise to the bait. "Agreed," she said.

Mrs. Daventry, who had been hovering while effecting to be deaf, suddenly exclaimed, "Well, thank heaven for that! Come along, children. Let's take our seats before the play begins."

She led the way to the crush of glittering fashionables who were entering the King's Theater.

The play was by Sheridan, *The Rivals*, and though Jo had seen it many times, she still found herself laughing at Lydia Languish's antics. But there was more in-

volved in going to the theater than the play on stage.
During the intermissions, people strolled in the corridors and stopped to chat with friends and acquaintances, much as they did when driving in Hyde Park.

It was hard not to be impressed by the glamorous
surroundings and the equally glamorous patrons in
their satins and gauzes. But it wasn't all one-sided. She
had made an impression as well. She recognized it in
the gleam of appreciation that flashed briefly in
Waldo's eyes when he introduced her to his friends.
The whole experience made her feel as though she'd
been in hibernation and was just awakening to the
sights and sounds of the world outside her burrow.

Now she was beginning to sound like Lydia Languish, and even knowing it did not dim her pleasure. It
was a glorious, exciting occasion, made all the more
agreeable because Waldo was there. It was easy to understand why her aunt had taken such a liking to him
when he'd taken her in to supper.

During the last intermission, Mrs. Daventry met up
with a friend from Greek Street, and she waved Jo and
Waldo on so that she and Mrs. Nairn could have a
good gossip. Jo suspected her aunt's motives, but there
was nothing she could do.

They were returning to their box when they came
upon Viscount Morden, who was with a party of
friends. At sight of them, his face closed up. Lady Margaret, however, who was by his side, greeted them
warmly. The viscount had no option but to introduce
them to his companions. Only two of them were of interest to Jo: Lord and Lady Brinsley.

Waldo already knew them, quite well by the sound
of it, and as they chatted of this and that, Jo made a
veiled perusal.

There was a marked resemblance between the earl

and his son. Their features were blunt, but not unpleasant. Where the viscount's hair was brown and receding at the temples, however, the earl was almost
bald, except for a fringe of white at his ears. He was
perhaps close to seventy, but not infirm. His back was
straight and his presence commanding. Jo judged that
very little got by his eagle eye.

Her gaze shifted to take in Lady Brinsley. She was of
average height and her dark hair was liberally shot with
silver. Although she must have been in her sixties, her
sensitive face still held remnants of the beauty she must
have been in her youth. Where her husband and son
exuded health and confidence, however, she seemed
frail.

Jo's gaze shifted again, to the lady who had been introduced as her ladyship's companion. Miss Dunn was
not much younger than her mistress, stern-faced, and
solid. She was standing very close to her ladyship, giving Jo the odd impression she was either her ladyship's
gaoler or her nursemaid.

Her attention was brought back to the conversation
when she heard Waldo mention Chloë's name.

"An odd business," the earl said, addressing Jo.
There was no interest in his eyes that Jo could detect.
He seemed to be talking as a matter of form. "Victor
mentioned that Lady Webberley was missing. I wish I
could help, but neither I nor any member of my family
has the least idea of what became of her after she left
Brinsley Hall."

Jo said, "It *is* an odd business. But someone must
know something, whether they know they know something or not." She looked at Lady Brinsley, but Lady
Brinsley looked back at her with blank eyes.

Waldo said in his easy way, "This matter is too serious to discuss here. I should be obliged, Brinsley, if you

would be at home tomorrow afternoon so that we can discuss this in private." He looked at the viscount. "I'd like to talk to you too, Morden."

The earl silenced his son by raising one hand. To Waldo, he said sharply, "I've already told you we know nothing. There would be no point in discussing this in private."

Now Waldo sounded merely bored. "Fine. If you prefer to talk to a magistrate, that can be arranged."

Brinsley looked as though he would like to strike Waldo. With considerable restraint, he evened his breathing. "That won't be necessary," he said. "I'll be at home tomorrow afternoon."

As though oblivious of the undercurrents of hostility in this exchange, Lady Brinsley said, "Lady Webberley is one of my dearest friends. I hope, Mrs. Chesney, everything turns out for the best."

Brinsley silenced his wife with a look. She averted her eyes and edged closer to her companion. Jo looked at the viscount, but there was nothing to read in his expression. Only his betrothed seemed distressed.

Like the well-bred people they were, they smiled, nodded, and went their separate ways.

When the Brinsleys were out of earshot, Jo said, "What an unpleasant man! And I don't think much of his son either. Who do they think they are?"

"Aristocrats," replied Waldo with a smile. "They believe they were born to rule, and they don't suffer lesser mortals questioning their word."

"Does that apply to Lady Brinsley also? I thought Brinsley was very callous, silencing her with a glare."

"Yes," Waldo said thoughtfully. "But I think she has found a way of escaping her unhappy lot." To Jo's questioning look, he replied, "Opium. You can see it in her eyes. Her pupils are pinpoints. It's not as uncommon as you might think, and it's easily available."

"Laudanum," she said. Every medicine chest had a bottle of laudanum. A drop or two in a glass of water could ease pain or help someone sleep. One had to be careful to use it only as prescribed by a doctor or one might become addicted.

She said, "But why would Lord Brinsley allow it, or doesn't he know?"

"He must know. He's not a fool. I suppose he allows it because it's the only way Lady Brinsley can function."

"Miss Dunn," said Jo, thinking to herself.

"The companion? What about her?"

"I think she's a nurse."

They were almost at their box when Jo's eye was caught by the lady she had noticed in Hyde Park, Mrs. Walters. She was clothed in violet again, but this gown was more elaborate, and more daring. It was a deep amethyst silk with a low bodice that bared more of the lady's bosom than Jo thought was decent. Her dark hair was threaded with diamonds. By her side was a stout little gentleman who gazed at the world with an affable eye. When he caught sight of Waldo, he beamed.

Whether Waldo had seen the couple or not was debatable. He had opened the door of the box so that Jo could precede him inside, but, in spite of his hand on the small of her back urging her forward, a contrary spirit had taken hold and she dug in her heels.

"Waldo," she said sweetly, "aren't you going to introduce me to your friends?"

He gave her a long, narrow look. "If you promise not to do anything that will land us both in Bow Street."

She stared at him blankly, then, catching his drift,

said in a tight little voice, "I think your conquests have mounted to your head. I'm not interested in creating a scene. In fact, I'm not interested, period."

Laughter gleamed in his eyes. "Liar," he said, and before she could come back at him, he turned aside to greet the couple who were bearing down on them.

Waldo made the introductions with practiced ease. Mrs. Caroline Walters and Mr. Bruno Walters, he intoned politely. It surprised Jo that a woman of such compelling beauty should be married to such a funny little man. She liked Mr. Walters at once. He joked, laughed, and smiled a lot. Mrs. Walters's expression was very different. She dismissed Jo with a flick of her lashes and fixed those predatory eyes on Waldo as though he were her next meal. It took all of Jo's considerable control to keep a smile on her face. It occurred to her, fleetingly, that if she were wearing Chloë's red dress, Mrs. Walters would have to take her a little more seriously.

When they entered the box, Waldo said, "I'm entitled to my past, Jo. And that's all I'm going to say on the subject of Mrs. Walters."

She replied coolly, "Try telling that to her husband. He may not be as complacent as you."

For a moment he seemed puzzled, then he chuckled. "Caro isn't married. She's a widow. Bruno is her brother-in-law."

"Oh." When she thought about it, that made sense.

"So you see, our short-lived affair hurt no one."

But that did not make sense to Jo. If the affair was over, Caro Walters didn't appear to know it. Or maybe it was bravado. No woman could relish the position of discarded mistress.

"Jo?"

Her eyes jerked up to meet his. "Don't look to me

for sympathy," she snapped. "I'm sure you won't be lonely for long. Men like you never are."

Mrs. Daventry entered the box at that moment, was instantly aware of the chill in the atmosphere, and kept up a monologue of good-natured chitchat until the curtain went up.

Jo was still thinking of Waldo and Mrs. Walters when she got ready for bed. It seemed inconceivable to her that a woman who could attract males like a flame with moths should settle for an affair when she was free to marry. Unless, of course, she prized her freedom above everything. When a woman married, all her money and property came under her husband's control. In that case, why not embrace the single life as she had done?

Idiot! Not all women were as cold-blooded as she. Some craved passion as much as she craved making a success of her newspaper. Each to his own.

She thought of Waldo and sighed. Whether he knew it or not, he deserved better than a string of affairs with women like Caro Walters. He was more than a handsome seducer of women, more than a charming rake. He had many fine qualities that she truly admired.

She sat on the edge of the bed and gazed into space, cataloging all that she found to admire in Waldo's character. Before she could prevent it, she had a flash of recall. She was in his arms and he was kissing her passionately. Her lips burned; her breasts felt heavy; her nipples were so sensitive that she had to palm them to ease the ache. Heat was spreading through her, making her tremble. A tiny moan escaped her lips.

On a cry of alarm, she shot off the bed, hurried to

the washstand, and doused her face and body with cold water.

The following afternoon, as arranged, Waldo called on Lord Brinsley in his palatial home on Piccadilly. The house itself, like many of its neighbors, was completely hidden from the street by a high brick wall that made Waldo think of a cheerless prison. He had to pass through the outer gate first, make his way across a huge courtyard that could have served as a parade ground, and up a long flight of marble steps to the front door. He counted twenty steps, and by the time he got to the last one, his lame leg was aching like blazes.

The door opened before he could use the knocker, and the butler, who was expecting him, asked him to wait for a moment while he advised his lordship that Mr. Bowman had arrived. Waldo took the opportunity to take in his surroundings. The grand entrance hall, with its elaborate coffered ceiling, took up two stories. The pictures on the walls were reputed to be priceless. The carvings on the staircases were by the famous Gibbons. The furniture was the best that money could buy. The house and its contents served to inform visitors that they had entered the domain of a proud and privileged family. And this was only the Brinsleys' town house. The estate in Oxfordshire was far superior to this in every way.

All this wealth and the privilege that went with it would one day pass to one person: the son and heir. Much the same could be said about himself, though by the Brinsleys' measure, his wealth would hardly make a showing.

It was an iniquitous state of affairs. His class took

their wealth for granted, as though it were divinely ordained. His own family, he supposed, was better than most. His father's tenants were well looked after; his mother and sisters worked tirelessly for the church and various charities. It would take more than that, however, to close the vast gap between rich and poor. Things had to change.

The butler returned at that moment and Waldo followed him across a vast expanse of cold marble to the earl's library. The library was as big as a ballroom. The earl came forward and waved him to a leather armchair. The viscount was there, smiling for once. This was a big change from last night at the theater.

The earl said, "I hope the front steps did not give you too much trouble? If I'd only thought, we could have met at one of my clubs."

The earl's condescending smile as much as his words set Waldo's teeth on edge. It was deliberately done, this reference to his lame leg, and meant to put him in his place. Since he wasn't here to quarrel but to get answers, he let the aggravation pass.

"Don't apologize," he said. "The exercise was good for me."

When the superficialities were dealt with, the earl said, "Last night, my mind was preoccupied. Lady Brinsley's health continues to be a cause for concern. If I was abrupt, I apologize. Of course, Victor and I wish to help you in any way we can." He looked to his son for confirmation.

"Naturally," replied the viscount on cue.

"Naturally," repeated Waldo, trying not to sound cynical. "Then you can begin by telling me how Lady Webberley appeared when she was at Brinsley Hall. Was she in good health? Did she mix with the other guests? Was anything said that appeared to upset her, any reason at all for her to quit the Hall in a hurry?"

Lord Brinsley seemed at a loss. He hadn't paid much attention, he said finally, because it wasn't his kind of party and he'd left early to return to town. The guests were his wife's friends, members of the Horticultural Society, he believed. He'd hardly exchanged more than a few words with any of them. He felt more at home with the men, though it was the wrong time for a house party. No fishing and no shooting. Only conversation, cards, and billiards. An altogether boring event.

"Except that mother seemed to enjoy herself," the viscount added. "And that was the object of the party."

"Perhaps," said Waldo, speaking his thoughts as they occurred to him, "I should be putting my questions to her ladyship."

Two spots of color appeared on the earl's cheeks. He met Waldo's eyes with a cold stare. "Obviously," he said, "I haven't explained myself very well. My wife is in no condition to be questioned about anything, let alone the regrettable disappearance of one of her friends."

The earl hesitated, apparently groping for words for something he would rather keep to himself. Finally, he said, "Her ladyship has always had a nervous disposition. She suffers from melancholia. I thought the society of a few close friends would be good for her. And it was, up to a point. But she has not been the same since she learned that Lady Webberley has not been seen since our house party. You may imagine how that affected my wife. So you see, Mr. Bowman, I cannot allow anything to disturb her peace of mind."

This did not wash with Waldo, not entirely. Keeping his voice level and inoffensive, he said, "I'm sorry. It must be a great worry to you. I trust her ladyship will be well enough to attend your wedding, Lord Morden."

The viscount's eyes were bright with amusement and what might have been a challenge. "I'm sure she'll make the attempt. It's every mother's dearest wish, isn't it, to see her son married to some eligible girl? Besides, the wedding isn't for another month. I think my mother will be well enough by then."

Though the words were unsaid, the image of a shady lady made a vague impression on Waldo's mind before disintegrating. Not, thought Waldo, the sort of girl the Brinsleys would approve for the son and heir. He wasn't tempted to retaliate. He looked at the viscount and felt a fleeting twinge of pity. From the day of his birth, he'd been groomed to step into his father's shoes when the earl died. He doubted that the viscount was allowed to choose his own breakfast, let alone the girl he would marry. It made Waldo reflect that maybe his own father wasn't so bad after all.

The viscount went on, "In any event, my aunt will be there to assist my mother, so the wedding will go forward as planned."

Another twinge of pity passed over Waldo, not so fleeting, more troubling. He could well believe that whatever the earl and his son planned would go forward with or without the countess's presence. Maybe that's why she suffered from melancholia. Her position in the family was negligible. Had it not been for her companion, she would have been isolated.

The earl leaned forward in his chair, drawing Waldo's attention to him. "Do you have any other questions you wish to put to us, Mr. Bowman?"

"Several."

He began with the hired chaise that was supposed to take Chloë to Stratford. At the end of twenty minutes, having learned all that he was going to learn, which was precisely nothing, he thanked them and left.

From an upstairs bedroom window, Lady Brinsley watched Waldo traverse the courtyard. When the porters closed the great iron gate after him, she shivered.

"I hate this house," she told her companion. "It's like living in a prison. It reminds me of the asylum."

"Hush now, Elinor. And it isn't an asylum. It's a hospice. You must try to think of more pleasant things."

The speaker was Miss Dunn, her ladyship's companion. She was sitting at a sofa table, pouring tea.

"I *have* tried," said her ladyship, "but it's no use. It's this house. I wish I was in my conservatory at the Hall."

Miss Dunn put down the teapot and crossed to the window. With one arm around Lady Brinsley's shoulders, she shepherded her to an upholstered chair in front of the fire. "What you need is a nice cup of tea. Things always seem better after a cup of tea."

Her ladyship sank into the chair and accepted the proffered cup and saucer. She smiled faintly. "How long have you been with me now, Harriet?"

"You know yourself. Since before you were married."

Her ladyship shook her head. "Before I was married. I can't remember a time before I was married."

"That's because you were so young. You were only eighteen when you married the earl."

She'd been the envy of her peers. Girls, that's all they were, knowing nothing of men or the ambitions that drove them. Her misfortune was to have been born an heiress. She wasn't allowed to marry where she loved. Her father had seen to that. She'd been sold to the earl. Her father considered it a fair bargain, his money for a title. His daughter would be a countess, and his grandson would be born an aristocrat.

Harriet had the good fortune to have been born poor. No man wanted to take on a wife without a dowry. They'd made a life together of sorts, she and Harriet. But she feared that she was slipping away again, into the twilight of unknowing. That mustn't happen. She had to leave this place soon.

Her eyes darted around the room. "A drop of laudanum," she said. "That's all I need to settle my nerves."

Her companion took the cup and saucer from her, set them on the table, then grasped her ladyship's hands. She spoke gently, soothingly. "We're trying to wean you off laudanum, Elinor, don't you remember?"

Her ladyship blinked several times, then inhaled a slow calming breath. "I remember. It's not over yet, is it, Harriet?"

"No. It's not over yet. But don't upset yourself. You know that I would never let any harm come to you or yours."

The countess let out a long sigh. The fog in her brain lifted, and for a moment or two she saw things with blinding clarity. "I know I have to be strong. This time, I won't fail, will I, Harriet?"

Miss Dunn smiled. "No, not this time," she said.

Chapter 17

Viscount Morden felt the color drain out of his face. He couldn't believe what he was reading. Chloë's column was back in the *Journal.* For the last few weeks, the paper had carried an apology for its absence, informing readers that Lady Tellall was indisposed. Now she was back with a vengeance, and his name was at the top of the list.

> *Congratulations to Lord Morden and Lady Margaret Kintyre on their engagement. It looks as though it will be a June wedding. What is the bride to wear? More on that little secret in my next column.*

But that was nothing compared to the report about Lady Webberley.

He wanted to tear the paper to shreds, but that would only draw attention to himself. He was in his club and the steward had just delivered the papers to his table along with a glass of port. He despised the *Journal* and never would have subscribed to it had he not discovered that Chloë was Lady Tellall. Even her pen name disgusted him. But she'd embarrassed him once before in her column, and he wanted to make sure that it didn't happen again. He could not have it delivered to his house. He didn't want his father to see it and start asking awkward questions. So he had it delivered to his club.

The print seemed to blur before his eyes. He felt sweat bead on his brow. If anyone had stopped to talk to him, he wouldn't have been able to say a word. As long as he appeared to be reading the newspaper, however, no one would disturb him. It was one of the unwritten rules of gentlemen's clubs.

He scanned the back page again. The report said that Lady Webberley had been seen on the ferry to Calais and speculation was rife that she was meeting someone in Paris.

How could this be?

It couldn't be. It was impossible. Chloë was dead. He'd killed her with his own hands and afterward hidden her body and her boxes where no one would ever find them. Then he'd cleared her room of all her personal belongings to make it look as though she'd left as planned.

Now that he was over his shock, he was beginning to think clearly. He knew for a fact that Chloë was dead. That meant someone else was writing her column.

It had to be Jo Chesney.

He mustn't lose his head. No matter what she suspected, she couldn't prove anything. No one could. But she could make things very difficult for him.

Tiresome busybody. Something had to be done about her.

That wasn't the only thing that worried him. If anyone ever found out that he had a subscription to the *Journal*, they might make the connection between Chloë and him. He didn't want that to happen. He must be above suspicion. He would cancel his subscription at once.

On the other hand, he wanted to keep himself informed of what was being published in Lady Tellall's name. There must be another way to get the paper. Bates would know what to do. He would ask Bates.

He left without touching his port and without tipping the steward.

Jo sat back in her chair and tried to think positively. No matter how she came at it, however, she was no further ahead in discovering what had happened to Chloë. A week had passed since the *Journal* came out. She was looking over letters that had been sent in response to Lady Tellall's latest column. They'd arrived yesterday from Stratford, so this wasn't the first time she'd read them, but there was little here to spark her interest. Several correspondents claimed to be the Shady Lady who "had taken London by storm," to use Lady Tellall's own words. Another correspondent confirmed seeing Lady Webberley on the ferry going to Calais, while another claimed that she had gone to live with the nuns on the isle of Iona. But there was one letter that Jo had to take seriously. It was from Lady Kintyre, whose daughter, Lady Margaret, was betrothed to Viscount Morden. Her ladyship wrote that she had not been amused by the coy reference to her daughter. The betrothal was supposed to be a secret until the night of the Brinsleys' ball. She had ruined what should have been the happiest night of Lady Margaret's life.

Jo didn't feel the least bit contrite. Everybody and his wife knew that the couple were betrothed. If her ladyship wanted to take offense, she should look to herself. Lady Margaret should have her own ball to mark her betrothal. No wonder the Kintyres were one of the wealthiest families in England. They were skinflints.

The last sentence in Lady Kintyre's letter amazed Jo. *Please cancel my subscription.* Jo knew that the *Journal* had many subscribers in London, but not of her ladyship's standing. It made her wonder who else was on the list, and she decided to ask Mac when she sent him the next episode in the life of Lady Tellall.

That is, if she went on with it, which was by no means certain.

With elbows on the writing table, she cupped her hands over her eyes. They were now well into May and there were still no leads that would help them find Chloë. She'd come at last to accept the fact that Chloë was dead. What she couldn't accept and what gave her no peace was the growing realization that they were never going to find Chloë's body or her murderer.

She breathed deeply and sat up. She wasn't ready to give up yet. Maybe something more was needed than Lady Tellall's column. The authorities weren't any help either. They took the stand that they couldn't do much without a body. But what if she wrote a piece for the *Journal,* like an advertisement, asking directly for anyone having information about Lady Webberley's whereabouts to write to the *Journal*? As an incentive, she could offer a reward.

On that thought, she cleared the letters away, found the pen cutter, and sharpened the nib of her pen. After a moment's reflection, she put the pen down. She had to think this through. She didn't want to be inundated with letters from curiosity seekers or, worse, cheats and swindlers. She would ask Waldo's advice.

Jacob Fry knew that he'd never get a better chance to complete his assignment. He'd never killed a woman before, but he didn't feel queasy, not when the fee for doing the job would set him up nicely for the next twelve months. With that kind of money, he could go to America and start a new life. The prospect was tempting.

He'd been watching the house for days and had decided now was the time to act. This was Sunday, a sleepy, sunny Sunday afternoon. There were few servants about and only one gardener, but he'd already taken care of him. The aunt and boy might be a problem, but nothing he couldn't manage. There was no sign of Bowman or his curricle. Not that it mattered. Anyone seeing him would take him for one of the gardeners, and he wasn't going to kill the girl with witnesses present. It would be a quick and silent kill so that he could slip away before anyone raised the alarm.

He could see her sitting at the little writing table in the room that looked out on the terrace, the room with the French doors. He wondered what she could have done to deserve the sentence of death. He didn't think about it too long. The sooner this was over, the sooner he would be out of here.

Hunching his shoulders, with his hat pulled down over his ears, he made his way to the French doors.

Jo looked up with a start. Someone was on the terrace, outside the glass doors. Her heart subsided when she realized he must be one of the gardeners. Rising, she went to unlatch the door.

He had a potted plant in his hands, a sickly plant, one of Chloë's precious orchis. Jo knew what he wanted before he said a word. He wanted her to tell him what to do to bring it back to health. They were all out of their depth here, she and the gardeners, even Sykes. They knew how to look after English plants, but not these delicate specimens.

He held out the plant for her to take. With a sheepish smile, he said, "Mrs. Paige asked me to take a look at it. All it wanted was a little water. Perhaps you'd be good enough to give it back to her? It should be fine now."

Jo accepted the plant, her head tilting as she stared down at it. This plant couldn't belong to the housekeeper. It was one of Chloë's prize plants. She gave those as presents to a few select people—that is, to those who knew how to take care of them. She and Mrs. Paige were no gardeners, so they'd never been considered for this high honor.

She looked up with a smile and said as casually as she could manage, "Irises don't make very good house plants, do they?"

"Not," he said, "unless you knows wot you're doin'."

So he didn't know the difference between an iris and an orchis. Where did that leave her?

Panicked. Ready to bolt or scream the house down. Not that it would do her a bit of good. There was no one nearby to help her. This was Sunday. Half the servants had gone home to be with their own families, and the other half were eating their midday meal. Aunt Daventry was having a nap, and Eric, thank the Lord, had gone off with Waldo to row down the Thames to Westminster Bridge. There was no Harper now, no extra gardeners. As time passed, they'd all become complacent.

She pulled herself up short. This was absurd. Why would anyone want to harm her? She didn't know, but she remembered Chloë's warning. She could be in mortal danger.

Abruptly, her panic subsided. She was still afraid, but her mind was crystal clear. She couldn't afford to give him the benefit of the doubt, not when his strength outmatched hers. She had to even the odds.

Her pistol was primed and ready. The trouble was, she'd become complacent too, and she'd left it in the cupboard under the stairs where they kept umbrellas and other outdoor paraphernalia.

Gently, slowly, so as not to provoke him, she retreated a step. "I'll make sure Mrs. Paige gets this." She hardly recognized her own voice.

His eyes crinkled at the corners. "You do that, Mrs. Chesney."

She had to turn her back on him to reach the door, but her feet refused to move. His eyes had strayed to the brass candlestick on the sideboard and she knew, sensed, what was going through his mind. He was seeing it as a weapon.

"On second thought," she said, "you take it."

"What?"

His hands came up automatically to take the clay pot she thrust at him, but Jo didn't stop there. With an almighty shove, she sent him staggering back through the open glass doors and onto the terrace. In the next instant, she whirled herself around, snatched up the pen cutter that lay on the writing table, and was through the door to the hall. With a bellow of rage, he went after her.

He reached her as she swung open the door to the

stair cupboard. His hand caught at her dress, dragging her back. Instinctively, she lashed out at him, using the pen cutter as a dagger. It caught him below the eye, slicing his cheek open. He let out a howl, part pain, part anger, and sent her sprawling to her knees with a blow from his fist. The pen cutter fell from her hand and went clattering over the parquet floor, coming to rest against the wall.

She didn't take time to think. She didn't have the breath to scream. Fueled by terror, sobbing, she rolled and came up on her knees.

Blood dripped down his face and blotted his white shirt. He stared at his bloodied hands, then he looked at her. His expression was feral as he advanced upon her. She heard a door open and close in another part of the house. When it momentarily drew his attention away from her, she saw her chance and seized it. Surging to her feet, she reached into the cupboard and snatched up her reticule.

With the pistol braced in both hands, she faced him. It wobbled alarmingly, as did her voice. "If you come one step closer, I'll blow your brains out." And to show him that she meant it, she leveled the pistol and pulled back the hammer.

Either he didn't believe her or he was too enraged to be intimidated. Her finger tightened, but she could not bring herself to shoot. The thought of snuffing out someone's life made her stomach heave. She tried to scream, to bring servants, someone, but her throat was so tight that all that came out was a harsh sob.

There was a sound of a door opening nearby. Someone called her name. Eric! She was afraid to take her eyes off her assailant. Her throat cleared. "Stay back," she screamed. "Stay back, Eric."

He didn't understand. She could hear his feet as he

walked toward her. "What is it, Aunt Jo? What's wrong?"

· "Go on, then," said the man, sneering at her. "Pull the trigger. You can't do it, can you?"

Where, oh, where was Waldo? Had he dropped Eric at the door and then left? She glanced at Eric. That one moment of distraction cost her dearly. Fry grabbed for her arm and twisted the pistol out of her hand.

"I knew you couldn't do it," he said.

A voice from the door to the morning room said laconically, "No, but I can. Put the pistol down or I'll shoot to kill. Stand away, Eric."

It was Waldo at last.

Fry's eyes narrowed to slits the second before he spun round. Jo screamed. Two shots exploded simultaneously. Only one found its mark. A look of surprise crossed Fry's face. He looked down at his chest and touched his fingers to the spreading stain. He took a step toward Waldo, then slowly keeled over.

"Damn," said Waldo, "I'd hoped to take him alive."

Jo gave one horrified look at the shapeless heap on the floor as she ran to Eric and gathered him in her arms. Waldo pocketed his spent pistol, picked up Jo's pistol, and laid it on the hall table before going to join them.

Eyes swimming, she looked up at him. "Thank God you were here."

He touched his fingers to her cheek in the softest caress. His look was arrested, warm, intimate.

The house erupted into motion and noise. Servants burst through the baize door and came to a sudden halt. Mrs. Daventry appeared at the top of the stairs shrieking for Jo. Mrs. Paige cried that someone should fetch the constable. One of the upstairs maids took one look at Fry's body and quietly fainted.

The rest of the day passed in something of a haze for Jo. Officers from Bow Street arrived and took statements. The man who attacked her, she learned, was the gardener who had cleared out after the first break-in. One of Sykes's apprentices was found in the outside privy, badly beaten but still breathing. On the outside, she was a model of fortitude. On the inside, she was close to the breaking point.

One thing gave her some consolation. Eric had come out of the experience unscathed. He went off with Mrs. Daventry, chattering about his part in apprehending the villain. He didn't realize that Fry was dead. He thought the Bow Street officers had taken him to prison, and they let him go on thinking that.

Waldo indicated that he intended to stay the night, and she was glad of that too. It relieved her of having to be in charge. For a little while, all her burdens and anxieties could be turned over to his capable hands. So, after picking her way through a dismal dinner, she excused herself and retired to her chamber.

Not long after, Libby arrived with a glass of warm milk laced with laudanum. Jo drank it back, then climbed into bed.

In spite of the laudanum, she slept fitfully. In her dream, Chloë wasn't dead, she was in hiding. All Jo had to do was find the right door and she would find Chloë behind it.

Before turning in for the night, Waldo cleaned, loaded, and primed every gun he could find in the house. There were only four of them—his and Jo's, and a pair of dueling pistols that were kept in a velvet-lined box in Sir Ralph's former library. That gave him only four shots, one from each gun. He'd heard of a minister up in Scotland who had invented a gun that could fire more than one shot before it had to be reloaded. With a weapon like that, a man could afford to take chances. As things stood, every shot had to count. Reloading took time.

He left one dueling pistol in the morning room—in the top drawer of the sideboard, among the silver cutlery—and the other in the cupboard under the stairs. He pocketed the other two pistols, poured himself a large glass of brandy, then picked up his cane and went upstairs.

He wasn't the only one up. Sykes and his gardeners were posted at the downstairs doors. Lamps were lit on both floors. He blamed himself for what had happened. He should never have called off Harper or relaxed his vigilance. He wouldn't make that mistake again.

A bed had been made up for him, on his instructions, in Eric's chamber, though there were plenty of other rooms he could have used. He wanted to be close to both Eric and Jo. They had adjoining rooms. He didn't care what anyone thought of this arrangement. For his own peace of mind, he wanted to be within hearing distance if someone else decided to take a potshot at her.

His pent-up fury dissolved when he walked into Eric's room to find Jo hovering over the bed. Her hair was loose around her shoulders. She was wearing a Paisley shawl over her nightgown and her feet were bare. Her appeal to the sensual side of his nature was powerful, but she wasn't the only woman he had lusted after. What was staggering was how she could make him feel.

Though her eyes were shadowed with fatigue, she gave him the sweetest smile. "Surely," she said softly,

"Mrs. Paige could have done better for you than that."
She pointed to the trundle bed that took up one corner of the room.

As softly as she, so as not to waken Eric, he replied,
"Mrs. Paige offered me my choice of rooms. I chose to
be close to you and Eric."

"Thank you," she said simply.

While she gazed at Eric, he studied her. He thought
of what might have happened if he had not walked in
on Fry when he did, and his hand curled menacingly
around his brandy glass.

"Waldo," she said, "I must talk to you. Shall we go to
my room?"

He balked. "The servants will be scandalized. We
can talk in the morning room."

Her eyes blazed. "What do I care what the servants
think? After all that's happened here today, that's the
least of my worries."

Without a backward glance, she pushed into her
own room. Waldo left his cane but held on to his
brandy and obediently followed her. She left the door
ajar and told him to be seated.

"Waldo—"

"Sit down," he ordered, "or I shall get a crick in my
neck looking up at you."

She sat on the edge of the bed and came to the
point at once. "I want you to take Eric away from here.
I want him to be safe. You have sisters he could go to.
Or maybe your mother might take him. It's not that I
don't want him. You must know that. It's just that I
want him to be safe, and he won't be safe as long as
he's with me."

When she stopped, he replied, "I was thinking
much the same thing. My mother will be happy to have
him."

She sat back, obviously astonished by her easy victory. "Well," she said, "that's settled, then."

"Not quite." He took a sip of brandy before going on. "I want you to go with him. I don't know why you should be surprised. You can't imagine I would leave you here to fend for yourself when there have been two attacks on you already. This isn't the time for bravery, Jo. This is a time for caution."

"I wasn't brave," she said fiercely. "I was stupid. I had a clear shot at him—Fry, I mean—and what did I do? I let him take the gun away from me. If you had not been there..."

"But I was."

Arms hugging herself, she went on, "I think, deep down, I believed he would back off. But he didn't. What kind of man takes such chances?"

He said seriously, "One who thinks that women don't have it in them to shoot an unarmed man."

"Women like me," she said bitterly.

"Most women," he corrected, "and there's no shame in that."

"Hah! Easy for you to say. Can you imagine how I felt? I didn't know you were there. I thought it was just Eric and me. I never want to feel so helpless again. Never!"

"Women aren't the only ones who can feel helpless."

She looked up at him with an arrested expression. "But you sounded so confident, so... so in command of the situation."

He showed her his hands and made them tremble. "Does that look like 'confident' to you?"

He'd hoped to win a smile from her. Instead, tears welled up. She took one of his hands in both of hers and, with the tips of her fingers, traced the lines on his palm. When she turned his hand over, she found the scar from an old knife wound. She gazed at the scar for a long, long time, then slowly brought his hand to her lips and kissed it.

Waldo, never at a loss with women, was transfixed. In other times, with other women, he wouldn't have hesitated to take things one step further. But this was Jo.

She gave him a searching look. "I don't want to be alone," she said. "Would you ... would you sit with me for a little while? It would help if I knew you were there."

He was flattered. No. He was humbled. And amused. He'd had the odd fantasy about spending the night with her, and it seemed that his fantasy was about to come true. But on her terms.

She wanted to hear the sound of his voice, so he read to her from *Waverley*, one of Scott's novels that he found on the table beside her bed. When her breathing was slow and even, he stopped reading, but a moment or two later her lashes fluttered open and he had to start over.

When she was sleeping soundly, he checked on Eric, then removed his jacket and neckcloth and made himself comfortable on one of the upholstered armchairs. He sipped his brandy slowly to make it last.

Thoughts flitted in and out of his mind. Jacob Fry. The attack on her, and who had ordered it and why. But the thought that kept coming back, the thought that left him shaken, was how important this slip of a girl had become to his happiness.

From now on, he promised himself, he would take better care of her. He didn't want her to put herself in harm's way by asking questions about Chloë. He didn't want her living in this house with only gardeners to protect her. He wanted her at Palliser, where half the footmen were former soldiers who knew how to handle guns and take care of themselves in a fight. He wanted her where he could keep a close eye on her.

Tomorrow, he decided, he would take Jo and Eric to his mother, and if Mrs. Daventry wished to go with them, so much the better.

Before going off to his own makeshift bed, he took one last look at her. There wasn't much to see, only the tip of her nose and her glorious mane of red hair. He stood there staring down at her, with a foolish smile on his face.

Chapter 18

They set out for Palliser Park the following morning. Waldo had sent a servant ahead with a note for his mother, explaining briefly why they were coming. Jo was anxious. As she told her aunt in the carriage, what had seemed like a good idea at breakfast had lost its gloss the closer they got to Palliser Park. It was asking a great deal of Lady Fredericka to take in three strangers at such short notice. Eric didn't think it was asking too much at all. Uncle Waldo had invited them, so it must be all right. Uncle Waldo couldn't comment. He was on the box with his coachman, with a great blunderbuss cradled in his arms and a pistol stuffed in each pocket.

Jo's fears were groundless, as Mrs. Daventry had predicted. Lady Fredericka was waiting for them in the great marble entrance hall to welcome them to her home. She didn't make a fuss and she didn't bombard them with questions. She was solicitous, but she was also matter-of-fact.

"You'll be quite safe here," she said, "and you must stay until this dreadful business is settled. Leave it to Waldo. He has connections. He'll get to the bottom of this."

As Waldo went off to speak to his father, Lady Fredericka led the way upstairs. Jo held on to Eric's hand. It was a beautiful Palladian house in a beautiful parklike setting, but she couldn't help being anxious about Eric. She remembered how she'd felt as a child, when she was left with first one relative then another. It didn't matter how kind they were, and they were all kind, generous people. A child needed stability.

"Luncheon will be served in half an hour," said Lady Fredericka. "Quite informal. Just come as you are."

She left as a bevy of maids came to help them unpack. Eric's room was right next to Jo's and had a clear view of the lake.

"Maybe Uncle Waldo can teach me how to swim," said Eric, his eyes sparkling. "Or maybe there are boats and we can go fishing."

Mrs. Daventry and Jo exchanged a quick look. "I do believe," said Mrs. Daventry, "that Eric and I think alike. This is a grand adventure, and we're determined to make the most of it." Her smile suddenly died as a thought occurred to her. "Oh, dear, I didn't mean that the way it sounds. It's just that I'm glad we're here and not at Chloë's house."

"And I," said Jo with feeling, "am glad that you decided to come with me when you might have gone home to Greek Street."

"I wouldn't dream of leaving you when you need me. I mean it, Jo. I'm not leaving you till this whole ugly business is settled."

Jo's throat closed up, but before she could clear it, the luncheon gong sounded. Waldo was waiting for them at the foot of the stairs with his sister Maude. As Maude showed Mrs. Daventry and Eric the way, Waldo fell back a little so that he could talk to Jo.

"I've warned my family not to pester you with questions," he said. "And I know they'll do everything possible to make your stay comfortable."

Touched by his concern, she let her hand rest briefly on his arm. "Don't worry about me, Waldo. I'm fine, really I am."

It was an exaggeration, but she felt that, after all he'd done for her, she owed it to him to appear, if not unscathed, at least on the road to recovery. Uppermost in her mind was the memory of last night. He'd read to her from some boring tome till she'd finally drifted into sleep. All her troubles faded just because he was there beside her. When she'd wakened in the morning to find him gone, she was disappointed.

She supposed she wasn't the first female to waken in the morning and be disappointed because Waldo was no longer there.

Swallowing a sigh, she marched into the dining room.

Standing at the head of the table was Waldo's father. Waldo made the introductions. Jo was aware that she was being carefully measured, then Mr. Bowman smiled, not a superficial movement of his lips but a genuine expression of warmth, and Jo felt herself relax. He was a striking-looking man, of an age with his wife, above-average height, and bore a vague resemblance to Waldo, though Mr. Bowman's eyes were blue and his hair was rapidly giving way to gray. There was a keen intelligence in those blue eyes, Jo thought, and humor too.

"Well, well," he said, "we regret the reason that brought you all to Palliser, but not the fact that you are here. We hope your stay will be a pleasant one and that you will treat our home as though it were your own. Please, Mrs. Chesney, take the place by me, yes, and you too, Mrs. Daventry."

Jo made some suitable rejoinder, as did her aunt, and they went to the chairs Mr. Bowman indicated. No one was seated yet. They were all standing. Jo looked around for Eric, but there was no sign of him.

There was one person still to be introduced, a gentleman in his late thirties. His coloring was fair; his eyes were as blue as Mr. Bowman's. There was an easy charm about him that Jo found herself responding to.

"And this," said Waldo, "is my cousin, Thomas Bowman. You'll meet his daughters later, Jenny and Marion. Eric went with them. They're having lunch in the conservatory, I believe."

Looking at Jo, Thomas added, "Except they think it's a jungle. When they've finished lunch, they're going to hunt for snakes and poisonous insects. So you see, they'll be wonderfully entertained."

Jo nodded and smiled, and decided that she liked Waldo's cousin. He was telling her all this so that she wouldn't worry about Eric.

At this point, Mr. Bowman signaled the footmen to come forward and help the ladies with their chairs. When everyone was seated, he said, "Thomas is the member of Parliament for Burnham. When the House is in session, he spends most of his free time at Holland House, just a stone's throw from here. We're honored to have him with us today."

Thomas grinned. "Hardly free time, Uncle. There's

a great deal of House business gets done at Holland House."

Mrs. Daventry said, "Lord Holland is a Whig, is he not?"

Mr. Bowman nodded. "There have been Whigs at Holland House for generations, whereas at Palliser House we've always been Tories—until, that is, the present generation." He looked pointedly at his son and nephew. "Need I say more?"

"No, you need not!" declared Lady Fredericka. "You know the rules, Julian. We do not discuss politics at the dinner table. It is bad for your digestion."

Mr. Bowman and his wife exchanged a long, challenging look down the length of the table. He said gently, "Then am I permitted to talk about the succession?" To Jo, he said, "You see here, Mrs. Chesney, my heirs: Waldo, who is a bachelor, and Thomas, who is a widower. At the rate they're going, there will be no male Bowmans left to carry on our line."

Waldo said, "That's not a good enough reason to get married, Father."

To which Thomas added, "I wouldn't swap my girls for sons even if you offered me the position of prime minister."

To which Mr. Bowman replied, "I am hardly likely to do that, you being a Whig. As you know very well, I'm talking about duty, not your lovely girls."

From the other end of the table, Cecy called out, "What's wrong with girls, Papa? Don't we count?"

Her father let out a long-suffering sigh. "Of course you do," he said, "but when you marry, you'll take your husband's name. That's all I meant."

Her ladyship let out an audible snort. "I don't see what's so special about *your* name," she said, addressing her husband. "If I had my way, I would have kept my own name when I married. The Howards go back as far as the Bowmans, yes, and did not change sides when you-know-who came to the throne. We Howards know how to be loyal."

"Mother!" Waldo was shaking his head and laughing at the same time. "Mind your tongue or you'll have us all hanged for treason."

Jo did not know where to look. She was on tenterhooks, wondering who would enter the fray next. She could tell that her aunt was as disconcerted as she. No one else at the table, however, seemed to find anything amiss in these heated exchanges. She studied each person discreetly. When her eyes met Waldo's across the table, he smiled and shrugged helplessly. She took that to mean that this was how his family usually conducted itself and there was nothing anyone could do about it.

There was a respite when footmen served luncheon—crimped salmon, croquette of chicken, with sprouts and lobster salad—but the respite was only to last for a few delicious bites.

It was Maude, in her quiet way, who picked up the gauntlet that her father had thrown down. "Once women get the vote," she said, "there will be no stopping us. We shall keep our own names, enter the professions, become members of Parliament, and leave our worldly goods to whomsoever we choose. But nothing can be done until we get the vote. What do you think, Mrs. Chesney?"

Jo choked on a sprout, reached for her glass of wine, and took a long swallow. When she could breathe again, she looked at Maude as though she'd stabbed her in the back. It came to her, by degrees, that Maude hadn't asked for her opinion out of mischief or for a joke. She really wanted to know what she thought.

And so did everyone else at the table. All eyes were on her.

She cleared her throat, a delaying tactic to give her time to think. "If we passively wait for men to give us the vote," she said slowly, putting her thoughts in order, "it will never happen. And they're the ones with all the power. Only they can change the laws. It seems to me that we should make things so difficult for them that they'd be glad to give in to our demands. Our trouble, of course, is that we are too passive. We must be active. We should start demanding access to the professions. We should set up our own businesses. We should lobby our members of Parliament to change the laws so that we have control of our own property. When men see that we won't give up and that we are as intelligent and as capable as they are, they'll have to give us the vote."

"And if we won't?" interjected Mr. Bowman with a decided challenge in his eyes.

"Then I suggest," retorted Jo, caught up in the thrust and parry of the debate, "that all women take immediate steps to become as I am. A widow, Mr. Bowman. We widows enjoy privileges that married women can only dream about."

When the laughter died away, Mr. Bowman said, "I see I am outnumbered by Whigs and Radicals, and in the sacred halls of Palliser no less! I also see my wife signaling me to move on to a neutral topic of conversation. The floor is open. Who would like to begin?"

They all looked blankly at one another except for Mrs. Daventry. She filled the silence nicely. "Cecy," she said, "your sister tells me that your presentation to the queen will take place next week. Are you permitted to tell us about the gown you've chosen for this exciting occasion?"

Cecy needed no prompting, and for the rest of the meal the conversation was all of the joys and pitfalls of court life.

"I can't believe I said that," said Jo.

"What?" asked Waldo.

Luncheon was over and they were sitting on a bench beside the man-made lake, watching the children feed the swans with scraps of bread. Thomas and Maude were close by, on the lawn behind them, setting things up for a game of croquet.

"At the dining table," said Jo, "when I advised all women to become widows like me. I didn't mean it, of course. I only said it to score points off your father."

Waldo said gravely, "We were all very impressed."

Her eyes narrowed on his face. "You're laughing at me!"

He touched a hand to his lips. "Ah, no. This is an old war wound, a nick from the point of a bayonet. I always look as though I'm amused."

"Fustian! Your eyes don't lie, Waldo. You're definitely laughing at me!"

He chuckled. "You're a dangerous woman to know, Jo Chesney. I shall have to watch what I'm thinking when I'm with you. But you're wrong to think I'm mocking you. I'm amused, because you did what few people have ever done. You debated my father to a standstill." He caught her curious look and shrugged. "My father was one of Mr. Pitt's closest associates, when Pitt was prime minister—both Tories born and bred. So you see, he learned how to be an orator from a master."

"Your father was a member of Parliament?"

"Not elected, no. But, he was part of the inner circle

that Pitt relied on to draft policies. When Pitt died, my father retired from public life."

Things were beginning to take shape in her mind. "But you and your cousin, Thomas, are Whigs?"

"That's what comes of having Lord Holland as our nearest neighbor. His uncle, Charles James Fox, was a frequent guest there, along with other outstanding Whigs. This was long before I went off to war, you understand. I was just out of university when Thomas and I were invited to some function at Holland House. Over billiards, we met some of the most liberal-minded men of our day, liberal and brilliant. They opened our minds to ideas that were new to us. We were very young, very impressionable. Some years later, when there was a bi-election in the borough of Burnham, Thomas was elected. I had canvassed for him. You can imagine what my father thought of that."

Her mind was going back and forth, slotting things into place. She spoke slowly, "This can't be the quarrel that has caused so much bad feeling between you and your father? This can't be the reason you became a soldier and went off to Spain?"

"Why can't it?"

"Well . . . because it's only politics. People don't stop speaking or hold grudges because they hold different points of view. That's childish."

"Only politics!" Waldo repeated and let out a rich laugh.

Thomas joined them at that moment. "What's the joke?" he asked.

When Waldo told him, he, too, began to laugh. "In this family," he said, "one's politics are on a par with one's religion. Bowmans have been Tories since the days of the Cavaliers. Waldo and I have broken with tradition. That makes us heretics in the eyes of the older generation."

Jo said, "That's not so unusual, is it? The older generation is always finding fault with the younger generation."

"It caused a rift," replied Thomas, then fell silent.

"It seems pointless, in retrospect," Waldo said, "but at the time it was all very serious."

"Bad feelings all round," agreed Thomas.

A long silence fell, companionable, and they watched the children feeding the swans.

After a while, Waldo stirred. "It's all water under the bridge now. We've all mellowed in the last few years."

"If that's the case," said Thomas, "what's to stop you taking up where you left off—with the party, I mean? There are bi-elections coming up. You could stand in one of them. You'd be an asset to us in the House." When Waldo looked skeptical, Thomas grinned and added sheepishly, "Grenville asked me to sound you out."

"I can't think why. I've been out of things for—how long is it now—eight or nine years? I know how to fight battles. I know nothing about politics."

Thomas said, "I take your point, but your years as a soldier give you the kind of experience that is invaluable. At least think about it. *Seriously*, I mean, won't you?"

Waldo hesitated only a moment. "I'll think about it."

"Good. Anyone for croquet? I promised the children we'd play. Maude has gone to fetch the others."

"I'd like that," said Jo.

As Thomas went to gather the children, Jo and Waldo walked up the incline to the turf. Waldo said,

"You're not the only one who can read eyes. I know what you're thinking, Jo."

She stopped and turned to face him. Eyes wide and bright on his, she said, "Go on, then. Tell me what I'm thinking."

"You're impressed. You're thinking that if Lord Grenville wants me to join his party, I must be a worthy fellow."

That's exactly what she was thinking, but there was an edge to him that put her on the defensive. "What's wrong with that?"

"Perhaps you'd like to see my war record? That's impressive too."

She couldn't think of an amusing rejoinder, so she said nothing, but inside she was fuming. She felt as though he'd given her a set-down, and she couldn't understand it.

After a thankfully uneventful dinner, Jo went upstairs to check on Eric. He was in his nightshirt, newly bathed, and sitting up in bed waiting for her. The maid was tidying up, but Jo told her she'd take care of things, so the young maid bobbed a curtsy and left.

Though not precisely awkward around Eric, Jo wasn't always comfortable either. She felt fiercely protective of him, but she lacked, she supposed, a mother's instinct to kiss and pet. And she was never more aware of this lack in herself than at his bedtime.

But there were other ways to show she cared. As far as possible, she read to him every night. She sat beside him on the bed. "Do you like it here?" she asked.

His eyes locked on hers. "Yes," he said.

He was a happy, well-behaved boy. Everyone said so. There was something wrong with this picture, but Jo couldn't put her finger on it, and now Maude had stirred up her doubts. *How do you get him to be so polite?* she'd asked. *My sons are holy terrors.* And Thomas had made a similar comment, not to her, but to his daughters. *Look at Eric! He doesn't make a fuss just because it's time to go to bed.*

But he wasn't always well-behaved. He could be a holy terror too, like the time he'd broken into the *Journal* offices and later had thrown onions at her in Holy Trinity's churchyard. Had he changed toward her just because she'd saved him from Mr. Harding? Was he good because he was afraid that if he misbehaved, she would send him back? No child should have that hanging over his head.

She wished she could talk things over with Waldo, but he was behaving very oddly. She would never have believed he could be so moody. He spoke to her only when she spoke to him first. It had taken her two hours to realize what he was doing, then she was furious with herself for being so pleasant to him.

She pushed Waldo and his moodiness to the back of her mind and concentrated on Eric.

"This is Uncle Waldo's home, did you know?"

He nodded. "He says I can stay here as long as I like."

That gave her a pang, but she kept her voice light and easy. "What do you want to do, Eric?"

He looked surprised at the question. "I'm going to stay with you, Aunt Jo. Jenny says I have to because you're Papa's sister."

Jenny was eight years old and the elder of Thomas's daughters. Jo didn't know how to begin to sort out the tangle of a child's logic, so she didn't even try. Instead, she said, "I just want you to know, Eric, that you're never, *never* going back to Mr. Harding's school, and that's a promise. Do you believe me?"

Round-eyed, he nodded.

It was perverse, but she was beginning to feel that if he would only do or say something naughty, she would be easier in her mind.

She smiled brightly. "Time for your bedtime story," she said. "Look! I found this book in Mr. Bowman's library and he very kindly loaned it to me."

"Is it about the Trojan War?" he asked eagerly. "Uncle Waldo said he would lend me his very own book about the Greek heroes."

"Oh, he did, did he?" She did not consider stories of blood and gore to be suitable for a child of Eric's tender years. She held up the book in her hand. "These are Greek stories too—Aesop's fables. Wouldn't you like to hear about the tortoise and the hare?"

"I already know it. I have Papa's book with his name in it. I know all the stories by heart."

"Your papa?" This was something new. He'd never mentioned his father before now. "Do you remember your papa, Eric?"

"No. Mam told me. He brought presents for me at Christmas and on my birthday."

"I see." She tried to sound casual. "Who read the stories to you, Eric?"

"Mam did." His little face puckered. "But that was before she fell ill. She was in bed a long time, then the angels came and took her to heaven."

Jo felt something twist inside her. She imagined herself as that young mother, knowing the end was near, knowing that she had to give up her son to the care of others.

Eric was watching her. She swallowed the lump in

her throat and said cheerfully, "Heaven is a good place to be."

"That's what Mam said. Are you going to read me a story?"

There was something in his eyes that gave her pause, something that told her this wasn't the time to press him. She set the book down. "Move over," she said. This done, she climbed onto the bed and stretched out beside him. "You know all Aesop's fables by heart, do you?"

He nodded.

"Fine. Then *you* tell *me* the story about the hare and the tortoise, because it's one of my favorites."

Half an hour later, Waldo found them curled up together, fast asleep. The book had fallen to the floor. His first impulse was to shake Jo awake. His mood was swinging between temper and alarm. Mrs. Daventry, in all innocence, had offered him the latest copy of the *Journal,* and on the back page what should he find but Lady Tellall's column. He knew what that meant. Jo had taken over from Chloë.

Just thinking about it made him want to roar. She didn't understand the danger she'd put herself in, but he did. Now he understood why Jacob Fry had been sent to kill her. Chloë's murderer—and he was sure Chloë had been murdered—must have read the *Journal* and leapt to the conclusion that either Jo had found Chloë's diary and was getting her information from it or that she knew something without realizing its significance and might well publish it one day for the whole world to read.

The paper was rolled up in his hand, and he absently tapped it against his leg as he stared at the

woman and child. Gradually, his softer feelings began
to stir. They looked so innocent, so helpless, so much
in need of a protector, but that didn't make him feel
any happier. There was too much at stake, too many
things that could go wrong.

He moved closer, fascinated by the sight of Eric's
fingers entangled in her hair. These two were fast becoming inseparable. How had he allowed things to go
this far? Because, of course, he couldn't deny Jo whatever she wanted. It gave him pleasure to please her.

She, on the other hand, wasn't so easily won over.
She had only one standard for measuring a man—her
husband, the inestimable, saintly John Chesney—and
no man could live up to that.

His thoughts drifted to the debate at luncheon and
the sparkle in her eyes when she'd challenged the
comforting fictions men cherished about women.
He'd wanted to laugh out loud. What was curious was
that she was quite unaware of what she had revealed.
Whatever the truth about her marriage to Chesney, she
had changed and there was no going back.

Or was that only what he wanted to believe?

He gave a grunt of derision, mocking himself, and
left the room.

Chapter 19

It was the day of the Queen's Drawing Room, the day that Cecy was to be presented to Her Majesty in St. James's Palace, and the whole house revolved around the preparations for this grand occasion. Cecy, her mother, her father, Waldo, and Maude—all had to be got ready, and servants flitted from room to room, some with various costumes draped over their arms, others bearing the accessories that were essential for correct court dress. The presentation was to take place in the afternoon and afterward there was to be a celebratory dinner at the Clarendon Hotel, to which Jo and her aunt had been invited.

Jo was taking everything in, making mental notes for Lady Tellall's next column, subject to Waldo's approval. When he'd discovered that she'd taken over the column from Chloë, he'd been coldly furious and called her all kinds of a fool. She'd accepted his harangue meekly because he seemed so certain that it was Lady Tellall's taking up her pen again that had provoked the attack on her. She'd been too clever for her own good, he'd told her. She'd insinuated that she knew more about Chloë than she did. Someone wanted to silence her and had damn near succeeded! From now on, anything she wrote for the *Journal* had to be submitted to him first for his approval. She was so shaken, she was only too happy to agree.

She was now in Cecy's room, helping her get ready for her presentation. All she had to do was hand items to the abigail as they were needed. Lady Fredericka was there as well, but since she was already dressed, her movements were so severely restricted that her role was reduced to issuing orders.

It was like walking into a painting of a former era, a painting where the figures came to life. Jo remembered her grandmother wearing a dress that resembled the one her ladyship was wearing, and everyone said that Grandmother was hopelessly out of vogue even then. It had a hooped skirt, low bodice, fitted waist, and yards of embroidered silk. These court gowns were more formal than Grandmother's and came with a long train that was attached at the waist.

Everyone's nerves were stretched, especially Cecy's. She was complaining bitterly that she would never manage to walk in a hooped skirt with its long train, and Jo inwardly sympathized with her.

"Nonsense," said Lady Fredericka, not roughly but not gently either. "If I can do it, so can you. Watch."

She deftly draped her train over her left arm. In her right hand, she held her fan, another essential accessory for formal court dress, as Jo had discovered.

"Are you watching, Cecy? Take slow, small steps."

Her ladyship walked forward slowly, her carriage supple and graceful. "Curtsy to Her Majesty." She made a deep curtsy to the abigail, whose hand flew to her mouth to stifle a giggle. "Then curtsy to the prince regent," and she curtsied to the bedpost. This time Cecy giggled. "And slowly take a step to the side before moving away. Remember, Cecy, never turn your back on the queen or any member of the royal family. Just gracefully fade away."

"You forgot something, Mama."

"I did?"

Cecy nodded. "You forgot to kiss the queen's hand."

Her ladyship laughed. "So I did. Something always goes wrong. You can count on it."

Alarmed, Cecy cried, "What can go wrong?"

"Oh, little things. Your feathers may come undone, or your train may tear. That happened to one unfortunate girl the year I was presented. No one noticed till she was right by the dais where the king and queen were waiting. The poor girl's nerves were so overwrought that she burst into tears, picked up her train, and fled. There was no need for it. The pages are there to help."

"What if I sneeze, Mama?"

"Sneezing isn't allowed."

"But what if I can't help it?"

Her ladyship sighed. "Ignore it as though it never happened." She walked to her daughter and put her arms around her. "I felt exactly as you when I was presented, and so will every other young woman at the Drawing Room today. So you see, you're in good company."

Cecy gave a fluttering sigh and smiled.

There was a knock at the door, and a moment later Mr. Bowman entered. He, too, was dressed in garments of a former era—black satin knee breeches, dark blue embroidered silk coat, and embroidered white waistcoat. What Jo had not expected was the small sword at his side and the silver wig. His ensemble lent a wickedly rakish air. His resemblance to Waldo was more striking now.

He crossed to Cecy. "To mark the occasion," he said, and he fastened a diamond necklace around her throat, then he turned her to face him and nodded approvingly.

"Oh, Papa. It's lovely. Thank you." Her voice was teary.

His voice was thick. "Your mama and I are so proud of you, Cecy, not because you're beautiful—which you are—and not because you're clever—which you must be because you're Mama's daughter—but because you turned out just the way we wanted." He kissed her on the brow.

"Oh, Papa!"

"No tears!" declared her ladyship as everyone began to sniff and search for handkerchiefs. "Now see what you've done, Julian!"

Smiling, her husband dried her tears with his own handkerchief. "Thank you," he said simply.

"For what?" She took his handkerchief from him and blew her nose.

"For raising such fine children."

"We were lucky, Julian."

"Yes, we were lucky."

It was a private moment, and Jo sensed the unspoken messages that passed between them. She didn't know why she envied them. They were an atrocious family. They loved and hated on a grand scale. They excelled at debating. If one said something was black, the other would say it was white. Sometimes they were too loud. They quarreled constantly and were not always quick to forgive. Then why did she find them so attractive? They'd been kind to her, of course, gener-

ous beyond anything, but so had the relatives who had
opened their homes to her when she was a child.
There was something about the Bowmans that defied
description.

"Time to go," said Mr. Bowman. "The carriage
awaits. Cecy, take my arm."

He and Cecy led the way. Jo and the maid followed
well behind. In the entrance hall, a small group clus-
tered, waiting for them. Mrs. Daventry and Thomas
were there with the children. They were not going to
court, so they were not dressed for the occasion.
Maude looked stately, her regulation white feathered
headdress fluttering like the sails of a sailing ship.
Waldo was resplendent too, but unlike his father, he
didn't appear to be at ease in court dress. He kept ad-
justing his wig and small sword.

There were more kisses for Cecy, then they went
outside to the carriage.

Eric said, "Aren't you going with them to see the
queen, Aunt Jo?"

"No," she said. "The queen forgot to send me an invitation. But I don't mind. Aunt Daventry and I have
plenty to do here. And we'll be going to the Clarendon
later for dinner."

"Where will I be?"

Thomas's elder daughter, Jenny, answered his question. "With us, silly. Don't you remember? Uncle Julian's
groom is going to show us how to take care of the foals."

Waldo managed a quiet word with Jo before he entered the carriage. "I've sent a man to Chloë's house to
get those back copies of the *Journal* you told me about.
Read them through. See if anything strikes you as odd."

"I see. I'm to spend my afternoon poring over old
copies of the *Journal* whilst you are cutting a dash at
court?"

He stared at her hard, then chuckled. "Believe me, if I could, I'd change places with you. Drawing Rooms are boring. I'll be standing for hours on end, talking to, for the most part, tedious people about tedious, trivial subjects. Cecy's part will be over in five minutes, and I may not get a clear view of her anyway."

"Then why go?"

He cocked his head to one side, studying her. "Because it's important to Cecy that I should be there."

It was on the tip of her tongue to say *How kind* or something equally inane, and though she meant it sincerely, she feared another set-down, so she merely smiled.

"I'm reading your thoughts again, Jo."

"Oh, go to blazes!"

He laughed. "I'll see you later, then, at the Clarendon. And remember to read through those back copies of the *Journal*. Mark anything that looks odd or interesting. Now get back before you're trampled in the stampede."

Someone must have signaled the butler, for he opened the doors and a crush of laughing servants streamed down the steps and into the courtyard. As Waldo hastily entered the carriage, his father threw a handful of silver coins in the air. Only the butler and housekeeper kept themselves aloof from the fun. Everyone else made a dive for the coins, including the children. Jo came up with a shilling.

As the coach moved off, another handful of coins was thrown in the air.

Silver for good luck, Jo thought. *I hope it rubs off on me.*

At St. James's Palace, the queen had yet to make an appearance, so everyone stood around in little groups, speaking in hushed tones while they waited. Waldo was talking to his father when someone brushed against him. It was Viscount Morden.

"Bowman," the viscount said and bowed.

Waldo inclined his head. "Morden," he said. "What brings you to the Queen's Drawing Room?" He couldn't imagine anyone coming to such an event unless it was to support a sister or a wife as she made her curtsy to the queen, and he knew that Lady Margaret had already been presented.

The viscount smiled. "Why does anyone come to court," he said, "except to keep abreast of things, and to see and be seen."

Waldo concealed his distaste behind a bland smile. There were plenty of others like Morden who thought that rubbing shoulders with royalty added to their consequence. "It's hard to see anyone in this squeeze," he remarked casually.

He waited, sensing that there was more to come. He was right.

The viscount said, "I happened to read an extraordinary report about Lady Webberley in some provincial paper. It said that she was seen taking the ferry to France. Does this mean she has turned up and we all worried for nothing? What do her friends say?"

The result of this little speech was to focus all of Waldo's considerable intelligence on Morden, though he did not betray it by the blink of an eye. A secret-service agent whose expression revealed what he was thinking did not last long in His Majesty's service.

He deliberately frowned. "This is the first I've heard of it," he said. "Where did you read this?"

"Where?"

"What was the name of the paper?"

"Oh. I believe it was the *Avon Journal*. My mother

showed it to me. Someone had given it to her because she was anxious about Lady Webberley's disappear-ance. I was hoping I could assure her that the report is true?"

There was nothing remarkable in the viscount's concern for his mother, and Waldo might have be-lieved him except that his words were too pat, his eyes were too intense. It struck him, then, that it wasn't Lady Brinsley but the viscount who wanted to be reas-sured.

Now he was thoroughly confused. Did Morden want the report to be true or untrue? If he was the killer, the report wouldn't matter to him because he would know that Chloë was dead.

He couldn't be the killer. It was too far-fetched. What motive could he have? On the other hand, he was present at that fateful house party.

"If I hear anything," said Waldo, "I'll let you know."

They parted company then, and Waldo rejoined his father. Mr. Bowman studied his son's expression, then glanced over at the viscount. "What did he want?" he asked.

"I don't know," replied Waldo thoughtfully, "but I mean to find out."

The footman who had been sent to Chloë's house to fetch back copies of the *Journal* returned also with let-ters from Stratford and a traveling box with Eric's name on it. The housekeeper had him bring every-thing up to Jo's chamber, but Jo did not get around to examining them till it was almost time to get ready for dinner at the Clarendon.

She opened the package from Mac Nevin first. It contained the circulation lists she'd asked for and a note to the effect that everything was going well at the *Journal*, though there were no more letters for Lady Tellall respecting Lady Webberley. Setting the lists aside, she went on to the next letter.

It was from Mrs. Sutherland, the vicar's wife. She wrote satirically that Eric's grandmother had made a miraculous recovery, but not so miraculous that she wanted Eric back. She was simply too old to look after the boy. Besides, they were practically strangers. He was better off at boarding school.

The letter went on:

> *I'm sure Mrs. Foley's illness was just a ruse to get rid of Eric and save face at the same time so that no one could claim that she was coldhearted. The vicar doesn't like to hear me speak unkindly of the woman, but I know it's true. She doesn't want any reminders of Eric, hence the box with the few things he possesses. I think what you are doing, Mrs. Chesney, is truly admirable and selfless.*
> *May God bless you.*
>
> > *Respectfully,*
> > *Adelaide Sutherland*

Jo thought the ending to the letter was rather flowery, especially as she hadn't done very much for Eric, or at least nothing that Mrs. Sutherland could have known about. She was sure Waldo wouldn't broadcast the fact that she'd rescued Eric by attacking his headmaster, not when she'd ended up in Bow Street for her trouble.

The passage about Mrs. Foley didn't surprise her. She'd allowed Eric to go to a monstrous boarding school, without a protest, when his mother died.

Coldhearted didn't do her justice. She was a nasty piece of work.

There were other letters, but nothing of interest, so she lifted the box onto the bed. It wasn't very heavy. She could easily have carried it to Eric's room and let him have the pleasure of opening it himself. What made her hesitate was a distrust of Mrs. Foley's motives. She had never liked the woman, and after reading Mrs. Sutherland's letter she liked her even less.

On that thought, Jo undid the leather strap that fastened the box and lifted off the lid. There was very little there: a change of clothes, a pair of well-worn leather boots, some books, and a box of toy soldiers. One of the books was Aesop's fables. On the flyleaf, she found the inscription Eric was so proud of. *To Eric, many happy returns, from Papa.*

Her heart did a little flip-flop. The writing seemed familiar. It made her think of John's script. He always used the Greek *e.* But many people did. It didn't mean anything.

Thoughts tumbled into her mind, impressions of Waldo. He had told her very little of Eric's parents, especially the father. She had respected his reticence. He was only protecting his ward's privacy, as any guardian would.

She scolded herself for the little seed of suspicion that had sprouted in her mind.

John couldn't possibly be Eric's father. She knew that Eric was born two months before her wedding, when John was courting her. She *knew* John. He was too decent, too honorable to abandon a woman who was expecting his child.

She thought of the flowery ending to Mrs. Sutherland's letter. *I think what you are doing is truly admirable and selfless*. She thought of how much Mrs. Foley disliked her.

And she thought of how her imagination was inclined to run away with her, and she was ashamed of what she'd thought.

But her imagination wasn't wrong. She found it tucked inside a shirt, a folded piece of vellum, a letter from an attorney to Sarah Foley, outlining his client's provisions for her and his son, Eric. The client's name was John Saxon Chesney. He'd settled one thousand pounds on Sarah Foley, in trust, for life, and the same for his son, Eric Foley. She didn't recognize the signature at the bottom of the letter.

Numb with shock, she sank into a chair and stared unseeingly at the document in her hand. Several minutes were to pass before she stirred. Things that had puzzled her were beginning to make sense: Mrs. Foley's hostility from the first day she'd arrived in Stratford as a new bride; John's frequent jaunts around the county without her, *to gather local color for the Journal*, so he'd said; and more recently, Eric breaking into the *Journal*'s offices, then pelting her with rotten vegetables.

That wasn't all. Waldo must be involved too. When he applied for guardianship of Eric, all this must have come to light. He should have told her. She shouldn't be the last one to know. She must be the most gullible woman who ever lived.

She sat there unmoving, head bowed, trying to understand what could not be understood. The man she had loved with her whole heart, the man she had revered, had lied to her. He'd been her whole life, but he'd had a life apart from her, a secret life. The pain hurt so deeply, it was staggering.

Then anger came, not a trickle, but a deluge. Those

were not tears of self-pity that burned her throat. They were tears of outrage and wounded pride. She wanted to hurt him as much as he had hurt her. For ever after, she would remember him with loathing.

That was the hardest thing to bear. Memories she had cherished, memories of John, tore at her heart like poisoned barbs.

It was too much. She jumped to her feet and ran from the room.

The night belonged to Cecy, so Waldo forced himself to a gaiety he was far from feeling. Jo wasn't there, and all through dinner he found his thoughts wandering to Palliser. According to Mrs. Daventry, Jo had gone out for a walk, had been caught in a sudden squall, and had come home complaining of chills and a headache. She sent her apologies and hoped to see them all at breakfast tomorrow.

Everyone commiserated, then everyone forgot about Jo, except for Waldo.

To one of his asides, Mrs. Daventry responded in an undertone that she thought there was more to it than that, that something had upset Jo but she wouldn't unburden herself and had insisted that Mrs. Daventry come on to the party.

Waldo brooded. He was thinking about his conversation with Viscount Morden, remembering the attack on Jo a few nights before. He'd thought she'd be safe at Palliser; now he wasn't so sure. What could possibly have upset her?

As soon as the toasts were over, he made his excuses and left. There was no question of his hiring a horse and riding out to Palliser in his fancy getup, so he took the carriage that had brought Thomas and Mrs. Daventry and as soon as he arrived home told the coachmen to turn around and go back to the Clarendon.

The light was fading and candles had been lit. His first order of business was to divest himself of a suit of clothes his grandfather would have been proud to wear. He'd already removed the wig and stuffed it in his pocket. He'd dispensed with his small sword as well but had left it in the carriage. No doubt Thomas would find it and return it to him. He despised these antiquated rules of court dress and etiquette. It was enough to make a man a republican.

His suite of rooms was on the ground floor: a bedchamber, dressing room, and a parlor that had been turned into a study. He entered the darkened room with the grace and silence of a cat and paused, an ingrained habit from his former life as a spy. But it was more than habit that made him pause this time. It was instinct. Someone was waiting for him. He could smell the faint aroma of lemon, could hear the soft sound of someone breathing.

When that someone moved, so did he. He realized his mistake as soon as he rolled with his assailant and came up on top. His assailant was a female, and not just any female.

"Jo!" he said furiously. "What in blazes do you think you're doing?"

"I want you to make love to me," she said tremulously.

Chapter 20

*H*e was sure his heart stopped. This couldn't be Jo speaking. "What did you say?"

"I said I want you to make love to me."

It *was* Jo, and he hadn't misheard her. He brushed his body against hers in a purely masculine response he was powerless to resist. She was in her night clothes, and he could feel the soft swell of her breasts against his chest.

He cleared his throat. "You know you shouldn't be here alone with me."

And they shouldn't be sprawled on the floor, limbs entwined, like cavorting lovers. He should help her up and get her back to her room before the others got back.

When he helped her to a sitting position, she winced. "I think," she said, "my ankle is sprained."

He could well believe it. He'd fallen on her like a mighty oak that had been felled by a thunderbolt. "Put your arm around my shoulders and I'll help you to the bed."

After depositing her on the bed, he turned away to get a candle.

"Where are you going?" she cried.

"To light a candle."

She captured his hand and brought it to her cheek. "Waldo, don't leave me."

In the semidarkness, he could just make out her features, the sculpted bones, and her hair falling around her shoulders. He felt transfixed. She was so soft and womanly, so much more than he had ever hoped to find in a woman. And, at last, it seemed that she wanted him as much as he wanted her.

"Jo," he said, and there was wonder in his voice.

He sat on the bed beside her. His hand trembled as he brought her chin up so that he could look into her eyes. They were in shadow.

A flicker of doubt crossed his mind. He'd arrived home with a sense of urgency, a suspicion planted in his mind by Mrs. Daventry that something might be wrong. He'd allowed himself to stray, or he'd been deliberately led astray. Which was it?

"I can't see your eyes," he said, "so you'll have to tell me what you are thinking, Jo."

Her voice was very low. "I'm thinking I want us to make love. What more is there to say?"

He lifted her hand, turned it over, and kissed her palm. He smiled when he heard her breath quicken. "You can tell me why you've had a change of heart. Mrs. Daventry said you seemed upset when she left you. What happened here today, Jo?"

"Do you question all your lovers like this before you take them to bed?"

A jarring note. His fingers tightened on her wrist with enough force to make her wince. "Tell me!" he commanded.

She jerked her hand out of his grasp and massaged her wrist. He could feel the temper rise in her, then, as quickly as it came, it burned itself out. "Something did happen," she said. "I came to see how alone I am, how friendless. Oh, I know it's my own fault. I haven't even kept up with my own family, not really. These last few years I've become obsessed with keeping the *Journal* going. Suddenly, it didn't seem like a good enough reason for cutting myself off from everyone. Cutting myself off from real life is what I mean."

She rubbed her cheek on the sleeve of her gauze robe before going on. "I went for a walk to think things over and was caught in a sudden downpour. I was chilled to the bone. I stayed home because I wasn't up to company. I just couldn't face everyone in my confused state. So I took the time to think about what I really want. And I came to a decision." She looked up at him with the same shadowed eyes. "I decided that I didn't want to be alone anymore. I wanted to start living again. I wanted you, Waldo."

It wasn't exactly what he wanted to hear. "Is it me you want, Jo, or will any man do?"

She gave a teary chuckle. "I don't know any other men, so I guess you'll have to do."

There was a heartbeat of silence, then he said dryly, "Didn't anyone ever tell you that honesty isn't always a virtue?"

She went perfectly still. Even her breathing became inaudible. When she spoke, her voice strained for flippancy and failed. "I don't want honesty, Waldo. I don't want us to become best friends. I just want an affair."

Her shoulders lifted in a tiny shrug. "I thought it's what you wanted too."

She was his for the taking. It's what he'd always wanted.

Then why did he hesitate?

Because she was coming to him for all the wrong reasons.

He bowed his head as he weighed her words. This was a complete reversal of everything she stood for. She didn't want honesty. She didn't want a friend. She wanted an affair.

And then he knew. He *knew*!

He went to the mantel and got a candle lit, then he lit several other candles around the room. When he came back to her, she was on her feet, her flimsy negligee clinging enticingly to her curves. She had certainly dressed for the part of seducing him.

His voice was like velvet. "How did you find out?"

Her lashes swept down. "Whatever do you mean?"

He reached out with one hand and forced up her chin. "Look at me!"

When she gave him her eyes, he nodded. "So you found out about your dear departed husband and you thought you'd punish him by seducing me?"

She slapped his hand away. "The thought of seducing you never once entered my mind. How is it possible to seduce a rake? I thought you wanted this. Evidently, I was wrong."

"Don't bandy words with me, and don't call me names or I might return the compliment. Oh, yes, there's an ugly word for you too, Jo."

She sucked in a quick, shaken breath, then her hand lashed out, but he caught it in midair, blocking the blow. "Let me go," she cried. "You're hurting me."

"I'll do a damn sight more if you continue to provoke me. Now, sit down and answer my question."

He had to admire her courage. Though fear leapt to her eyes, she subdued it and walked with a straight back to the chair he indicated. There was no pretense now of a sprained ankle.

Chin tilted and eyes unfaltering on his, she said, "I can't see the point in discussing this."

"Can't you? Then you're not as clever as I thought you were. I want answers—that's the point. So start at the beginning. How did you find out?"

There was no attempt at prevarication now. "Eric's grandmother, quite deliberately, sent on a letter that she knew would fall into my hands, a letter from an attorney to Eric's mother outlining the provisions John had made for her and her child." A thread of bitterness entered her voice. "But of course, you must know all this."

"That must be obvious. I could hardly apply for guardianship of Eric without learning all there is to know about his background."

Her voice rose alarmingly. "And you never thought to tell me?"

"And disillusion you about a husband you worshiped? What would be the point? Besides, messengers of bad tidings generally come to a sad end. Just look at you now. Your eyes are flashing. Your teeth are clenched. John Chesney is beyond your reach, so you'd like to punish me instead."

Her hands balled into fists.

He nodded. "That's what this is about, isn't it, Jo? He may be in his grave, but you still want to punish him. Well, I want no part of it."

He waited for her to refute his words, but when she sat there stony-faced, he turned away and walked to a table with glasses and a decanter of brandy on it. After pouring himself a generous measure, he took a long swallow, then another. If she was disillusioned, so was he. He'd thought better of her than this. Her only use for him was to punish her husband for his sins.

When he heard her sniff, his softer feelings began to stir. He could never be angry with her for long. Naturally, she was angry at Chesney. She had every right to be. If only she would leave him out of it.

"Look, Jo," he said gently, turning to face her, "Chesney wasn't a bad man. He tried to do the right thing by the girl, didn't he? And he tried to do right by you. Besides, it happened before he married you, and that was the end of it."

A moment before, she'd been the picture of misery. Now she sprang to her feet, every muscle tensed. "Are you defending him?" she demanded incredulously.

"No. I'm trying to be fair to him."

"Well, you might try being fair to me. He was my best friend. We vowed always to be honest with each other, yet he visited that woman all the time we were married, and he never said a word."

"He visited his *son*."

His words made no impression. "He lied to me! He said he was in one place when he was in another. He had a son, for God's sake. Eric was born before we were married. Don't you think I had a right to know?"

"Yes, I do. But if you had known, what would you have done?"

She drew in a long breath. "We'll never know now, will we?"

He gave a short, disbelieving laugh. "Come now, Jo. Don't lie to yourself. Chesney knew what you would do. You demand perfection in those who are close to you, and no one can live up to that. You haven't kept up with your family. Your friends have fallen away. You said so yourself. Oh, I think Chesney knew you would turn him away, so he concealed the truth from you. I can almost feel sorry for him. He must have loved you very much. It couldn't have been easy living on a pedestal. I know I couldn't. Then, of course, I'll never be asked, will I, Jo?" He gestured with one hand to the bed. "My role would have been insignificant. Any man would have served your purposes." He gave a slight shrug. "Contrary to what you may think, even I have scruples. Thank you, but no thanks."

He could feel the little pulse beating inside his cheek. There was a tremor in his hands. He bolted his drink and set the empty glass down with a snap. At that moment, he didn't like himself very much. He'd wanted to hurt her, and it seemed he had succeeded. Her face was ashen. Her eyes were luminous with tears. Her breathing was quick and fast.

Remorseful now, he held out his hand in a gesture of appeal. "I didn't mean it, Jo. You hurt my pride and—"

Without hearing him out, she picked up her skirts and left the room.

When they reached the turf, Waldo slackened the reins and allowed his stallion to have its head. They'd made this ride many times in all kinds of weather, though rarely in the dark. He welcomed the danger. The wildness in the wind suited his mood perfectly. Setting his heels to Mercury's flanks, he urged him on.

Powerful muscles bunched and strained, then Mercury lengthened his stride and was soon soaring effortlessly across the sward. It wasn't only the excitement Waldo craved. On horseback, there were no restrictions on a man who was lame. He felt whole again, and as reckless and as daring as the horse he rode.

The excitement wasn't enough. It couldn't drive from his mind the picture of Jo as he'd last seen her, only a few hours ago, white-faced and shaken. There was no excuse for him. What the devil had got into him? Women had offered themselves to him before now and he'd let them down gently if they didn't appeal to him.

That was the trouble. Jo did more than appeal to him. He ached for her. And because she'd humbled his pride, he'd lashed out like a sulky schoolboy. That wasn't quite right. A schoolboy didn't have his finesse. A schoolboy didn't know how to twist the knife to cause the most pain. She'd confided in him, and he'd taken those confidences and used them against her.

How low could a man get?

There might have been some truth in what he'd said to her, but it wasn't the whole truth. She took too much upon herself. She hadn't abandoned her family; they had abandoned her. And she wasn't without friends. Chloé came to mind. When Jo committed herself to someone, she didn't count the cost. Then there was Eric.

He didn't envy John Chesney one bit. The threat of exposure must have nagged at him constantly. Waldo could sympathize, but he could not condone. All the same, Chesney was a decent man. He'd done the right thing by Eric and his mother. If only he'd had the courage to face up to Jo, everyone, including himself, wouldn't be going through hell right now.

For the next little while, he gave himself up to the wildness inside him. They plunged down dales and vaulted over hedges. Lightning streaked across the sky, turning night into day, but that did not slow them, nor did the driving rain. They made the circuit at break-neck speed.

As they neared the house, he saw a light at an upstairs window. He knew it came from Jo's chamber. Everyone else had gone to bed long since. Why was Jo still awake?

He slowed Mercury to a walk, then reined in, his eyes still on the light in Jo's window. What was she thinking, feeling? If he'd kept his mouth shut, they'd be together right now, in his chamber, in his bed, and he was damn sure he could drive the thought of John Chesney clear out of her mind.

He felt the beat of his blood at every pulse point, the slow rise and fall of his chest. The ache inside him was like a physical pain. There was only one cure for what ailed him, and that was Jo.

He'd never been fainthearted with women, but he'd held off with Jo because she was still wedded to the memory of her late husband. It occurred to him now that he and Chesney had much in common. They'd both allowed Jo to call the shots.

He'd be damned if he'd allow that state of affairs to continue. He wheeled his mount and headed for the stable block.

Sleep was impossible, so she'd risen from her bed and tried to read, but that was impossible too. She ached all over. It was sheer luck that he hadn't broken any of her limbs when he'd fallen on her and sent her crashing to the floor. Though she hadn't sprained her ankle, there was a nasty gash on it. That's what came of tangling with a man who wore silver buckles on his shoes.

She was seated at her dressing table, examining herself in the looking glass for little scratches and abrasions she'd taken when she'd fallen to the floor. None of them amounted to anything except the scrape on her ankle.

Her shoulders drooped as the memory of the humiliating scene in Waldo's chamber came back to her. He had willfully misunderstood her. She wasn't denying that she was upset at what she'd found out about John, but she wasn't using Waldo to punish John.

Or was she?

She'd told Waldo the truth as she saw it, that she'd wanted to—what? She couldn't remember what she'd told him. But she knew how she felt. She'd wanted to do something reckless, to step outside the boring character of Jo Chesney and seize life before it passed her by.

Maybe Waldo knew her better than she knew herself. Maybe she *had* wanted revenge on John. Waldo had been harsh, and maybe she deserved it.

She found a set of tiny bruises marching across her chest. She supposed she got those from the silver buttons on his coat. And silver was supposed to be lucky? She scanned the top of the dressing table for the silver shilling she'd picked up in the courtyard. Having found it, she threw it with all her might into the empty grate, where it bounced and rattled before sinking into the cinders.

So much for luck.

She stared at her reflection again, at a shadow on her left cheek, and groaned in mortification. If it turned black and blue, she didn't know how she'd explain it away. Was it a shadow or was it a bruise? She couldn't see clearly in this light.

She snatched up her hand mirror—silver again—
and crossed to the mantelpiece, where a candle was
burning. The light shone full on her face. It wasn't a
bruise. It was only a shadow. She angled the mirror to
get a better look, but it wasn't her own face that was reflected back at her. It was Waldo's.

Her hand trembled. Her throat closed. For one in-
sane moment, she thought she'd conjured him out of
thin air. She hadn't heard the door open. How had he
got here? But the voice that spoke to her wasn't an illu-
sion.

"I couldn't leave things as they were. I came to apologize."

Those tears were clogging her throat again, and that
made her cross—cross and weak and trembly. She put
the hand mirror on the mantel and turned to face him.
He was standing by the door that gave onto the servants'
staircase. He wasn't wearing a jacket, and his dark hair
looked damp and windblown. He looked as vulnerable
as she felt.

Waldo didn't feel vulnerable so much as staggered.
It wasn't her beauty that struck him or the fact that she
was wearing a transparent nightgown, unbuttoned to
the waist, which revealed far more than he wanted to
see when he had something serious on his mind that
had to be said. What staggered him was the awful realization that he might, against all reason, possibly be
seriously obsessed with this woman, and there wasn't a
damn thing he could do about it.

"Don't apologize," she said. "I deserved it."

He made a motion with one hand. "I didn't mean
half of what I said."

That brought a fleeting smile to her lips. "Which
half *did* you mean?"

He didn't smile. "I can't remember what I said, but if it hurt you, I didn't mean it."

She felt the prickle of tears. He shouldn't be apologizing. The fault was hers. She hadn't made him understand. She took a step toward him, then another. When she was close enough to touch him, she halted. "I didn't mean to hurt you either." She stopped to swallow. "But I mean what I said. I've been alone too long. There's no joy in my life. I thought you could teach me how to find joy again."

His fingers stroked her cheek; emotion darkened his eyes. "I thought you could do the same for me."

Suddenly, something that had seemed so hard was easy. She wasn't an innocent young girl. She knew what she was doing and what to expect. With a long, sighing breath, she twined her arms around his neck and lifted her face to his. "Don't talk. Just kiss me."

As his lips brushed hers, heat flamed within her, making her ache for more. It had been so long, so long.... She wanted joy, but she wanted more. Just for a little while, she wanted to forget all the troubles that plagued her. She wanted the oblivion only Waldo could give. Her hands slid to his shoulders and drew him closer.

He laced his fingers behind her head, holding her steady as his lips sank into hers. When her body yielded to the pressure of his, her softness melting against him, he drew her to the bed.

Eyes on hers, he divested her of her gown and tossed it to the floor, then quickly shed his own garments. His hands trembled as they skimmed over her. She was soft and supple, her skin as smooth as silk. There was no seduction. She gave him kiss for kiss, touch for touch. She was eager, more than eager, and that made him smile.

"Easy," he said. "Easy. We have all night."

He tried to soothe her with softly murmured words and gentle caresses. It didn't help. In fact, it did the opposite. She was turning to fire in his arms, racing for the end when they'd hardly begun.

This wasn't what he wanted. He wasn't looking for the ease a woman's body could give him. He could find that with any woman. He wanted Jo. He wanted what was in her mind and heart. He wanted to cherish and savor, and be intimate with her in every sense of the word.

She could feel his heart thundering against her hand, could hear him murmuring that she was going too fast for him. He was going to stop, and that was the last thing she wanted. She couldn't understand it. He had hardly touched her, yet she was hovering on the edge. In another moment she would shatter into a thousand pieces.

Holding his face with both hands, she kissed him again and again, each kiss more abandoned than the last. He was searching for his control when her hand slipped between their bodies and closed around his sex. For one moment more, he held her off, but he'd left it too late. Her needs overwhelmed him, her passion found an answering beat in his own body.

"Is this what you want, Jo?" he asked hoarsely.

His hands and mouth were desperate to learn all her secrets. She was wild and sweet and wet with wanting him. He couldn't remember wanting this much, needing this much. He rose above her and positioned her for his possession. Her eyes were dark and unfocused, her hair a fiery halo around her shoulders. With head thrown back, he drove into her, fusing their bodies into one.

Jo sucked in a breath as pain streaked through her.

By degrees it subsided to a dull ache. She hadn't expected this. It had been so long since a man had made love to her.

He went perfectly still, watching emotions chase themselves across her face. On a shaken laugh, he got out, "Don't tell me you've changed your mind? I don't know if I can stop."

In answer, she wrapped her arms and legs around him, locking him to her. There was no answering smile on her lips. "If you stop now, I'll kill you."

His smile gradually died. "I'll never stop," he said, "so you'd better make up your mind to it."

His words hardly registered. He moved, raising on his arms to make his penetration as deep as he could make it. Her body arched and trembled beneath his. Then coherent thought disintegrated as they streaked toward a mindless release.

It took her a long time to get her breath back. Now that the madness was over, she didn't know where to look or what to say. Her behavior was completely out of character. She'd never felt that kind of desperation. With John, making love had been pleasant. With Waldo, she'd been wild and free. Now she felt awkward. What on earth was she going to say to him?

They were still on the bed, but covered now by the quilt, and he was propped on one elbow, gazing down at her. What did he see? What was he looking for? She chanced a quick look up at him, then looked away. There was a guarded expression in his eyes, and he was chewing on his bottom lip. One of them had to say something before the silence became deafening, and it seemed that someone had to be her.

"You can take that look off your face, Waldo," she said lightly. "I'm not expecting a declaration of love."

Something flickered at the back of his eyes, but he said in his easy way, "Well, that's one problem I won't have to worry about."

Disappointment shimmered through her, but she brought it quickly under control. She had to remember that Waldo did this kind of thing all the time. She was only one among many, and a novice at that. Did all men crave variety?

She looked at him and looked away.

"What?" he asked.

She shrugged.

"Jo." He tipped up her chin with his index finger. "Tell me!"

She said slowly, "I was thinking about Eric's mother—you know, Sarah Foley, wondering what she was like. I don't suppose you happened to find out..."

Her voice trailed to a halt when he abruptly threw back the quilt and got up. He dressed with quick, efficient movements, then turned to look at her. His face was pale and his eyes were vivid with anger. She strained back against the pillows when he put one hand on the bedpost and leaned over her.

There was nothing easy about his voice now. "To answer your question. Yes, I found out about Sarah Foley. She was a simple, kindhearted girl and a loving mother. But we both knew this already, didn't we, Jo, because Eric is a happy, normal little boy. To answer the question you didn't ask, no, I didn't happen to find out whether your husband kept up his affair with her after he was married to you. To tell you the truth, I wasn't interested. He's dead, Jo. So is Sarah Foley. Accept it. And *never* make me a party to your revenge again."

She said quietly, "That is so unjust. Revenge had nothing to do with it. I had a stray thought about Eric's mother, all right?"

But it wasn't all right. His mouth twisted, and with a grunt of derision, he left her.

Chapter 21

*I*t was the morning after Cecy's presentation, a
time when everyone was usually up and doing,
but today Jo was the only one to come down for
breakfast. Evidently, no one was expected, for there
was very little set out on the sideboard. She helped herself to toast and scrambled eggs and washed it down
with tepid coffee.

The children were up. She could hear their shrieks
through the open window. Cup in hand, she wandered
over and looked out. They were trying to play cricket with
only one bowler-cum-fielder and two batsmen. They were
shrieking because Miss Tanner, the girls' nursemaid, who
was acting as umpire, had declared that the batters were
both out!

She turned when she heard the door opening. Waldo
paused for a moment on the threshold. She could see at
once that there was a change in him. He wasn't cold or
aloof, but there wasn't the familiarity she had come to

expect. His eyes were flat, his smile lacked warmth, his greeting was perfunctory.

There was a change in her as well. She felt awkward and tongue-tied and not only because last night she'd behaved with all the finesse of a cat in heat. She couldn't understand how everything could have gone so wrong. All he helped himself to was toast and marmalade and a cup of coffee. When he sat down at the table, he indicated a chair, inviting her to be seated. "I want to talk to you," he said.

She refilled her coffee cup first, then took the chair he indicated. "I want to talk to you as well."

"I see your sprained ankle has healed?"

She almost took exception to his cynical smile, but she wasn't up to bickering, so she merely nodded. "Do you want to begin or shall I?"

He let out a weary sigh. "If it's about last night—"

"It isn't about last night. In fact, I think it would be better if we pretended that last night never happened. I've already erased it from my memory and I hope you'll do the same."

"Consider it done."

He took a sip of coffee as though he'd done no more than agree to post a letter for her. A tiny shard of glass lodged in her heart.

"Is that all?"

"No," she said. "I want to talk to you about Eric." She took a moment to frame her words. "It's about the letter," she said finally, "the one from the attorney to Eric's mother. Why did Mrs. Foley wait so long before she passed it on to me? Why now? Why not when it came into her possession, which I presume was when Eric's mother died?"

"As I understand, she assumed that she would have control of the money that had been settled on her daughter. When she realized her mistake, she no longer wanted the boy."

Bitterness welled up in her. "Is that all Eric meant to her—money?"

"Apparently." He was crumbling a piece of dried toast between his fingers, but he was watching her. "But that's not why she sent you the letter."

"No. I've thought about that. I think she blames me for coming between John and her daughter." She stopped, afraid to go on, afraid to revive their quarrel, but there were so many questions she wanted answered.

He said abruptly, "Look, it's not my place to divulge all the salacious details of your husband's past. If you want to know more about Sarah Foley, ask the vicar. Anything I know, I got from him."

"The vicar! Is there anyone in Stratford who didn't know about Sarah Foley, apart from me?"

"I have no idea. Is that all?"

It would have given her great pleasure to shock the indifferent expression from his face, but nothing came to mind, so she said instead, "No, we still have to talk about Eric."

"I see. Now that you know whose son he is, you no longer want him. Well, I tried to dissuade you from the very beginning. I knew it was a mistake to allow you to become too attached to him. But nothing has changed. He'll go to a good school. In the holidays, he'll go to my sister Maude or he'll come here."

"Nothing has changed?" She was as derisive as he. "*Everything* has changed. He's John's son. I have more claim to him than you."

"You want Eric?" He sounded incredulous.

"Yes."

"Jo." He shook his head. "I don't think you've thought

this through. Can you tell me, honestly, that knowing who he is won't make a difference? You have so much bitterness fermenting inside you, some of it is bound to spill over." His mouth twisted. "As I should know. I won't let you make Eric a victim in this war between you and a ghost."

She could feel her hands clenching into fists, and she quickly linked her fingers so she wouldn't betray herself. Pride kept her eyes dry and her voice level. "I have never understood why you want to be Eric's guardian. A little boy doesn't fit into your life. You'll only see him in school holidays."

"Yes, so you've told me on more than one occasion. However, as I remember, the role was foisted upon me by *you*. One thing you should know about me, Jo— when I take something on, I see it through. Which brings me to something else I agreed to take on for you—finding out what has happened to your friend Chloë."

She didn't want to leave things like this. She wanted to defend her character, show him how wrong he was in all his assumptions. She wasn't at war with a ghost. Yes, John had hurt her, but bitterness wasn't fermenting inside her. Last night she'd given vent to her feelings, and some of the poison had drained away. In time, she would get over it. That's all she needed, a little time.

Those flat, hard eyes that stared at her indifferently did not encourage her to explain herself. "Fine," she said. "Let's talk about Chloë."

He had set things up in a corner of the library—a long table set out with pens, paper, and ink pot down one side, and on the other, the back copies of the

Journal and the circulation lists that Mac Nevin had sent on. Ruggles was there, and he got up from the table when he caught sight of her.

"Mrs. Chesney," he said. "It's a pleasure to see you again."

She was pleased to see him as well, not only because he was a pleasant, well-mannered gentleman, but because she and Waldo would have to stop sniping at each other when company was present.

She bobbed him a curtsy. "Mr. McNab," she said. "Is that the list of the *Journal*'s London subscribers you have in your hand?"

"It is, and I've found something." He looked at Waldo. "Morden's name is here, but not his title: Mr. Morden, Wattier's Club, Bolton Street."

Jo said, "Viscount Morden?"

"The same," said Waldo. "Now, isn't that interesting?"

Both men were smiling. Jo said, "You think..." She paused as her thoughts took shape. "You think that Morden was behind the attack on me, that he read the piece I'd written for Chloë and decided that I was a threat to him?"

"That's exactly what I think," said Waldo. "I think that he knows Chloë is Lady Tellall and that you are her publisher as well as her closest friend. He must think that you know more than you do. No, hear me out. At Cecy's presentation yesterday, Morden made a point of talking to me. He'd read the piece you'd written in the *Journal*, though, of course, he pretended that he'd got the information secondhand."

"Well, of course," said Ruggles. "He'd hardly admit to subscribing to a—" He observed Jo's expression and hastily amended what he'd been about to say. "Eh... a...provincial paper."

"Not up to the *Times*, I suppose?" she said acidly. She looked at Waldo. "Go on."

"To cut a long story short, he said that he hoped that the report of Lady Webberley taking the ferry to France was true, but I got the distinct impression he was lying. I think he hopes the story is false. I think he knows where Chloë is, you see."

Hope leapt to her throat. "He knows where she is hiding?"

He answered gently, "No, Jo. I'm sorry. What I should have said was that he knows where Chloë's body is hidden, because he put it there."

She waited for the shock of his words to spread through her, but all that she felt was a dull ache. She'd already begun to accept that they were never going to find Chloë alive.

She said, "What do you mean—he hopes the report is false? He must *know* it's false if he killed Chloë."

"I think you've planted a doubt in his mind."

"A doubt?"

"I think he's beginning to wonder whether he killed Chloe after all."

"Supposing I accept what you say—and I'm not convinced yet—where is all this leading?"

Waldo smiled. "We're going to panic him into leading us to Chloë's final resting place."

When she shook her head, Ruggles added, "It's a long shot, but what have we got to lose?"

She looked at the table with everything neatly set out on it. "Tell me what you want me to do," she said.

Her job was to write the copy for Lady Tellall's next column. She had more than enough to go on with Cecy's presentation and the snippets of gossip Lady

Fredericka had passed on. The real point of the exercise, however, was to insert something about Chloë that would panic her killer into believing that she might be alive and the only way to verify it would be to check on where he'd hidden her body.

That was supposing he read the next issue of the *Journal*.

The word *far-fetched* kept drumming in her brain, but the certain knowledge that her coconspirators were anything but amateurs gave her some grounds for hoping that they knew what they were doing.

She looked over at Ruggles. His job was to scour the *Journal* for every reference to Viscount Morden or anything that struck an odd note. They'd been working for hours. Waldo, meantime, had taken off with Harper for Brinsley Hall to scout the area, he said, for likely places for hiding a body. He was due back the following evening.

The thought of Chloë lying unmourned in unhallowed ground made her blood boil.

Ruggles looked up and caught her eye. "I'm almost finished."

"Me too." There was a fresh pot of coffee on the table, so she reached over and topped up their cups. "This is supposed to sharpen your wits," she said, "so drink up."

He let out a sigh. "I need something. I'm not making much sense of this."

"What is it?"

"A reference to the viscount's birthday last year. Only Chloë got it wrong. She says his birthday was in December. She makes the correction a few weeks later. *Many apologies to Viscount Morden and his family,* etc., etc. Morden wasn't born in December. He was born in June."

He passed the relevant pages to Jo. She read them, then shrugged. "I can't see that this makes much difference. It's the kind of slip anyone could make. It doesn't mean that he was born out of wedlock. Now, that *would* mean something. But everyone knows that his parents were married for years before he came along."

"All the same, it's odd and worth a closer look."

She turned slightly in her chair to get a better look at him. She knew that he and Waldo were roughly the same age, but Ruggles's red hair and freckles made him look boyish. Yet he was a seasoned soldier, having served with Waldo all through the Spanish Campaign. It was rumored that they'd been some sort of spies. She might have believed it of Waldo. He was turning out to be far more complex than she had at first realized. But she couldn't see Ruggles as a spy. He looked so pleasant and trustworthy.

He was watching her too. "What is it?" he asked.

She smiled sheepishly, as though she'd been caught out in a white lie. After a moment's hesitation, she framed her question to be as inoffensive as possible. "What was it like in Spain? For you and Waldo, I mean? I know you worked for British Intelligence or something. . . ."

"Or something," he agreed, a smile in his eyes.

This was getting her nowhere, so she asked bluntly, "What exactly did you do?"

He stifled a yawn. "It was all pretty boring," he said, "and not at all as most people imagine. We decoded messages, questioned witnesses, and did much the same as we are doing here. I suppose you would call it police work."

"Oh. I see."

"I'm sorry to disappoint you."

"I'm not disappointed, because I don't believe a word you've said." She smiled to soften her words.

His eyes flared. "It's all true."

"Perhaps, but it's not the whole truth. Keep your secrets, Mr. McNab. I had no business quizzing you like that. What I should have done was thank you for helping out like this. So thank you, and I mean that sincerely."

Faint color tinted his cheeks. "My pleasure, ma'am. Nothing at all. No need to... that is..."

She rescued him by saying, "Shall we get back to work?" When he nodded, she went on. "I've written something out that I think will suit our purpose, but I'd like your opinion."

After picking up one of the sheets of paper she'd been working on, she read, *"The rampant speculation about Lady Webberley is over. She writes from Paris that she has no plans to return to London in the near future, not until after her memoirs are published. Yes, dear reader, her ladyship has sold her memoirs to a prestigious London publisher, who is bringing them out in August. Be prepared for scandals that will rock both court and government circles. And remember, you heard it first from Lady Tellall."*

She looked up at him. "What do you think?"

"If that doesn't panic Morden, nothing will."

"Won't he suspect a trap?"

"Possibly. But even if he does, he'll want to verify it, and he can only do that by going back to the scene of the crime."

"So, what do we do next?"

"We send your notes by express to the *Journal* so that Morden can read them in the next edition of the paper."

"It won't arrive in London for at least a week."

"Then, hopefully, all hell will break loose."

* * *

Waldo and Harper arrived at Henley as dusk was falling. After tipping the postboys for getting them there in record time, they took rooms at the Swan and repaired to the taproom, where they hoped to meet some of the locals and pump them for information. Unfortunately, it was a quiet night, and the few locals who came in regarded them with suspicion. Their landlord, however, proved to be extremely helpful after he observed that Waldo was a man of expensive tastes with the money to indulge them. Only the best rooms would do for Waldo, only the best dinner and the most expensive brandy the inn had to offer.

Their cover story was that Waldo had engaged Harper, a well-known landscape gardener, to design a garden for him along the lines of the gardens at Brinsley Hall.

"That is," said Waldo, "if Lord Brinsley will allow us to view the gardens. I'd heard that he wasn't very obliging. Still, we thought it was worth a try. You'll have another?" He passed the opened bottle of fine cognac across the table to the landlord.

"I don't mind if I do," replied Mr. Pike, obviously gratified by the gesture, "but only a small one."

Harper didn't mind having another one either. He didn't know the first thing about gardening and was hoping that he would fade into the background so that he wouldn't be put on the spot.

Considerably mellowed, Mr. Pike told them what they wanted to know, that there would be no objection to them viewing the gardens, or the house if they wished, because the Brinsleys had gone up to town.

"There are always plenty of visitors to the Hall," Mr.

Pike said, "but when the family is in residence, they don't show the house."

"The Brinsleys are well known in Henley, then?" asked Waldo.

That got the old boy going and, as he sipped his drink, he gave Waldo a thumbnail sketch of the most prominent family for miles around, beginning with the old earl, who had died the year before his grandson was born.

"Now *he* was a colorful character," the landlord said, a shade of admiration in his voice. "Larger than life, if you know what I mean. Aye, and he had an eye for the ladies, or so my father told me." He chuckled. "Everyone liked him in spite of it, but the poor sod practically bankrupted the estate with his wild living. The present earl, well, you might say he learned from his father's mistakes."

"Not as colorful?" Waldo observed.

"And not as well liked either, though, to be fair, he's a much better father than his own father ever was. His son is the apple of his eye."

"And," Harper cut in, "his mother's too, I suppose."

"I suppose." There was an element of doubt in the landlord's expression. "You know, she was never right in the head after he was born. It was tragic, that's what it was. The birthing was too much for her. My wife says it happens sometimes."

Harper said, "If the old earl practically bankrupted the estate, how can they live so well? They're as rich as nabobs."

The landlord laughed. "His lordship married a bottomless well of money. Her ladyship was an heiress."

At this point, Waldo made an oblique reference to the house party, but Mr. Pike was no help there. Brinsley Hall was only two miles along the road, and guests were unlikely to stop at an inn when they were so close to their destination.

When they got up to leave, he said, "Mention my name to Wallace. He's the head gardener. Tell him Pike sent you and you'll get a warm welcome."

The following morning, they hired horses at the local hostelry and were soon on their way to the Hall. They might have rented a buggy, but Waldo thought that would restrict their movements. A horse could take them where a buggy could not.

The house was reached through a long avenue of mature oaks.

"It looks like an abbey," said Harper, somewhat awed.

"It is. It used to be known as Holywell Abbey. There was a spring that was thought to be holy because it had miraculous powers. The Romans got here first, then the monks came and built their abbey."

"Sounds as though you've been here before."

"When I was at university," Waldo agreed. "I had a friend who was interested in Roman antiquities. Unfortunately, there's little left of what the Romans built."

Harper squinted against the rays of the sun. "The abbey looks old to me."

"Well, it is. It was built in the fourteenth century."

"Bloody hell! I'll bet there's a lot of nooks and crannies in that house that would make a good place to hide a body."

"It wouldn't stay hidden for long, Harper. Think of the stench."

They found the head gardener directing his under-gardeners in the delicate task of transplanting seedlings from the hothouse to the garden beds. Wallace was a pleasant-faced man in his forties with the ruddy complexion of someone who was out of doors in all kinds of weather. He seemed to know what they wanted before they had said more than a few words. He could not spare the time to take them to the ruins, he said, but he had a map of the grounds that showed where everything was. They thanked him, accepted the map, and jogged off to the shade of a sycamore, where they reined in.

After studying the map, Wallace's words began to make sense. Visitors didn't come in droves to see the gardens but to see the ruins of a bygone era.

"Seems," said Harper, "like there's no end of places to hide a body, inside *and* outside the house. Look here—the old chapter house, the refectory, the almshouse, the old well house, and so on and so on. They can't be still standing, can they?"

"I doubt it, but their foundations will be hidden underground."

"And look here! There was a Roman villa on the grounds at one time, and other things I've never heard of. What does it mean?"

"It means," said Waldo, "that Brinsley Hall is steeped in history going back before the Romans. There must have been settlements here from time immemorial."

"So what do we do?"

"We explore, Harper, we explore, then we ask to see the house."

After seeing over the house, they returned to the Swan, where they ordered an early dinner and hired a chaise for the return journey to Palliser. They ate their dinner without being aware of what they were eating. Waldo was making notes with a pencil in the margins of the map Wallace had given them. They talked back and forth, trying to narrow down possible sites, but they couldn't get around the fact that that still left them with, as Harper said, a lot of territory to cover.

On the drive home, they fell silent, each lost in his own thoughts, and the closer they got to Palliser, the more Waldo's thoughts turned to Jo. He was beginning to think that she was a lost cause. After three years, she still hadn't got over her husband's death. He wondered if it would take her another three years to get over his betrayal.

He could almost appreciate this reversal of roles. Women had never played an important part in his life. He liked them. He admired them. He enjoyed their company. But he'd never wanted more than a casual affair. And that's all Jo was offering when, for the first time in his life, he wanted more.

On that dark and dreary thought, he closed his eyes and drifted into a light sleep.

He stirred when their chaise turned into the gates of Palliser. It was dark, but he could see lights flickering through the trees. He wakened Harper. "Something is wrong," he said.

Harper looked out the window. "Those look like men with lanterns."

Waldo's gaze had moved to the house. Lights were blazing from all the windows. Alarm coursing through him, he shouted to the driver to spring the horses. In the next instant, the whip cracked and they went thundering along the drive to the house.

Chapter 22

As he climbed the front steps, his mother and sisters came out of the house to meet him. Mrs. Daventry was hovering behind them.

"Where is Jo?" he asked sharply.

Lady Fredericka took his hands in hers. "It's not Jo. It's Eric. She went into his chamber before going to her own bed and found that he was missing. We've searched the house and now they're searching the grounds. Jo is with your father and Thomas. She insisted on going with them. They'll find him, Waldo. They must."

Maude said, "It's only a small boy's prank. He's run away from home because of some silly quarrel. It happened with my own son once. You remember, Mama? Derek came home late at night and we didn't even know he was missing."

Cecy began to cry quietly.

Waldo, who had been thinking along the lines of an abduction, let out a pent-up breath. "When was he last seen?"

"After supper. Jo read him a story when he went to bed. It was only later that she found him missing."

"Who did he quarrel with?"

Everyone looked at Mrs. Daventry. She had got hold of a ribbon and she stood there, the picture of misery, absently winding it through her fingers. "He overheard you quarreling with Jo," she said, "and got the idea that...that if he went away, you and Jo would be friends again."

"He heard us quarreling?"

"You were having breakfast. The children were playing hide-and-seek, and Eric hid behind the holly bush outside the window. Jenny told me."

Waldo stifled the profanity that sprang to his lips. He could well imagine what a sensitive child like Eric would make of the quarrel he'd overheard.

He saw that the others were looking to him for guidance, so he kept his voice calm and steady. "He can't have got far. I'll find him. Mother, why don't you see that there are sandwiches and something to drink for the men when they come in from the search? And make sure there's plenty of coffee for me and chocolate for Eric."

When they were out of earshot of the others, Harper said, "Where are we going?"

Waldo stopped to let Harper catch up with him. "We're going to the stables to get horses."

They were almost at the stable block when Jo came out of the shadows, accompanied by Waldo's father. Mr. Bowman had a lantern, and when he held it up, Waldo could see the lines of exhaustion in his father's face.

Jo didn't speak. She simply walked into Waldo's arms.

Mr. Bowman and Harper exchanged a look, then edged away to give the couple a little privacy. Neither Waldo nor Jo spared them a glance. Their moment was intensely private.

Jo said, "We've looked everywhere and can't find him. He's so small, and the park is so big. I thought if he heard me calling his name, he would come out of hiding. But what if something has happened to him? What if he can't call out because—" She couldn't complete the thought, so she shook her head.

"You're sure he ran away?" He could see how close she was to collapse, so he didn't voice the word *abduction,* though the thought that Morden might be behind Eric's disappearance was still running through his mind.

She grasped his meaning at once. "No. He hasn't been abducted. Things are missing from the kitchen— a pork pie, a loaf of bread, cheese. And Jenny told us that Eric was crying because he heard us quarreling."

"That makes things simpler. Nothing has happened to Eric. I am almost sure that I know where to find him. I'll bring him back to you safe and sound."

"How can you know where he is when I don't?"

"Because Eric and I have had many man-to-man conversations. And this isn't the first time he's run away. He ran away from school and got himself to Stratford, didn't he?"

She nodded. "So where is he?"

"I think I'll find him at the parish church."

He prevented her from asking more questions by the simple expedient of issuing orders. "Father, don't call off the search yet, not until I return with Eric, but get Jo up to the house and get her warm. She's shivering. In fact, you both look done in, and you're both wet."

"We were at the lake," his father explained, "and got too close to the edge."

"I see. We'll talk about this later. I haven't time to talk now."

When he turned to leave, Jo cried out, "But I want to go with you!"

"You can't ride in your state, and I can't wait for you to change. Father, see that she does what she's told."

She was ready to give him the sharp edge of her tongue, but to the surprise of everyone present, he kissed her swiftly, full on the lips, and moved off in the direction of the stables before the others had come to themselves. Even Harper was left staring.

When he caught up to Waldo, he said crossly, "I thought you was supposed to be lame?"

"What? Oh." Waldo slowed his steps. "I can move when I want to. It's a case of focusing on the problem at hand."

"Is that what you was doing with Mrs. Chesney? I thought you was hard on her."

"Harper," said Waldo patiently, "you were a soldier, you had men under your command. What did you say to them when they were on the verge of collapse?"

After a moment's thought, Harper said, "Did you mean what you told her about finding the boy?"

"I meant it. But that was Waldo Bowman, master spy, speaking. Now let's see if I've lost my touch."

"Master spy," said Harper, and made a small sound of derision.

Mr. Bowman left Jo in Mrs. Daventry's capable hands with strict instructions that she was to change out of her wet clothes, then he went to his dressing room to do the same. Lady Fredericka arrived a short while later to find him changed and sipping a neat whiskey. She had a thousand questions she wanted to ask about Eric. All she'd been told was that Waldo was sure he would find him at the nearest church. When she saw her husband, however, looking pale and drawn, she said quickly, "You're not keeping something from me, are you?"

"How do you mean?"

"About Eric."

"Oh, no. Waldo seemed quite confident that he would find him at the church."

"Well, that's a relief." When there was no response, she went on, "Are you all right, Julian? You're very pale."

"Put it down to fatigue."

She sighed. "Yes, it's been an awful night, for Jo as well."

"She was a regular trooper. Not a complaint out of her. Then Waldo came on the scene, and it seemed for a moment or two she would go to pieces."

"But she didn't?"

"No. I thought Waldo was a bit hard on her, but it did the trick. Well, you saw her. She's a plucky little thing."

A moment of silence went by. Finally, Lady Fredericka said, "But that's not all. What is it, Julian? What's bothering you?"

He heaved a sigh. "I think they're lovers, Freddie."

Her ladyship cocked her head to one side. "What makes you say that?"

"If you'd seen the way they looked at each other and the way he held her and the way he kissed her. A blind man could tell they were lovers."

"You're surely not shocked?"

"I'm not shocked. I'm disappointed. I want to see Waldo with a wife, not another mistress."

"I don't think Waldo would like to hear you call Jo by that ugly word. I think he loves her."

"Then he should do the honorable thing!"

"Am I hearing right? Don't you remember what it was like to be young and in love? You did a lot more than look at me and kiss me, and I was much younger than Jo."

He spoke with a touch of asperity. "We were engaged to be married. The banns had been read."

Her ladyship snorted. "What a poor memory you have! It was only because I wanted more of your kisses that I agreed to marry you at all. You seemed so sedate and proper and not the kind of man I could be happy with. Until you kissed me."

On the point of taking umbrage, he saw the twinkle in her eyes, and chuckled instead. "And you were precocious. You led me astray."

"We led each other astray as I remember. Ready? We should go down."

He bolted his drink and set the glass on a dresser. "I can tell by that look in your eye that you want to give me some wifely advice. Out with it, then."

Though there was no necessity for it, she adjusted his neckcloth, then looked up at him. "Be gentle with Waldo. I think he would offer for Jo in a minute if he thought she would have him. So I don't want to hear any high-blown debates at the dinner table about the old values or modern morality, or whatever. You told me that we'd raised fine children. So trust them, Julian. That's my wifely advice."

His eyes searched hers. "I know I spoiled the girls. Tell me the truth, Freddie. Was I too hard on Waldo?"

She thought for a moment, then said seriously, "I

love my son just the way he is. I'm not saying he is perfect. Well, nobody is. But in the things that really matter, he is as solid as a rock. Does that answer your
question?"

The gravity in his expression gradually dissolved. He
offered her his arm. "Is it permitted to talk about the
weather at the dinner table?" he asked.

"Just as long as you don't turn it into a debate."

Smiling, they went to join the others.

Jo was standing at one of the long windows in the
front of the house, a shawl draped around her shoulders, staring at the long drive, waiting impatiently for
the moment when Waldo should appear. Occasionally
someone spoke to her, but she answered in monosylla-
bles. She'd been to church once since arriving at Palliser, both she and Eric. It was just off Kensington High
Street. In her mind's eye, she was covering the distance
as though she were riding alongside Waldo.

St. Mary Abbots wasn't that far away. They should
have been home by now. Something must have—

Before she had completed the thought, she saw
movement on the drive, then the sound of men cheer-
ing.

She whirled around, her eyes searching for Mr. Bowman. He was smiling. "The men wouldn't cheer," he
said, "unless the boy was safe and sound."

With a little cry, she picked up her skirts and ran
from the room. She met Waldo as he was coming up
the steps with Eric nestled in his arms. "The vicar
found him," he said, "sleeping under the cloisters. He
recognized him, of course, and was just about to bring
him home when we arrived. He has something to say to
you. Well, Eric, what do you have to say to Aunt Jo?"

Tears stood on Eric's lashes. He blinked them away, and stretched out his arms. "I want my aunt Jo," he said.

The apology came later, when he was tucked up for the night, but it wasn't so much an apology as a commentary on what the vicar had told him, that by making *them* sad, he had made his mother sad too, and all the angels in heaven. He wished, he said, that they could all live together, then everyone would be happy.

Waldo probed gently, and it soon became evident that what really troubled Eric was the thought that they were going to send him away to school again.

"That settles it, then," said Waldo with his disarming smile. "You'll go to school as a day boy and come home every night, or we'll find a tutor for you and you'll study at home."

The tears that were never far from Eric's eyes dried. "And will you and Aunt Jo be there?"

Waldo glanced at Jo, then said without hesitation, "Who else would be there if not your Aunt Jo or I?"

Eric smiled. "And you're going to teach me to ride?"

"I said I would, didn't I?"

"May I say good night to everyone?"

Jo answered. "It's very late. Everyone has gone to bed except Uncle Waldo and I."

"Then may I have another cup of chocolate?"

"Well, I suppose—"

"No," interjected Waldo, "you may not." Then to Jo, "This is getting too close to bribery for comfort." He pulled the quilt up to Eric's chin. "Off to sleep with you now, and tomorrow we'll have a long man-to-man talk."

In the corridor, Jo said in hushed tones, "We need

to talk about Eric, before you have that man-to-man talk."

"I know. But if you think about it, Jo, the answer to our dilemma is staring us in the face. In fact, I think it would be the perfect solution."

His lashes veiled his expression and there was a stillness about him that she found confusing. The word *marriage* hovered in her mind, but she discarded it. Neither of them was ready for that. In her own case, she didn't think she'd ever be ready.

She said carefully, "You mean that I'm to have Eric and he'll go to you in the holidays?"

His eyes went hard and flat. "The last time we had this discussion," he said, "it was overheard and we both know what happened next. Let's keep it for a more appropriate time and place. Good night, Jo." He turned to descend the stairs.

"Wait!"

"What is it?"

"At least tell me how you knew that Eric would make for the church. How did you know where to find him?"

"It was what he did the first time he ran away from Harding's school. He said that, before his mother died, she told him that if ever he got in trouble or lost his way, he was to go to the nearest church and tell the vicar."

"I see. That makes sense. If you can't trust a vicar, who can you trust?"

"What is it, Jo?"

She gave a tiny shrug. "The more I hear about Eric's mother, the more I find to admire in her. How could John have—"

He turned away abruptly. "We'll talk in the morning," he said.

Baffled and hurt, she stared at his back as he descended the stairs. "What did I say?"

When there was no answer, she marched to her own chamber and closed the door behind her with a snap.

If he heard the name John Chesney one more time, he would shoot himself.

This was Waldo's thought as he flicked the ash from his cheroot and blew out a plume of smoke. He was in his office, just off his bedchamber, going over the notes he'd made at Brinsley Hall. The trouble was, he couldn't concentrate. He was still thinking of Jo as he'd last seen her, not half an hour ago, on the stairs. It did not sit well with him that one provoking slip of a girl had the power to break into his thoughts no matter what he was doing.

A look from her, a word, and he was putty in her hands, and those were ruthless hands. He was supposed to be a fearless warrior. Wellington had said so in his dispatches from Spain. Yet, here he was, licking his wounds after a tussle with a ghost. How could he fight a ghost?

He couldn't, and he wasn't going to try.

Frowning, he picked up the map of the grounds of Brinsley Hall. After a moment's reflection, he made a notation in the margin. After another moment's reflection, he stroked it out. This was useless. He should go to bed.

He tossed the stub of his cheroot into the empty grate, pushed into his bedchamber, and came to a sudden halt. She was there, Jo, wearing that filmy negligee again, looking like she had just stepped out of his deepest, darkest fantasy. She was sitting in one of the armchairs that flanked the grate.

"What are you doing here?" he asked abruptly.

"Waldo, that was churlish," she chided, "and not like you at all. But to answer your question—I'm here because . . ." She sighed, got up, and walked toward him. "You're making this very difficult for me, standing there all silent and brooding."

"If you knew what was good for you, you wouldn't be here at all."

The bite in his words made her falter a little, but she'd come too far to turn back. It had taken her a little while to work things out, and now that she had, she was prepared to humble her pride and accept his barbs without a murmur of protest.

She said softly, "I'm not thinking of what's good for me or what's good for Eric. I'm thinking of what's good for you. That's why I can't marry you."

He had a repertoire of smiles he could use to devastating effect. The cynical twist to his lips matched the cynicism in his voice. "I don't recall asking you to marry me."

"Not in so many words. If you had, I would have been tempted to say yes."

"You would? I mean, why would you?"

She was toying with the buttons on his waistcoat, so she missed the little muscle that tensed in his cheek. "Well, it wouldn't be because it was the perfect solution to our problem of who should have charge of Eric." She looked up at him. "I couldn't marry a man I didn't respect and admire, and I respect and admire you. In fact, I enjoy being with you."

He touched his fingers to his brow and shook his head. "If you're looking for a best friend," he said, "you can count me out. I've no wish to step into your husband's shoes. Is that all? Because if it is, I should like to go to my bed."

The barbs were sharper than she'd anticipated, but she could tolerate them, up to a point. Keeping her voice easy and inoffensive, she said, "No, it's not all. I don't want you to step into John's shoes. I haven't changed my mind. I'm not looking for a husband. I want you to be my lover."

"Your lover! So we're back to that, are we?"

"What is *wrong* with you?" she cried out, her patience—never her strong point—at an end. "One minute you're kissing me and comforting me, and the next all you want to do is quarrel. If I mention John's name, you foam at the mouth."

Violence flashed in his eyes. "I don't want to hear about John Chesney, do you understand? If I never hear his name again, it will be too soon for me, so don't mention it in my hearing."

At first, she was crushed, then she was angry, blazingly angry. She was baring her soul to him, trying to explain why she wasn't the right woman for him, and all he could do was sneer in that nasty way of his. If he had one sensitive bone in his body, he would see that she needed to be comforted, not reviled.

Her chin lifted. "John, John, John," she said.

"I'm warning you, Jo!"

She put her hands on her hips. "John, John—"

She heard the rush of his breath before he clamped his arms around her and crushed her mouth beneath his. A moment later, they broke apart, stunned by the ferocity of that kiss. His eyes were wildly dilated; her breath was coming thick and fast. They stared, they shook their heads, then they fell on each other as though they were locked in mortal combat.

He'd promised himself that the next time they made love, he was going to show her that the pleasure could be slow and easy. But he was in the grip of some

primitive emotion that had nothing to do with pleasure. He wanted to drive every vestige of John Chesney
from her mind and heart. He wanted to fill her with
himself, stamp her with his own impression so that it
would be *his* name she remembered and only his.

Still locked together, they edged to the bed and top-
pled upon it. His mouth on hers filled her with heat,
waves of it, submerging her in sensation. It was just like
the last time, yet it was different. Waldo was different.
She could taste the desire on his lips and something
else, something wild and desperate.

On an impatient oath, he dispensed with her negligee, then yanked her nightgown to her waist so that he
could feast on her breasts. At the first touch of his lips
and tongue, she gasped, but as he continued to play
with her, she writhed and arched, offering him more.
Never had she known such desperation. Every touch
and caress made her ache to feel more. "Waldo," she
said, "Waldo," trying to convey her urgency.

When he heard his name, he laughed softly, his
warm breath fanning across one distended nipple as
he laved it with his tongue. That soft laugh dispelled
some of the sensual haze that enveloped her. Rising to
her knees, she loomed over him and began to tear at
his clothes. He was as eager to be free of them as she
was to free him. When he was down to bare skin, he
rose to his knees beside her on the bed.

It wasn't urgency she felt now so much as awe. He
went perfectly still as her hands brushed over powerfully
corded muscles and hard flesh. Her fingers lifted when
she found the long scar that ran from his shoulder to his
navel. It wasn't the first time she'd seen him naked, but
that other time was a blur. Her hands dipped lower.

He grasped her wrist before her fingers could close

around his member. "Oh, no," he said. "Not this time. This time, I lead, you follow."

Teeth gritted, she said, "Waldo Bowman—" then she shrieked when he rolled with her on the bed.

He came out on top. Smiling, eyes glinting, he said, "You've caused me a lot of grief, Jo, but finally you're beginning to make up for it."

"I could say the same about you."

He was smiling when his lips met hers, but the smile disintegrated when he took her cry of arousal into his mouth. He had never wanted like this. His heart was racing, his blood was pounding, he could hardly get his breath. It wasn't enough for him. He wanted her to feel everything that he was feeling, to ache as he ached.

He pinned her arms above her head and exploited every pleasure point he remembered, her throat, her ears, the underside of her breasts. He dipped lower toward the heat between her thighs. She didn't struggle or fight him. At every caress of his lips and tongue, she sobbed with pleasure, little sounds that drove him wild. He was obsessed with her, with her scent and flavor, with the softness of her skin, the silky feel of her hair. *Mine*, he thought, *all mine*, and wondered what she would do if he dared voice what he was thinking. The thought made him smile.

Her mind was storing up impressions—pictures, feelings, sensations—that she would take with her when she left this place, impressions that would warm her when she was alone once more. She hadn't known that a lover could make her feel strong and helpless at the same time, or that he could be both greedy and generous. Not a lover, but Waldo. She would never forget him. He might think that he could forget her, but she was going to show him how wrong he was.

On a half moan, she rolled, freeing her hands and

rising above him. His body fascinated her. He had learned all her secrets, now she wanted to learn his. She pressed her lips to his throat, to his shoulder, and traced the path of his scar with her tongue. As she dipped lower, she could hear his breath straining in his lungs, could feel the rise and fall of his chest. She prolonged the torture, reveling in her power. No one had ever wanted her like this. She wanted everything from him and more.

Suddenly, she felt herself spinning, and he was over her, pinning her to the mattress. She could see his face in the candlelight, heavy-lidded and harsh with passion. There was something important she wanted to tell him, but the thought wouldn't form, so she murmured his name instead.

Eyes locked on hers, he spread her legs. The muscles in his arms bunched and strained as he slowly entered her. She had braced for pain, but there was no pain this time, and her breath came out in a long, shuddering sob.

His lips sank into hers in a slow, proprietary kiss, then he thrust deeply, fusing their bodies into one. Sensation became unbearable, then burst through her like shattering crystal. He watched the rapture take her, then followed her over the edge.

Breathless and dazed, Waldo collapsed against her. They lay for long minutes, panting, trying to get their breath. Finally, he rolled onto his back and gazed up at the ceiling. There was a big smile on his face. He knew how to make her forget about John Chesney.

"What are you smiling about?"

She was sitting up, leaning over him, her hair veiling her breasts. Her lips were swollen from his kisses. She looked dazed and love-sleepy, just the way he wanted her to look.

He reached out and dragged her into the shelter of his body. "I'm smiling," he said, "because you made me happy. Don't I make you happy, Jo?"

It seemed a tepid word to describe the storm of emotions he had aroused in her. "Very," she said.

"Then," he turned into her, "why don't we make a habit of it? Marriage, Jo. If we were married, we could make each other happy morning, noon, and night, and no one could object."

She freed herself from his arms and sat up, half turned away from him. Her breathing was still ragged. "That's what I was trying to tell you before you pounced on me. You need heirs and I can't give you one. That's why we can't marry." She looked at him over her shoulder. "Or was I mistaken? When you mentioned 'the perfect solution' earlier, what did you mean?"

"Exactly what you thought I meant."

"There you are, then. I was married for four years but never conceived. We know that my husband had a child. When you add it all up, what it amounts to is that I'm . . . well, incapable of having children."

"I don't accept that. Four years isn't that long. But if children meant so much to you, why didn't you marry again?"

"Because I loved John, of course! And I didn't know you existed, did I?"

He realized that she'd told him far more than she'd meant to. Biting down on a smile, he anchored her with one arm across her breasts, her back resting against his chest. "Oddly enough," he said, "begetting heirs has never been one of my ambitions. And I have an heir— my cousin, Thomas."

"Tell that to your father. He won't be too happy to see Palliser Park go outside the family."

"Thomas isn't outside the family. Besides, how will my father know?"

"What?"

"He won't be here to see it unless, God forbid, I die prematurely. No more about heirs, Jo. You know it's just a convenient excuse. Either you want to make a life with me or you don't."

She turned in his arms so that she could see his face. "Let's not argue. Let's not make promises we can't keep. I'm happy with the way things are."

The tension in him suddenly relaxed. He took her face between his hands. "Oh, Jo. What a coward you are. There is only one good reason for us to marry. One of us has to be the first to say it, and I've decided it should be you."

The words, *I love you*, hung on the air. She gulped down a breath. "You're talking in riddles."

"Am I? Then let's stop talking. You wanted us to be lovers. So love me."

She was about to protest that she hardly had enough energy to keep her eyes open when his fingers found her and gently probed. A wave of heat flamed through her, making her gasp for air.

"You were saying?" he asked, a smile in his voice.

He took her words into his mouth. And not long after, apart from little moans and sighs, speech became impossible.

•

Chapter 23

*I*t seemed to Jo that their investigation into Chloë's disappearance had slowed to a halt. There were any number of things that struck odd notes, but nothing solid to go on. Now all their hopes were pinned on Morden panicking when he read the piece she'd written for Chloë's column, the piece about Chloë selling her memoirs to a prestigious London publisher.

She still wasn't convinced it would work. If Morden had killed Chloë and disposed of her body, he would know he had nothing to fear. You couldn't tell Waldo that. Morden, he said, was worried about something that was connected to Chloë, and even if all they did was discover what it was, it might lead them to Chloë's final resting place.

She wanted time on her own to think. As a result, she'd called a halt to her involvement with the Bowmans. While they'd gone off in various directions, she had sat down at the writing table in her chamber and thought of nothing but Chloë. It always came back to the same puzzling things: What happened to the chaise that was to take Chloë from Brinsley Hall to Stratford? Where was Chloë's notebook? Where was her box with all her clothes? Why was there a delay in her letter arriving at the *Journal*'s offices?

If she could answer those questions, she would have the answer to who murdered Chloë and why.

Sighing, she got up and stretched her cramped muscles. There must be something she could do. She hadn't talked to Lady Brinsley, but it wasn't for the want of trying. Whenever she called at the house, she was told that her ladyship wasn't receiving visitors. She'd already talked to Lady Langston, and Ruggles had questioned all the other guests at the house party. So where did that leave her?

She had nothing to lose by calling on Lady Brinsley again. And if she wasn't at home, she knew where she would get a warm reception. Lady Langston was always pleased to see her.

She'd forgotten about Harper. He was her bodyguard, so when she sent the footman to get some sort of conveyance to take her to town, Harper came with it, a one-horse buggy with enough room for only two people. She'd hoped that the head coachman might give her Lady Fredericka's spanking new phaeton with its big yellow wheels and matched pair of white horses, or "grays" as the horsey set liked to call them. Still, beggars couldn't be choosers.

Harper kept one hand on the reins, reached down the other, and hoisted her in. "She may not look like much, but old Bess here," he patted the side of the coach, "is as solid as a house. They don't make 'em like her anymore. She won't tip over in a gust of wind or when we turns a sharp corner, not like those fashionable curricles and phaetons that are all the rage."

She could tell from his tone of voice that he didn't think much of "fashionable." He was looking at her, waiting for her to make some comment. And then it came to her. Waldo had told her that Harper's first love was coaches—building them, driving them, restoring them—and that when he finally retired from the service, he was going to go into business with a friend, restoring broken-down coaches.

"She looks splendid," she said, injecting enthusiasm into her voice. "Is this one of the coaches you've restored, Mr. Harper?"

It was all the encouragement he needed, and on the short drive to town, he gave her a running commentary on all the improvements he'd made to make Bess first in her class.

Things turned out as she expected. Lady Brinsley was not receiving visitors, but Lady Langston gave her a warm reception, though, the maid said cheerily, it wasn't the best time to call. There were workmen in the conservatory taking measurements for a new, improved heating system, but her ladyship never turned away visitors, and so it was.

"Any news of Chloë?" was the first thing Lady Langston said when she came into the room.

"Nothing definite." Jo knew she had to tread carefully here. She didn't want to say anything that might jeopardize Waldo's plan for entrapping Morden. "The latest gossip is that she's in Paris."

"Yes, I heard that too."

This was said with such a long face that Jo was prompted to say, "But you don't think so?"

"I *hope* it's true, as all her friends must, but I can't shake the awful suspicion that something dreadful has happened to her, and Elinor agrees with me."

"Elinor?" Jo straightened in her chair. "You mean Lady Brinsley?"

Lady Langston nodded. "You just missed her. She's helping me with plans for my conservatory. I was hoping to model the heating system on the one in her conservatory, you know, in the manner of the Romans? But I think it's going to be too expensive. Those Romans had slaves to do all the work. I'll have to pay workmen's wages."

Jo wanted to talk about Lady Brinsley, not conservatories, and knew that if she wasn't careful they'd be talking about gardening till the cows came home. With Harper it was coaches. He and her ladyship were both fanatics in their different ways.

She said vaguely, "We could learn a lot from the Romans."

"That's what Elinor says."

This was the opening she wanted. "I'm surprised that Lady Brinsley was well enough to visit. I heard that she wasn't receiving visitors or going out and about."

Lady Langston laughed. "Oh, Elinor would receive you soon enough if you came bearing a rare plant or were a member of the Horticultural Society. But, to be fair, she's not that well. She doesn't care for London, and if it were not that she had to make the effort to attend parties and so on for her son's betrothed, I doubt that she would come up to town at all."

When Jo did not respond but merely looked thoughtful, Lady Langston said, "Is something wrong?"

Jo flashed a smile. "No, no. It's just that I was hoping

to talk to her about Chloë, but the maid always tells me that her ladyship is not at home."

"And now you know why."

"Will she be coming to see you again? If so, perhaps you wouldn't mind if I came too?"

Her ladyship's plump cheeks bunched as she smiled. "I'll do better than that," she said. "I'll take you to see her tomorrow, if you can spare the time. We're all going out to the Hall to view the gardens. We've been invited to stay the night, but you don't have to if you don't want to. It's not that far away. You could leave before dinner and be home in time for a late supper."

"Who has been invited to the Hall?"

"The members of our little gardeners' group. We're all avid gardeners, but there aren't too many of us. I know Elinor would be delighted to see you. Some famous gardener whose name I can't recall is going to speak to us about landscape design. Don't let that put you off. It's all very informal."

The polite thing to do was make an excuse for why she could not accept. To attend a private party without the hostess's knowledge would be an act of unmitigated impertinence. On the other hand, finding out what had happened to Chloë was more important than offending Lady Brinsley. Add to that the lure of speaking with some of the people who had been at the house party, and she didn't see how she could refuse.

Lady Brinsley solved her dilemma. "The invitation was extended to anyone who is a member of or a friend of our society, so no one will think it odd to see you there."

"Thank you," Jo said, "I should like that very much."

Lady Langston beamed. "Who knows, perhaps we'll make a convert of you and adopt you into our little society."

It wasn't until after refreshments were served that Jo managed to steer the conversation away from gardening and back to Chloë. It was impossible to be diplomatic, so she asked her questions straight out, but her ladyship was no more help this time than she'd been the first. She didn't know about the chaise or Chloë's notebook or Chloë's letter. Everything seemed normal on the morning of their departure.

It was time to go.

Lady Langston walked Jo to the door. They were both subdued, both thinking of Chloë. Lady Langston said, "We made a wager, you know, Chloë and I. That last night, before going to bed. It was all good fun. I won and she lost. She said she'd pay me when she got back to town. It seemed so normal. We were looking forward to the summer. How could things have gone so wrong?"

Jo said something soothing, but what she wanted to do was pounce. This was the first she'd heard of a wager. She said casually, "What did you wager on?"

"The viscount's birthday. Chloë said that he was born the day his grandfather died, but I knew she was wrong. I was there at the old earl's funeral. Elinor was there too. There was no baby. I think she'd given up hope by then of ever having children. The viscount was born six months later."

Jo felt as though she'd just inhaled a powerful stimulant. All her faculties sharpened. This was one of the odd items that had cropped up in Chloë's column. "What did Chloe say?"

"She was under the misapprehension that the old earl died in June, on the same day that Victor was born. But of course, he died the December before that."

"How did you settle the argument?"

"I asked the viscount. He said that I was right and Chloë was wrong. I think the confusion came from Elinor. It's no secret that her nerves are not very strong. She takes something for them from time to time, and that's when she becomes confused."

"And when she's not taking something for her nerves?"

Lady Langston sighed. "She cries a lot. It's a vicious state of affairs, isn't it?"

When she had seen Jo out, her ladyship returned to the parlor in a thoughtful frame of mind. On thinking over what she'd said, it seemed to her that she'd made Elinor out to be much less than she was. No one could be more lucid and enthusiastic than Elinor when she was talking about gardening. But Mrs. Chesney would see for herself at Brinsley Hall.

On that thought, she sat down at her writing table and penned a note to her dear friend, advising her that she had invited a young friend, Mrs. Chesney, to attend their little assembly. All going well, she thought they might add another member to the Horticultural Society.

That should cheer Elinor, she thought, and signed her name. They were always on the lookout for kindred spirits. She got up, called for a footman, and told him to take her note at once to Piccadilly House.

The viscount knew all about his mother's plans to retire to the country. In fact, he had put the idea into her head. He reckoned that the Hall was where she could do the least damage. Her mind wandered. She had become so indiscreet that she could no longer be trusted. The day was coming when he would have to decide what to do about her, but not until *after* the wedding. Meantime, he monitored her letters and visitors.

He arrived home to dress for dinner and stopped by the hall table to collect the post. One note, obviously hand-delivered, was addressed to his mother. The porter told him it came from Lady Langston. The viscount could not hear Lady Langston's name without gnashing his teeth. It was her careless remark about his birthday that had been the spur for what followed. He was curious to see what she was up to now.

He took the note and a package that had come by express from Stratford and went upstairs to his study. He knew what was in the package. It would be the latest copy of the *Journal* that Taggart had sent on, and because it was sent by express, it would have reached him a few days earlier than if it had been sent by regular post. Bates had arranged everything, and all that remained to be done now was to cancel the subscription that went to his club.

He read the note first and was appalled, then he was furious. His mother had not told him that she had invited guests to the Hall, the same guests who were present when Lady Langston made her wager, and now this! The Chesney woman was to be one of the party.

Jo Chesney an avid gardener? He didn't believe it. Jo Chesney was a thorn in his side. She was trying to ferret out information for that unscrupulous paper she published. Or she was trying to entrap him.

Sweat had broken out on his brow. He mopped it with his handkerchief and tried to think what he should do. It was too late to stop his mother. She had already left. But it wasn't too late to call on Lady Langston and tell her that his mother wasn't fit to host a gathering of the blasted Horticultural Society. And how had his mother managed to invite people to the Hall without his knowledge?

He had to think calmly and rationally and not act out of temper. He said the words over and over in his mind until gradually a measure of control returned. Setting aside Lady Langston's note for the moment, he opened the package from Stratford. As expected, it contained the latest copy of the *Journal*, with Lady Tell-all's column.

He scanned the back page and soon found what he wanted, another reference to Lady Webberley. Chloë was in Paris and had sold her memoirs to a prestigious London publisher.

His hand trembled; he couldn't breathe, not in fear but in fury. If she had been standing in front of him, he would have killed her again and taken great pleasure in doing it. They'd once been lovers. He had indulged her. He had told her things about himself he'd never told another soul. The deceiving bitch had stored everything away in her phenomenal memory to use against him when it could hurt him the most. She wasn't going to get away with it.

For a full minute, he sat with his elbows on his desk and his clenched fists pressed to his brow. Gradually, the angry color in his cheeks receded and his breathing evened.

He was back to the same old dilemma. Was Chloë dead or had she somehow survived and crawled out of the pit he'd put her in?

Impossible!

Then this must be a trap, engineered by the Chesney woman to discover where he'd hidden Chloë's body.

He felt tears start to his eyes, as though he were a little boy again. Papa wouldn't like to see those tears. Papa didn't like boys who whined or made excuses. He had to be manly. He had to stand on his own two feet and make Papa proud of him. He must never forget that he was a Brinsley. It was the family name as well as the title. Earl Brinsley—that was his father's title, and one day it would be his.

He took several calming breaths, then pushed back his chair and got up. There was only one person he could confide in, one person who always took his part, right or wrong, and that was Bates. He found him in his dressing room, laying out garments for that evening's entertainment—dinner with friends at Wattier's.

Bates took one look at his master's face and pushed him into a chair. "What you need," he said, "is a shot of brandy to get your color back. You're as white as parchment."

It was good to be fussed over, good to be listened to without fear of looking stupid or ridiculous. After a few sips of brandy, he felt more like himself, but he would be the first to admit that Bates always had a calming effect on him. He couldn't remember a time when Bates hadn't been there for him to lean on.

Slowly at first, then with gathering confidence, he told Bates about the Chesney woman and Chloë and how he couldn't decide what to do for the best. He didn't go into details but spoke, as always, in the same vague terms.

He'd come to the right person. After a thoughtful silence, Bates said, "You're never going to have any peace of mind until you know whether this Lady Webberley still has the power to hurt you. We'll go to Brinsley Hall. Do what you have to do there, then we'll see."

"But what if it's a trap? What if Jo Chesney wrote that piece in the *Journal* hoping that I would lead her to Lady Webberley?"

Bates shook his head. "If it's a trap, she's not going to spring it until after her newspaper comes out here, and that's not for a few days yet. She can't know that you've already got a copy and know that Lady Webberley is going to publish her memoirs."

"But—"

Bates spread his hands. "You're not the one who is going to walk into a trap. She is. She's not expecting you to act now. Only after you read her piece in the *Journal*. Anyway, maybe it's not you she suspects. Maybe it's someone else, maybe one of your mother's other guests."

There was a short silence, then Morden nodded. "It's possible."

"Then we'll take her unawares, won't we?"

The viscount thought briefly of Jacob Fry and the debacle he had made of taking Jo Chesney unawares. This time there would be no mistake. This time, he would take care of her personally.

He looked into Bates's kind eyes. "Yes, we'll take her unawares," he said, and smiled.

When lessons were over for the day, Jo joined the children for a game of cricket on the immaculate lawns. Five minutes with the inestimable Miss Tanner as umpire put her staunchly in the children's camp. The woman was a fiend. She couldn't seem to understand that they weren't playing cricket for the county but for fun.

Her eyes never strayed far from Eric. Maybe that was why Miss Tanner came down so hard on her. She wasn't paying attention to the game. He seemed to be having a good time. His best friend wasn't Jenny, who at eight had adopted airs and graces that befitted her advanced years, but Marion, five-year-old shy little Marion, whose protector he had become.

Her thoughts slipped, as they often did, to Eric's mother. Sarah Foley had done a fine job of raising this boy. She wished she could say the same for his father.

A sour note, she inwardly chided. She had to get over her bitterness. And, to be fair, though Eric couldn't remember his papa, when he spoke of him it was with kindness. No doubt he got that from his mother as well.

The cricket match stopped when two riders appeared on the drive. Waldo and Thomas had returned from Tattersall's, where they'd gone to look for a pony for Eric. It was a secret, which was just as well, because there was no pony in tow.

When they saw the two riders, all the children jumped up and waved their arms. Her own heart did a little flip-flop, and that made her impatient with herself. She couldn't be in love with Waldo. She knew what love was. It's what she had felt for John. This was different. She didn't trust it to last.

Harper came out of the stables when the riders dismounted. She saw him confer with Waldo and wasn't surprised when, not long after, Waldo came to get her. Harper would have told him about her visit to Lady Langston, and she was eager to talk to Waldo too.

A light drizzle began to fall, so everyone made for the house to take cover. Waldo followed the children only so far, then turned aside and led Jo to the old ivy-covered gazebo that overlooked the lake.

She wasn't interested in the scenery. She said at once, "Lady Langston was—"

He stopped her with a kiss—slow, proprietary, and devastatingly sweet. He was smiling when he lifted his head; she was having trouble breathing.

"Lady Langston was...?" he prompted.

"Lady Langston," she began, but the thought disintegrated. He was kissing her cheeks, her ears, her chin. She was offering her lips, but he wouldn't take them.

When his hand cupped her breast and squeezed, she hauled out of his arms. Panting, she got out, "Stop this at once! Someone may see us."

He looked around. "No, only the swans."

When he took a step toward her, she backed away. "Waldo," she cried, "will you listen? I have something important to tell you."

He captured her in his arms. "Nothing," he said, "is more important than this."

He wasn't smiling now. He was serious. He was going to take her here, in broad daylight, in a rickety old gazebo that was open to the elements. All he was waiting for was a sign from her.

It wasn't decent. She couldn't allow it. That's why she moved closer, so that her breasts were crushed against his chest. That's why she drew his head down and sealed his lips with hers.

Their bed was cushions from a wicker sofa that Waldo scattered on the floor. He was gentle, then not so gentle when he felt the passion rise in her. They didn't have time to undress. Desire turned suddenly to desperation, taking them both unawares. He adjusted their clothes and entered her. The pleasure became unbearable, the leap to abandonment happened in a heartbeat. Her cry of release echoed his own as he emptied himself into her in deep, hard thrusts.

Long minutes passed before he slipped from her body, allowing her to sit up. She adjusted her drawers; he adjusted his trousers. They sat on the cushions, arms folded, with their backs against the front of the sofa.

"I can't believe we just did that," she said.

He kissed the nape of her neck. "You'll get used to it."

She turned quickly, eyes narrowing on his face. "I don't *want* to get used to it! It's too much. It's too overpowering, too . . . too everything."

He looked reflectively into space. "You may be right. I can see us in a snug little cottage, in front of the fire, surrounded by children . . ." He glanced at her. "No, I can see from your face, no children, only Eric. Can we have dogs? I'm almost as fond of dogs as I am of children."

"Bowman," she said, "do you never give up?"

He turned his head to look at her. "Do you want me to?"

She spoke with more honesty than wisdom. "I don't know what I want."

"Good."

"That's good?"

"It means we're making progress."

She finally got to talk about Lady Langston when Eric was in bed. It had stopped raining, so she and Waldo went for a walk around the perimeter of the lake.

"So, what I'm asking myself," she said, "is this: What difference does it make when Morden was born?"

"I think Chloë could have answered that question. That's why she had to die. What we're looking at here is a powerful motivation."

"I know, but nothing comes to mind. I mean, if Morden wasn't the legal heir, I could understand it, but his parents were married long before he was born. Years, in fact."

He took her hand and linked it through his arm. "And Lady Langston thinks that Morden's mother may have confused the issue?"

"Yes. And confused Chloë. It seems innocent enough to me. What do you think?"

"Oh, I disagree. I think it's anything but innocent. Let me think about it, all right?"

"Fine."

"Anything else?"

"I'm going to see Lady Brinsley tomorrow at the Hall. Lady Langston invited me." She went on to tell him how it came about. Finally, she said, "It will give me an excellent opportunity to ask questions and look over the house. Why are you shaking your head?"

"It's too dangerous. It's exactly the same situation Chloë was in."

"Except that Morden won't be there. And even if he is, he won't have read the piece I wrote in the *Journal*, you know, the one that's supposed to panic him into doing something foolish."

"You're missing something important."

"What?"

"If Morden is older than he pretends to be, that means both his mother and father connived to hide that fact."

"So?"

"So it's a conspiracy, Jo. That means we have three prime suspects, not one."

"All the more reason for me to go."

"I'll think about that too."

It started to drizzle just then. "We could take shelter in the gazebo," he casually suggested.

He looked at her, she looked at him, then turned to look at the gazebo. "It's closer than the house," she observed.

They looked at each other again and started to laugh. "Well," he said, "what are you waiting for? Let's set the gazebo on fire."

Later that night found Waldo sitting up in bed, propped against the pillows, with Jo's softness nestled against him. In another few minutes, he would escort her back to her own room, before the house stirred. Meanwhile, she was sleeping and he was going over in his mind all that she'd told him about her visit with Lady Langston.

He had pretty well worked everything out. Morden was still his prime suspect. He knew why the chaise that was to take Chloë to Stratford had never been traced. He was certain that her body was concealed somewhere in the grounds of the Hall, somewhere close to the house. He knew the motive for doing away with her. What he hadn't worked out was how he was going to bring her killer to justice. Even if they found Chloë's body, all the evidence was circumstantial and had little chance of standing up in a court of law.

He might be forced to take the law into his own hands.

"Waldo?"

"I'm here, Jo."

She sighed and drifted off to sleep again.

He was wearing the softest of smiles. There was something deeply satisfying in hearing his name on her lips when she was hardly conscious of what she was saying.

Progress.

Take two steps forward.

But this time, there would be no going back, not

even if he had to take the law into his own hands with Jo as well.

The thought made him wince. As though she would allow it! As though he would want her against her will! He'd already decided on his strategy and he was going to stick to it. It wasn't a question of her coming to him willingly. That wasn't enough for him. If she couldn't give him her whole heart...

Since when had he started lying to himself? He would take her on any terms he could get.

He put his hand on her shoulder. "Time to get back to your own room, Jo."

She came to herself slowly, stretched, and sat up. "You sound cross."

"No. Just thinking. Someone has to keep an eye on you, so I've decided to come with you to Brinsley Hall."

She lifted her face to him. Her eyes were shining. "Thank you, Waldo. I was wondering how I could talk you into it."

"Seems like we both have the same problem," he murmured.

She didn't hear the irony behind his words. She had looked at the clock and was hastily dressing so that she could get back to her own room before the servants were up.

Chapter 24

Jo cast one comprehensive glance at her companions and tried to inject the same worshipful look into her own expression. Mr. Charswell, the landscape gardener, was practically a prophet, and these avid gardeners were his disciples. So she should look the part and not betray that she was bored out of her mind. And really, it wasn't as though the lecture was uninteresting. It was simply that she didn't have acres and acres of parkland to beautify. She had a small patch of garden. She didn't want to know how to design an artificial lake. She wanted to know how to get rid of aphids.

Harper, she was sure, was as bored as she. If he stifled one more yawn, she would be forced to tread on his toes. He was supposed to be designing a garden for her. She was on tenterhooks because his breathing was edging close to a snore.

Waldo was one of the party, but he hadn't stayed for

the lecture. He'd said that he had business in Henley and would join them later for dinner. That was just an excuse so that he could roam the grounds, narrowing down possible hiding places for a body.

The more she thought about it, the more incredible it seemed. The Brinsleys could trace their lineage back to the Plantagenets. Their home was as old and venerable as their blood lines. This seemed like the last place on earth where a murder would be committed.

The lecture was coming to a close and, uh oh, everybody looked as though they were bursting to ask questions. She tried to look intelligent when the speaker's eye fell on her.

She was saved by Lady Brinsley.

"I've arranged to have refreshments served on the terrace," she said. "We're a small group. We can ask our questions over tea and cake."

And they *were* a small group. They were, Lady Langston confided, fewer in number than they'd been the last time. Not everyone wanted to travel as far as Oxfordshire just to take in a meeting of the Horticultural Society. But if they didn't go to the Hall, they would hardly ever see Elinor, poor dear.

On the terrace, Jo managed to exchange a few words with the other guests. The Miss Boyds must have been in their sixties, but they made her think of kittens chasing blowing leaves. They didn't pursue a conversation to its end but were easily distracted by every stray word or thought. Lord Skene was bluff and hearty and his wife was the opposite, but for all that, it was easy to see that there was real affection there. There were two other couples, much the same as the Skenes. All in all, a convivial gathering of long-standing friends.

She wasn't sure how Lady Brinsley's stern-faced companion fitted in. Miss Dunn seemed to have only one interest, and that was to make herself indispensable to her employer. After a while, one forgot that she was there.

She couldn't fathom what Chloë had in common with these people, apart from an interest in gardening. Nice as they were, they were too old for her. Hardly had the thought occurred to Jo than she changed her mind. These weren't merely nice people. They were the salt of the earth. An interest in gardening may have brought them together in the first place, but they were like a family now. They really cared for each other. One only had to see how they'd rallied around Lady Brinsley to know that. In this company, she bloomed.

If Lady Brinsley suffered from nerves, no one would have known it. She seemed to be enjoying herself. She wasn't jumping up and down, but she was quite animated. And she hadn't blinked an eye when Jo, Waldo, and Harper had turned up on her doorstep. In fact, she'd made them feel very welcome.

When there was a lull in the conversation, Jo said casually, "What a pity Lady Webberley isn't here. Has anyone heard from her? Someone mentioned she was in Paris."

No one looked guilty or seemed put out by the question, but there was a shift of focus from the landscape gardener to Lady Brinsley, as though, of them all, she was the most likely to know the answer.

Her ladyship smoothed her hair back from her face and smiled artlessly. "I've heard the same rumor," she said, "and if it's true, I think Chloë has behaved abominably, and next time I see her I shall tell her so. But how like Chloë to go off to Paris without a word to anyone! One can't help envying her. She does what she wants when she wants without consulting anyone else's wishes."

There was no reproach in her voice. She might have been a fond mother excusing a daughter's foibles. It was a telling little speech. Jo wondered how much freedom Lady Brinsley enjoyed. Not much, by the sound of it. For a married woman, everything was subject to her husband's wishes, and some husbands were tyrants.

She was jerked out of her thoughts when she heard Harper's voice. He was talking to the guest speaker. She searched her mind for something to say to draw Mr. Chaiswell's attention away from Harper, who was more ignorant of gardening than even she was. Lord Skene got there before her. It wasn't gardening the gentlemen were talking about but coaches.

Harper caught her stare and winked.

Not long after, when the ladies rose to view the conservatory, there wasn't a gentleman in sight. They'd excused themselves to go outside to compare notes on their various coaches.

She was in her room about to dress for dinner when she got the shock of her life. A part of the wall opened, and a maid, carrying a pitcher of hot water, entered. Jo put a hand over her heart and sank down on the bed. "I'd thought you'd come through that door," she said, pointing to the door into the corridor. "You gave me such a fright."

"I'm sorry, ma'am. I did knock. Didn't you hear me?"

"Yes, but I didn't know there was a door there." She smiled to show there were no hard feelings. "It's what they call a jib door, isn't it?"

"Yes'm."

Jib doors were not uncommon and gave directly onto the servants' staircase, but she hadn't expected to find one in a converted monastery. But she shouldn't

have been surprised. The building was beautifully
made over, a pleasing blend of old and new. There was
a splendid, four-tiered Georgian staircase rising from
the great hall to the attics, and in the main rooms, one
would never have known that the house was once a
monastery. The chapel was all that remained of the
monks' church.

When the maid had set the pitcher of water on the
washstand, Jo said, "You're Anna, aren't you?"

"Yes, ma'am. Her ladyship sent me to help you dress
for dinner."

As Anna set out towels and soap, Jo said, "My friend,
Lady Webberley, was here just before Easter. Do you remember her, Anna?"

There was a slight hesitation, then Anna said, "I remember her."

Odd, thought Jo. She sensed a change in the maid.
Either she was afraid or she hadn't liked Chloë.

Or maybe Jo was imagining things. She tried again.
"Do you remember which room was hers?"

"This room was hers."

Jo's heart lurched. "*This* was Lady Webberley's
room?"

Anna nodded and looked down at the floor as a dull
stain spread across her cheeks.

Jo pushed herself off the bed and crossed to the
maid. "You're ashamed of something, Anna," she said.
Her voice was stern. The girl could not have been
more than fifteen or sixteen, but Jo did not let that de-
ter her. "It's something to do with Lady Webberley. I
think I know what it is"—she had no idea whatever—
"but if you don't confess, I swear I shall send for the
magistrate and have you arrested."

Tears welled in the maid's eyes and rolled down her
cheeks. "I made amends," she said. "I posted it and

paid for it out of my own wages, just like the priest told me to do." Her shoulders began to shake and she had difficulty getting the words out. "I know I sinned, but it wasn't a mortal sin. Please don't call the magistrate in. It will break my mother's heart if I'm transported."

A handkerchief wouldn't have mopped up that flood of tears, so Jo fetched one of the towels from the washstand and handed it to Anna. "I promise I won't send for the magistrate." This time, she spoke in a kindly voice. "So sit down in that chair and, when you've come to yourself, tell me the whole story."

Anna obeyed.

"Let me get this straight," said Waldo. "The maid found Chloë's letter to you and kept it for almost two weeks before posting it?"

"Poor Anna. It weighed on her conscience to such a degree that she confessed the sin, her word, to her priest. Luckily, she'd kept the letter. He told her to post it and her sin would be forgiven. It cost her eightpence, so you see, the penalty was quite severe. I doubt that she earns more than eleven or twelve pounds a year."

They were out on the terrace, leaning against the balustrade, watching the sun set. Behind them, the French doors were open and they could hear the buzz of conversation as the old folks—as Waldo called them—played cards. Lady Brinsley was playing the piano, something soft and tragic that suited her soft and tragic expression, and Jo wondered whether Lady Brinsley's famous nerves were at work or whether her ladyship was hinting them all off to bed.

"And she took the letter out of spite?"

Jo nodded. "Not only did Chloë not say good-bye to

Anna, but she did not leave the customary gratuity, you know, for services rendered. All she left was the letter addressed to me."

"What a mercenary wretch!"

"Not really. I think Anna's feelings were hurt. Chloë hinted that she might find a place for her in London, but that last morning, Chloë had cleared out, leaving Anna to face the other servants after boasting that she might be handing in her notice. It was an impulsive act that she regretted almost at once, but she didn't know how to put it right."

"Mmm." He rubbed the bridge of his nose with his index finger. "I think you're taking her part. No. It's more than that. I think you admire her."

She shrugged. "Perhaps I do. Only someone with a good heart could feel such guilt and shame. A heartless person would have destroyed the letter and never given it another thought."

His smile was reluctant. "She's still a wretch. She lied to Ruggles. She didn't know anything, she said. What I'm asking myself is why she made a clean breast of things to you. What did you say to her to get her to confess?"

Her smiled was complacent. "You're so clever, you figure it out!"

"You threatened her?"

"A little. But that's not why she confessed. She was mortally afraid before she entered my chamber."

His clever eyes were on her. After a moment's thought, he said, "It was your name. She knew you were Chloë's friend because she posted the letter and saw your name on it."

Her smile vanished. "Now you've spoiled my triumph. Yes, it was my name. She thought I had come to denounce her to the authorities." She gave him a sharp look. "Which I'm not going to do. She acted rashly, but she's sorry for it, so that's the end of it."

He spread his hands. "I won't say a word."

"Good."

He sighed. "Are you sure she knows nothing about Chloë's diary?"

"Very sure. I searched the room, but of course, I didn't find anything. I didn't expect to after all this time." There was a silence, then she went on, "She left nothing behind but that letter. I know Chloë. She wouldn't have forgotten to leave a gratuity for the maid. She was always thoughtful that way. She might forget to thank her hostess, but not the maid."

She looked up at him. "She left her room in a panic. The letter proves that. So does the lack of a gratuity for the maid. I'm finally convinced that she's still here."

His hand covered hers and squeezed. "We'll find her, I promise you."

Their conversation was interrupted by a figure who suddenly appeared on the other side of the balustrade. It was Harper and he was breathing hard.

"Guess who has just arrived to add a little spice to our party?" He took in their surprised stares and grinned. "Yes, the viscount himself. I haven't seen him, but Ruggles did. He followed him all the way from town."

"Where is Ruggles now?"

"Hiding in my room," replied Harper.

"Good. Tell him to stay out of sight until I find out what's going on."

Jo said, "I don't like the sound of this."

Waldo held her gaze for a moment, then smiled faintly. "Jo, you'll have three of His Majesty's crack agents guarding you. Don't you have confidence in our abilities to protect you?"

"Yes, but who is going to protect you?"

They laughed, thinking she'd said something witty, but she meant every word.

The viscount did not join his mother's guests. A footman entered, whispered something in her ladyship's ear, but no announcement was made regarding his presence. Evidently, the viscount had no wish to be part of his mother's house party.

Tea was served, and shortly after they all trooped off to their beds except for her ladyship and her companion. They went to the chapel for prayers, as they did every evening. Waldo managed a quick word with Jo before they parted to go to their different chambers.

"Lock yourself in," he said. "I'll be along to talk things over as soon as the coast is clear."

Once in her chamber, she lost no time in doing what Waldo advised. There was one problem. There was no key in the jib door, and that alarmed her. Ever since she'd heard that the viscount had arrived, she'd felt shivers of apprehension. This wasn't supposed to happen. He wasn't supposed to be here until he'd read her latest tidbit about Chloë in the *Journal.*

She told herself she wasn't being hysterical when she pulled her box out of the closet and found her pistol. This was the act of a rational woman, especially one who had been attacked once before. She checked to see that it was primed and ready, then sat in a chair waiting for Waldo to arrive. She had only one shot. The thought turned in her mind. After she fired her pistol, she would be defenseless. She needed something else as a weapon. After stewing for a moment or two, she got up and went to the fireplace. The poker would do very well.

Now that she had two weapons, she returned to her chair feeling a mite less panicked.

Time passed. She wondered what was keeping Waldo. When the doorknob rattled, her heart lurched so violently, she could hardly breathe. If she hadn't been expecting Waldo, she would have picked up her skirts and run through the jib door. She was in half a mind to do just that when she recognized his voice.

"Jo. It's me, Waldo. Let me in."

When she opened the door, both Waldo and Harper slipped inside.

"What's going on?" she asked. "Why are you here, Harper?"

He gave her a huge grin. "I'm going to stay in this room, as quiet as a mouse, hoping you-know-who will come creeping in, then we'll have the bastard, if you'll excuse my French, Mrs. Chesney."

Her heart leapt to a gallop, and she put a hand on her breast to slow it. "You think he'll try to kill me?"

Waldo saw the fear-bright eyes and the pallor of her cheeks, and he put his hand on her shoulder to steady her. "It could all be very innocent," he said. "Maybe he won't try to do anything at all."

"Then what is he *doing* here? I mean, no one was expecting him. He was supposed to be fixed in London for the Season."

"We don't know. Maybe it's a coincidence. Maybe it's not. But now that he *is* here, I think he'll try to verify whether Chloe is where he put her. And if he doesn't, we've lost nothing. But we'd be fools not to anticipate his next move. So we are going to do exactly what we planned to do if he walked into our trap. And when you think about it, this is better than we planned. We have access to the house. At this very moment, Ruggles is stationed in the room opposite the viscount's suite and will know the moment he leaves it."

"Much good that will do if the viscount's room has a door like that." She pointed to the jib door.

"It doesn't. The house has three servants' staircases, but only two rooms with a door that gives directly onto one of those staircases: yours and Lady Brinsley's. All the other doors lead onto corridors."

She was impressed. "I had no idea you were so accomplished. It would never have occurred to me to check the staircases. So you really were a crack British agent."

Harper's only comment was a short, sharp snort.

"So, what do we do now?" she asked.

"Harper stays here; you're coming with me. We're not going far, but you'll need a coat or something to keep you warm."

She went to the closet, got her cloak, and put it on.

"Where is your pistol?"

"Right here."

"Good girl."

"Where are we going?"

"To my carriage."

"You're not sending me away?"

He made a small sound of impatience. "Of course not. You're going to be our scout."

She liked the sound of that. "Lead on!"

Waldo led her through the jib door and onto the servants' staircase. There was enough light from wall sconces to make everything out. It wasn't as grand a staircase as the one that began in the great hall, but it still had four tiers. They were on the landing of the second tier. On the same landing was another door that they had to pass before they came to the stairs.

Waldo stopped and said, "This is the door into Lady Brinsley's chamber."

"How do you know whose chamber it is?"

"Because the door is unlocked, like yours, and naturally I went in and had a look around."

"You were taking a chance, weren't you?"

"Not really. I knew her ladyship was in the chapel."

Jo looked back the way she had come, then looked at Waldo. "What if," she said, "Chloë came this way? Maybe Morden did go to her room that night and she ran from him. She could have come here for help or to hide."

"Well, we know she didn't get help, and I think Morden made sure of that by choosing his time with care."

She got the point at once. "When his mother and her companion were in the chapel."

"Yes. And where would she hide? He could come in either door at any moment and find her."

She looked at him hard. "But?" she prompted.

He smiled. "But she might have had time to hide her notebook before he caught up to her."

Her mind was working frantically. "Supposing you're right, do you think Lady Brinsley found the notebook?"

He began to laugh. "If Chloë left the notebook there—and it's a big if—then I think her ladyship must have it. Harper and I searched her chamber and found nothing."

"But—"

He put a finger to his lips. "Work it out for yourself," he said, "but no more talking till we are in my carriage."

And with that, he began to descend the stairs.

Chapter 25

There were no horses harnessed to the carriage. Waldo had located it right next to the old tithe barn, which was now the coach house, so as not to arouse suspicion. It made an excellent observation post.

From this vantage point, they had a clear view of the house, or as clear as they were likely to get when the only light came from outside lanterns hung on poles or from the few windows on the upper floors where people had yet to retire for the night. In that obscure light, all the trappings of modernity faded away and the house looked as it might have when it was first built, centuries ago, a magnificent monastery to serve God and all the inhabitants in neighboring villages.

Jo had learned that Holywell Abbey was the original name of the building until it passed into the hands of the second Earl of Brinsley. What monstrous conceit on his part to rename it after himself, monstrous and profane. The thought chilled her and she gathered her cloak more closely about her.

Waldo's voice was hardly as loud as a whisper. "Whatever happens, Jo, I want you to stay here until either I or Ruggles or Harper comes to fetch you."

"You think something may go wrong?"

"No. But I don't want to be distracted by worrying about you."

"I thought I was to be your scout?"

"And so you are. Just make a mental note of anyone who looks suspicious and report it to me when I return."

"What about the viscount?"

"You're to leave him to me."

It didn't sound like much of a job, and she was beginning to wonder whether he was purposely putting her out of harm's way. He would have known that she would want to be part of what was going on. But somebody had to be the scout, she supposed.

After a while, she said, "How do you know that Morden will come this way? What if he comes out by another door?"

"It doesn't matter which door he comes out. Ruggles won't be far behind him. He'll signal to let us know where he is."

"A signal?"

"An animal cry—distinctive—so I'll know it. Now, no more questions. Let's not give our position away."

One by one, the lights in the upstairs windows winked out. Time passed. A time or two, she tried to speak, but Waldo silenced her with a gesture. He was completely focused on the house and grounds. She studied his profile. In that gloomy interior, he didn't look like the Waldo she knew. There was no charming smile, no humor in his eyes or expression. Everything about him was stern and harsh. Now, finally, she believed all the rumors she'd heard about his war record. He wasn't a slightly tarnished Prince Charming. He was a slightly tarnished knight in silver armor.

She stifled a smile. It seemed sacrilegious to smile when they were hoping to unmask a murderer. She should be as vigilant as Waldo. And she was, for a time, but when there was no signal from Ruggles and no one left the house, she let her mind wander.

She heard rain pattering on the roof of the carriage. The fragrance of new-mown grass wafted through the open window. The breeze was soft with the promise of summer. A time or two, she yawned. She felt safe with Waldo beside her.

She lurched out of sleep on a jolt of terror. She couldn't breathe. When she struggled, the hand on her mouth relaxed.

"Don't make a sound," said Waldo, "or our quarry may take flight."

As awareness came back to her, she nodded and inhaled a long breath. She'd been dreaming of Chloë, a mixed-up dream where Morden was the abbot and he was walling Chloë up in a tomb. It was her turn next, and all her supplications to the monks went unheeded.

Waldo's hand covered her shoulder. "Jo, are you all right?"

She blinked up at him. "I am now. So it's started, then?"

He moved slightly, giving her a clear view of the window. A man was detaching the lantern on the pole closest to the back door. She couldn't make out his features because his back was to them.

"How do you know it's Morden?"

"Because," said Waldo, "Ruggles gave the signal. You have your pistol?"

"Right here." It was cradled in her arm.

"Remember what I told you. Stay here and keep out of sight. If anything goes wrong, fire the pistol and I'll come running."

A moment later, Waldo left the carriage by the far door. There was no sound. Both doors were unlatched. Minutes passed, but there was still no sound. She could see Morden because he was carrying a lantern. Her eyes trailed him as he took the path to the gamekeepers' cottages. Not far behind him were two shadows, Waldo and Ruggles. She watched until they all merged into the night.

Her heart was beating very fast.

She knew the lay of the land because Waldo had been here before and had made a map of the area. Beyond the gamekeepers' cottages was the home farm, with its pastures and woodlands. There was a stream there that fed into the Thames at Henley, but it wasn't deep enough to submerge a body.

"Chloë," she breathed out, a catch in her voice, "where are you?"

She heard something, some movement at the back door, and she hastily drew back from the window. Another figure emerged from the house. He, too, went to one of the poles with a lantern on it. As he reached up to detach it, the light shone full on his face. It was Morden.

She was stunned. Then who—*A decoy!* He had sent someone ahead of him to lay a false trail. For one panicked moment, she thought of shooting her pistol. That would bring Waldo and Ruggles back. But it would also scare off Morden, then they would never find Chloë.

That left Harper, but by the time she got to him, Morden could be out of sight. She fretted for a little while longer, but when Morden began to move, she knew she had no choice. As soundlessly as she could manage, clutching her pistol in her hand, she left the coach as Waldo had done, by the far door.

It didn't take her long to figure out where Morden was going. The conservatory, detached like Chloë's, was served by a wide path. It wasn't far from the house. He kept to the path, while she took cover in the stretch of shrubbery that bordered it. She waited until he had entered the conservatory before she moved, then she picked her way around a dense clump of rhododendrons and looked through a pane of glass. She couldn't see him, but she could see the haze of the lamp as it penetrated deeper into the conservatory. Then it stopped moving.

He must have reached his destination, Chloë's final resting place.

She was rigid with fear. She knew what she had to do next, but her feet refused to obey the commands of her brain. This wasn't supposed to happen. She wasn't supposed to confront Morden on her own. But if she didn't do it, no one else would, then he'd get away with murder.

It was that thought that steadied her. He had murdered Chloë. He had snuffed out a life without remorse. He had sent someone to kill her too. Who would be next? Waldo? The killing had to stop.

Move, she told her reluctant feet, and they obeyed her. The door was ajar. She slipped inside and paused. The light was far ahead of her, but she couldn't say where exactly because she didn't know the layout of the conservatory, not with any certainty. All she could remember from the visit earlier that afternoon was that it was a maze of twisted paths—twisted paths, towering palm trees, banks of flowers, and ancient artifacts to remind people of the house's proud history, as though they could forget.

Many minutes passed before she marshaled enough confidence to move. She had taken only a few halting steps when she heard the door behind her close. Someone was close by. She could hear him breathing. Her pistol was in her hand but she had yet to cock it. Blood was pumping to every pulse point. She had stopped breathing. The sound of her pistol as she pulled back the hammer was unmistakable. She whirled herself around, but she was too late. The blow caught her on the side of the head, and her pistol slipped from her nerveless fingers. Then she was seized and dragged toward the light.

Waldo became suspicious when their quarry climbed a stile and began to traverse the pasture behind the home farm.

"What is it?" asked Ruggles.

Waldo looked back the way they'd come. "We've come too far," he said. "Morden couldn't have carried a body this distance."

"What if he forced her at gunpoint?"

"Too risky. Someone might see them, some of his tenants or the gamekeepers. They were out that night looking for poachers, remember? Morden would have known it. No. This doesn't feel right. He must have concealed the body closer to the house than this."

"Then what is he doing now?"

"I don't know. But I think he's cleverer than we gave

him credit for. I don't think he has fallen into our trap.
I think we may have fallen into his."

"You think he'll ambush us?"

"I don't know. You're sure this is Morden we are following?"

There was a short silence, then Ruggles said, "I recognized his coat. There are so many capes on it, he
looks like a coachman."

Another silence, then Waldo said, "I'm going back.
You go on. But don't take any chances. Kill him if he
tries anything."

"No quarter asked or given?"

Waldo didn't respond. He was moving fast, in spite of
his lame leg, making for the coach where he'd left Jo,
calling himself all kinds of a fool for underestimating an
enemy.

Ruggles climbed over the stile. "Just like the old
days," he said, and he quickened his pace to keep up
with his prey.

"Last time," the viscount said, "I had everything prepared in advance. All I had to do was knock Chloë on
the head and toss her into the drain. This time, you'll
have to give me a few minutes till I get things ready."
He straightened and looked at Jo. "I must correct myself on one point. I had to go back to her room later
and clear it of odds and ends—her toiletries and so
on—so that everyone would believe she'd packed up
and left. I gave that little bag to my valet to dispose of."

He was speaking to her in a normal, conversational
tone of voice, as though they were in his mother's
drawing room. Only they weren't having a reasonable
conversation. A few moments ago, he'd attacked her.
The pain in her head was needle-sharp, and her throat

hurt where his fingers had squeezed when she'd tried to scream. Nausea was making her stomach heave.

If she hadn't felt so weak, she might have made the attempt to escape. Meanwhile, she was breathing slow and deep, trying to get her bearings. She was sitting on the tiled floor, her back against a stone urn, and he was standing by the sundial, one of the prized artifacts, beginning to dismantle it. He'd warned her that if she tried to stand or made a sound, he would kill her.

What she couldn't understand was why he hadn't killed her already.

She choked back her fear. Panic wasn't going to save her. She had to find a way to put off the awful moment when he'd do to her what he'd done to Chloë.

"Chloë—" She cleared the lump of fear from her throat and tried again. "You're wrong about Chloë. She's not dead. And only I know where she is."

She thought the lie would gain her some time, until she realized how easy it was to dismantle the sundial. The top came off, then the pedestal, and he was down to the base. Soon he'd know the truth and know that she'd lied to him.

"You almost had me convinced," he said, "until you came out here." Hands on hips, he stared at her, a malevolent smile on his lips. "You wanted to find Chloë? Well, I'm going to show her to you."

He was lying about one thing. If he was convinced that Chloë was in that drain—what drain?—he wouldn't be here. He would know she was dead and he had nothing to fear. Calling him a liar wasn't going to help her. She had to think of something else.

The base was harder to move than the other pieces. She watched him grunt and strain as he tried to shift it to the side. The beds of pansies were crushed beneath his feet. It flashed through her mind that when Waldo saw those crushed flowers, he would know where to look for her.

Horrible thought! She squelched it at once. "You're not going to get away with this," she said. "My friends will be looking for me."

He straightened, shook his head, and began to laugh. "Try again, Mrs. Chesney. I sent them on a wild-goose chase." He looked at his watch. "They won't be back for at least an hour. My valet will see to that."

They'd followed the valet and not Morden. He'd tricked them all. She'd never leave this place alive. Terror rose in her throat. He saw the look on her face and laughed. "No one will ever find you, because no one knows this place exists. I found it when I was a boy, when workmen were repairing my mother's conservatory."

"What is it?" she asked hoarsely.

"The bathhouse of the old Roman villa. It's all that's left to show that the Romans were once here, that and the few artifacts you see. It's where the spring was. In later years, they called it Holy Well because the waters were supposed to have miraculous properties."

His little speech was so well rehearsed, she could imagine him giving it to curious visitors who came calling. Even now he was boasting about his remarkable heritage. He couldn't help himself.

Miraculous waters. That's what she was praying for, a miracle.

"Holywell Abbey," she said dully.

He laughed. "So you see, you and Chloë will be resting in holy ground."

He was going to kill her. That smiling monster was going to kill her. When he found Chloë's body, it would be all over for her. There would be no reason to keep her alive. She had to make her move before he removed that stone base.

"You're wasting your time," she said, and was surprised at how calm she sounded. "She's not in there. You thought you'd killed her, but you didn't. She found a way out and made her way to Paris. You're ruined, Morden. Her memoirs are to be published—"

He silenced her with a violent motion of one hand. "Lies! All lies! I read your piece in the *Journal*. You thought you would entrap me, but it's you and your friends who walked into *my* trap."

So, he knew about the *Journal*. It didn't matter. She had to go on with the lie. "She's in Paris, I tell you. She found another way out of your drain and came to me in Stratford. I helped her get to Paris."

"And how did she leave Brinsley Hall?"

The question brought her up short. *Tread carefully*, she told herself. Aloud, she said, "By chaise, I presume. She didn't say."

"There never was a chaise!" Spit was flying from his mouth, and she cringed from the fury in his face. "She asked me to send a servant to Henley to order one for the next morning, but I didn't do it. I knew she wouldn't be going anywhere."

She could see Chloë's last moments as if she'd been there. He'd invited her in here, maybe to talk things over. Chloë was frightened. Jo knew that from the letter. But what choice would she have had if he insisted? As for him—what had he told her? Chloë's grave was already waiting for her. All he had to do was, as he said, *knock Chloë on the head and toss her into the drain*.

Her fear was suddenly engulfed by a stronger emotion, a white-hot fury to match his own. She rose to her feet and faced him without flinching. Her voice was shaking, her breathing was labored. "There was someone here who helped her. I don't know who. She refused to tell me. And if Chloë didn't go to Stratford by hired chaise, you may be sure that same someone helped her get away from here. Go on. Move the stone and tell me that Chloë is still there."

Color charged into his face, then slowly receded. "No," he said, "my mother wouldn't go that far."

He dropped to his knees and heaved the base of the sundial to the side. She watched him in a daze, her mind in a whirl. His mother? What did he mean by that?

Her thoughts scattered as he let out a roar and turned on her. His face was twisted with fury. "Where is she?" he yelled. "Where have you hidden her body?"

She flinched when he grabbed her by the shoulders. He shook her so roughly that her teeth rattled. Then his words registered, and nothing could quell the wild leap of joy. Chloë wasn't in that drain! It was quite possible that she was alive! Hope cleared her brain and renewed her strength.

She butted his nose with her head, then shoved at his shoulders like a madwoman. He howled in pain and stumbled back. She didn't wait to see more. Picking up her skirts, she bolted down the aisle to the exit.

She knew she couldn't outrun him, so she didn't make for the house. The ruined refectory was hard by the conservatory. She turned aside and made for it. There were no lights to guide her here, so she crouched down behind one of the broken-down walls, ears straining to catch the sounds of pursuit.

He wasn't running, but she could hear him breathing. He must be very close. At any moment, she expected to feel his hands on her as he dragged her into the light. She had stopped breathing. *Breathe*, she told herself, and she inhaled a quick breath.

She heard the crunch of leather on gravel and spun round to look the other way. A huge shadow was looming over her. She shrank back against the wall, her hands searching for something, anything to use as a weapon. The rocks were too big, slabs from the wall. She could never lift them.

His voice was savage. "You bitch! You'll pay for all the trouble you've caused me."

Powerful hands hauled her to her feet. She opened her mouth to scream, but the scream died to a whimper when he sent her staggering to the ground with a vicious blow from his hand. She shook her head, trying to clear it. He hauled her to her feet again.

"Now, bitch," he said, "tell me where Chloë is or I'll break every bone in your body before I put you in the drain and close it up again."

Waldo went first to the coach where he'd left Jo. When he found it empty, he was numb with fear. He'd underestimated an enemy, and that was inexcusable. Calmer thoughts took hold. He mustn't jump to conclusions. Jo could have grown impatient and gone back to the house. She might have done any number of things. He must hope for the best but act as though the worst might have happened. That's how he'd been trained to think as an agent.

His eyes were accustomed to the dark and he could make out shapes within shadows. The conservatory was in darkness. His gaze shifted to the refectory. There wasn't much left of the refectory where the monks once dined. Only a few broken-down walls and the stone pulpit. He almost missed it. A shadow moved. Now he was completely focused. He was moving before he heard what sounded like a kitten mewling, before he heard a man's voice raised in anger.

When he got to the outer wall of the refectory, he

stopped and listened. Morden was threatening to break every bone in Jo's body. His pistol was useless in the dark. He pocketed it and vaulted over the wall.

The viscount caught the movement and threw Jo violently to the side to face this greater menace. Waldo feinted to the side, then lashed out with his foot and caught the viscount in the stomach. Morden's breath tore out of his throat and he sank to his knees, doubled over. When Waldo's foot lashed out again, the viscount was ready. As though galvanized by sheer animal instinct that told him this would be a fight to the death, he blocked the blow and brought Waldo crashing down. Locked together, each trying to gain a stranglehold, they went rolling over the rocky ground.

"Jo," Waldo panted, "get Harper. Just get away from here! Go!"

She didn't obey. She hovered like a cursed hummingbird. He wanted her to be safe, because if things went badly for him, Morden would turn on her.

He was distracted by his fears for Jo, and that was fatal. The viscount twisted away and suddenly kneed Waldo in the groin. Pain exploded through his body and he relaxed his grip. Morden seized his advantage and heaved himself to his feet. Panting, sucking air into his lungs, he felt on the ground and came up with a block of stone that had once formed part of the wall.

This was what Jo had feared might happen. Waldo was down and this monster was going to kill him. That's why she had disobeyed Waldo's command.

Her heart was in her mouth as she watched Morden lift the stone slab over his head. He didn't see her coming. She launched herself at him, and her momentum sent them both flying back. Morden hit the ground with a sickening thud. She landed on top of him. He made a feeble attempt to rise, then he was still. She scrambled off and ran to Waldo.

He was still groaning when she helped him to sit up. "I think I've knocked him senseless," she said.

"Get a lantern and let's have a look at him."

"Will you be all right? What if he wakes up?"

"I have my pistol," Waldo responded dryly. In fact, his pistol was already in his hand, and he would have blown a hole in the viscount if Jo hadn't taken a flying leap at him.

When she returned with the lantern, it was obvious that the viscount would never wake up again. He was on his back, staring up at them with unseeing eyes. He looked mildly surprised. Waldo examined the body, then straightened.

"His neck is broken. Now how are we going to find Chloë?"

A shudder ran over Jo, but she didn't waste time in analyzing what she was feeling. That would come later. She looked at Waldo. "I know where he put Chloë, but she's not there. Come, I'll show you. Put your arm around my shoulders. I'll help you."

Though Waldo didn't need her help, he meekly followed her orders. He rather enjoyed being fussed over. It made him feel cherished. A man could be too capable.

When they entered the conservatory, Jo had the eerie feeling that they were walking through a petrified jungle. There was no breeze. Nothing stirred. She knew one thing. Conservatories would not figure prominently in her future. She wanted no part of them. They were bad luck all round.

She led him to the Roman drain and told him about the sundial and how Morden had found this place. He lowered the lantern into the gaping hole. "At one time," he said, "a Roman slave would have cleaned this drain out. That's why it's so wide and deep."

"What about Chloë? Morden said she wasn't there, but I didn't see with my own eyes."

"She's not there, Jo." He got up and came to stand beside her. "But at least we've solved the puzzle of her boxes. They're in the drain."

She said dully, "There was another bag of her toiletries and so on. He said he gave it to his valet to dispose of."

"Yes. He was very thorough. But not thorough enough. He missed the letter and he missed the diary."

Weary beyond bearing, she pressed a hand to her eyes and swayed into him. He felt so good and solid and clean. She was turning into a watering pot and she couldn't seem to stop herself. "Where is she? What's happened to her?"

He dried her tears. "We're going to talk to the one person who could possibly know where Chloë is."

"Who?"

"The one person who knows every nook and cranny in the conservatory."

"Lady Brinsley," she said.

"Yes, Lady Brinsley."

Chapter 26

They didn't meet with Lady Brinsley for another hour. Waldo needed the delay to arrange things to make Morden's death look like an accident. He was thinking mainly of Jo. He didn't want her to come under suspicion of murder. Lord Brinsley was well connected. He could make a great deal of trouble for her if he wanted to.

Ruggles had returned from the chase after bagging the valet, who was locked up in one of the cellars until they could decide what to do with him. Now Harper and Ruggles had the distasteful task of putting things back together in the conservatory and disposing of Morden's body to make it appear that his death was an accident brought on by himself. They transferred him to his bedchamber and set the scene to make it look as though he'd tripped over a small hassock and had broken his neck when he fell on the fireplace fender.

Jo had tidied herself, but other than that, she'd had

little to occupy her time but her thoughts. When Waldo came for her, she felt as confused as ever. Strangely, she no longer felt tired, though it was very late and the house would soon be stirring. Until she discovered what had happened to Chloë, there would be no rest for her.

Waldo noted her pallor and the dark circles under her eyes, and he cursed himself for being the cause. He should have taken better care of her. He shouldn't have left her alone to fend for herself.

In his mind's eye, he was seeing that open grave, picturing how it might have ended if Jo's luck had run out. Fear tightened his chest, then was swallowed up in anger. He'd told her not to leave the carriage, and she'd disobeyed him. He wanted to shake her. No. He wanted to hold her, just to reassure himself that she was safe.

He settled on a kiss, a long, slow embrace that was far more eloquent than words. She understood. The same feelings pulsed through her. She didn't want him to be a hero. She just wanted him to be safe.

When they drew apart, he rested his brow on hers. "Are you going to give me those words yet?"

"I'll think about it."

"Wrong words. Be careful you don't run out of chances, Jo. A man can wait only so long."

"I thought we were going to see Lady Brinsley?"

"Then let's not keep her waiting."

Lady Brinsley had been told to expect them. She was fully dressed, as was her companion. They were in a small parlor off her bedchamber. The fire had been lit, and a tray with teapot and crockery was set on a small, round table. They had hardly sat down when Miss Dunn poured the tea, then quietly left.

Lady Brinsley opened the conversation. "Your man said that you had something serious you wished to say to me, Mr. Bowman. What is it?"

"Morden is dead."

Jo almost gasped. This was no way to break the news of a son's death to his mother. She looked at Waldo's stern face, then looked at Lady Brinsley. The shock and grief she expected to see were not there, only a curious kind of acceptance, as though it was what her ladyship expected to hear.

"How did it happen?" asked her ladyship.

As blunt as before, Waldo replied, "He was going to kill Mrs. Chesney and put her body with Chloë's. Mrs. Chesney fought back. Morden fell and hit his head against a stone. I've had the body removed to his own room. When the authorities come calling, they'll think he fell against the brass fender. So, you see, there won't be a scandal."

There was a long silence. "Thank you for that."

Jo was beginning to feel that she was a spectator at a badly performed play. The actors were saying their lines woodenly, as though they didn't understand their significance. She had no patience with this.

Leaning forward in her chair, she said forcefully, "I'm sorry for your loss, Lady Brinsley, but you must understand that your son was a bad man. But I'm warning you now, I don't care whether there is a scandal or not. All I'm interested in is my friend Chloë. You seem to know that your son put her in that dreadful hole in the conservatory. She's not there now. So where is she?"

The harsh lines on the older woman's face softened. A ghost of a smile touched her lips. "I wanted to tell you," she said, "because you've been such a good friend to Chloë. But I was afraid of what Victor would do. I hid her at the hospice. She's not herself yet, but she is improving every day."

"What hospice?"

"The one that's in the Convent of the Sacred Heart on the outskirts of Henley."

Jo slumped back in her chair. This was too easy. She couldn't believe it. She looked at Waldo. "Can this be true?"

The answer she wanted was in his eyes. "Yes, thank God," he said. "You can believe it."

All the emotions she had suppressed these last weeks suddenly swamped her. There were no tears, but her shoulders began to heave as she fought to draw air into her lungs. Then she was in Waldo's arms, looking into his stricken face. She struggled to get the words out, to tell him what she was feeling, but all she could say coherently was his name.

Jo was all for going to the convent at once to see with her own eyes that Chloë was all right, but this wasn't feasible. No one would let her into the hospice at this time of night. As Waldo pointed out, it was still pitch-black outside and unsafe to travel. Besides, he had a great many questions he wanted to put to her ladyship.

After replenishing their teacups, Waldo asked Lady Brinsley to tell him exactly what happened the night Chloë disappeared.

After a long silence, her ladyship said, "I think you know what happened, Mr. Bowman, or you've worked everything out."

Jo looked at Waldo, who was nodding his agreement, then she returned her gaze to Lady Brinsley. Slightly aggrieved, she said, "Well, I haven't worked everything out, so please go on, Lady Brinsley."

"Where shall I begin? There's so much to tell."

Waldo said gently, "Begin with the conversation after dinner. What was said that last night that incited your son to try to murder Chloë? We know that Chloë was panicked, because she wrote a note that later came into our hands. What happened? What was said?"

She said bitterly, "Nothing of any importance! It was all in Victor's mind. Chloë didn't care whether he was the legitimate heir or not." She took several shallow breaths before going on, "It was Lydia's comment that started it. His birthday is next month. She wanted to wish him a happy birthday in case she didn't see him before the day arrived. Chloë made a comment about Victor having been born the same day his grandfather died. Lydia corrected her. She knew that the old earl died in December, six months before Victor was born. Chloë was puzzled. She thought the two dates were the same, Victor's birthday and his grandfather's death. It's what Victor had told her, but that was before he discovered that she was Lady Tellall."

"And, of course," said Waldo, "if he was born the day his grandfather died, he couldn't be your son."

"No," she whispered. "He isn't my son."

"Go on."

"Chloë—or rather, Lady Tellall—wished him a happy birthday in her column, oh, it must be two years ago in December. Victor came to me. That's how we discovered Chloë wrote for the *Journal*. He hadn't told anyone else. I told him to leave it in my hands. I wrote to Lady Tellall pointing out her mistake. Victor was born in June. The correction was made, and that, we hoped, was the end of it. Until the last night of the house party, when Lydia made her wager."

Jo was baffled. "What difference would it make? Even if Chloë broadcast it to the world, it would only be Chloë's word against his."

Waldo said, "There are such things as records, Jo, parish records that are kept by the bishop. Forgeries are not that hard to detect."

Lady Brinsley said, "Apart from that, think of the scandal. But it would never have come to that. Chloë is not vicious, and she would never have done anything to hurt me."

Waldo said, "So Victor was born in December, the day his grandfather died."

"Yes, but not to me. I was at his grandfather's funeral, as was Lydia. There was no baby and no talk of a baby. So when Chloë related what she thought was a nice little anecdote about Victor's birthday, Lydia corrected her and they made the wager. Not only that, but Lydia made much of the fact that only legitimate heirs could inherit the title and estates."

Jo asked slowly, "Was Victor adopted, then?"

Her ladyship gave a sad smile. "No. If we had adopted him, he could not have inherited the title, and that would not have suited my husband. He is inordinately proud of his heritage and wanted to pass it on to a son. You see, Mrs. Chesney, Victor *was* his son. His mother, I believe, was quite respectable. She died when he was only a few weeks old. I was childless and likely to remain so. I was more than happy to take the boy and pretend that he was mine. But it had its problems. I had to pretend I was with child. I had to leave the Hall—well, I think you know what I mean."

Jo nodded. She would have had to leave all her friends and family and go, under an assumed name, where no one would know her. And after a suitable interval, she would have returned home with her husband by her side and a baby in her arms.

"Tell us," Waldo said gently, "what happened after everyone went to bed that night. Did you go to the chapel?"

She smiled faintly. "Yes, as I always do. I'd overheard the conversation between Lydia and Chloë and I was on edge, not because I thought Chloë would expose our secret, but because I was afraid Victor might do something foolish—threaten her, I don't know what. The toruble was, you see, that he knew about his birth, knew that he was his father's natural son and that I was not his mother."

When she paused, Waldo said, "You told him?"

"Oh, no. He learned it from his father, quite inadvertently, when he turned twenty-one and my husband had drunk too much champagne. It's one of the memories that my husband cherishes, that on his father's deathbed he was able to tell the old earl that a son had been born and their line would continue." She gave a brittle laugh. "If Victor had been a girl, none of this would have happened. Only sons count when a man has a title and great estates to pass on. Well, Victor knew that his grandfather had died the December before he was born, so he came to me and bullied the whole story out of me. To this day, his father doesn't know that Victor knows he was illegitimate. He was too drunk to remember, and Victor would do or say nothing to change things between them. He worships his father."

This picture of the father–son relationship was so pathetic that Jo had to look away. She was beginning to pity them all, but none more than Lady Brinsley.

Waldo said, "So you left the chapel. Then what?"

"I went to Chloë's room, but the door was locked and she did not answer. I was worried now, so I thought I'd try the servants' door. I had to go to my own room first to get to the servants' staircase. I found her notebook just inside the servants' door."

Waldo and Jo exchanged a quick glance. This was exactly how they had imagined it.

Her ladyship went on, "I knew she must have put it there for a purpose, so you can imagine how I felt. Her bedroom door was locked from the inside, so it seemed to me that she must have gone down the servants' stairs either to the kitchens or outside. I sent Harriet—that is, Miss Dunn—to the kitchens while I went outside to look around. That's when I saw Victor coming out of the conservatory. I hid in the shrubbery until he'd entered the house. Not long after, Harriet joined me. We took one of the lanterns and entered the conservatory."

There was a long silence as her ladyship tried to compose herself. "We searched everywhere and found nothing. I was on the point of giving up when I remembered the old Roman drain. Victor had fallen into it as a boy, so we had it covered over with the sundial. I knew he had an ungovernable temper, but I couldn't believe he would go that far." Her voice grew less steady as the memory came back to her. "When we got to the sundial, however, the plants around its base were completely trampled. I was sure then that he had killed Chloë and put her in the drain."

Her voice became slower, less distinct as she went on, "I was ready to rouse the house and call in the authorities. The only loyalty I felt to Victor came from my sense of guilt. If he was spoiled and indulged from the day he was born, I had a share in the blame. Not that I had much influence. My husband saw to that. If I'd been a stronger character—" She broke off and shook her head. "But I never believed he was capable of murder until that night."

"But," said Waldo, "you didn't call in the authorities?"

"No. Harriet thought she heard something, that maybe Chloë was still alive, so we worked feverishly to take the sundial apart. And as it turned out, Harriet was right."

"You *moved* the sundial?" Waldo asked, astonished.

Lady Brinsley gave a shaky laugh. "Even I find it hard to believe, in retrospect. At the time, I seemed to have the strength of a Samson. Panic will do that to a person. And it was sheer panic that gave us the strength to lift Chloë out of that dreadful hole. She was in a very bad way. We didn't stop to think. How we got her back to my room, I shall never know."

Tears were now streaming down her face. "If I had accused Victor, no one would have believed me. I had no credit, you see, because I was known to suffer from dementia. That's how I came to know about the hospice. Over the years, I've spent weeks there at a time as a patient. Some people call it an asylum, and I suppose it is. My one thought was to keep Victor away from Chloë until she was well enough to tell the authorities what happened that night."

She dashed away her tears with the back of her hands. "So we kept her in my room until Victor left for London two days later. Harriet is an accomplished nurse, as good as a physician. She took care of Chloë until we could transfer her to the hospice."

Waldo said slowly, "The hospice that you generously support and where no questions will be asked?"

Lady Brinsley lifted her proud head and gave him

back stare for stare. "I see we understand each other, Mr. Bowman," she said.

Jo was shaking her head. "But it has been almost two months since Chloë went missing. Why is she still there? Why haven't you gone to the authorities?"

Her ladyship's gaze shifted to Jo. "Because Chloë has not completely recovered yet. I told you she was in a bad way. She suffered a concussion that was so severe, she was unconscious for two weeks. She had broken ribs and a broken arm. And there is something else. She has no memory of that night. The last thing she remembers before waking up in the hospice is driving to the Hall in Lord Skene's carriage. The convent doctor says that she may never remember what happened to her."

"How much have you told her?" asked Waldo.

"I gave her her notebook, and it seemed to jog her into remembering odd moments of that house party. She knows someone tried to kill her—well, I had to tell her that to explain why we were keeping her sequestered in the hospice. But I didn't tell her that I suspected Victor. The doctor doesn't think we should put ideas into her head. He thinks we should wait until she remembers by herself. Besides, until you came here tonight, there was always a niggling doubt in my mind. After all, I was not there. I did not see Victor attack Chloë. But now I have no doubts."

She smiled at Jo. "She told me to expect you. She said that you would move heaven and earth to find her. She wanted to write to you, but I advised against it. Of course, I didn't suspect you of being implicated in the attack. But until her memory had returned, well, I thought it best not to let anyone know where she was." Tears glistened in her eyes. "But I must say, she is very fortunate to have you for a friend, Mrs. Chesney."

Waldo said carefully, almost too carefully, "Chloë is fortunate to have you as her friend also, Lady Brinsley. What you did was quite extraordinary."

Her ladyship's head lifted. Her gaze was as direct as his. "Thank you, Mr. Bowman," she said. "Chloë is very dear to me. I think of her as the daughter I always wanted but never had."

He smiled. "I'm sure you do."

When they were in the corridor and Waldo was escorting her to her own chamber, Jo said, "What was that last exchange all about?"

"What exchange?"

"Don't pull that innocent face with me. You practically accused Lady Brinsley of being Chloë's mother."

"No. All I did was raise a question that was puzzling me. Why would she go to such lengths for someone she hardly knows? All they have in common is a love of gardening. It was Lady Brinsley who mentioned mother and daughter. But you know Chloë better than anyone. Could it be possible?"

"Not as far as I know. I mean, I don't know much about her early life. Like me, she was an only child. She was happy. That's all I know."

They were at her door. He fixed her with his steady gaze. "It's Lady Brinsley's secret, Jo. Don't pry. You may do more harm than good."

"I'm not prying. I'm just speculating, and I picked up that habit from you."

He laughed.

"Still," said Jo, "she didn't waste much sympathy on her son, did she?"

"Ah, but he's not her son. Not only that, but she was never allowed to get close to him. His father saw to that. I'm not surprised she was stricken with bouts of dementia. They closed her out. She was nothing but a cipher to them. And these last two months must have been a torment. I think there was more to the delay in calling in the authorities than Chloë's loss of memory. I think she was hoping that she was wrong and Morden was not a killer."

"Some hope."

He shrugged. "You never gave up hope that you'd find Chloë. Sometimes hope is all we have. Look at me."

She pretended she hadn't heard that last remark. "Why were you so hard on her, at the beginning, I mean, when you told her Morden was dead?"

He shrugged. "I wanted to see her reaction. For all we knew, she could have aided and abetted him. After all, it's her secret too."

"Chloë was lucky to have her on hand. Which reminds me. When are we going to see Chloë?"

"Not for some time. No, don't argue. There are a number of things I have to do before we can go."

"Such as?"

"Such as concoct a plausible story to explain a body in a bedchamber and a valet locked up in a cellar. After the magistrate and his constables have come and gone, then we'll go see Chloë."

"How long will it take you to arrange that?"

"Not long. Why?"

She looped her arms around his neck. "Hurry back. I don't want to be alone. I want to be with you."

Her flippant tone lacked conviction. He understood only too well. After a battle, the soldiers who survived experienced some of the same emotions she was experiencing now. She had faced her own death. Now she wanted life in all its abundance. And so did he.

A slow smile touched his lips. "Ruggles can handle things," he said, and with that, he swept her into her room and shut the door on the world.

Lady Brinsley was standing by the window, gazing at her own reflection in the dark glass. She wasn't sure what she was feeling—guilt, remorse, and, if she were honest with herself, a sense of relief that it was finally over and she hadn't had to betray her son to the authorities.

That's what had tortured her for these many weeks. Victor wasn't the only guilty party here. If anyone should go to trial, it should be his parents for raising a son who thought he was the center of the universe.

Tears dampened her lashes, but she wouldn't give in to them. If she started to cry, she would never stop.

She turned as Miss Dunn entered the room, and smiled when she saw the teapot her companion was holding. Harriet was a firm believer in the efficacy of tea to solve all problems.

When they were drinking their tea, Miss Dunn said, "Are you going to tell Chloë the truth now?"

"That I'm her mother? What would be the point? She has many fond memories of her own mother. I would only be an interloper. I don't want to change things between us. I won't risk losing her altogether. Besides, once she knows who attacked her, she may decide that she doesn't want to know me at all."

Miss Dunn stirred her tea. "I see," she said. "That's to be your penance, is it, for what Victor did to her?"

"No. That's to be my penance for Victor."

"You didn't make him the way he was. He made his own choices, chose his own path."

"Harriet... pass the sugar."

Miss Dunn sighed. The conversation was closed, at least for the present. She said, "We had better rehearse what we're going to say to the magistrate when he gets here."

"Yes, and to the earl. He'll never get over the loss of his son."

"What will you say to him?"

"Exactly what we tell the magistrate."

The magistrate had only one constable with him, and they accepted the evidence that was presented to them without demur. The valet, who feared the hangman's noose, was only too eager to verify that he found the body when he came to wake his master with his morning cup of coffee. The police doctor was satisfied and so he would tell the coroner. After expressing their condolences to her ladyship, they left.

There were other arrangements to make, but those were left in Ruggles's capable hands, and Waldo and Jo set off for the hospice late in the afternoon. Jo had a note from Lady Brinsley, which she gave to the porter at the door. If they hadn't had the note, they wouldn't have been allowed in.

When Jo walked into Chloë's room, she caught back a gasp. Her friend was in an invalid chair, as pale as chalk, and looking as though she hadn't eaten in weeks. But that wasn't what made Jo's eyes hot with tears. Chloë's beautiful hair had been shorn and was no more than a cap of soft down, like a nestling's feathers.

She must have made a sound, because Chloë turned. She looked at Jo blankly, then, as recognition dawned, gave a tremulous smile. "Jo," she said, her voice unsteady, "why are you wearing my best walking dress?" and she dissolved into tears.

They both laughed, they both wept and hugged, but gradually emotion was spent and they began to talk.

Chloë said, "Is Lady Brinsley with you?"

"No. Waldo Bowman brought me here. He's waiting outside the door. Lady Brinsley is at the Hall." She took her friend's hands. "Something dreadful happened. Lord Morden died this morning—"

Chloë's whole body jerked. She seemed to have trouble breathing, then her words came out in a rush. "I'm not sorry he's dead. He's the one who did this to me. I didn't know how I was going to tell Elinor. She has been so kind, so generous." Emotion overcame her and she couldn't go on.

Jo said slowly, "I was told you'd lost your memory."

Chloë nodded. "I did, but it came back to me in odd snatches. And when Elinor gave me my notebook and I read the last entry, I remembered everything, how he'd forced me to go to the conservatory, the choking fear in my throat because I knew he was going to kill me"—she drew in a shallow breath—"and that's where my memory ends, until I woke here one night with Elinor by my bedside. The pain in my head was excruciating. I couldn't talk. I couldn't see clearly. I couldn't move. I was bound like one of those Egyptian mummies. But Elinor was there, that night and every night those first few weeks, anticipating my needs. How could I tell her, when I finally got my memory back, that her son had tried to murder me?"

"I think she must have known."

"Because she read my notebook? I don't know. Mothers are always the last to see the bad in their children." She looked out the window onto a small, sunlit courtyard. "And there's nothing in that last entry that indicates Victor might try to murder me. All I wrote about was the wager."

Jo was puzzled. "Then why did you run from him?"

Chloë plucked at a loose thread on the blanket that covered her legs. "It was only as I thought about it that I realized what it meant. Victor could not possibly be the legitimate heir. If there's one thing he prizes above all others, it's his heritage. I could well believe that he'd kill to keep his secret.

"He was already at my door. I hadn't time to do more than write you a few lines.... I don't know what I was thinking. I just wanted someone to know what was happening to me."

Jo put out her hand and squeezed her friend's arm. "Thank God you had the presence of mind to leave your notebook in Lady Brinsley's room. That's what saved you."

Chloë shook her head. "I had to go back for it. I left it in the writing table with some idea that one of the maids might find it. But I changed my mind. I really was in a panic. I had no idea I was leaving my notebook in Lady Brinsley's room or I might not have done it. She is, after all, his mother. I just wanted to make sure that if anything happened to me, someone would read my last entry and make the connection." She gave a teary sniff. "As it was, I wasted precious moments, and when I finally ran outside, he was there, waiting for me."

The thought was too awful to dwell on, so Jo tried to distract her friend. She said lightly, "You should have sent word to me, telling me where you were."

"Jo, I couldn't write, even if I wanted to. My arm was broken. I was as weak as a kitten. And I was afraid that you might lead him straight to me. He knows—knew— you are my closest friend. I was beginning to be sorry that I'd penned those few lines to you. Did you ever receive them?"

"Yes. That's what got me all fired up. I'm practically a member of Special Branch. If it hadn't been for Waldo Bowman, Morden would have got off scot-free."

"I always liked Waldo. One day I'd like to thank him, but not looking like this." She touched a hand to the down on her head and smiled wryly. "Not until I get myself a wig. You know me, Jo. I always was vain."

Why Chloë's attempt at humor should bring tears to her eyes baffled Jo. She groped in her reticule, found her handkerchief, and blew her nose.

Chloë said, "You haven't told me what happened to Victor."

"I killed him," said Jo.

Chloë's mouth was a round *O*. "Are you serious?"

Jo nodded. She was still sniffing back tears.

"In that case, I'm not going to say one word about my best walking dress. You may keep it."

Jo gave a watery chuckle. "All the clothes I've been wearing in town are yours. I had to borrow them to catch a murderer."

"Now, this I must hear. Start at the beginning and tell me all about it."

Jo took the chair beside the window and did as Chloë asked.

Chapter 27

Chloë went home to convalesce with Jo, not to her own house in town but to Stratford, so that Jo could catch up on what had been happening with the *Journal* in her absence. Leastways, that was the reason she gave the Bowmans, and nothing they said could persuade her to stay on. Waldo made it easy for her. He let her take Eric on the clear understanding that this was only a temporary arrangement. After Cecy's ball, he would join them and they could decide then on Eric's future as well as their own.

He seemed to understand that she needed time alone. So much had happened to her in the last two months. So much had changed. Sometimes she felt like a stranger to herself. She had to find out who Jo Chesney was and what she really wanted to do with her life.

"Two months ago, I had my life all mapped out," she told Chloë. "I knew exactly who I was and where I was going. I was happy. Now..." She shook her head. "It's not the same. I'm not the same person."

They were in the garden, sunning themselves over tea and scones. Mrs. Daventry had taken Eric to feed the swans on the river to keep him occupied. This was supposed to be a holiday, but he missed Waldo and he missed the girls, or "his cousins" as he was now calling them. He couldn't understand why they couldn't all be together.

Only Chloë seemed to be thriving. In the last little while, she had filled out and got her color back. She was wearing a wig and could walk unaided. At the moment, she was content just to soak up the sun.

She opened her eyes and looked at Jo. "What about the *Journal*? I thought that became your life after John died."

"It did, but it's lost its appeal. I thought I was indispensable, but it turns out I'm not. I was away for two months and they managed quite well without me. Now Mac is talking about bringing the *Journal* out twice a week. He has all sorts of plans he is eager to get started on. I was once like that."

"Ah," said Chloë.

"What does that mean?"

"It means that you've finally come to accept that John is gone and your life is no longer tied to his. If you go on with the *Journal*, it must be because it's what you want to do, not because it's what you think John would want."

"I've already accepted that my life is no longer tied to John's." She batted away a fly as she bit into a scone. "But the *Journal* is important to me. It's part of who and what I am."

"Yes, change is always difficult, isn't it? And when

there's no going back, it can be quite frightening. Doubly so for someone like you."

Jo almost took umbrage but thought better of it. "You're right. I don't like change. I like stability."

"Change is inevitable. You can't stop the clock or turn it back. Life moves on."

"I'm aware of that, but I am what I am." She gave a helpless shrug. "I don't want to start something new unless I know I can succeed or unless the odds are in my favor. I don't want to end up with nothing."

There was a moment of silence, then Chloë said, "I see what you mean. John was a safe bet; Waldo is a gamble."

Jo's voice cooled. "We were talking about the *Journal.*"

Chloë laughed. "I don't think so. We were talking about what you should do with your life. Of course, I'm the last person to give advice—"

"At least we agree on something!"

"But as your friend, I feel duty-bound to help you know your own mind. We already know your heart is taken."

Jo stared at her friend long and hard. Finally, when it was evident that she couldn't stare Chloë down, she capitulated. "So, I've lost my heart. But I refuse to lose my self-respect. I know Waldo loves me *now*, but how long will it last? How long before he becomes bored with me? I've read your columns. I know of his reputation with women."

"There you are, then. He's a scoundrel, so you shouldn't marry him."

"I didn't say he was a scoundrel. In fact, he's the opposite."

"There you are, then. Marry him."

"You're no help at all."

Chloë laughed. "What do you want me to say? That

there's no risk involved? There's always a risk, as you should know. Look at John. No, I won't belabor that point, but I will say this. It could be that Waldo is going through the same kind of soul-searching, and if I were him, I would have a few qualms about taking on a lady like you. Who knows what you'll get up to next? You've led him a merry dance these last two months, have you not, risking life and limb for both me and Eric? Not that I'm objecting, of course. I'll be eternally grateful for what you did. However, Waldo's case is different. If he wants a safe, quiet life, then my advice is that he should steer clear of you."

Jo chuckled. "Point taken," she said.

She spent the next few minutes putting the teapot and crockery on the tray and generally tidying up. She looked at Chloë, hesitated, then said, "He said that you exaggerated, that he wasn't anything like the rake Lady Tellall made him out to be."

"Well, he would, wouldn't he?" Chloë's eyes twinkled. "That's what all men say when their pasts catch up to them. No, Jo. If you're going to take a chance on Waldo, you'll have to take the bad with the good."

"I don't know why I'm discussing this with you."

"Neither do I. Your mind is already made up."

Jo made a harrumphing sound and, with the tray in her arms, stalked back to the house.

Chloë reached for a letter that had arrived earlier, a letter from Lydia Langston, and she read it again. The next meeting of the Horticultural Society was to be at Lydia's place so that she could show off the improvements to her conservatory. Chloë wasn't sure she was up to it, not after what had happened with Victor. In fact, she had developed a phobia to hothouses.

There was also news of the Brinsleys. The earl, Lydia wrote, was a sad little man. He'd suffered a stroke and became agitated whenever his wife came near him. As a result, Elinor had left the Hall and taken up residence in the dower house in Knightsbridge. There was talk of Elinor and her companion doing a grand tour of Europe. Her friends, of course, were aghast. Elderly ladies did not go off jaunting all over Europe as though they were young men just out of university.

She wouldn't try to dissuade Elinor from embarking on a grand tour, thought Chloë. She would applaud. What did age matter? Life was precious. It was a sin to waste a minute of it. That's one thing she could say of herself. She had tried to live her life to the full. She had learned that from Ralph, and she refused to allow one nasty, horrible specimen of humanity to blight her life.

Of course she would go to the next meeting of the Horticultural Society. Not to do so would be cowardly, and she was no coward. She wasn't going to let Victor defeat her.

Her thoughts drifted to Jo and Waldo. She wondered what she would give them for a wedding present.

This was Cecy's night, and Waldo tried to find a measure of satisfaction in his sister's happiness. He could hardly believe how grown-up she looked, grown-up and beautiful. Only yesterday he'd thought of her as a child. Tonight, she was a woman. Ruggles seemed to have noticed the difference as well. He was paying her too much attention. He'd have a word with Ruggles before the night was out. Cecy was too young for that sort of thing.

He tried to remember himself at Cecy's age. He and his friends were just out of university. They'd thought they could change the world. A large dose of reality had blunted their hopes. Now he'd be content if he could change the heart of one headstrong, outspoken, unconventional female.

Maybe he should have settled for second best. He could have marshaled enough good reasons to persuade her to marry him. They could make a real home for Eric, she could continue to run her precious newspaper, and she would have unlimited access to his bed.

And vice versa.

That should count for something. His little Puritan had a passionate nature to match his own.

But he wanted more. He wanted her heart, and if he couldn't have that, it would be an empty victory.

He helped himself to a glass of champagne and wandered out to the terrace. Thomas was there, smoking a cheroot. He found another in his pocket and handed it to Waldo, knowing without asking that it would be accepted. They were close friends as well as cousins.

"What's bothering you?" Thomas asked. He offered his own cheroot so that Waldo could light his.

Waldo leaned against the balustrade and blew out a stream of smoke. "What makes you think anything is bothering me?"

"Your limp is showing. It always gets worse when you're upset about something. Is it Mrs. Chesney?"

Close friends or not, Waldo had no intention of discussing Jo with anyone—not his mother, who had been quizzing him, nor his father, who had been suspiciously circumspect, and certainly not an older cousin who hadn't a tactful bone in his body.

"No," he said emphatically, "it's not Mrs. Chesney."

"Is she still grieving for her late husband?"

"I said it's not—" Waldo gave up. "I don't think so. As for my limp, that's the result of fatigue, not an unquiet mind. I've been running around like a pack-horse, fetching and carrying for this blasted ball. That's why my limp is more obvious."

Thomas took a long swallow from the glass in his hand. He said reflectively, "Then if there's nothing between you and Mrs. Chesney, I think I may try my luck." He smiled into Waldo's eyes. "My girls need a mother, and they're fond of Jo. I think we would suit very well. What do you think?"

As pleasant as his cousin, Waldo said, "If you go near her, I'll make you regret it."

Thomas cocked a brow. "It's like that, is it?"

"Name your seconds."

This was greeted by a hoot of laughter. Thomas took a last puff of his cheroot and threw the stub into the shrubbery. "I never thought I'd see this day—Waldo Bowman mooning over a woman. Don't let her get away, Cousin, because if you do, I'll go after her. I'm quite serious." And with another hoot of laughter, he sauntered off.

Waldo took a savage draw on the cheroot between his teeth and succeeded only in bringing on a fit of coughing. He tossed the cheroot away, drained his glass, then he tossed that away too.

He didn't like the way Thomas had described him, but like it or not, it was the truth. For the first time in his life, he was in love. He hadn't been looking for love, and if he'd known it was lying in wait for him when he walked into the *Journal*'s offices to confront Jo, he would have given Stratford a wide berth. But he'd met Jo, and he'd found more than a pretty woman to share his bed. Something inside him had shifted and changed him forever. He knew she felt the same way, and he couldn't understand why she wouldn't admit it.

Thomas was right. He shouldn't let her get away. He'd been a fool to give her time to come to things on her own. First thing tomorrow—

"You win. There's no getting round it. I love you, Waldo Bowman."

Waldo closed his eyes. When he opened them, she was standing right in front of him. The gown she was wearing was a red silk that shimmered when she moved. The color did wonderful things to her hair and skin. She looked happy and confident and breathtakingly beautiful. He couldn't help smiling. The picture he'd had in his mind of Jo a moment before was as he'd first seen her, hair tied back with a ragged ribbon, ink on her nose and smock, and green eyes spitting fire. How could he not help loving her?

"Now, that's an odd smile," she said. She touched her fingers to his lips. "What are you thinking?"

He kissed her fingers. "You know what I'm thinking. It's been two weeks."

"We must be made for each other. We think alike."

"Why don't we do something about it?"

"I told you we think alike."

"What are you thinking about?"

"Mmm?"

She was looking up at the canopy over the bed, floating back to reality. The strains of the orchestra playing a waltz came to them faintly from the terrace. She could feel his heart beating against her palm. His words registered and she looked up at him through her lashes.

She said in a languid tone, "I was thinking about the *Journal.*"

He said dryly, "As I've told you before, honesty isn't always a virtue."

She thought, at first, he was joking, but he wasn't smiling and his eyes were intense on hers. She raised herself on one elbow so that she was level with him. "I've sold it," she said, "to Mac Nevin, and I was reveling in this tremendous sense of freedom I feel. I don't think I could have told you I loved you as long as I was tied to the *Journal*."

He was appalled. "But you're the driving force behind the *Journal*. You turned it around and made a success of it. I know how much it means to you."

"That's true, up to a point. But it wasn't my paper, was it? It was John's. As long as I was tied to it, I was tied to John. Now I'm free to follow my own heart."

She sat up, plumped up her pillow, and sat back against it. When he did the same, she went on, "Don't think I'm bitter about John. I made my peace with him yesterday when I took Eric to his grave. I've done a lot of thinking and see now that I wasn't blameless either."

She smiled faintly. "It will always grieve me that he never thought he could tell me about Eric. For all that, I will always remember that we were happy together." She combed her fingers through her hair as she thought about it. "I know that you think I put John on a pedestal, but that isn't entirely true. The truth is, he put *me* on a pedestal, and I tried to be the kind of wife he wanted. That was easy, because I didn't know who I was, not really. It wasn't until after I became a widow that I began to think for myself, but, oh, it was a slow, painful journey."

She looked up at him. "Have I ever told you about my parents?"

"You mentioned them. Why?"

"I'm sure you know all there is to know about them.

I never wanted to live like them or be like them, so I went to the other extreme, and that was a mistake too."

She stretched and turned in to him. "But that's all in the past. I finally know who I am and what I want. I love you, Waldo, with my whole heart."

He said quizzically, "Will you accept the word of a rake like me when he tells you that he loves you too?"

"A rake? Pooh!" she scoffed. "You got that from Chloë's column, and you know how she exaggerates. Besides, you hadn't met me then, and I can assure you, Waldo, there will be no more shady ladies in your life. Only me."

He let out a shout of laughter and dragged her into a passionate embrace. When he finally lifted his head, he said, "Jo Chesney, you amaze me. Does this mean you will marry me?"

"Of course." She added provocatively, "I could never give up Eric."

"Ah, Eric." He relieved her of his weight and said seriously, "You took him to his father's grave?"

She nodded. "I don't want Eric to be ignorant of his real parents. Of course, I was thinking of the Brinsleys. Morden learned the truth about his parents on his twenty-first birthday. Can you imagine how he must have felt? For the first time, I pitied him. We're not going to do that to Eric. He's going to know the truth about his parents from the outset."

He smiled at her vehemence. "What truth is that?"

"That his parents were good people, that they loved him and wanted him, that they would have married except that there was some impediment, so eventually John married me."

"What impediment?"

"I'll think of something, or we can say we don't know. Waldo, a boy should know that his parents wanted and loved him. That's the only heritage that is worth passing on. And it's true. They did love him."

He was amused. "How much of this does Eric understand?"

She heaved a sigh, then smiled. "Not much. Only that his mother and father loved him. But when he starts asking questions, we must know how we're going to answer him. All I'm saying is that he should know the truth."

"You don't need to convince me. I agree. Where is he now?"

"Where do you think?" She shifted to get a clearer look at his face. "He's here. When he knew I was coming, he made such a fuss, I had to bring him with me. He's been moping for two weeks, demanding to know when you were coming to Stratford or when we were coming to you. Aunt Daventry and Chloë were glad to see the back of us."

There was a big smile on his face. "I liked that boy from the moment I set eyes on him."

Her sigh was soft and a little rueful. "I didn't. In fact, I didn't like him at all, and the same goes for you. I knew you were both going to cause me trouble, and I was right. On the other hand, it shows how wrong I was. You and Eric are the best thing that ever happened to me."

That little speech was rewarded with a slow, hot kiss that was edging close to passion. After a moment, Waldo raised his head. "Sounds to me," he said, "that you did a great deal of thinking when you were in Stratford."

"Well, I did, and it was worth it. Now I feel at peace with myself and at peace with the world." She nestled her head in the crook of his shoulder. "What did you do when I was away?"

"Oh, I thought about you too."

She looked up at him. "And?"

"And I came to the conclusion that you're the most perverse, stubborn, exasperating woman I know. I can't think why I want to marry you."

She smiled when she saw the laughter in his eyes. "I might say the same about you."

"And that I'm desperately, hopelessly, helplessly in love with you."

She wound her arms around his neck. Briefly, her mouth touched his. "How desperate?" she whispered.

"I'll show you."

The Journal, July, 1817 (an extract from London Life)

Lady Tellall takes great pleasure in announcing the marriage of her good friend Mrs. Jolie Chesney to Waldo Frederick Bowman, Esq., at St. Mary Abbots Church, Kensington. Mr. Bowman, his bride, and their adopted son will be making their home in Marylebone. At present, they are in Ireland, visiting the bride's parents, Sir Vivian and Lady Moore.

Mr. Bowman, who comes from a long line of parliamentarians, is a candidate in the bi-election for West Hockham. Both his wife and his cousin, Thomas Bowman, will be canvassing on his behalf. This should make for interesting if not fiery debate in the family home in Kensington. Mr. Bowman, the elder, is a Tory. The younger is a Whig.

Mr. Bowman, Sr., told me personally that he is very proud of his son and that, though they take their politics seriously, their debates have always been conducted in a spirit of lighthearted banter.

I tried not to betray my skepticism.

Following the church service, there was a reception at

Palliser Park. Everybody who is anybody was there, including my dear friend Lady Webberley. Sad to say, her memoirs are not be published after all. The project was dropped when her publisher was threatened with an action for slander. Who made the threat? Lady Webberley, perhaps wisely, refuses to say.

Remember, dear readers, you heard it first from me. More to follow.

About the Author

Best-selling, award-winning author Elizabeth Thornton was born and educated in Scotland, and has lived in Canada with her husband for over thirty years. In her time, she has been a teacher, a lay minister in the Presbyterian Church, and is now a full-time writer, a part-time baby-sitter to her five grandchildren, and dog walker to her two spaniels.

Elizabeth loves hearing from her readers.
If you wish to receive her newsletter, e-mail her at: *elizabeth.thornton@mts.net* or visit her web page at: *http://www.elizabeththornton.com*.